Christina Mou

LAYERS

NOVEL

Ἀκακία
PUBLICATIONS

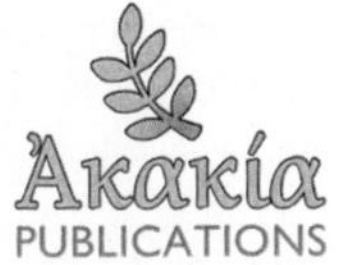

Published in England by AKAKIA Publications, 2018

CHRISTINA MOUTSOU

LAYERS

NOVEL

ISBN: 978-1-912935-01-7

Cover Image:
Source: "La Tailleuse de Soupe", François Barraud
Mixed and Designed by AKAKIA Publications

19 Ashmead, Chase Road,
N14 4QX, London, UK

T. 0044 207 1244 057
F. 0044 203 4325 030

www.akakia.net
publications@akakia.net

2018, London, UK

Profoundly committed to the better life, the promiscuous,
like the monogamous, are idealists.
Both are deranged by hope,
in awe of reassurance, impressed by their pleasures.

Adam Phillips, *Monogamy*

To my late father, Georgios Moutsos,
who always believed that I would write it.

Contents

Layer 1

It is said that when we touch pitch we are defiled.
But when we touch, or are touched by, another's story,
that also affects our being, and more radically.

Salley Vickers, *The Other Side of You*

1
Therapy

London, February 1998

'I'm in a lift', Eleni says to Laura towards the end of her Thursday morning session. 'It goes up and up, it shrinks around me and then squeezes me out into the void, nobody there to catch me.'

'How many times have you had this dream?' Laura mumbles, moisture making her eyes look like shiny leaves after the rain.

'I don't remember, but it's always the same. It started the night before I first walked into your room last October.'

Anyone who's ever been to therapy for any more than six weeks will know that there are sessions that get forgotten as soon as you walk out of the door and those which get replayed in your mind like a broken record, in which the first three lines of the song are repeated again and again. Eleni would remember that session with Laura in mid-February, the boring week that came in following the excitement of her birthday, for years to come. What she could still not remember was the order that things happened or rather were said, as happenings in therapy take shape in words.

Yet, her memory of that session consisted of snapshots pushing to the surface one by one, like bubbles allowing the sun in before bursting.

In fact, there was hardly any sun at all that February day. By that time in her therapy, Eleni had taken to sitting on the large floor cushion, which she was not sure was meant for patients, but which Laura had consented to letting her use with a nod. Diagonally across from her, Laura was sitting in her slightly reclining therapist's chair, and just above her head was the roof window, one of Eleni's favourite features in Laura's room. She always thought lofts were cosy, almost womb-like. Eleni lifted her gaze to the window so that she could discern a tiny sunray the colour of sickly yellow ochre. It was the first light she noticed that day, and it was past two o'clock. There must have been some silence, but she remembered her mood, the hopelessness of her obsession for Yves still ruining her mind. She must have complained about it, said something like, how come four months into the therapy and I am still thinking of an irrelevant loser that I will never ever be in love with? Would this symptom ever show any signs of improving? It must have been shortly after that, while trying to trace the sunray outside the window, when Laura said:

'Well, perhaps now is your turn to ruminate over your father, a man who ruined so many women's lives.'

Though Eleni did not get where this was coming from, she had no trouble recollecting the contempt for her father in Laura's voice and how that led to all the other images creeping in. She told Laura how drunk she was that summer night in Paris when she had walked with Yves on shiny warm cobblestones with only as much as her slippers, shorts and T-shirt on; how she could not know then that that night would change her life for ever. That the encounter with Yves would take things away from her like her father had done to women in all his dangerous liaisons. Then she remembered the rustling leaves echoing in the empty studio after Nicolas had left for work that morning, and how she knew that he could not stand her depression, her writer's block; how petrified she was that he would leave her and then nobody else would ever love her again. And yet, as Laura said, Nicolas's impatience with her moods did not make her feel loved in the first place, did it?

Floods of tears, it was one of those sessions, the floodgates had opened for good.

When Eleni stood up, just about feeling her numb legs, crouched as she had been on the bean cushion, Laura came close, touching her shoulder lightly. 'The lift no longer has to throw you out, now that you are coming to see me, I promise', she mumbled. Eleni would remember the cracks in Laura's voice for years to come.

Yet, once she was out, coat wide open and gaze looking inwards, the wind stabbed her in the chest, and the void was there again.

2
The beginnings

Athens Airport, April 1972

When he opened his pack of Assos cigarettes and realised that there were only two left and no kiosk nearby to get any, Dinos decided that waiting for the flight to arrive had now become unbearable. He looked around him standing as he had been in the middle of the arrivals lounge for any staff nearby that could have an earful of his thoughts about Greek airline services. For lack of a better option as no staff were in sight, he headed towards the canteen, while wondering if he could swallow any liquid at all. The knot in his throat would show no signs of unclenching.

'Still waiting for the London flight, sir?' the young bright-eyed waitress asked him, while handing him his extra-sweet, extra-strong Greek coffee. At least she had not double-checked that he had indeed ordered it 'extra sweet', like most male waiters, who exercised the little power they had by making him feel uncomfortable that, despite being a man of a certain standing, he did not choose to have his coffee bitter, as though bitterness was a brand of masculinity.

'Yes, I am, unfortunately. I usually have my coffee at Syntagma Square, sitting comfortably at a white-clothed table, but instead I'm still here, hopping from one foot to another, wondering why we are given no information about this flight being so late.'

'Do not worry, sir. Olympic Airways flights are always late', the girl smiled wryly.

'That makes me feel better, thank you. I'm not a frequent flyer, you see, so I don't know. All I know is this weather: cloud all over, no visibility at all. Do planes manage to land in such weather?'

'I know, it's dull weather for April. But for planes? They can handle much worse.'

It was an unusually cloudy day for mid-April in Athens mirroring the mood his early morning exchange with Leonora had left him in, just before he set off for the long drive from Thessaloniki to Athens.

'Do you seriously believe that this woman is going to give you her baby, just like that?' she had asked him.

Her sarcasm always got to him straight away. 'Have I not shown you the documents, Leonora?' he had mumbled under his breath. 'Eleni Hatzis, officially my baby ... And yours', he had added hastily.

'I will have to see it to believe it. I'm afraid she may turn out to be just after your money in the end.'

He had refrained from slamming the door behind him, swallowing down the 'fuck off' bubbling on the surface of his tongue. This moment in time was too perilous for letting his rage loose. Things were fragile, they could go either way.

'Just get yourself ready for the baby's arrival, Leonora, will you? I'd better go now, since you are trying so hard to wind me up.'

Leonora was more right of course than he would ever want to admit. The baby was not yet legally theirs. Antonopoulos, his long-term solicitor and his compatriot from the Peloponnese had made it clear to him. 'No adoption can have legal standing nowadays before the baby is four months old, Dinos. The law gives the birth mother this length of time as a minimum to sort her head out. Bide your time, Dinos', he added. 'You are already the baby's father legally, we have made sure of that. It's just a matter of time before your wife can adopt her as well.' But how much more time could he bide? After giving birth in early February, Nefeli had looked after the baby in London for nearly six weeks. Any more than that and the transfer would have become impossible.

Nefeli did not say as much, but he knew she was disappointed that he had not gone over to visit her in London after she gave birth. Her romantic dreams about the two of them and the baby together as a unit seemed to have got rekindled. She could not see that this was just a fantasy, it could never be. He was a married man, to start with. Then again, the baby needed the right home to grow up in. She was part of his family and all its intricate but honourable history of landowning.

He sat down now on a nearby bench, letting out a sigh of relief. It made a difference to come across somebody kind like the waitress in the canteen, especially if this somebody happened to be a young woman with bright eyes and smile.

He made sure he tipped the girl well. Her eyes looked even brighter when she saw the note that he discreetly placed in her hand.

Sipping his coffee slowly, he found himself engrossed in his thoughts. How will Mother react when she sees her granddaughter, he wondered. He had deliberately chosen to give the baby her name to appease her. Yet he had not avoided her critical gaze, the 'you are just like your father' words coming out of her mouth yet again. It was hard to be in the same room with her for more than a few minutes without losing his temper.

He lit his penultimate cigarette and inhaled deeply. When his parents separated, after his father ran off with his girlfriend, both of them fighting for the Communist Party in the civil war, Dinos was forced to accompany his heartbroken mother and his younger sister to their relatives in the north of Greece. *A true scandal it was those days to be an aristocrat, a landowner, and to side with the lefties, let alone to leave your wife and children for a loose unmarried woman wearing trousers as though she was a man,* his mother still repeated nowadays, a good twenty years later. He was barely seventeen when they left the village heading north, and yet he had to fend for himself and for his mother and sister. And now Nefeli thought that he was going to fend for her too.

The thunder burst not far from the window. To his surprise, the knot in his throat loosened as the rain started hitting the ground. He could almost smell the earth, the thirsty, dry soil meeting the water. Only he was not near fragrant spring blossoms on the farm of his childhood before his parents' marriage fell apart, but in a barren field in the middle of nowhere, meant to receive his new baby packed in a metal bird coming down from the waterlogged sky.

He had had enough. He got up, stabbing the cigarette decidedly on the shiny silver upright floor ashtray next to his seat, and walked in search of the nearest information desk. How funny to be so worried that the plane had crashed. For all he knew, Nefeli and the baby, his baby, might not even be on it. He brushed this thought away, almost like a fly sitting on his crisp white collar. It could not be. Nefeli was like an open book whose pages he had access to.

Nefeli was handed to him, almost like a Christmas present, on a December day just past his thirty-sixth birthday, two years ago. Theo, Nefeli's godfather, one of his credit buyers, had brought her over to his office.

'Here is my favourite goddaughter,' he told him, 'a truly special girl. Not very good at typing, but a quick learner and a true beauty too.'

Nefeli became his secretary and she turned out to be better at it than he thought she would be. It was then that the idea came to him that he could get her pregnant and keep the baby. From catching her gaze when she thought he wasn't looking, he knew that she would not be hard to persuade to sleep with him. He was a handsome man, women were after him.

'Olympic Airways flight number 7375 from London has now landed', a loudspeaker announced just as he was about to reach the information desk.

He jumped up. She is here; they are here.

3
Sweet adolescence

Thessaloniki, 25 January 1986

My dearest diary Jardin,

Last night I had the strangest of dreams:

I was looking at my face in the big silver mirror by the entrance hall and through the mirror I could see that I had a hole in my head, and through the hole I entered a space with two interconnecting rooms. I walked through the first empty room into the second room, where two middle-aged men in religious gowns were sitting down on what appeared like thrones, one of them holding a sceptre. 'Tell me the truth', I said. 'I want to know the truth.'

The man with the sceptre stared at me with magnetic, dark eyes. He shook his head. 'No.'

***

'Your dream is like *Alice in Wonderland*', Lea said while they were walking along the seafront, the city's humid wind piercing through their coats. They were downtown like every Saturday morning. The familiar scent of Thermaikos's city waters, a mix of seaweed, salt and dirt rose to Eleni's nose giving her pleasure. She loved the city and the sea. As she walked with Lea along the seafront heading from the old harbour to the White Tower, the cars and banter from the cafés facing the sea buzzed on their left-hand side. Lea liked to talk in riddles, and sometimes, Eleni thought this was the only reason she was quickly becoming her best friend, the only worthy point of reference in the overall distasteful all-girls private her parents had planted her in without so much as her consent.

'Alice in Wonderland?' Eleni said, puzzled.

'You know, like another reality you are just about to discover.'

The magic of their stroll downtown evaporated quickly for Eleni, when they stopped at the ice-skating café at Lea's insistence. Why did Lea love so much to mingle with the posh lot from their school, Eleni wondered. Teenage girls dressed in stupidly expensive all-American brands, flirting desperately with the boys from the 11th High School who frequented the café, perfecting the act of spending their wealthy parents' money. The only bit that was worth it there was the ice-skating itself; Eleni had said to Lea as much.

'I have to go', she mumbled less than an hour after their arrival at the café. 'You know what my parents are like, we have to sit down to lunch together on weekends and all that stuff.' The dream had played on her mind all morning.

***

Lunch was boring again.

'This is the most delectable cut of beef you ever had,

Eleni. My friend Kostas, the butcher, reserved it especially for me.'

'I just want pasta with cheese.'

'But you have to try the beef.'

They all went on eating quietly, as though there was nothing more important in the world than the steaming pile on their plates.

When Eleni and Lea had walked along the seafront earlier on that morning, Eleni could already anticipate her return home, where she was expected for lunch in a couple of hours. She would start heading uphill, away from the sea, the washing lines getting more frequent the further up she was, the smell of fabric softener blending with car fumes in her nostrils, the sun not always making it through the drying clothes on the first floor balconies. When she would take the final turn into her street, she would see the alley where her mother would not allow her to play when she was little along with the other kids of the neighbourhood, and the wide wooden and glass front door of the block of flats where she lived, standing out as the poshest in their tiny street. She would then look up trying to spot their fifth-floor balcony. Since as far back as she could remember, she loved living on the fifth floor. She considered it with pride. 'The higher, the better', her father would always say. There was only one more floor above them, the so-called privileged penthouse. Still, Eleni had a sense that the fifth floor was just the right identity for her family. Not quite at the top, but almost. It helped that she never got to know the neighbours who lived above. She only said hello to Mrs Christou, the lovely old lady who lived just below them and who smiled at Eleni every time they met outside the communal lift. The fact Mrs Christou had given her permission to make noise, as she was just a child after all, was yet another advantage of living high in Eleni's eyes. This was all of course before the age of six, when she still considered it a privilege to be the only child of her parents. She didn't like her dad much at all after that, not sure why.

'You are still not eating any of the meat, Eleni', her father's voice scratched her ears as though from far away.

'It's in tomato sauce swimming in olive oil. You know I don't like that', Eleni grunted.

But he did not know, that was the problem. He had not even begun to notice what she liked to eat in the fourteen or so years that she had been around. Her mother had put it right: 'All men are selfish pigs.' All her father really cared about was cooking for himself, as he so loved his food, and then trying to convince her that it was good for her. She was so sick and tired of seeing him day after day in the kitchen waiting for her after school, trying to force-feed her. Why could they not be like a normal family: Mother cooks, Father goes to work?

The piece of stewed beef that he had with apparent optimism placed in front of her, lay untouched. Eleni took a look at it filled with disgust. She could almost feel inside her mouth the oily red sauce coagulating around the meat. *Look, man, notice! I am not eating your beef casserole. Come on, man, get out of the house, go to your business, to your girlfriends that make you feel so important. Give us some breathing space.*

***

After lunch, Eleni walked down the corridor to her room. Since she had finally conquered her right to her own teenage room previously used as her father's TV abode, Eleni had been reminded of how dark the corridor had seemed when she was little. At the age of fix or six, she would lie in the middle of her parents' big bed, look out into the long, snake-like corridor, and despite the flickering of the light from the living room and the TV projecting different shades of blue from the living room's half-open door, the shadows would still form. In the corner, just before the opening of the kitchen, she could always make out the shadow of a wolf. Now, from the conquered castle of her teenage room on the other side of the corridor, she could still discern the dip before the kitchen door and notice the shadows gathering there, even in the middle of a bright afternoon.

'Was I a breech or a head-down baby, Mum?'

It was the time for their post-lunch chat, just before her mother would retire for her long midday siesta, the time of day that Eleni had always found the most deadly. Eleni had been waiting for her in her room patiently, while she could hear the clattering noise of dishes being put away coming from the kitchen. It had been for a couple of weeks now that she had wanted to know more about her birth. As much as she hated her school, there were the occasional teachers that would just get through. Their new Biology teacher was one of a kind. She had spent the last class telling them all these fascinating facts about how babies were born. It really seemed to Eleni like a miracle.

'Mum? I asked you a question', Eleni said impatiently. Leonora had not moved or made a noise, sitting up stiffly at the end of Eleni's bed. She seemed to be staring at the turquoise wall that Eleni had imposed after much debate with both her parents about her right to decorate what now was her own room. Could she not just get over it?

'It's been a long time I've been thinking of telling you, a long time that I've been living in fear that you would hear it from someone else, that they would break the news to you and hurt you.'

'Mum, what are you talking about?' Eleni said in surprise.

'I tried to tell you when you were five but you would have none of it', her mum went on, as in a trance. 'I know you are definitely the wrong age now, in adolescence, and I am dreading how you will take this, how it's going to affect you.'

'I don't understand what you are talking about, Mum. Have you gone bonkers?' Eleni mumbled, feeling a strange numbness spreading slowly all over her body.

'You asked me earlier on about your birth. How exactly you were born. Well, I don't know all the details of that because it wasn't me who gave birth to you. I took you when you were very little, only two months old. I still remember that day. Your wide blue-green eyes, how you stared at me when I took you in my arms ...'

Eleni felt her hands going cold and her body stiffening. 'Are you saying that you are not my mother?' she asked quietly.

'Of course I am your mother. Who else could your mother be? I changed your nappies and I rocked you to sleep and you kept me up night after night. Mothers are those who bring up a child, not those who give birth to her.'

'So my father is not my real father either?' Eleni mumbled, trying to restrain the tears that were quickly filling her eyes.

'It's quite complicated, a bit of a mess, a mess that's certainly not only of my own making. You are adopted, but only on my side. Your father is your biological father.'

'I don't understand', Eleni murmured in a shaky voice.

'Just before your father and I were going to get married, I got pregnant. You know that his mother didn't really want him to marry me. His mother and all the supposedly upper-class aunties, they all thought that their prince could not possibly marry a simple girl from a family of the lowest class of peasants, those who cultivated tobacco. I was not even a pretty girl. "What does he see in her?" I overheard them saying.'

'That's mean! You were pretty, I have seen pictures.'

'Well, I was small and dark, not a tall, blonde, statuesque goddess like his mother. I could never measure up to her, you see. Anyway, I just knew that if I married him being pregnant with his child, they would all say that I had blackmailed him. I was very proud then. I was just about finishing my Medicine degree, I was going to be a professional, an independent woman, why on earth would I need to blackmail someone into marrying me? I had an illegal abortion. It went wrong –'

'Stop! Why are you telling me all this?' Eleni yelled at her.

She wanted to stand up and leave the room, but her legs had turned to jelly like in a scary dream.

'What I am trying to say is that I was not able to conceive after the abortion. We tried, month after month and year after year from our mid-twenties to our mid-thirties. It made us unhappy. Your father kept saying, "What's the point of making all this money and having no one to spend it on?" Every day that passed, I craved a baby. I thought of the aborted baby, it was a boy, I was sure. Was I being punished for aborting him? We had all these things in our lives, successful careers, lots of friends, eating out in expensive restaurants, and yet nothing was right. There was this longed-for baby we could not have.'

'I could not care any less about your longed-for baby', Eleni shouted, her voice finally breaking into a silent weep.

'Don't cry, my darling. This is a conversation that's been long overdue. So, one day your father came home and said to me, "I've got a baby for you. Do you want it?" Of course it was not as simple as that, not at all. He had got someone pregnant, one of his girlfriends. He had researched it all, her family tree and everything, and he got her pregnant deliberately.'

Eleni had been crying for all this time and her mother did not even seem to notice.

'You know, this is all perfectly legal nowadays', Leonora continued. 'Surrogate mothers, they call them in America. I read an article about them. They get paid to carry a baby for an infertile couple. That's all it was. But of course, it was done in your father's usual, messy way. He has never been good with boundaries. Paying her off, cutting off ties and that's it.'

'So who is she? Who is the woman who gave birth to me?' Eleni asked, letting the tears and snot roll down her face and land on her not-that-white-any-more angora pullover, the one she had just reluctantly received from Nefeli as an early birthday present.

'Oh … I don't know. One of your father's girlfriends, I suppose. I do not want to know about them, as you must have noticed. I never enquire. It's an addiction really, it has almost killed him a couple of times – and then he always comes back to me, asking me to save him.'

Eleni got up abruptly. She needed a wee so badly that it felt like her body was being ripped apart. She continued checking into the toilet every ten minutes for the rest of the afternoon.

Leonora had now stopped talking. Tears rolled down her cheeks as she sat still on the side of Eleni's bed. In her mother's presence, Eleni felt numb, as though she did not inhabit her body at all. Every time she went to the toilet, she took time to look at her image in the mirror. Her face seemed totally new to her. 'Who am I? I have not come from my mother's body. I am not my mother's daughter', she mumbled to her reflection between sobs. 'Who am I?'

4
Birth

London, March 1972

Nefeli did not know how long she had been standing still over the white cot in row number three of the nursing ward, her eyes glued on the baby's pale yellow face turned on the side, her skin almost translucent under the lamp.

'Would you like to give her her next feed, as you are here?' The voice over her right shoulder and next to her ear startled her. 'We need to wake her up now. She is such a sleepy-head.'

'Sure', Nefeli mumbled, turning to face the white-collared nurse. She recognised her face from previous visits. She was one of the few kind ones, as one could discern from her calm blue eyes.

The baby had been in hospital for almost five weeks. Pathological jaundice, the doctor had said, probably due to being slightly premature. Nothing to worry about, he said, and yet it had proved mysteriously slow to clear. Nefeli had been visiting her every day. Well, to start with every day, then every time she had to go to hospital for check-ups and appointments with the social worker. She had been there, bending over her hospital cot, with the fluorescent lamps on, which made her look even more darkish yellow than she already was.

This baby did not look remotely like anything she had imagined. She didn't look like her baby. Two fair, handsome people producing a yellow-faced Chinese-looking baby? Were the doctors sure that there was nothing wrong with her other than the jaundice? Maybe she had some kind of disorder? She had asked them so many times. She should not have drunk the glass of beer that Mrs Marika kept offering her with lunch. 'Beer is good for foetuses', she would tell her. 'It helps them grow bigger.'

She had loved being pregnant. It was a floating experience, like being immersed in a dream from which she did not have to wake up. It had been the only time in her life that she had felt pampered, loved even. The last six months in London had been amazing. She would attend her daily English classes in Covent Garden religiously and then she would stroll down Oxford Street, occasionally buying clothes for the baby in neutral colours. Only the best, exactly as she was instructed by 'The Prince'. She could not resist stopping in the brightly lit superstores. She would spend what felt like hours staring at the endless counters of elegant brands of make-up and perfumes. Estée Lauder was her favourite. Once a week she would get back home with a new acquisition in a crispy, perfumed paper bag. She had to be careful with her money though, she wouldn't like to have to ask him again for more. Still, what a thrilling sense of freedom it gave her. She had never had so much money before to spend on the things she liked.

Occasionally she would walk further, all the way to the river. Once, she even crossed Waterloo Bridge and found herself on the south side; but then she lost her way a bit and by the time she was all the way back to Wood Green, Mrs Marika seemed on edge. 'We have been waiting for you for lunch', she told her. 'I began to get really worried that something had happened to you.'

All these lovely lunches that Mrs Marika prepared for her while she'd put her up for the last six months. She had not known that food could taste that good. She would even make her bed for her, which despite her initial embarrassment she had grown accustomed to accepting with ease. Sometimes she caught herself wishing that this was where she had grown up. Even Mrs Marika had told her once, patting her tenderly on the shoulder that she had become the daughter she never had. Mrs Marika had been the only female presence in a house accustomed to the rumble of four boisterous boys, all of whom, bar the youngest, had now left home. She could see Mrs Marika's sorrow, every time she talked about her eldest, the one who took a gap year in India after finishing his first degree and who ended up accepting a permanent job in Bombay.

'What is a Greek-Italian boy doing in India? It is full of disease out there, Son, come back home', she would tell him, sighing.

'I am a British citizen, Mum, lots of us out here. You wouldn't believe how cosmopolitan it is', he would invariably reply.

Nefeli could always see tears in Mrs Marika's eyes when she related a version of this dialogue. The other two sons were both at university, and it was only the second eldest, Anthony, who studied architecture in London, who would occasionally join them for lunch. But he had opted to share a flat with friends rather than stay with his parents – all down to Mrs Marika's generosity of course, who was paying some of the sky-rocket rent on his trendy London apartment-share with her hard-won savings. He was Nefeli's least favourite out of Mrs Marika's sons, as she found him snobbish and full of himself.

'Hey Nefeli,' he would tell her, with a considerable hint of irony in his voice, 'now, that your English has improved, come and visit Notting Hill. It is still a bit grotty, but it just has the right kind of vibe. Rock bands in the making', he would add in a daydreaming voice. 'We are rewriting history. We are changing the world. Not like the rotten feel around here. I tell you, north London suburbia sucks.'

'I am perfectly happy here', she would reply. 'And I am so lucky to enjoy your mother's amazing cooking now that you all, apart from Spyros, have left home.'

Mrs Marika would always intervene at this point, sighing. 'None of them likes my cooking, they don't like Greek food. You see, this is why every time Anthony is visiting, I cook English food. I have to apologise to you for this, Nefeli, boiled stuff is so tasteless. But my sons' favourite is not even that. They all prefer American hamburgers and those disgusting-smelling Indian curries.'

'Your English cooking is so tasty, Mrs Marika', Nefeli

would say, and Tony, as he preferred to call himself, would get ready to make his way out, giving the two of them an unfriendly look and chatting with his father about football before finally exiting in a rush, giving his mum a quick peck on the cheek.

'Don't be a "moany", Mum', he would tell Mrs Marika jokingly before leaving.

It seemed like all of Mrs Marika's energy had now been invested in Nefeli, as even her youngest, still at home, was most of the time locked in his room, supposedly studying for his university entry exams while the sound of rock music would get the walls of the house vibrating.

'You need to rest and eat well to produce a healthy baby', she would tell her, bringing some toast dripping with butter to her room only two hours after they had finished eating a large lunch. Only once did she appear to be in a more sombre mood.

'I wonder if I am doing the right thing hiding this from your mother', she told her. 'What is happening in your life is a very serious thing and I don't know if you realise it. Have you thought what it will be like to give your baby away just like that?'

Nefeli remained silent, looking down at the floor and refusing to lift her eyes. She was hoping that Mrs Marika would stop talking soon and return to her normal cheerful, caring self. But she did not stop.

'Are you sure this is what you want to do, Nefeli?' she persisted. 'You could stay here for a little bit longer with the baby if you wanted to, until you sort yourself out. But in order to do so, I need ...' She hesitated. 'We need to talk to your mother.'

Nefeli interrupted her. She was upset now. 'I told you when I first came here that if you talk to my mother I will go and stay somewhere else. I only came to stay here to please her, because she was worried about me living abroad, and then I saw what a nice person you were and I decided to stay over and to trust you with my secret. My first plan was to move out as soon as I found a place, you know that. I thought I explained everything to you when I first came, so I don't understand why we are having this conversation now. I do not even see this baby as mine. I am carrying it for a couple who cannot have children and I am getting paid for it, I told you that. It would not be right to keep it. It would be like stealing money.'

'Or so you are told. Every woman has the right to keep her baby', Mrs Marika said sternly.

'Not if she has accepted money to give it away. This was my passport to London, to learning English. This is the life I have always dreamt of. Don't you see how good it is for me?'

Just as Nefeli had thought that the matter was finally settled once and for all, Mrs Marika interrupted her.

'Why does he keep calling you every day then?' she asked, looking her straight in the eye. 'What are all these long, whispering phone calls about? You are having an affair with a married man and he is going to break your heart, Nefeli.'

She was right of course, kind of right anyway. Part of her wanted to give the baby over as soon as she was born and continue with her life in London, build a life here, study and find a job and marry someone later on. Would Mrs Marika help her settle if she chose to stay longer? she wondered. Another part of her, almost despite herself, kept thinking of him. The burning, fleeting moments of guilty sex, the cuddles in the office when they thought no one was looking, all the promises of the things they would do together. She missed him terribly and she was bitterly disappointed and hurt that he had not come to visit her as he had promised. She did not believe his excuses about being too busy with work. She knew what the real reason was: his wife, of course. He had to be very tactful with her now that he was preparing the adoption, she could sense as much.

From the beginning of the new year, Mrs Marika had tried to prepare her for going in to hospital and giving birth. It wouldn't go unnoticed, she had said to her, that she was a young single mother and she was not prepared to lie. She would have to tell them the truth. She had been spared the check-ups: Mrs Marika was so experienced; she had given birth to four healthy boys. She had told her to watch out for the baby's movement, and after a while the kicks inside her stomach could not be missed. Sometimes, especially in the last month, she had been woken up in the middle of the night by what felt like a punch to her innards. Hmm, not the gentlest of babies, she had thought to herself. A prospective boxer, perhaps?

Troublesome, though, this baby's birth was not. It slid out like a fish eventually. All the pain and the anguish happened before they arrived at the hospital. What was happening to her that night? She kept going to the toilet every ten minutes, passing copious quantities of water. It felt like her insides were being ripped apart. She was convinced that either she or the baby or both of them were going to die. Eventually, around five a.m., Mrs Marika was woken up by all her comings and goings and she found her lying on the floor of the living room, bent in two, to the degree that was possible with that big belly of hers.

'You are in labour', she said, without managing to conceal the panic in her voice. 'We must go to hospital right now.'

'But I am not due yet, it cannot happen yet, it is not possible', she mumbled.

'It doesn't matter. It can happen early, and it will, any time now. We need to go', Mrs Marika replied, rushing about and gathering her things as though she was about to check in to hospital.

She was in no way ready to give birth, but the worst was to follow. Mrs Marika could not have prepared her for the extent of interrogation that she would endure soon after the ordeal of birth. As soon as she declared that she was a single mother, a twenty-year-old as well, she was booked for a visit from the social worker. And even before the social worker's visit, she noticed the nurses' hostile glances, the contempt in the tone of their voice when they spoke to her.

'She is one of those, a teenage mother', she had overheard one of them whispering to another. Who were these people and what was their right to question her decisions? She did not even live in this country, so surely they should have no say about how she lived her life. And then the social worker turned up at her bedside, just as she was about to drop off after the sleepless night of agony she had had. She pretended that her English was not good enough to have a conversation, but then the social worker, a stern-looking woman with long grey hair (why would anyone keep their hair long and grey?) offered to find her an interpreter.

This was the worst possible scenario, Mrs Marika told her discreetly after the social worker had left her bedside. 'The local Greek community is very small here, Nefeli. Everyone knows everyone. I hope you understand that my position is delicate. Hosting an unmarried pregnant girl will be much frowned upon by all the church-goers. People may even gossip that I am doing it for money.'

Nefeli was alarmed. She had caused Mrs Marika enough trouble already.

'We are just here to make sure that you realise what the implications of your decision are', the social worker said to her during her second visit the next day, looking her piercingly in the eye, once Nefeli had consented to explain to her the situation. 'Handing your baby over for adoption is an irredeemable decision. You can never change your mind. You lose your baby for ever. Do you understand?'

She had a feeling that everyone around her, including Mrs Marika standing at the far corner of the room, looking down, was expecting an emotional reaction from her, like bursting into tears or losing her temper; but she would not give it to them.

'Yes, I understand', she kept saying, smiling. But the social worker would not let it go, not until she got her to agree to at least a single session of counselling.

'"Counselling"? What on earth is that?'

5
Paris breeze

Paris, June 1992

Eleni had always found it hard to move about in her tiny cupboard of a room, which was why she chose to sit still most of the time she spent there during the interim semester of her art degree in Paris. 'The cupboard room' was not a name she had come up with. Vivienne and Yves had always liked to crack a joke about her room and how only a sweet little girl like her could fit into it. Vivienne had at least made a good job of painting it bright white and matching it up with a narrow white single bed that stretched the length of the long side of the room from door to window. It had been an exercise in intimacy, sharing this bed with Nicolas during the many long weekends they spent together, when he came to visit her from London. His long legs would stretch out on to the window sill where some of her few possessions had been squeezed and squashed. The window sill also doubled as her desk through pushing a white polished board over the radiator and fixing it at the level of the sill. She would then unfold the plastic chair that also lived by the radiator. Thankfully, the small wardrobe across from the bed was fitted. Still, if she left its doors open, they created a tight square blocking the space between the wardrobe and her bed.

She found herself standing in the centre of this square, while slowly and painstakingly packing up all her possessions, the clothes she had worn for the last six months in Paris from heavy winter to a glorious summer. She had to finish packing up almost everything before this evening, as Vivienne and Yves were organising a farewell party for her and Nicolas was arriving before seven the following morning. She had to be ready, as they were setting off early to catch the train to Amsterdam, their first planned stop during a month of travel round Europe by train before finally reaching Greece at the end of July. This was a dream come true, her and Nicolas going travelling together. They so deserved it after all the hard work they had put into their degrees. Especially Nicolas, as he had passed his finals with a First.

Eleni felt a shadow darken her excitement. She had not worked all that diligently in the last six months in fact. She had been too busy spending most of her time in Vivienne and Yves's flat, partying. Her attendance of university classes had been minimal, and so the few students who had started saying hello to her at the beginning of the semester had forgotten who she was by the end of it. Her dissertation was good though, her tutor had said; her written French was excellent. She was still waiting for her mark, but it would be a pass for sure. Yves had offered to help her out and read through it, but she had surprised herself by stubbornly refusing. In the end she gave it to him to read after she had submitted it, and she smiled politely upon hearing his playful protests about why she had kept all this interesting work away from him.

She was never too sure what to make of him. Vivienne and Eleni had become close, almost from the beginning of her stay in Paris. She always knew that she liked friendships with older women, never being bothered by an age gap. But an older man like Yves, Vivienne's partner, she did not know what to make of him. She was stunned when he told her during one of the wine and cheese evenings at their flat that he was thirty-seven. Thirty-seven only? Vivienne was not one for revealing her age, but she must be fifty at least, Eleni thought, not that much younger than her mother.

She seemed to have found in Vivienne's ground-floor apartment her own private bohemian Paris that she had always dreamt of. So many early summer nights, full of electric blue light well into the late evening, she had spent in their flat as the guest of honour. She was the only one invited out of all the tenants. They asked her to be discreet, not wanting to give the impression that she was being favoured. She had even been invited to the big party Vivienne had given for her birthday, full of the Parisian high society of artists and art dealers. She still remembered vividly that larger-than-life guy, apparently an old sweetheart of Vivienne's, holding her hand open and reading her fortune. 'Your career will flourish, my darling,' he had told her, 'but not many men will truly love you, one or two at most.' What a thing to say to her – it still hurt when she remembered.

During these nights full of happenings, Yves was always there, at Vivienne's side, as always cheerful and witty, showing off his multilingualism. It was only Greek that escaped him, he had said to her; six languages he spoke fluently, and now that he had met her he would get to learn some Greek too. He was always busy being the host along with Vivienne, but he would never lose sight of her, never forget to fill her glass with some more red wine. Yet, in quieter moments, when she and Vivienne would get engrossed in one of their long conversations, he would discreetly withdraw.

Vivienne had made no secret of being fond of Eleni from the beginning of her stay. The moment Eleni had walked in accompanied by her mother to view the little bedsit that had just become vacant, Vivienne had known instantly the truth, she told Eleni much later on. 'I knew you were adopted, sweetie', she had said, patting her on the shoulder. 'I have an eye for such things.' Eleni was not used to people guessing. If anything, most people would make comments about how her mother and Eleni looked alike, out of default, it seemed, as in truth, they looked nothing like each other, Leonora, dark-coloured and small, with delicate, symmetrical facial features, and Eleni, much taller, strong-boned, with a fair complexion, green olive-coloured eyes and her father's wet-hay hair and oval face.

It was Vivienne's dreadful history that had helped her guess the truth about Eleni. She had been the adoptive mother of a baby boy who was no longer there, as after her acrimonious divorce with her ex-husband, apparently a well-known art dealer, he removed the child and flew to another country, to live there with his biological son and his lover who was the child's birth mother. The privilege of owning a three-storey house near the vibrant Jardin du Luxembourg was the only remaining trophy out of Vivienne's failed marriage. 'Ten years of mothering my son,' Vivienne had said to Eleni during one of their long conversations, 'and look, I am now left with an empty nest. There is no day that passes by that I don't miss him.'

It was the first time Eleni had heard a story so similar to hers. She had cringed at the idea that her own story could have had the same outcome, her father fleeing with Nefeli and taking her along with them, when she was too young to have a say. She could barely begin to imagine how unhappy this would have made her. She depicted living with her father and his mistress as living with two people completely blind and deaf to her needs.

Vivienne had not given her much more than the basic outline of what went on. Eleni could see how painful and raw it still was for her. 'He took my son away', she kept saying to Eleni, as though she had found in her not only an eager listener, but a temporary replacement for her loss too. Was it more comfortable, Eleni wondered later on that night, to focus on Vivienne and her story than to see clearly what was coming?

***

'Chérie, un peu du boeuf?' Vivienne offered, holding a piece of extremely rare roast beef over her plate.

Eleni cringed. She had nibbled on crumbs of cheese and some deliciously mustardy lettuce salad for most of the farewell dinner Vivienne had organised for her, allowing Yves to fill her glass again and again with ruby red wine. Her mind was like a cinema screen, one scene following another in quick succession. All the little wonderful moments filling the canvas of her stay in Paris, and now it was all coming to an end. She had no appetite for food, just for wine.

'Non, merci, je n'ai pas faim.'

She sensed Vivienne giving her one of her piercing looks. 'You have lost so much weight lately, Eleni. I hope you are not becoming anorexic. It is a bit of a trend nowadays, you know. Young, beautiful girls like you, losing their appetite and then their health.'

Eleni did not like that side of Vivienne. She found her superior gaze, full of 'I know it all from experience', distasteful and intrusive. She had noticed before that Vivienne assumed she had the right to exercise it on her younger guests.

'I am not an anorexic. It's just that I don't like anything bloody on my plate', she dared to reply, and almost instantly regretted her rudeness. She had indeed lost a lot of weight in the last few months. Some of the summer trousers she had brought with her had become so loose around the waist that they were in danger of rolling off her hips unless she kept them in place with a belt. She could never eat much when in a state of infatuation, and she had grown deeply infatuated with Paris as the time wore on.

'Eleni has had to become slight in order to fit into her

room', Yves jumped in, and everyone round the table burst out laughing.

Was he trying to save her, or embarrass her even more? Eleni wondered; but she could not help but feel grateful that the tension between her and Vivienne had been diluted.

It was a few minutes past midnight and the party had just dispersed. Eleni was pottering about in the little kitchen upstairs across from her bedsit, when she heard steps coming up. It must be Vivienne coming to say goodbye, she thought. Vivienne had retired early saying that she was tired, and the party went on for a little bit longer without her, but Eleni could not shake off the feeling that she had retreated into her bedroom because she was furious with her.

'Fixing yourself another drink?' Yves's smooth accent came from behind her left shoulder, close to her ear.

'Oh God, no! I was just tidying up. I have an early start tomorrow.'

'Oh ... I was wondering if you would fancy a drink downtown, a last-night-in-Paris drink?' he said.

Eleni could hear his breathing and hers for some time, as though they were both suspended in space, before he lifted his hand and very gently and slowly removed a lock of wavy, sun-touched hair from her face, his eyes focusing gently on hers.

'Oui', she heard herself saying. Had she really said yes?

After the two of them sneaked out of the house well after midnight, he took her bar-hopping to the kind of bars only locals know about. By the time they reached the second bar, he was visibly drunk, talking manically to the fellow customers about his trips to Africa. She seemed to have missed most of what he was saying about Morocco. By this time she was tipsy herself, although she had hardly had more than a few sips since they left the house. In the intoxicated state of mind she was in, alcohol was not necessary or desirable.

It was when they left that second bar that the inevitable happened. They stopped in the middle of a wide pavement and started kissing passionately. Eleni could sense the few remaining late-night pedestrians passing close by and gazing at their intertwined figures. She could feel her braless breasts loose under his touch as he fondled them, only her fine black T-shirt separating her skin from his hands. Then he had her lying down on an old wooden box abandoned on the side of the pavement, leaning over her gently until she could feel his erection between her legs. They kept stopping to kiss and touch before ending up in another bar off Pont Neuf. Eleni could not help but wonder if their next stop after this would be his *pied-à-terre,* as he called the little flat he had insisted on keeping, despite Vivienne repeatedly telling him, even in front of Eleni, that it was a complete waste of money.

It must have been past four in the morning when they started looking for his car. 'I have lost my mind with you', he mumbled, clearly in a drunken state. 'No woman has made me forget where I have put my car before.'

She was feeling much more distant now. The alcohol had worn off along with her arousal and she was beginning to be painfully aware of what she had done. When she had left the house, she had been so anxious not to encounter Vivienne that she did not stop by her room to grab her watch or her purse or even to put her shoes on. Her alcohol-induced euphoria had made it okay to walk out of the house penniless and wearing her plastic summer slippers, but it now began to dawn on her how vulnerable she had made herself. She was completely dependent on him. What would Nicolas do when he arrived, if she was not there to open the door for him? He would have to wake Vivienne up.

'I really have to head back very soon', she told him as they walked up and down the cobbled streets holding hands and looking desperately for his car.

It must have been around then that it happened. They were suddenly circled by a gang of young North Africans. It was possible that they had been following them for some time – neither of them would have noticed, oblivious as they were to the outside world. Eleni was reduced to a wordless infant as they talked to him, pushing into his space, asking him for something again and again. She felt terror like a hand clenching her stomach. Her legs felt frozen, paralysed. Finally, it dawned on her that they were asking him for money and he was trying to talk them out of it. They were surrounded, and there was nobody else around to call to for help. They were at their mercy.

One of them finally turned to her and said in heavily accented French, 'Do not worry, we will not touch you. It is only the French we have it in for.'

How did he know she was not French? She had not talked at all. Had he assumed that she was a prostitute of some sort? She started hoping that Yves would just give them the money and it would all end, but then she saw the first punch go into his face. Blood ran down his nose and she screamed. She tried to go to his side, but they were all around him, not letting her get any closer. The circle had closed around him, leaving her out. She thought there might have been another two punches after that, and suddenly they were off, as abruptly as they had come. He was doubled up on the pavement in tears, his face covered in blood. 'They took all my money', he wept. 'I had a month's earnings in there.'

She helped him up, trying to steady him. 'Yves, you must remember where you put your car. Please try to concentrate', she told him as gently and firmly as she could. They both started at the noise of the brakes of a taxi turning the corner and stopping right in front of them.

'Do you need a ride?' The taxi driver popped his head out of the window. 'Are you all right, man? Do you need me to take you to hospital?'

'Oh, no, I am all right', Yves mumbled. 'But yes, please, we desperately need a ride.' They both got in and he leant forward to give the taxi driver instructions, keeping one arm round Eleni's shoulders.

'How are we going to pay?' she whispered to him once the taxi set off. 'I have no money on me.'

'Don't worry, I will sort it out', he reassured her, while still visibly trying to find his bearings. He held her and kept her tight by his side. 'Je suis desolé', he kept saying to her. She felt like giving him something, she didn't know what.

She kept kissing him on the mouth as she squeezed into his side during the twenty-minute ride home. She was not sure, in the darkness of the taxi's back seat, if it was saliva, tears or blood that found its way into her mouth.

***

It was 6.10 a.m. Eleni was lying in her narrow single bed, now in her pyjamas, not having bothered to cover herself with the duvet, although she was shaking all over. With the curtains drawn back as she had left them the day before, she saw the sun rising and breaking through light white cloud. Nicolas should be here any minute now. They had just about settled into coupledom, settled into seeing sex not as novel and exciting and something to experiment with, but as an expression of the intimacy they felt with each other. It was not long ago that her body had finally got used to his, and she was looking forward to the familiar routine and the exciting pleasure of their union. How had she managed to break all this in three hours? She did not believe that it would feel the same ever again.

6
The scent of things to come

Thessaloniki, June 1983

Leonora was walking swiftly towards the school keeping her head down, engrossed in her thoughts. She must not be seen by her daughter, not before it was time to pick her up anyway. How would she account for picking her up from school, something she had not done for years, out of the blue, just like that? She finished work early, she could say, and she wanted to see whether Eleni fancied taking her to town for a true kasseri toastie and freshly brewed coffee ice cream in Aristotelous Square. These were Eleni's favourite treats, which she adored matching up with the glimmering view of the nearby open sea. Eleni always loved an enticing view to enjoy her food with, and Leonora could not blame her. She only wished her own life allowed for pausing and getting perspective.

Still, it would look odd. She didn't want to clash with her. She had known better than to do that from the time her daughter was only two years old. Trying to tell her what to do, to oppose her, never worked. She had had to refine her diplomatic skills from very early on. She had to get her to do something in a roundabout way, make it look like it was not her idea at all, like it was Eleni's own invention.

She had managed to appear calm and composed even during Eleni's most unreasonable and prolonged tantrums. Like that time when Eleni was five and she packed a rucksack with her favourite toys, saying that she was leaving for ever, she was never coming back to this family that she didn't like. She had let her get out of the flat, shut the door behind her, and heard her going down the five flights of stairs. Then she went down herself and waited calmly by the front door. She knew she wouldn't go as far as the end of their little street that led onto the main road, busy with speeding cars. Yet it was quite a bet to take.

This time though, things were much more perilous. How had this mess cropped up out of nothing? This time round, she had to be very careful and vigilant with the school and with what she conveyed to Eleni. She just wished that she didn't have to handle all this alone as usual, that she didn't have to think it all through carefully and strategically, to make sure that she was protecting them all as a family, but most of all that she was protecting Dinos yet again. He was like an overgrown child, so vulnerable in his mood swings, either up in the clouds or down in the dark doldrums, and never quite able to handle things, to stay in touch with reality.

She stopped at the last crossroads in Iasonidou just before the school, letting a car pass. The dark iron, ominous-looking school gates had become visible now on her left. It should be easy to work it out with Eleni, she didn't have to worry about it. She would just say that she had to catch the shops before closing, had found herself downtown and had thought of picking her up to give her a treat. But if she preferred to go skating with her friends instead, she could still go: she hadn't come here to be obstructive to her plans.

All these hours of skateboarding after school had to stop anyway. A gang of prepubescent children disappearing for hours after school into the vast grounds of University Town, nobody keeping track of them, supervising them. Now that they were getting close to puberty it was all about boys and girls and who fancied whom – Eleni would tell her as much. The plan was to go private for secondary. The school had been chosen already, a traditional all-girls secondary, but Eleni had not been told. Well, her father had tried to tell her, and it ended up in disaster as usual. 'I am going to go state for secondary with all my friends. How could you even dare to think otherwise? I know why, you just want me to be unhappy', Eleni had said in a shrill voice, holding back her tears; and then she had left the kitchen, banging the door behind her and stomping her feet.

She was buzzed into the school. Her mind was spinning. She needed to concentrate on the meeting with Eleni's teacher. She needed to be polite but firm with him. Not threatening, not overtly threatening at least, but putting her request across to him. She had to convey to him that his attempt at pastoral care had failed. His intervention had been both intrusive and unwelcome. Surely the headmaster would be thoroughly disappointed to hear that one of the wealthiest and most respected families that this inner-city school had ever attracted was leaving feeling rather embittered.

Anyway, what happened was still mind-boggling to her. She had befriended Eleni's teacher and his wife when Eleni had first joined the school. In fact the couple were the only positive asset to the school, teachers by ideology, deliberately choosing to work in a school with an unusual number of children with complex needs, from impoverished backgrounds or from broken families. They both regarded their pastoral role in the school very highly. She had even tried to support their work by organising charity events at the hospital. She wouldn't have normally told them that Eleni was adopted, but she knew that they had already noticed. They were that kind of people with an eye for a child's darker secrets and concerns about how these might affect their development.

And yet she had not anticipated that he would call Eleni into his office to talk to her about her family. Thank God she was rather good at mind- and face-reading, especially where her daughter was concerned. That day, she had come back from school unusually early.

'How come you did not go skating with your friends today?' Leonora had asked her, sensing the upset through her daughter's tight-lipped face even before risking the question.

'Not in the mood', was Eleni's unforthcoming reply.

'Did something happen at school? You seem a bit upset to me', Leonora had persisted. And then it all spilled out: about how Mr Manos had called her into his office and asked about her family, prompting her to confide in him. Thankfully, Eleni was not one of those secretive, introverted children. It did not take much for her to confide in her mother.

She turned the door knob of the main school building and let herself in. Her stomach was churning. It felt like walking into one of the hospital's large interdisciplinary meetings, knowing fully well that somebody's throat was on the line, and, depending on whether this person was your friend or your enemy, you had to play it right or else your own throat would be next.

Mr Manos rose politely to greet her as she entered the room, and he pulled a chair away from the desk, gesturing for her to have a seat.

'Mr Manos,' she said, getting straight to the point, 'do you realise that my daughter took an overdose two days ago? The overdose in itself was not serious, she didn't need to go to hospital or anything, especially since I am medically trained and I know what to look out for, but I am sure that you would agree with me that the act is very serious.'

'Indeed! I cannot believe that Eleni did such a thing. I have to admit that I have been in a state of shock since hearing about it. Eleni is one of the happiest, most settled children in our school. She is full of life.'

'Quite. She is a happy child, as you just said. That is precisely why I was really puzzled when I heard that you called her in your office and you interrogated her about her family and her problems. I was very unsettled, to say the least, when I heard about it, but I decided not to confront you at the time.' Leonora took a deep breath, and felt the adrenaline running high in her body. 'I would not have brought it up at all, as I know full well what good work your wife and you do for the school, if it was not for what happened after, what Eleni did.'

'Are you saying, Mrs Hatzi, that Eleni took an overdose as a result of me talking to her? Is this what she said? I was very gentle with her, you know. We had a good conversation.'

'Yes, sure, a conversation about "the family secret". She didn't know what to make of it. Oh, and about the problems in her parents' marriage. All relationships have their problems as you know, Mr Manos, but I can assure you that my husband and I are doing, have always done, the best for Eleni. You yourself told me how impressed you were by her knowledge of geography and natural history. That is because my husband and I have travelled a lot with her. My husband has been teaching her about nature and animals as well. He tells her wonderful stories about his traditional upbringing in the countryside. We have always bought her the best toys, and many, many books. Last summer my husband took her downtown to Barbounakis bookshop. He wanted to buy her books for her summer holiday reading. You know how many books they came back with? Thirty! He was struggling to carry them. But she read them all, if you want to know, before the summer break was over. She loves reading.'

'I know all this, Mrs Hatzi. I have every trust that Eleni's academic development will be exceptional.'

'And then, she is a child who loves joining the adult world as well. So we take her out to expensive restaurants with us. She loves to eat game and to try unusual cheeses. My husband always talks to her about how the food she eats grows and why eating seasonal and local is best. His knowledge of such things is profound. Yet, despite being raised so differently from most children in this school who have never been in a restaurant or to a foreign country in their entire life, she is happy to blend in and she has made many friends. She is a child fundamentally happy in herself. This is why I don't understand why you chose to unsettle her.'

'Mrs Hatzi, please let me try and explain. I agree with you that Eleni is fundamentally a happy and settled child – and please permit me to say that this is also due to our work at the school. She did not come across like that when she first joined the school. She was very shy, lacking in social skills with her peers, but this is not unusual in an only child. However, she is approaching puberty very fast and she has formed a close friendship with another girl who is also precocious in her development, like Eleni. My impression is that the two of them are already treading in deep waters and may run into difficulties once they leave this school and start secondary. Believe me, I have seen it happen to some of my brightest pupils, those with the greatest of potential. But also, I am particularly vigilant with Eleni because I know that she has such a complicated history to handle and come to terms with.'

'Don't you think it is the place of her family, her parents, to deal with that?'

'Well, yes and no. Good teaching can play a very helpful role too. But Mrs Hatzi, I have still not made myself clear. I had no idea, I was astonished in fact, to realise that Eleni did not know about being adopted. Once this was clear to me through our conversation, I did not push any further and I made sure that I did not reveal anything myself. I have to admit that it was naïve of me to assume that Eleni knew about her history, but I had assumed that, as you are a well-educated professional woman, you would have told her already. It is common knowledge. Isn't it? And also, I am sure you will have heard it yourself that the best time to tell a child is in their early childhood, so that they develop with the knowledge as part of their growing identity.'

Leonora interrupted impatiently. 'I know all this, Mr Manos. If you want to know, I tried to tell Eleni when she was five and a half and it did not work. I am her mother, and we are very close, so permit me but I have to use my intuition in such matters. What I came here to discuss is what you are prepared to do to repair the terrible thing that happened two days after you interrogated her: Eleni's overdose and all its after-effects. I am sure you will appreciate that such a serious matter should normally be referred to the Head. I would be within my rights to complain or at least to raise a question to Mr Papastylianou about the effect your intrusive act had on Eleni and on our family life. But I think that we will agree on one thing, that it is best for everyone concerned, and for Eleni especially, not to escalate the matter any further, and to resolve it here between ourselves.'

'I am sorry but I don't understand. I am not clear what you are asking of me.'

'Well, let's say what happened was an accident, a misjudgement on your part. You meant to help, not to harm, but as you can see, your intervention was indeed harmful despite your best intentions.'

'Mrs Hatzi, I very much doubt that Eleni's overdose had anything to do with my intervention. It is rather unfair to blame me for Eleni's complicated history and the fact that it has started affecting her. Eleni and I have always had a very good rapport, as I am sure she will have let you know.'

'Even worse. You are someone that she looks up to and trusts, and you chose to stir things up for her before she was ready to handle it.'

'On the contrary, I stepped back in order not to stir things up for her. Perhaps it is this knowing and not knowing that is the most disturbing and dangerous thing for her. Have you thought about that?'

'It would be hard to argue, Mr Manos, that a girl in your class who takes an overdose at an unheard-of age for doing such things just two days after you spoke to her about very delicate matters clearly outside your role and responsibility as her teacher was nothing to do with you. It is somewhat preposterous for you to assume so, don't you think? Anyway, the problem we have now is that almost all the parents in the school, or at least in Eleni's class, know about it. I have received phone calls. This is clearly not good for our family right now, but nor is it good for the school's reputation, or yours as a teacher either.'

'I see. You are quite right.'

'It is fortunate that my husband was away on a business

trip while all this happened. He is very sensitive in matters that concern Eleni, you know. He would have made a big fuss at the school. He would use his friendly connections with local politicians and the council – so many of them come from his village in the Peloponnese. You would not want that to happen, not after all the hard work you have been putting into this school.'

'Mrs Hatzi', he interrupted, his voice sounding impatient. 'What is it that you are asking of me?'

'I am receiving phone calls from mothers who are concerned and who want to know what happened to Eleni. This has been testing my patience, and I hate the sense that there is gossip about our family. Perhaps you could call some of the parents in. You will know the ones who like to gossip. You could say that there was a concern about a friendship between two girls in the school and that you tried to intervene but your intervention was not entirely successful. You could say that the matter is under control now, and ask them to be discreet and to stop talking about it. Reassure them, do whatever it takes.'

Mr Manos had leaned his head to the right and he seemed engrossed in intense thinking. 'Mrs Hatzi, this does not sound entirely unreasonable, and it might actually be a good idea. Let me mull over it. I will think about the best way to handle the gossipy parents. But with your permission, I need to talk to Eleni again. I need to find out what it was that upset her so much.'

'No. I totally object to that. Eleni is in a delicate condition right now. Anything could upset her. I, as her mother, am keeping a close eye on her. She has always talked to me. You do not seem to realise it, Mr Manos, but your intervention was a mistake. It unsettled our family's equilibrium. Believe me, it has not been easy to raise this child. Not as easy as having a half-hour conversation with her during the school break. Eleni and her history are a matter for her parents to deal with.'

'I have to respect your wishes, Mrs Hatzi, although I have to say that I don't agree with your view of things. I will try to assist you as much as I can in the matter of the other parents. If I have any concern, though, about Eleni's well-being – and I will also keep a close eye on her – I will have to call you in again.'

'That's fine', she said, and she got up, giving him a firm handshake and smiling coldly.

7
The encounter

London, March 2010

Eleni looked at the clock sneakily, trying not to wake Nicolas up. Four a.m. She had been tossing and turning all night. She could not believe that it was happening again. After all these years of therapy, having declared herself cured, and here she was, lying awake in the middle of the night thinking of a stranger. It is almost an irony to stay awake in the night when you are the mother of a baby and the baby has been sleeping through, she thought to herself.

She got up as noiselessly as she could to check on Chloe again. It was the third time already, and if she was not careful she was going to end up waking her. Chloe was a light sleeper, like her. She stared at her small body stretched out in the cot, her arms spread trustfully out. Every time she would wake up to check on her since she was tiny, she would feel her heart pumping hard for fear of finding a baby who was no longer breathing.

The anxiety had become worse in the last few months after the dreadful incident. She had woken up in the middle of the night only to find Chloe on her breast. This was ordinary enough, as Chloe was fed on demand and she was still then sleeping in their bedroom, her little cot with the rails down on its one side next to her side of the bed. And yet she just knew that something was wrong. Had she rolled over her and smothered her? It had probably been the pain that had woken her up rather than a mother's instinct. She had switched on the side-table lamp, still unsure of what she was looking for. Chloe had given her a toothless, tummy-full-of-milk smile. But when Chloe had pulled back ready for a middle-of-the-night play session, she saw it. The blood had crusted over her nipple, the raw skin red and exposed.

The few weeks that followed were even more nightmarish than the sleepless night she was having now. Chloe would have been tested anyway when she was about a year old; and the transmission risk was so small, about five per cent she was told, not worth losing sleep over. What about now, though – now Chloe had swallowed her blood? Was not having a mother with a history as messy as hers heavy enough for the little girl? Could she also have passed to her daughter on top of her complicated history a degenerative disease that she would have to carry for life? Some people should never have children, was her first thought when she discovered the crusty blood and realised that it stung like a stab.

It was barely dawn when she began moving Chloe into her own nursery the following morning. Nicolas thought that she had lost it.

'Did you not say you wanted to keep her in our room for at least a year?' he had tried to reason with her.

'That was before I discovered that I, her own mother, am a danger to her well-being', she had said between sobs.

'The risk is still very small, Eleni.'

'Oh, really? That's exactly how I got it. And she is only a tiny baby with an incomplete immune system.'

All she wanted from him was to hold her, but at the times that her despair caught up with her, he would always try to reason with her at best; or even worse, get exasperated and angry.

It took her at least a month to believe the test results indicating that probably Chloe had been spared for good. In order to manage her fear that she could be harmful to her own daughter, she had found the distance of traditional nursing in a strict routine and the baby having her own space at night reassuring. Yet her anxiety had not subsided since. She stared at Chloe from over her cot, the intensity of her love hurting her bones. She had heard it said, before having her, that babies make up for everything when they are asleep; but she didn't get it then. Well, you hardly get it before having them, do you.

Four forty-five a.m. Chloe would be up soon. How many times had she thought that she was finally slipping into sleep, only to be pulled away from it again, replaying his voice, its tone, its hue, what he had said to her last, replaying it all in her mind throughout the night. 'I think you are getting it', he had said. 'You seem to know intuitively what being a therapist is about. Few people get it, you know.'

'Art and Psychoanalysis', the workshop he was running was called. 'I am not a therapist, nor do I want to be one', she had replied.

Why did she have to be so sharp and rejecting in her reply to him?

There was something rather self-centred, though, in his statement that she would make a good therapist. Why did he assume that she wanted to be one?

'I am an artist', she told him. 'I only have an academic interest in psychoanalysis. That's all.'

She avoided telling him how many years she had spent in therapy, all those painful, sorrowful years going through all the details, all the complexities of her history again and again and going back for more. How many years had it been that she could not even imagine what it would be like to wake up without the heavy feeling in her chest, the sense of dread of having to face yet another day, as though being alive sat on her chest like a stone.

'Why are you not sleeping?' Nicolas said to her, turning abruptly to face her in the dark and making her jump out of her skin.

She hesitated. 'I am worried about my father', she replied, feeling a double load of guilt. Not only was she lying, but she was also not thinking about her father when she should have been. At least if that had been what was keeping her awake all night, it would have made sense.

'He will be all right, go to sleep', Nicolas murmured, and he drifted back, putting his arm around her waist.

Her mother had called her yesterday. They had had yet another doctor's visit. 'They don't expect him to live much longer', her mother had said to her over the phone. 'His heart and his lungs have given up, they are both well beyond any hope of recovery.'

She was drifting off to sleep, snuggled up with Nicolas, when the sound of his voice came back to her ears. It felt like a light touch on her skin.

'Come and do the workshop next week then', he had said. 'It is mostly aimed at artists.'

His face and his voice were so familiar. Where did she know him from? Did he remind her of Yves, of that night in Paris? He did not look even remotely like him, only in age. He had given them a small autobiographical note which included his year of birth. It was an unusual thing to do, to tell everyone his age. Maybe it was a show-off thing. He wanted to stress, to tell us all that he had grown up in the sixties, a flower-child. 'Make love, not war', and the rest. Nearly eighteen years between them, nearly eighteen years between her father and Nefeli, his almost-teenage love.

She had done her maths the other time as well, after that fateful night in Paris. And through her first year in therapy, while ruminating about everything, she'd had plenty of time to do the maths. All her sums had pointed to the fact that, on that fateful night on the Rive Gauche, she was probably exactly as old as her birth mother would have been in the month, even possibly the day of her conception. That night in Paris, she had nearly risked her life going out with a man as old as her father would have been on the night of her conception.

This was what happened to her when she was sleep-deprived. She got into maths. Everything in her mind turned to numbers. She could not help but wonder whether it was a psychiatrically classifiable trait. What would Leonora think? She would class it as obsessional for sure. That was it: her obsessional tendencies had come back.

She looked at the clock again, six a.m. She had stayed up all night thinking about a stranger, calculating the age difference between them. How on earth was she going to face the day that would begin in an hour or less? Chloe had been sleeping through, which meant that she would be well rested and full of energy in the morning. She was going to get three precious hours of babysitting in the afternoon – hours during which she should do some work, get in touch with things. Would she end up using those hours for sleeping? How tedious!

She turned onto her other side and fell into a painfully deep, dreamless sleep exactly as the first purplish-grey light of dawn started seeping through the white shutters of their bedroom window.

8
Dying

Thessaloniki, March 2010

He lay in bed with the mask on. The pale skin of his face felt puffed up through the mask's harsh plastic pressing against the sides of his nose. He could feel his distended stomach spreading on both sides as he lay on his back, his legs nearly alien to him, paralysed, stick-thin as they had become, emaciated through years of heavy steroid use. Through his half-closed eyes he could see his left arm, covered in bruises, a collection from his repeated hospital stays in the last few months. It was only two o'clock in the afternoon, but the shutters were drawn in and the bright ceiling lamp was on, even though he drifted in and out of dozing. The only noise in the room was the sound of the oxygen ventilator, and his legs occasionally shuffling against the bed sheets that no longer felt crisp.

Leonora tiptoed in. He sensed her standing at the end of the bed looking at him, trying to determine whether he was asleep or not.

'What?' he said just as she was about to walk out again.

'Oh, I thought you were asleep. It is just that the doctor

called. He said that he is running a bit late, but he should be here by three.'

'What time is it now?'

'Five past two. Do you want something to eat? It is getting past lunch time, but I didn't want to wake you up; A soup maybe? I could put something together quickly.'

'Can you cook me the courgette casserole with potatoes?'

'What?'

'That courgette casserole that my mother used to make, you know. Fresh courgettes picked from our farm, my favourite childhood dish.' The taste as he spoke filled his mouth.

'I wonder if you are hallucinating a little bit, Dinos', Leonora said, as though talking to herself.

'For God's sake, I am not hallucinating, my mind is as clear as ever. It is just this body that is all wrong. You asked me what I want to eat. This is what I want to eat!'

'But – but where can I find courgettes in early spring? I would need to go downtown, and even then it is unlikely. This is a midsummer dish. Did you forget?'

'In the spring the courgettes started flowering in our garden. My mother would stuff the courgette flowers with feta cheese and fry them in olive oil. You never find such delicacies in these northern lands where I have ended up. The courgettes were still small, but deliciously fresh, and so were the new potatoes coming out of the land. My mother's cooking was the best in the world.'

'Besides,' she said 'we are waiting for the doctor,

remember? You can't get up and buzz him in.'

'I am not hungry, thank you. It is just that this is all I want to eat before it happens.' Couldn't she see that his body was well past hunger? he wondered. Hunger is for the living.

'You must eat something though. It is no good to eat nothing.'

He tried to sit up. He tried to take the mask off. She rushed to help him. Even with the slightest exertion, he felt breathless.

'You are not supposed to take the mask off', she said, panic palpable in her voice. 'Not with how bad it has got. Let's wait for the doctor and see what he says.'

'I am dying, Leonora.'

'Don't say that. You will fight this one too. You fought so many of these health scares before. You will make it, just think positive.'

'Have you called Eleni?'

She hesitated. 'No, not yet. I don't want to upset her. We are waiting to see what the doctor says, remember?'

'Call her now. She may want to see her father before he dies. It takes time to travel over from London. I need to see her, say my goodbyes before it happens. I don't have long left, Leonora.'

'Okay, I will call her as soon as the doctor leaves. I promise.' She paused. 'Shall I call Her as well?' she added hesitantly.

He struggled to breathe now. He put the mask on again and lifted the bottom rim slightly off his face, directing his voice to escape through it.

'Who is "Her"?' he asked, his voice breathless at the end of the short sentence.

'You know! *Her*', she said, as though uttering her name would make her feel sick. 'Do you need to see Her?'

'Do you mean Nefeli?'

He put the mask on properly and breathed in and out heavily. He could hear his voice coming through it altered, deep, as though from far away. 'No, I don't need to see her', he said steadily. 'It is over. She's gone off with him and she's done herself in for ever. She's gone,' he repeated, 'literally, gone – gone from life.'

'Well, you are done in too since she left', Leonora said, looking down. 'I thought and thought about it, and as much as I would like you never to see her again, as unpleasant as it is for me, I think it may do you some good. Maybe she is the cure you need, the only one who can save you. I am willing ...', she stopped to swallow, and her voice trembled. '... to give it a try for your sake.'

He felt tired beyond belief now. 'I need to lie down', he said. 'Help me turn on my side.'

On his side, he felt an edge more comfortable, as though it was just about bearable to be in his body. He pulled the bottom of the mask off again so that his lips were exposed.

'You don't understand. You never got it, did you, what this relationship was about? You think it is about my jealousy and heartbreak and me being stubborn, not wanting to see her because she's gone off with someone else. I only wish she had done that earlier, before I got into this state. She drank my blood slowly throughout my life. I am the one dying, Leonora, but you seem to forget things.'

'Forgetfulness is soothing sometimes.'

'Are you forgetting that she was here, in this bedroom not that long ago, only last summer? She was visiting almost every day then. Did you forget that?'

'I am trying to.'

'Did you think this was all about our love, holding hands and the rest? She had already gone off with him then. God, this woman is so disturbed. She waited all her life to get off with someone and look who she picked, an ex-prisoner, a complete bastard.'

'You shouldn't get over-exerted', she said mildly.

'The only reason she used to come and visit last summer was money. Every day she came and she asked me for money. 'Give me some money,' she would say, 'I need it for my pension.' Every day I would put some money in my pyjama pocket and give it to her before she left. You know that sum of money that went missing and you suspected the cleaner? I think it was her. She knew where we kept it. I spent all my life trying to help this woman and all she was after was my money.'

'She has written to Eleni though. I didn't want to tell you, but she did.'

'What has she got to say to her?'

'I don't know. Eleni did not say any more. She no longer talks to me like she used to, you know.'

'Eleni, oh, Eleni', he sighed. 'That was the other thing. She told me one of the last times that I saw her, probably the time she stole the money, I could see that she was up to something, you know. She was wandering around the flat and I said to her, "Are you looking for something?" Anyway, that time, she said to me that Eleni truly hates me, not a love-hate thing, an intense father–daughter relationship as I always wanted to believe, but true hatred. "Eleni wishes you dead", she told me. Eleni, my Eleni, my little girl hates her dying father.' He began a painful weeping that burned the centre of his chest.

'Please try not to get upset. None of this is true', Leonora said, getting interrupted mid-sentence by the loud noise of the door buzzer.

'It is the doctor', she said in a high-pitched voice. She patted his hand quickly before leaving the room to answer the door. 'Forget about her. All you need to do is fight this last fight', she said tenderly.

9
Separation

Thessaloniki, August 1977

Eleni was at her mummy's office in the hospital. It always felt like a special honour to spend the morning at her mummy's workplace. If she had it her way, she would be there much more often. She loved the hospital, with its beautiful lime- and cherry-blossom-scented garden that overlooked the town centre and Thermaikos Gulf. On a spring or summer day like today, she loved sitting on one of the bright red benches in the garden, chewing a freshly baked koulouri that her mummy had bought her from the canteen and looking down at the blue-green glimmer of the sea spreading as far as she could see, merging with the sky at the horizon. The beauty of the landscape would be somewhat spoilt by the sight of the inpatients popping out into the garden to smoke a cigarette and to sip their coffee. They were often there with a family member making sure they were steady on their feet and carrying their bottles of serum for them, taking care so that the drip would not come loose.

Eleni did not mind the lack of ride-on toys in the garden or the absence of other children to play with. In fact, she almost enjoyed the company of adults more. She was so used to it by now, and it often meant that she received special attention. The images of some of the patients visiting the garden, though, would leave a lasting imprint in her memory, like a bad smell that she could not shake out of her nostrils. Some of them had their arms covered in bruises, or they looked very frail as they walked slowly, supported by crutches. Even worse, some of them had their faces or a limb deformed as a result of a bad car accident that had left them spending weeks in hospital. She would always try not to look at them, but sometimes she would find her eyes fixated on a missing limb or a monstrous-looking burnt face, and it was not unusual then to receive a nasty look back that would make her want to run away and hide.

The other thing she loved doing when in her mummy's work was to walk by her side when she went out on the ward tour. People would greet her mummy with respect. They would say, 'Hello, Doctor', or even, 'Hello, Director', and they would nod their head. Her mummy was the head of the whole clinic, and Eleni always felt so proud walking next to her. She seemed such an important person. Many of the people who greeted her mummy, mostly women, but occasionally some men too, would exclaim in delight when they noticed that Eleni was standing next to her, holding her hand and waiting patiently. They would bend down to her level and talk to her, say how much she had grown or how beautiful she looked in her bright new dress. Often they would look in their pockets in search of some chocolate or candy to give to her, or they would promise that they would pop by her mummy's office later to give her a little present. Eleni always felt shy during these encounters. She hardly ever replied, despite her mummy prompting her to. The people's faces looked familiar, but she didn't remember the names of most of them and they all seemed to think that she should know exactly who they were. Yet she secretly enjoyed the attention. She had grown fond of a couple of the younger women in their navy-blue nurse uniforms, who would buy her her favourite chocolates with the Mickey Mouse characters printed on each bright, folded square.

On this late August morning though, there was no chocolate treat for her. Her mummy would not allow her chocolate in the summer, she said the heat could make it go bad, and there was no ice cream sold in the hospital canteen either. She was sitting in her mummy's big black leather revolving chair, behind her imposing mahogany desk, her legs barely reaching the end of the chair even though she had now brought her body forward on the seat so that she could draw comfortably. In front of her was an open colouring block, and she had chosen the page with Cinderella and the pumpkin carriage. Every now and then, she had to hold the page open, or else the air blowing from the revolving fan would shuffle the pages.

She had promised her mummy that she would sit at her desk quietly and do some drawing and colouring, after their long walk in the garden and around the ward. Eleni had begged her to take her to the locked place, but her mummy had refused. She said no children were allowed there. She had only taken her there when it was nearly empty and there were some nice people there, but not all of the people locked up in the cells were nice and some of them were capable of saying quite nasty things to a child that would upset her. Eleni had been taken only twice to the basement, where, after unlocking a heavy padded door, they could see a number of locked-up square cells. The first time her mummy took her there, the place was empty apart from the security guard at the entrance. Her mummy had chatted to him for a while. She seemed to know him well. He told her that they were expecting some inmates that afternoon. The place was dark. Eleni could see no windows. It smelt of iron and a bit like a closet that had not been opened for days. Despite her fear, Eleni had found the place fascinating. It reminded her of the dungeon in 'Hansel and Gretel'.

'Are there actual people that live in these cells?' she had asked her mummy.

'Of course, that is what the cells are for.'

'And why do they lock them in here? Is it a witch who puts them here to eat them later? Why don't you stop her?'

Her mummy laughed. 'These people have done bad things and they need to be locked up here so that they don't do any more bad things.'

'What bad things do they do?'

'They do things like steal money or try to hurt other people.'

'And why do they keep them in hospital? Are they sick?'

'That is a clever question!' her mummy said. 'The people we have here are sick, and they have done bad things because they are sick, so they are not really all that bad. We keep them here until they get better and they understand that they have done something bad and promise not to do it again.'

'Oh.'

After that, Eleni had always wanted to visit the dungeon place, but she had only been taken there once more, when there were two very young men locked up in two of the cells. Her mummy had chatted to both of them and she had promised to see them both separately later. They had not seemed that bad at all, but neither of them had paid any attention to Eleni. When they left, her mummy told her that these men were boys really, and they were here because they had taken some pills that made them do bad things. Eleni should remember, she said, when she grew up never to take any pills unless a doctor prescribed them for her.

As she was sitting on the edge of her seat colouring the pumpkin carriage orange, she could hear her mummy talking to her two secretaries in the adjoining office. Her tone seemed agitated. Eleni thought for a minute that she could walk closer to the folding door between the two rooms and stand near it to hear what she was saying, but she decided against it. She had promised her mummy to finish one page of colouring-in at least, before getting up. After all, she wanted the pumpkin carriage to look nice, and she was taking care not to colour outside the lines. After a short while, her mummy walked in.

'Eleni, Mummy has to go to the conference now. I am presenting a paper. I was just talking to the girls and they will be more than happy to entertain you.'

'I don't want them to.'

'Come on, it will be fun. Maria will take you to the canteen and you can choose a cake. Any cake you like.'

'I still don't want to.'

'It is only for a couple of hours, Eleni. When I come back, we can go to the hospital restaurant and have lunch. You love lunch here, remember? And we haven't been for a while.'

'I don't want to stay with Maria. I want to be with you', Eleni said, protruding her lower lip as she tended to do when she was upset. She could feel hot tears welling up at the edge of her eyes.

'But I have to go and present the paper, Eleni. I told you this morning, remember?'

'Yes, but ... but you always allow me to be with you when I come to your work. Take me home then. I want to go home.'

Her mummy sighed. 'But there is nobody to take care of you at home. It is only two hours, Eleni, come on.'

'No!' Eleni said, getting up and standing rigidly. She was feeling really upset now.

'Okay then', her mummy said, sighing again. 'I will take you with me, but you have to promise Mummy that you will sit very quietly in the theatre while Mummy is on stage talking. Do you promise, Eleni?'

'Yes.'

'Otherwise Mummy will be embarrassed and people will gossip about her. Do you want that to happen?'

'No. I will be very good, I promise.'

'Oh and one more thing: Maria, will be with us to sit next to you. Okay?'

'Okay.'

'You have to be very nice and polite to her', her mummy warned her as she walked into the adjoining office to talk to Maria. Eleni could hear her apologising and asking her to accompany them to the conference.

They all walked down the hospital's main corridor and through a heavy-looking door into an amphitheatre with semi-circular rows of seats one above another. Eleni had never been here before. The place looked very dark and serious and enormous. The amphitheatre was already nearly full. Eleni could sniff heavy perfume in the air and hear the rising noise of collective whispering. Maria took her by the hand and Eleni did not resist, although she could feel a pang of upset in her tummy when her mummy, after giving her a peck on the cheek, walked ahead and sat down behind the raised long table with many serious-looking men in suits sitting behind it, sipping water from short transparent glasses. Eleni noticed that her mummy was the only woman behind this long table.

What happened next seemed very long and boring to her. The men in suits kept talking and talking, using long, strange words that Eleni did not understand. The words they used reminded her of her mother's medical encyclopaedia at home, with its long list of diseases and the scary, ugly images that accompanied each section. Her mummy's turn came, and she talked in exactly the same language. It was as though she was talking in a foreign tongue.

Eleni had grown very bored and restless and had started kicking her legs up until they reached the seat in front of her, despite Maria having tried to stop her a couple of times, when the lights were suddenly switched off and a big white screen came down behind the long table.

'A movie!' Eleni exclaimed, only to get a 'Shhh!' from Maria and a few disapproving looks from people sitting nearby. What followed reminded Eleni of late-evening TV films she had tried to watch with her parents while they had chivvied her to go to bed. There were groups of young people in the film, most of them handsome-looking. Everyone had their hair long and straight and they were all slim and tall and wore tight turtleneck pullovers and straight-legged trousers opening wide at the bottom. Even the boys had long hair. They were sitting on cushions on the floor, smoking, drinking and chatting. There was laughing and chatter. It was, in fact, like a party. After a while, they started doing things that seemed strange to Eleni. They gave each other pills, which they swallowed. Then the colours in the room went blurry, then very strong, as though the TV was broken. The boys and girls started dancing and kissing on the mouth. At this point, Maria whispered in her ear that the film was not suitable for young children, and, if she wanted, they could go out for some cake in the canteen. Eleni would have none of it.

Her eyes were fixed on the screen. Everything in the room where the boys and girls were was wrong. The music was too loud, the room was swirling around, the colours kept changing, the faces became blurry. Then someone opened the window while everyone else kept dancing, and she could see how high they lived, right at the top of a skyscraper. The lights of the city outside were dazzling as they shone into the room. Suddenly, one of the boys threw himself out of the window. He was high up in the air, dancing. 'Look, he can fly!' Eleni said; but she could hear screams now, and then a bang, when his body reached the ground far, far below.

***

Her mummy took her to the hospital restaurant for lunch, as she had promised. She had checked in the morning, she said, and they had Eleni's favourite hospital meal, roast chicken with potatoes and rice pudding.

'They are reserving a portion of chicken breast for you, Eleni. It is popular and it will be the first to go otherwise.

'Are you okay? You have gone very quiet', her mummy asked her while Eleni was wondering whether she still had room for one more of the yummy potatoes and the rice pudding as well.

'I like the food here', Eleni smiled.

'I think it is because you like spending time with me.' Her mummy smiled back.

'Why could you not stay at home, Mummy, and look after me?'

'Because then you could not come here and be proud of me and my work.'

'I guess', Eleni said quietly, pushing the potato away with her fork. There was no room for it in her tummy after all.

'Eleni, I thought that as we are spending all day together today, it might be a good time for me to tell you something important.'

'What is it?' Eleni said, feeling curious. 'Can I have my pudding first?'

Her mummy hurried to fetch the pudding. She had remembered to put extra cinnamon on top, just as Eleni liked it. She tucked in.

'You know how you like to spend a lot of time with me because you feel close to me?'

'Because you are my mummy', Eleni mumbled with her mouth full.

'Yes, and a child's mummy is the person who takes care of her and who is close to her, but this is not always the person who gives birth to her.'

'Is it not a birdy that brings a baby to a mummy?'

'I guess that's a good way to put it. A birdy brought you to me. Another woman had you in her tummy and gave birth to you, but she could not keep you, so I chose to have you, because I very much wanted to have a baby. So a nice birdy brought you to me.'

'No way!' Eleni shrieked, standing up and throwing her spoon to the floor. She could feel hot tears running down her cheeks. She noticed her mummy looking around, seeming worried. She did not even know why she was so upset.

'You are my mummy, nobody else. If you ever dare to tell me this again, I will fly out of the window like a birdy, like those people in the film.'

***

Later on, when walking with her mummy back home,

Eleni asked her about the boy in the film.

'Could this boy really fly like the Bionic Woman?'

'Which boy?'

'The boy in the film who threw himself out of the window of the skyscraper. It was like he was dancing in the air at the beginning. Could he fly, Mummy?'

Her mummy paused and looked at her very seriously. She turned to face Eleni.

'Do you think flying is fun?' she asked.

'Yes, it is my dream to be able to fly. I would love to.'

'Listen to me, Eleni. Humans cannot fly, only birds and aeroplanes can.'

'It is not true. The Bionic Woman can.'

'That is only a fairy tale. That boy in the film had taken a pill called LSD and the pill made him think that he could fly. It was like he was dreaming. Pills like that are very dangerous and they can make people do bad things, like the people locked up in the dungeon.'

'Oh.'

'Do you promise Mummy that you will never try to fly like that boy? Do you?'

'Okay.'

'Do you know what happened to that boy?'

'No. What?'

'He was crushed on the ground and died.'

'How sad', Eleni said quietly.

They kept walking, looking for shade from the hot mid-afternoon August sun.

Layer 2

All the clouds confessed to the earth
A grief of my own took their place

And when in my hair the unrepentant hand
Grew melancholy

I was bound in a knot of sadness.

Odysseas Elytis, *'Climate of Absence'*

10
Therapy

London, February 1998

Eleni was curled up in the floor-cushion corner again, the analysis couch that she had invented for herself given the lack of a real one in the tiny room where Laura had seen her twice a week for the last month. Twice-weekly sessions were still a novelty for Eleni. Apparently, therapists working at the University Counselling Centre were hardly ever allowed to take on a client more than once a week, but an exception had been made for her. Laura had managed to persuade the management that Eleni needed long-term intensive therapy. So here she was, sitting cross-legged on the plump floor cushion, having managed to establish herself as a long-term case. Did this mean that she was a mad case too? Laura had not made her feel mad when she broke the news to her with a restrained smile of achievement.

Today, Eleni had managed to cycle across Russell Square and arrive at the Centre just one minute before the start of her eight a.m. Monday session. Laura had warned her that she could only fit her in for a second session if she accepted an early-morning slot, as they were unpopular with most students. Early morning was not a problem for Eleni, as she had been an early riser since she was little, to her mother's despair. An unexpected problem had cropped up though. These Monday sessions were the times when Laura seemed to go weird, Eleni had said to her friend Emma from college, who was asking her how her therapy was going over scones munched with late-afternoon coffee.

'What do you mean weird? What is she like?'

'Well, I have seen tears in her eyes sometimes. She is much more approachable, more real, on Mondays, but I wonder if it is me she is moved by or if she has a problem of her own, something personal that gets triggered in our session.'

'It doesn't sound good, you know', Emma had said, taking a sip from her coffee. 'I can't say for sure, as I never had therapy myself, but I imagine a therapist should always appear professional, neutral.'

'She also gives me a hug by the door, almost always on a Monday.'

'Does she touch you?'

'Sometimes ... It feels like being touched anyway ...'

'Eleni, get out of there at once. The woman is mad. She probably fancies you or something.'

Eleni almost choked on her coffee. 'Don't be silly.' She paused for a minute. 'I really like talking to her, you know. The things I have told her, I haven't told anyone else. She is very special to me.'

'And you are very special to her indeed!' Emma said,

suppressing a laugh.

'Don't be a tease', Eleni said, trying to hide her annoyance. They both giggled and kept munching on their scones.

'I was thinking about my father', Eleni mumbled, drawing her knees towards her chest. 'I am not sure why; I think the last session triggered something.'

'What were you thinking about him?' Laura asked, leaning forward.

'I've had all these memories of him in the last few days, from when I was very little. He used to play with me in bed then. "Aeroplane" was my favourite. I would put my belly on his feet and he would hold me high up by straightening his legs and then sway me. It was real fun.'

Laura smiled.

'This was all before I was six, I think. Everything changed after. He would take me for drives in his fancy car then, and take me downtown to his office where Nefeli was working and there were people coming in and out. It was all very exciting. They would let me wander off down the street. At the end of the street where his office was, there were steps leading down to a little church and I loved sitting there munching on a slice of bread with blue cheese spread. Can you believe it? Nefeli introduced me to Roquefort cheese when I was little and I loved it. I have never heard of a child other than me liking blue cheese.'

'It sounds like you also have fond memories of your birth mother from that age. Maybe liking blue cheese was a way of being linked to her.'

'Actually, it was more like she knew what I liked. I don't

remember her eating it herself. She just knew that I would like it.' Her head was lowered, but she still noticed Laura's eyes looking moist.

'Going back to your father,' Laura said, seeming to want to change the subject, 'do you know what changed how you felt about him? Was it that he was not nice to you at other times?'

'He could be frightening, but mostly he was nice to me when I was little. It was when I was a teenager that we clashed. It was his temper I think that made me not want to spend time with him. It was scary to watch. He was like a volcano; I waited and waited in terror for its next eruption, and I just knew that it would happen sooner or later. After witnessing a number of these eruptions, I started avoiding him.'

'What were the eruptions like?'

Eleni paused, trying to think. 'Once, I remember, he was driving me to his office and there was a lot of traffic. A taxi came too close and scratched the side of our car. My father took the taxi driver up on it, and rather than apologise, the taxi driver said something like "fuck off". Next thing I knew, my father was out of the car, pulling the taxi driver by his shirt, lifting him off his seat just with one arm through the taxi's open window, looking him in the eye, his face very close to him, and whispering "What did you just say?" Of course, the taxi driver seemed scared to death; he apologised and offered to give my father his insurance number to pay for the scratch. And after all this, my father was like "no, don't worry, it is okay" and he let him go. Thinking about it as an adult, I think I would have liked the taxi driver to pay for the scratch – it is fair I guess – but I would not have threatened him like that. This is what my father was like, extreme.'

'I get the picture.'

Eleni paused and covered her face as an image as vivid and raw as though it had only happened yesterday flashed in front of her eyes. She stayed like that for a while, absolutely still, hearing her squashed breathing and the discreet shuffling coming from Laura's chair.

'I wonder where you are in your mind, Eleni', Laura said softly.

Eleni tried to speak, but she swallowed hard instead. She felt a shiver go through her body, as though her temperature was about to rise rapidly. She pulled her legs even tighter against her chest, sinking deeper into the plump, bean-filled cushion, feeling the comfort of being held by soft material. She took a deep breath in and heard her voice coming out strained, disconnected from her body.

'I just had a memory, an incident that happened when I was little, since which I did not want to be alone in the room with my father any more. After that, I was absolutely attached to my mother, not ever wanting to part with her. I remember wishing that he would leave or die, just leave us alone. And dancing with her, singing this song about her and me escaping to a nice place, just her and me alone in the world. That's it; after I was six my mother was my world. I would not trust anyone else ...'

Laura interrupted here, her voice slightly shaky, her eyes still moist. 'Did he abuse you, Eleni?'

'Abuse? Do you mean sexual abuse? Oh no, God, no! He was not like that at all.'

'No?'

'He didn't even see me as a girl, I mean not in the way some fathers admire their daughters' looks and encourage them to be feminine. He would have loved me to be a boy, I think.'

Eleni covered her face and burst into tears. 'Sorry, it's too difficult today', she mumbled between her fingers. Laura leaned forward and passed her the box of tissues. Eleni wiped her nose, but left her tears rolling slowly down her cheeks and eventually leaving wet patches on her white T-shirt and dampening the shoulders of her grey cashmere cardigan.

'You have remembered something significant, Eleni', Laura said after a while.

'I was about six, I think. I was in my room and they were arguing. This was not the first time they had had screaming matches around the kitchen table when they thought that I was asleep. When it happened before, I would always pretend to be asleep when my mother came to check on me. She often did a lot of the shouting, screaming things at him like "take your whore out of my house". This argument was somewhat different though: she was not shouting as much. In fact there was much whispering and talking under her breath, and slowly, as though she wanted to make sure that he understood each word's meaning. The tension was palpable. I remember even at that age, I could feel strongly that something was wrong. I remember sitting up in bed in a state of high alarm, trying to overhear what they were saying, but the words were lost to me.'

'It sounds dreadful.'

'My heart was pounding hard against my chest. I wanted to go to the kitchen and beg them to stop arguing, but I didn't dare. And then, all at once, the shouting and screaming started and I heard him saying, "I am going to kill you, bitch, I am going to kill you." And then, silence, nothing. I leapt out of bed and ran to the kitchen as fast as I could and I found him with his hands tight around her neck. "Leave her alone", I screamed, and I tried to get between them, but he did not move. He had this mad, explosive look on his face. He let go of her soon enough though, and my mother leant forward and spat blood out of her mouth. She tried to talk, but no voice was coming out. Eventually, she turned to me and said in a choked voice that I could barely hear, "Look, this is who your father is."'

'This is truly horrible', Laura said, seeming disturbed.

'That night, I slept in the double bed with her, and he slept on the sofa in the living room. I kept waking up to check if she was alive.'

'It must have taken a lot out of you to share this, Eleni. How are you feeling now?' Laura asked after a silence during which they had both been looking blankly into space, trying to gather themselves.

'Better than what I expected, actually', Eleni said quietly. 'It's just this strange sense of shame. I am not sure why it feels embarrassing to talk about it, as though it's my fault somehow that I had to witness it.'

'This is the nature of abuse. It makes people blame themselves, as though it is their fault that they have become a victim of abuse.'

'I ... I also wanted to talk about something else as well today. Do we have time?'

'About ten minutes', Laura said, looking at the clock.

'You know the thesis I am writing on the female body in contemporary art? You know I am allowed to use my own art as part of it. I never knew before why I was so drawn to explore the female body through art anyway. It almost felt like an obsession. Both my parents disapproved terribly of my choice of studying art. I haven't even shown them my work. They would be embarrassed, they would not see it as art at all I don't think. Anyway, I always thought of my art as a good substitute for the kind of life that I would be expected to have: get married, have a baby, all that.'

'As an antidote to becoming a mother?'

'Yes, that's right. A lot of my art revolves around the pregnant female body and childbirth. No idea why, I've never been pregnant myself.'

'No idea why?' Laura interrupted.

'No. Do you?'

'I suppose I have a sense of why it might be ... but go on, we will get to that later.'

'Well, some questions have been creeping into my head about motherhood, what it would be like. Anyway, I couldn't possibly. I can't. Not in my condition. Also, it means getting tied down into a long-term relationship. I have many doubts about that too. No matter how good it may be with someone, it always ends up being something that isn't one's own choice. It becomes a habit, an addiction – like my parents' relationship –'

'I think what you are saying is that there is a desire emerging in you about becoming a mother and that this is something that you had not contemplated before', Laura interjected. 'I think this is important, Eleni; and it ties in with your art.'

'How do you mean?'

'I think your art is a way of connecting, making a link in your mind with your birth mother. It is like saying that what you and she share is important. It is the same with these new thoughts about becoming a mother yourself. The therapy is allowing you to get in touch with such thoughts.'

'Such thoughts scare the hell out of me actually.'

'Our time is up', Laura said, smiling sweetly, as though talking to a child.

Eleni got up swiftly and, gathering her bag and her coat, she headed to the door.

'You can take the time to put on your coat', Laura said. She came to her and held the coat for Eleni to put on in an almost theatrical fashion. She patted her on the back and arm before Eleni was out of the door.

11 Birth

London, March 1972

Things with Mrs Marika had not been the same since the baby's birth, and Nefeli wondered sometimes what she had done to upset her. In Nefeli's mind it had all started on the day she had come back from her compulsory counselling session feeling disturbed and drained. The woman had tried to appear friendly, but Nefeli had felt grilled. She was asking her all sorts of strange questions. What was her relationship with her parents like? what was her childhood like? had she been abused? (she had had to explain to her what she meant by that), and what was the first time she had sex like? Nefeli had given her the official story.

'My parents were happily married, but poor', she told her. 'I always felt that my horizons were restricted at home, but they wanted the best for me, which is why they encouraged me to find work in a property development office. It was a good environment for me to work in, with excellent prospects. That is where I met the father of my child: he was the company owner, my boss.'

'Right. Can you tell me a bit more about your relationship with this man?'

'Well, he was a womaniser, everyone knew it.'

'Did he put pressure on you to sleep with him?'

'Not at all. He was charming and kind to me, and I liked him.'

'And then what happened?'

'Well, then I had a relationship with him and I got pregnant. I didn't want a baby, but it took me some time to realise that I was actually pregnant. In fact he was the first to notice.'

'What do you mean?'

'He asked me if I had missed a period and he said that he had an eye for these things and that I looked pregnant to him.'

'And then?'

'Then he offered to pay my expenses to study English in London and to live here for six months, which was always my dream, if I was willing to have the baby and give it over to him for adoption, as his wife and he could not have children.'

'And how did you feel about it?'

'I was fine about it. It was a great deal.'

'Do you feel fine about it now?'

'Yes, it is a good deal', Nefeli had repeated with a steely voice.

'It all sounds terribly devoid of emotion to me.'

Nefeli could still feel the irritation in her stomach. How she had wanted to punch the woman in the face, to tell her that it was none of her business what she wanted to do with her life, that she had no right to interrogate her like this. But the interrogation had gone on. Would she be able to take care of her baby before flying to Greece? Had she thought that she might want to keep her? This was the absolute worst point of the session. The woman leaned forward, her silvery hair accentuating the cold blue of her eyes piercing through Nefeli.

'You have been given a unique opportunity and I am not sure that you realise it', she had said in a very serious voice, stressing her every word. 'In the past, young women like you had no choice to even reflect on whether they wanted to keep their baby. You should take your time to think about it very seriously.'

Nefeli surprised herself by bursting into tears, and she could not stop weeping. She hated crying in front of strangers. She felt that the woman had had it all her own way. She had in fact been right not to trust her, as just before ending the session the woman told her that she did not feel that she had gleaned enough information in this one session to let her take the baby home with her. Mrs Marika would have to sign and vouch for her, and she would not be allowed to live anywhere else in the UK with the baby without reporting to the social services.

When she went back home after the session, it was like the floodgates had been opened. She stormed into the house, seeing in her peripheral vision Mrs Marika preparing lunch in the kitchen through to her left. Nefeli went straight up to her room. She was feeling so fragile that even saying hello would make her burst into tears. A minute later there was a soft knock on the door and Mrs Marika walked in. 'Are you okay, Nefeli?' she asked. This was enough to cause a melt-down. Nefeli curled up in bed and wept silently, covering her face.

'I will be back in a minute' Mrs Marika said in a low voice. She walked out noiselessly. Nefeli heard her mumbling something to Mario down in the kitchen, and then she was back with her in less than a minute, walking into the room softly, this time not knocking first. Nefeli had not moved from the foetal position she was lying in, her face wet and squashed up against the pillow.

'What's wrong, Nefeli?' she asked. She waited for a while, and as she received no answer, she tried again. 'Is it about the baby? Is it that you now want to keep her? I told you before, you can stay here with the baby for as long as you want.'

Nefeli sat up abruptly and folded her arms across her chest. 'What's the matter with you all?' she said in a hoarse voice. 'The counsellor I have just seen was also going on about it: how lucky I am to have the choice to keep my baby and so on. As though it is a great thing to be young and single and saddled with a baby for the rest of your life. I never wanted a baby. I don't want to be a mother.'

'I see.'

'It's just that the session made me think for some reason about my own childhood, my mother and how much I hate her. The counsellor asked me about my childhood and I lied and said that all had been well.'

'And was it not?'

'My mother was a bitch. Sorry, I know she is your friend, but she was a bitch to me. Since I have been living here and I have seen how well you have treated me, it has made it even more blatantly obvious what I never got from her.'

'It is always much more difficult with one's own children, Nefeli.'

'Is it? I thought mothers were supposed to love their children the best.'

'Your mother loved you. I still remember how much, and with what pride she talked about you.'

Nefeli wiped the few remaining drops of her tears. 'Soon after my father left to go to work – the poor man worked so hard for all his life, you know – my mother, all pretty and made-up, would sit on the balcony chatting up the lorry drivers who stopped at the café below to have their morning break. Sometimes she would leave the house all dressed up and come back a few hours later in an uncommunicative mood. I remember I was about eight when she started doing this, and my sister was even younger. I wonder now what she was up to; was she picking the lorry drivers up for money?'

Mrs Marika interrupted. 'Nefeli,' she said, 'I am really shocked to hear all this. I have to say that my impression of your mother was ... is quite different. Could it be that you have got it wrong?'

'Wrong? Do you think I am wrong? Why has she never asked me where I found the money to come here for all this time? She has hardly ever called me to see how I am. She expects me to make a living the same way she did, don't you think?'

'Nefeli!' Mrs Marika cried, as though she was scolding a toddler. 'Your mother when I met her at the factory was a hard-working, honest woman.' She stopped, seeming slightly out of breath.

'I'm sorry. I didn't mean to upset you. I hope you know how grateful I am to you for everything you have done for me.'

'I have to say that I have not been very impressed by the fact that she has hardly called while you have been here. But then, I know their finances are always tight and phone calls to England are so expensive.'

'She doesn't want to know what's happening to me, Mrs Marika; that's the truth.'

'It was this little doubt I have had in me that has stopped me calling her myself and telling her all about your situation.'

'I am glad you haven't.'

'I want to tell you a story, Nefeli', Mrs Marika said after some hesitation. 'From the day your mother and I were working at the factory. She was pregnant then, with your sister, and you must have been two or three or something like that.'

'I was three and a half when my sister was born.'

'I remember how often she told me how sorry she was to have to leave you, even though she left you with family I think, but that the money was not enough and she was trying to make ends meet.'

'My aunt and uncle looked after me when I was little. I loved them', Nefeli said, having entered a kind of reverie.

'Anyway, one day you had an accident. You fell down the three steps in the back yard and grazed your face near your eye.'

'Oh, I know that', Nefeli interrupted. 'I still have a small scar. Here, look. It must have been a bad cut.'

'Somebody came all the way to the factory to tell her, one of your uncles, I think. He said that you were fine, not in any danger, but that they had taken you to hospital, just to be on the safe side.' Mrs Marika paused to catch her breath. 'Sorry, I think I will need the inhaler for my asthma soon. The old friend is visiting me again.'

'Mrs Marika, I did not mean to upset you.'

'It's not you, my girl. It's being a mother that's upsetting. You make all this effort and the result, well, you never know how they will turn out or if they will turn against you in the end. Anyway, I think she should have come home, but she was scared of losing her job. Being pregnant and getting a job was not easy in those days. She stayed, but tears kept rolling down her cheeks while she was working. "I can't afford to lose another one, Marika," she told me. "What do you mean?" I asked. "I have already lost him, my first. I was seven months pregnant when he came, but the doctors could find no heartbeat, he was born dead. They said he may have died a few days before. A beautiful, blue-eyed baby, my son."' Mrs Marika stopped and wiped a couple of tears from her eyes. 'That day, she told me, Nefeli, how special you were to her. You were the baby that came after that first one, just when she thought that she would never recover from the loss. So, that's how I know that you were ... are very special to her.'

Nefeli was sitting very still, listening carefully. 'Oh, that explains it', she said after a small pause. 'The lost baby was a boy ... I kind of knew about the lost baby, she kept talking about it, how beautiful it was, but it was always an "it", "the baby". It never occurred to me to ask if it was a boy or a girl. I was sick and tired of hearing about it as a child. I always felt that I fell short of that baby. Something about me being a girl seemed to bother her. Especially when I was a bit older and I grew very fond of my father.'

'She wouldn't mind that, would she?'

'Oh yes, she did. When I was little, many aunties and uncles admired my looks. I had hay-blonde hair and bright green eyes, they said that I looked like a beautiful kitten – I remember being called a kitten. But she never said a good word to me. It was clear after a while that she was jealous. The only thing she was after was getting to me. She loved confrontation. You are the only person that I have ever trusted, you and my father. But my father was always so overworked; he would come back home dead tired, and I didn't want to burden him.'

'Forgive me, Nefeli,' Mrs Marika said breathlessly, 'I really should go and look for my inhaler.'

***

Nefeli woke up with a start. Her heart was pounding hard in her chest. She had fallen asleep sitting up against the cold wall by her bed. Her neck was hurting – her head must have been hanging in an awkward position. She turned her anxious gaze down to her empty hands. 'Where is the baby?' She turned awkwardly to inspect her bed. No baby there either. Could she have fallen asleep and smothered her? She had promised Him she would take good care of her. How could she have failed so soon?

She got up and looked at where she had been sitting, as though she could have sat unwittingly on her baby. As she stood up, her gaze fell on the cot next to her bed, where Eleni was sleeping peacefully with her arms spread out, even though the bright ceiling lamp was on. The baby bottle she had tried to feed her with had rolled down next to the coffee table and a little milk had spilled on the carpet. Nefeli picked it up and placed it on the coffee table. Who could have put Eleni safely in her cot? she wondered. Mrs Marika? She looked at the bedroom door, which was firmly shut just as she had left it. Surely, if Mrs Marika had walked in she would have switched the light off at least. The clock on the coffee table showed ten past three a.m. She must go to sleep, she thought. It wouldn't be long before the baby woke up for her next feed.

She had been trying to give the baby her one a.m. feed (one every four hours on a strict schedule, as the midwife had said) when she must have dropped off. Eleni was having none of it. All she wanted to do was to wail the house down. Mrs Marika's youngest next door had been studying for his exams. She had caused enough trouble as it was already before bringing this little terrorist into their home. How would she survive this, trying to quieten the baby down for another month? Why did people ever have children if it was so difficult? She got up again and switched the light off.

There had been a certain edge to Mrs Marika since Nefeli had brought the baby home.

'You are fully responsible for the baby, Nefeli, while you

are staying with us', she had told her firmly when Nefeli had approached her to ask her how to prepare the feed on her first day back from the hospital. The midwife had shown her, but it was like she was watching a movie in a foreign language, and the words were not sinking in. Nefeli had flinched as though stung by a wasp.

'I breastfed all of mine, so I don't know much about feeds', Mrs Marika had added in a milder tone.

Almost despite herself, Mrs Marika had kindly offered to babysit a few times so Nefeli could have an outing. On these bright mornings, which felt like the world had taken on colour again, she would board the bus across the road for the long journey to the West End. By the time she was on the bus after Eleni's nine a.m. feed, almost always successful in getting a front seat on the upper deck, the roads were clear of traffic as they approached the less suburban parts of London, full of excitement and happenings. She loved mingling with the crowd in her flared trousers and raised platforms, both recent acquisitions from her post-pregnancy shopping trips, her blonde hair falling smooth and straight around her face. She loved walking about the West End, feeling cosmopolitan, enjoying the sense that before she opened her mouth to speak nobody would guess that she was not local. Mrs Marika had always teased her about how fair she looked. 'My English daughter', she would call her.

Nefeli turned on her right side to face the dark wall and drew the warm, fluffy duvet, still smelling of Mrs Marika's fragrant washing powder, towards her neck. Even in Mrs

Marika's well-insulated and generously heated home, she could sense the intense winter chill creeping through the window. Perhaps it had tuned in to the chill in her heart.

She started to drift off. Random images flicked through her mind. The sea promenade in Thessaloniki, shiny under the sun's rays. Walking up and down the promenade alone, her hair being ruffled by strong winds, when she found out she was pregnant; Dinos kissing her softly and holding her on his lap behind his big mahogany desk; lying next to him after sex; her mother and father giving her a tight hug at the airport, her mother not letting her out of her grasp and it becoming smothering – the plane was leaving, she needed to go; her breasts hard and sore, leaking, gouts of creamy liquid flowing out of them; her breasts are turned-on taps, oozing warm milk. Is she feeling turned on? Mrs Marika's sad face before leaving her bedroom two days ago. 'We mothers, we always get it wrong, it is the history of mankind', she had said to her in a soft voice.

Nefeli jumped up with a start at a sharp shriek. The baby was wide awake.

12
Sweet adolescence

Thessaloniki, February 1986

'Eleni, this is really not like you!' Mrs Antoniou cried. 'I am rather more in favour of your jitteriness and circus acrobatics in class. Can you get out of hibernation at once, please. We need your jittery mind in class today.'

Eleni blushed so much that she felt the redness go down her chest and her back. She had almost fallen asleep during Greek class, her favourite. Mrs Antoniou always liked to tease her and to accompany her compliments about Eleni being top of class with comments about her circus-monkey behaviour. She had enjoyed this in the past. It felt like someone was accepting her for her best and her worst all at once. But today, being dragged out of her dark space, being exposed in front of everybody like this, was a step too far. She could feel Mrs Antoniou's sharp gaze discreetly observing her for the rest of the lesson, but was relieved that she did not address her directly again.

In fact, Mrs Antoniou was spot on that Eleni had suddenly lost her passion for gymnastics and acrobatics in the last few weeks. This was her third year in this overall dreadful all-girls secondary, and since the beginning she had puzzled everybody by getting A+s in Greek, Maths, Biology and PE. It is unusual to be brilliant in such diverse subjects, some teachers would remark. At the same time, she had enjoyed being less than mediocre in the subjects that had not taken her fancy, at least not in the way they were taught at the school: Music, English, Chemistry, Art and Religious Education. Some of her teachers had complained to her mum that she was not making an effort, as she was clearly a brilliant academic student when she felt like it.

'I love art,' Eleni had replied to her mum 'but this is utter crap, learning how to decorate and embroider. I would happily skip the class all together. As for RE, why don't they teach us about Buddhism and Hinduism as well? I would be interested then. Who gave them the right to assume that I am an Orthodox Christian, huh?' She always enjoyed seeing her mother's exasperated look.

'It is all right, Eleni, to like some subjects more than others; just make a bit more effort in those you don't like, so that we don't get comments like that. You need to learn to be more diplomatic', she would say. But all this felt to Eleni like a different era from now, when she had her full spirits about her.

The way Mrs Antoniou taught Greek used to excite her so much that she couldn't keep still in her chair. Mrs Antoniou was quite right: if she could combine the class with gymnastics she would be bringing her most exciting subjects together: poetry, literature and gymnastics. But her passion for gymnastics seemed to have evaporated in the last couple of weeks. She had not gone to the gym, not even once, to practise in the last week, while she used to go in every single break, and in yesterday's athletics class she had felt as though she was tied to the earth by heavy chains. Unlike Mrs Antoniou, Mrs Petraki, the PE teacher had not noticed the difference, being too absorbed as usual in one of her self-centred monologues. However, she had stopped her in the corridor earlier on today to ask her if she wanted to start practising for an individual gymnastics performance for the end-of-year concert. Eleni had told her that she would think about it, but she had already made up her mind. No way. She wanted nothing to do with the end-of-year concert. She was becoming more sedentary than a fat cat lying in the sun.

If she continued to have the kind of nights she was having, she would start falling asleep in every single class and then everyone would know that something was wrong. In fact, she could sense that some of the teachers had noticed already. She had bumped into the Head the other day, who had patted her on the shoulder and said, 'Gear up, Eleni. The end of your final year is approaching fast. You are one of our top students and we need to show the world what we are made of.'

As though she cared to represent the school in any way. All she cared about was getting out of here as fast as possible. She knew that one day she would look back at these years and think that this was the worst period of her life. Forcing her to come to this school had been added to the long list of reasons why she hated her father.

Yet there were some nice things about the place, like her Greek teacher, and even the Head, who, she had a feeling, had a soft spot for her; and also the chance to exercise in vast fields. But she was now in danger of losing even the things she liked, due to this dreadful symptom that had emerged in the last two weeks or so. It had started a few days after her mother's disclosure. For the first couple of days, she had thought that she was fine, that nothing much had changed; but she also felt numb, as though there was a filter between her and the world. At moments she had felt like pinching herself, as nothing had tasted or smelt or felt the same against her skin. It was a physical handicap, as though she had lost all her senses at once. Yet the worst was to come.

She could not fall asleep. She would toss and turn, but nothing happened. It wasn't thoughts that kept her up, just an overwhelming fear of dying. She feared that if she closed her eyes and let go she would never wake up again. She would eventually fall asleep after having come to some acceptance that this could be her last night, only to wake up a few hours later shaking all over, as though an internal earthquake had taken place. After that, she would usually not sleep again until she could see the first milky light of day creeping through the gaps in the curtains. It was only then that she was able to truly let go and drop off, as though the light of day would ward off death. But this morning sleep was always short-lived, as she would have to get up for school.

Eleni jumped at the piercing noise of the school bell. At

last, she was released. Mrs Antoniou shot her another look, but Eleni felt reassured that she was going to let her be just this once, although not for long. She wondered if she should talk to her, tell her that something was up at home, but the thought filled her with panic. She tried to wander off unseen before anyone approached her. Although she was heading outdoors, she did not take her coat for fear of drawing attention to herself. She had done this in every single break for the last week. Willing herself not to feel the cold sharp wind against her ribs, and eventually managing to shrug off her chattering teeth as just another little nuisance.

She would wander off well beyond the courtyard where other pupils gathered to chat or play volleyball. She would reach the borders of the school field and walk along the fence. The ground was muddy and uneven. The penetrating wind against her chest, cutting her breath away, was the only thing that would help her feel awake, alive again.

She would always have to head back after ten minutes as she was not sure if the bell could be heard here. As liberating as her walk was, she felt so invisible that she wondered if anyone would even notice if she didn't go back to class at all. They probably would, as her seat would be empty and Lena with whom she shared a desk would alert the teacher to her disappearance. They would have no idea where to find her though. That would be funny. She could imagine the headlines in the local news: 'High-achieving but friendless school pupil goes missing in a posh school's grounds', it would read. It wouldn't make the best advertisement for the next intake. Thankfully for her, the school had apparently failed to obtain the necessary funds to develop the high school, and that meant that she would have to move schools next year.

Eleni was surprised to feel her tears being blown off her cheeks by the strong wind. She had not noticed that she was crying. What was it that she was crying about? She was not feeling sad. Her heart was pounding fast and all she could feel was anger that they dared to bring her into the world without asking her, and anger that she had to be at this school, again without being asked. She should head back. Her English class would be starting any minute. The last thing she wanted was for the teacher to notice that she was late and tell her off for the second time today.

13
The beginnings

Athens, April 1972

Suddenly, she was standing right in front of him, holding a baby in her arms. He did not recognise her for a minute or so: her hair, now much longer, was falling around her face in golden-hued strands. Still stunned, he gave her a hesitant peck on the cheek, but Nefeli stood on her tiptoes and hugged him round the neck with one arm, holding the baby on the other, and gave him a light kiss on the lips.

He tried to peer at his daughter, but he could hardly make out her face.

'This baby is swaddled like a mummy!' he exclaimed. 'I cannot even see her face. Is she alive?'

'Mrs Marika taught me how to swaddle', she said proudly. 'It keeps babies snug.'

'Oh. Was she much trouble during the flight?'

'I swaddled her right at the beginning of our trip, so she slept all the way. The only thing is that she was too sleepy to get her feed and she is now almost due for her next one.' She looked around her for a minute, spotting the carousel starting to get filled up with suitcases and other paraphernalia. 'Here', she said to him, passing him the baby. 'I have put her stroller with the luggage. I must go and retrieve it along with my suitcases.'

He sat down on a nearby bench with the baby in his lap, trying to concentrate on her features, see if there was something familiar in her face. She slept peacefully, from time to time half opening her mouth and poking her tongue out while turning her head to the side. Memories surfaced of his childhood on the farm. He had seen many babies then, newborns suckling at their mother's breast. It occurred to him that she was hungry. This poor baby was being sedated to starvation point. He started slowly taking her swaddle off, trying not to wake her up. Then, momentarily, she opened her sleepy eyes, and he saw himself in them.

'What are you doing?' Nefeli asked.

'Taking the swaddle off. The baby is very hungry but far too sleepy to know about it. We must get going, she will need her feed very soon.'

They were now in his Mercedes, driving fast towards the city centre, Nefeli sitting in the back with the baby on her lap. The only sound in the car was the rhythmic high-pitched cry coming from the baby.

'How long will it take us to reach the Hilton?' Nefeli finally asked. 'I think she is desperately hungry.'

'You should have fed her on the plane, Nefeli. This baby is crying as though she is dying. I can hardly bear it. Can you try to feed her now?'

'I prepared her a feed on the plane and I have no more sterilised water for another one.'

'This is really too bad, too bad', he murmured.

She hesitated. 'Well, if I was feeding her myself – I mean, if I was breastfeeding, it would be easy … Apparently, there are ways of bringing the milk back after it has dried out.'

He drove on silently, trying to suppress his irritation, trying to concentrate on driving. She had got even less mature since he had last seen her.

'I could try and do that, if you want me to. See if my milk will come back.'

He sighed and tried hard to speak softly.

'My head is about to explode from all this wailing. Can we talk when we reach the hotel?' And then (he could not help it), 'You know, though, that you cannot breastfeed a baby that you are giving away for adoption, don't you? Besides, you did not even want to breastfeed, remember? You said that it was primitive and that it would spoil your breasts.'

'I … I just don't understand why it has to be this way. Why can't the two of us have this baby? It's our baby after all.'

He drove on and they both stayed silent for a while. The baby had started to quieten down, letting out a sob from time to time, seeming about to fall asleep again, red-faced, sweaty and hungry. His mind was in overdrive. He was feeling upset, but not sure why. Something in her tone of voice when she said 'our baby' had really got under his skin. He had taken a good look at the baby when he took the swaddle off, when she had opened her eyes for him, bluish green eyes like the sea. These were definitely like Nefeli's eyes; but the rest of his baby daughter, the mouth, the nose, the face structure, even the expression in her eyes as she stared at him startled, everything else was so familiar. He had no doubt this was his baby. He had thought that she would start crying when she opened her eyes, but after the initial startlement she broke into a smile for him, and at that moment he had fallen in love with her.

Women – who needed them, when you could have the love of a baby? Adult relationships were far too complicated. He must promise himself, absolutely promise not to have sex with Nefeli tonight. Why did he always feel so muddled when it came to this woman? Strictly speaking what they had had was a professional deal that she had readily accepted. Yet every time he saw her, a part of him that he had tried to bury deep inside could not resist her. He had managed to keep the promise to himself not to visit her in London, partly due to Leonora, who was watching him closely. Yet he had ended up calling her every day, pretending to himself that he needed to know her whereabouts, to make sure that she kept healthy and the baby was safe. Sometimes they would be on the phone for over an hour, talking about her day, her trips to central London and what she had bought for the baby. At times it felt as though they were dating.

They finally arrived at the hotel. He helped her out of the car, the baby fast asleep in her arms.

'Can you hold her?' she said. 'I will get some bottled water from reception to prepare her feed.'

He sat down in the hotel lounge, holding his baby daughter in his arms. Eleni, like his mother's name. Not even giving this baby her name, though, had appeased his mother. This time round, he had tried his best not to get into an argument with her, and yet he had ended up storming out of the house, banging the door behind him. She had shouted after him, 'I told you not to marry this peasant woman, but to marry a girl of your class and social circle – so many such girls were after you. They would have given you not one but many babies, and not in this messy, dirty way.'

His mother was still an impressive-looking woman, elegant, but rigid, with a small waist and sturdy hips, her long golden hair, now turned grey, tied back in an elaborate do. Her large, olive green eyes were cold, but still bright. He jumped up. In fact, that was what his baby daughter's eyes had reminded him of, he now realised: his mother. Nefeli, his mother and himself, blended in one.

The baby had been stirring and grimacing for a while now. She did not seem happy. He had a strong feeling that she would start wailing the moment she woke up.

'Here is her feed', Nefeli said in a fake-cheerful tone. 'Pass her to me.'

The baby started feeding the moment Nefeli touched the bottle to her lips, and the suckling action seemed to drive her back to a deeper, more contented state of sleep.

***

He was lying awake in bed trying to keep his breathing as regular as possible. He didn't want Nefeli to realise that he was not asleep. It must have been around five o'clock in the morning, still pitch-dark outside, but he felt that it wouldn't be long before the first purplish grey light of sunrise of a probably cloudy April day penetrated the room. Nefeli had been up half an hour ago to feed the baby, but he had pretended to be asleep. They had had a conversation over dinner last night and he had explained his thinking to her thoroughly. It did not seem that by the end of the conversation she had much to say. Mrs Marika was much colder with her towards the end, Nefeli had said. She wanted her to keep the baby and she was disappointed with her that she was choosing not to.

'To keep the baby and do what?' Dinos had interjected. 'To become a single mother and a factory worker in London? Have you got any idea how tough such a life would be?'

'I thought about it and I did not feel that I was up to it', Nefeli said, her head lowered.

'Listen, you may come from a poor background, but your parents always wanted the best for you. That's why they sent you to me. I have a reputation for helping people.'

'And for being a womaniser ...'

'They were hoping that I would help you with your development, Nefeli.'

'And have you?' she asked sarcastically.

'Yes, in fact I think I have. Okay, there has been this attraction between us, but it was mutual, wasn't it?'

'Hmmm.'

'At times even initiated by you, and you knew that I was married all along. I never made a secret of it.'

'Why are we going through this?'

'Well, because I also did not make a secret of the fact that Leonora and I really wanted a baby ... And when you got pregnant, I was delighted because this could be the baby we had wanted. It was a good deal for you, Nefeli, spending all this time in London, broadening your horizons … And you know what, I would be happy to keep supporting you for a while. I could give you a lump sum every month for a year or so. If you want to go back to London and do some more studying, it should be possible for a while. I would have to see how many expenses crop up with the baby though. I am hoping to get my mother to look after her, but we will see …'

She had kept very quiet and towards the end of the meal she had burst into tears out of the blue.

'You don't love me, do you? I was so naïve to believe otherwise, to think this is what it's like to be in love.'

'I do … I mean, I care about you and there is also a strong attraction.'

'So why don't you leave her? Why don't you want to be with me?' she shouted.

Dinos looked around him. None of the other diners seemed to have noticed, but he still felt embarrassed.

'Can we keep it quiet?' he scolded her.

She was now visibly upset. 'I am sitting here listening to all this crap', she said in a lower voice. 'It's just fear and habit, Dinos. You are too scared to leave your wife and to be happy with me.'

'All right. Do you want to know the truth? The truth is that I could never be with you, because I would have to take care of two babies, you and Eleni. Leonora is a responsible, mature woman, who has been longing for a baby for many years now, while you could not even give this baby a feed on the plane and she was about to fall into a starvation coma.'

'You are being mean. I took good care of this baby. And if you want to know the truth, I did it for us. But I should have known better. All I ever was to you was the new catch to add to your portfolio of concubines.'

'Look', Dinos said, trying to save the day. 'The last thing I want is to argue with you tonight.' He was feeling tearful as well now, not quite knowing why. 'I will tell you something that you don't know about me. When I was the age you were when I first met you, nineteen, my parents had just split up and my mother was in a really bad way. She was counting on me for help and I had to pretend to myself that I was strong and I knew what I was doing. I had left school early, when they were still in the process of separating. All my teachers had said, "a brilliant mind being wasted". I remember I decided to travel all the way from the Peloponnese to Thessaloniki to get in touch with some relatives who could find me a job. I had to sleep rough for quite a few nights, Nefeli, and I will never forget the feeling.'

She was listening intently. 'I did not know any of this', she said in wonder.

'There is a lot you don't know about me. Anyway, I was so scared of stray dogs and other night animals – and people of course, as well. I remember lying on benches, covered with my jacket, looking at the bright stars in the very dark sky and feeling like a lost five-year-old. '

'Poor you!'

'You cannot imagine what this feeling of having nobody to protect you and take care of you is like. I wouldn't wish it on my worst enemy. That is why you should be grateful that I am willing to take care of you, as I am grateful to Leonora for the same. She is a stable person, you always know where you are with her. I am not going to leave her for anything or anyone.'

Despite his best intentions not to wake Nefeli up, Dinos could not resist turning onto his other side to be more comfortable. It would be morning soon, and they had a long drive to Thessaloniki ahead of them, but it felt like he had hardly slept at all. His body next to Nefeli's was too tense to let go.

His breathing got less regular as she rubbed herself against his back. She put her thigh on his hips and he could feel her hot breath behind his ear. 'I missed you', she whispered.

'We can't. What if the baby wakes up?' he whispered back.

'She won't. She just had a big feed.'

They were intertwined, trying to suppress the sighs of their lovemaking. His orgasm was so strong that it felt almost painful, as though his penis and his heart were going to explode.

14
Paris breeze

Thessaloniki, July 1992

It was the third time Leonora had come to Eleni's room in the last few days, having obviously stayed up to wait for her eventual return well after midnight. She would sit by the end of her bed and massage her feet, a ritual they had occasionally engaged in for as long as Eleni could remember.

'Your ankles are swollen. Have you been walking for long?'

'Yes, and we ended up in a crowded bar, we had to stand up. I don't like this new standing-up trend, it's silly.'

Leonora paused, seeming lost in her thoughts and then, out of the blue: 'Are you on drugs, Eleni?'

Eleni recoiled her legs and drew the light linen blanket higher towards her neck. 'What?'

'You heard what I asked you.'

'Mum, if your job gets under your skin so much, just change it. It is probably about time to retire anyway, isn't it? You are becoming paranoid.'

'I am not paranoid. I just know the signs too well. You have lost far too much weight, you look pale, wide-eyed, on edge. Besides, you smell of alcohol every evening.'

'I have two drinks every evening. That's all. That's very different from being on drugs.'

'I just know something is wrong. We can prevent it from getting worse at least, if you tell me now.'

Eleni started to lose her patience, although part of her was secretly enjoying the attention her mother was giving her. It reminded her of the times they were very close, times half lost now in the fading memories from her childhood.

'Tell you what? Duh, I've got nothing to tell.'

Since coming back home from her month-long trip around Europe with Nicolas, she had tried to eat more to please her parents, who were both concerned about her dramatic weight loss, but her weight had kept dropping off. It was the first time in her life that she could eat as much as she liked and stay as thin as she liked to be. Was it infatuation or heartbreak or both, she wondered, that were the best recipesfor weight loss? The only thing she thought her mother might have a point about was the alcohol. Since her stay in Paris, she had gone native and she would have a drink every evening. Recently, she could not tolerate it as well as she used to, and often it would give her stomach cramps and bouts of diarrhoea after only half a glass. She wanted to have a break and she only wished that Nicolas was not enjoying his daily drinking with her quite so much.

***

'What's up?' Nicolas asked her.

She could just about make out the worried look in his

moist eyes from the lit end of their cigarettes in the dark car.

'Nothing. Phew, this was intense!' she added hastily.

'Are you thinking about him again?'

'What? Who? ... No! Nicolas, that was only a silly one-off thing, you know that.'

'We had better get going. If somebody sees us now, they will still work out what we were up to, don't you think?'

'I must check myself properly when we are somewhere with more light, see that my clothes don't look disordered.'

He lifted the back of his seat and switched on the engine. She could see that he was impatient to get going. He was no longer there.

'Are you still interested to know what I was thinking?' Eleni said, stubbing her cigarette out.

'I guess.'

'In the last month, I have been feeling guilty all the time, Nicolas. I am feeling guilty towards you because of that silly incident ...'

He looked away. She paused.

'Hello, are you still there? Shall I go on or had we better leave?'

'I am listening, Eleni. What do you want me to do, look you in the eye all the time?'

'You were very good at doing that just a minute ago. Anyway, I was going to say that I have now started feeling really guilty towards my parents as well, even towards my father, and I usually don't give a toss what he thinks.'

'Why are you feeling guilty?'

'Look at us. We have taken up smoking this summer.

That was the one thing I had promised myself never to do. I don't want to end up like my father.'

'Are you saying I have lured you into bad habits? I'm only an occasional smoker, Eleni, and you should make sure you never become a regular one either. But why should that be my responsibility?'

'I never said it should. What's your problem today?'

'You are telling me that you are doing bad things with me.'

'No, I am doing bad things, full stop. Smoking, drinking every day, having sex in public places.'

'You didn't enjoy that?'

'It's dangerous, Nicolas. Especially for a woman.'

'Come on, let's get out of here then.' He got himself ready in the driving seat. 'By the way,' he said as they were setting off, looking straight ahead, 'I thought that you liked risky encounters.'

The main thing that had drawn Eleni to Nicolas was that she felt she could see through his detached exterior right to his vulnerable core from the very beginning. Once the intense physical attraction that had brought them together had mellowed, she was the first person he had ever opened up to. The first time he told her about the sudden death of his father from a heart attack right at the beginning of his adolescence, how he had come back from school and his father was no longer there, Eleni had tried to repress her tears, as she just knew how much he would hate her pity. And now, through what she had done, she had proven him wrong to have trusted her. It was the first time in her life that she was getting in touch with her own insanity. Her adolescence had been intensely miserable, and at times she could not believe that anyone could ever experience unhappiness as all-consuming and life-devouring as she did. But at least back then it made sense: she knew what the unhappiness was about. Whereas what she was doing now did not make any sense to her whatsoever. She had let her boyfriend down, while she was still intensely in love with him.

For a long time, she had grown accustomed to seeing her attraction to Nicolas as an unrequited love. They had accidentally met through friends of friends at university in London. Her friend Emma had known a friend of his and had made a point of introducing them: not only they were both Greek, but they also both came from Thessaloniki. The reputation he had was that of a loner. But she had kept bumping into him, and every time she did, her heart would flutter. Yet she had given up hope after a rather unglamorous quick drink they had together, when she had gathered the courage to casually ask him out. Talking about Einstein and why Freud was wrong and parting without even a peck on the cheek was not exactly her idea of a promising encounter with a young man she found attractive.

At the time there were a couple of mates from her year group that Eleni knew were interested in going out with her, and even worse, Nicolas himself had offered to fix her up with a friend of his who apparently fancied her. That was when she had lost hope; and yet, she could not bring herself to go out with someone else. And then, completely out of the blue, he had asked her out. She still remembered the trembling feeling in her legs when he approached her at the university café and said, 'Do you want to go out with me for a date?' She could not believe that he had said the word 'date'. But even then, even after numerous increasingly passionate dates, for a long while their liaison had felt like a mere sexual fling, and she was unsure of his feelings for her. And now that he had let her see his soft interior, which he would not normally let out into the light of day, she had decided to hurt him as much as she could. 'Fear of intimacy', she had accused him of suffering from. Was that her problem too?

The first day they had spent together in Amsterdam, after leaving Paris early that morning, she had spent trying to feel normal around him again even while an internal monologue was going on inside her about the events of the night before. Should she tell him about it? He would be so hurt, and even if she did not lose him, he would never trust her again. After all, it was not like she had fallen in love with someone else, was it? Yet the scenes from the night before were still being replayed in her mind, like forever-repeating snapshots of an intensely dramatic movie. She could not stand it. What was the point of being in a relationship if both of them lived in their own mind and there was no link? Besides, her parents' secrets and lies had marked her for life. She did not want a relationship like that.

The decision was finally made for her. They were sharing a bottle of red in a Dutch-style bistro when she burst into tears. 'I have been so preoccupied for the whole day,' she said 'and you have not even noticed. I don't think there is a point in this, we are not really connecting.'

'I noticed something was up this morning', he said, clearly hinting at their intense sex session earier on. 'I wondered then if you still like me …'

'Oh.'

'Did something happen with Yves?'

Eleni jumped out of her skin. Nicolas had given her no clue before that he knew Yves fancied her. Besides, she did not even know it herself before last night. How could he have known?

'How did you even know Yves fancied me?'

'A man always notices when someone else fancies his girlfriend', he said, half smiling. 'Did you sleep with him?' he added, his smile now frozen.

'Did what? No, of course not. Why would I?'

'I don't know, I have a feeling you like older men. You enjoy the attention. Do you not?'

And then, almost beside herself, she had proceeded to tell him the whole story. How she had not even noticed that Yves fancied her and that she was surprised when he asked her out. She had restricted her description of the sexual encounter to the kissing only, and how drunk she was when it happened. Then she told him all about the attack and how frightened she was that she could have been raped; and then the dread of the blood and the taxi ride home with no money after they had been robbed.

Nicolas had remained silent for a few minutes that had felt to Eleni like an eternity, and then he said as though talking to himself, 'Well, it's not really a big deal. You wanted a spectacular last night in Paris, and in the process you kissed another guy. Although, I don't understand why you had to. He's not even handsome, is he?'

The worst moment was when they had sex later on that evening. There was a look on his face that she had not encountered before, like a little puppy just having been separated from its mum. He was usually silent during love-making, but this time he kept asking her for reassurance that she was still into doing this with him and only with him. She promised herself silently never to do this to him again while they were together.

She was expecting that to be the end of the matter, as though if she confided in him, she would be granted absolution. Yet her last night in Paris kept haunting her. The look on Yves's face when he asked her out, Yves touching her braless breasts above her thin cotton T-shirt, Yves being attacked by the North African gang; kissing Yves and caressing his face during their taxi ride home. She could not help but wonder if he would write to her. He and Vivienne had asked her for a postal address for the summer during the farewell party they had organised for her, and she had advised them to write to her parents' address, as she was going to be moving halls of residence in the autumn.

Vivienne was very much on her mind too. Their long conversations sitting in the sun-drenched conservatory. She wondered, now, whether Vivienne had noticed it too, that Yves was attracted to her. Could it even be that she had overheard them leaving the house together after she had gone to bed, late that evening? She imagined Vivienne standing alone at her bedroom window, all the lights in the bedroom switched off, watching Eleni get into Yves's car. She could never go back to see her now. She could never take the risk.

Once they were back in Thessaloniki, she and Nicolas had continued to spend most of their days together. Being apart for more than a few hours a day felt like an existential threat. She was finding it hard, though, to come up with excuses for being out of the house most of the day in blazing heat, and she had not recovered her stamina since her starvation period in Paris. Her digestive problems were continuing despite trying to take more care of herself, and she would often have to search out a toilet in a rush when out at a café with Nicolas, which always left her feeling hopeless. One afternoon, she was hanging around at home for a bit longer than usual, partly to please her father – who kept complaining that she used the house as a hotel and that they hardly saw her – and partly to see whether lying down for a few hours during the hottest part of the day would make her feel any better.

After lunch, Leonora came into her room. 'Are you coming to interrogate me again?' Eleni had muttered in half amusement and half annoyance.

'I am worried about you. You don't look well.'

'Mum, I am okay.'

'Are you having too much sex?'

'You didn't use to be a bore like that, Mum. What is too much sex anyway, huh?'

'Do you remember to use contraception? I told you ages ago how devastating an abortion can be in a woman's life. Do you remember that?'

'Yes, Mum. We are using condoms, if you have to know.'

'Do you meet in his house?'

'No. Well, we tried his house once, but I could not stand it. His mother is like an iceberg and his house like a fossil museum. It would be really nice if I didn't have a tyrant for a father and we could spend some time here, but –'

'I hope you are not having sex in public places, Eleni. It is seriously dangerous. I told you the story about the forest serial killer, didn't –'

'I really do not want to hear any more horror stories. Can you stop it, please? If you are trying to scare me, get out now. I am trying to rest', she said, pointing at the door.

Leonora did not move. 'I really don't want to irritate you, Eleni. Can you just tell me, are you feeling well in yourself? Really well, like you used to?'

'When was that? I was always sickly, isn't that true? Just the wrong biological make-up, always delicate, falling ill at the faintest puff of wind?'

'Yes, but you were also a healthy child, Eleni, and now you no longer look healthy.'

'And I am not a child any more.' Eleni hesitated. She didn't know if she should volunteer any more information that could feed her mother's paranoia. 'I have been feeling a bit tired recently, but I think it is because of the homelessness that's imposed on me … Also, I have been having some diarrhoea. My digestion has not been right since I left Paris. That is probably why I keep losing weight.'

No further information was needed. Leonora spent the next hour on the phone arranging for Eleni to have some comprehensive blood tests the following morning.

A couple of days later, Leonora was on the phone again, seeming very agitated. Eleni assumed that she was talking about a crisis with one of her patients at the hospital, and she kept to her room. A moment later there was a knock on the door and Leonora stormed in without waiting for an answer.

'You are not well. You are obviously not well. I was right. I had to lie to your father and tell him that there was an emergency at the hospital, as I obviously did not want to worry him before we got to the bottom of this. But I will have to tell him eventually.'

Eleni felt somewhat dizzy and disorientated without quite knowing why. 'What are you talking about?'

'You liver enzymes are terribly elevated, seven times more than the normal level. This would explain all your symptoms, the tiredness, weight loss, paleness, stomach pangs, diarrhoea, the whole lot. It is a miracle you have not turned yellow all over. Hepatitis is the most probable reason. Hepatitis A is virtually non-existent in Europe. Hepatitis B or C are sexually transmitted or passed through blood-carrying syringes. What have you been doing to yourself, Eleni?'

Eleni was staring at her mother in horror, feeling numb at the same time. After a while, she began to come round from her trance-like state. 'What do you mean syringes? I haven't used any syringes. You are starting driving me mad now. Are you implying that I am a heroin addict or something?'

'You haven't?' Leonora said hesitantly. 'How did it come about then? Anyway, let's wait and see. Maybe there has been a mistake; we will do some further tests. In the meantime, you need to change your diet. No alcohol or fatty foods. Give your liver a chance to recover. You have an appointment with my friend Dr Spetsos tomorrow and he will go through with you a specific diet you need to follow. I was on the phone to him just now.'

'Yes, madam', Eleni said humorously, but she was still feeling numb and dazed, as though she had just been to the scene of an accident.

The tests were done privately the following morning, and hepatitis C was confirmed, the most recently discovered and most complex of all the forms of the disease. Although it was a long-term illness and its outcome depended very much on lifestyle, the chance of liver deterioration and cirrhosis or cancer in the long run was significant. Nicolas was tested as well, and to Eleni's relief he tested negative. She was relieved that he didn't have it, yes – but then where had she got it from? She had had boyfriends before, but he had been her first and only sexual partner.

She was lying in bed, about to fall asleep when the scene came to her mind like a screen memory: Yves bleeding in the taxi, her leaning forward and kissing him on the lips. She could not see much in the dark, but she thought that she had tasted blood in her mouth. In fact, that moment in the taxi, although not exactly erotic, was probably the most intimate moment between them. She now knew that it was what would bind them for ever.

Hepatitis C was actually transmitted through blood much more often than through sexual secretions. And in that moment of intimacy between them, he had quite literally got under her skin. She would have a lot of explaining to do – to her parents and to Nicolas and who knew who else … but certainly Nicolas to start with.

15
The scent of things to come

Thessaloniki, June 1983

Leonora was deeply engaged in an interview with a new psychiatric admission, a rather complex case, an on-and-off drug addict also with probable neurological disease, MS possibly, and a history of maternal abandonment in early childhood. Maria knocked on her door and popped her head in. 'Sorry to interrupt you,' she said, 'but Eleni is on the phone.'

'Tell her that I will call her right back', Leonora replied absentmindedly.

'She says it is urgent. Shall I ask her what it is?'

Leonora got up and walked to the adjacent office, as she did not want the new patient to overhear her conversation, apologising to him for the interruption at the same time.

'What's up?' she said rather impatiently into the receiver. 'What is it that you cannot find this time?'

One of the things that got to her most was Eleni's pseudo-independence. This was something she had in common with her father. What it meant in reality was that both Eleni and Dinos felt perfectly entitled to make their own decisions, often in spite of all available evidence, but they were not equally keen to take on the consequences of their actions, which would invariably land on Leonora's shoulders. Independence of spirit, but then taking others' support for granted when the going got tough. Since the moment she had first laid eyes on her, she was determined to bring Eleni up in the best possible way. And that first moment of staring at each other's eyes when she had received Eleni had convinced her that this was a child that needed her and only her. This baby could not be let down again. At that first fleeting moment of eye contact, it was like saying to each other: 'From now on, we will be the most central people in each other's life and we will have to make the best of it.'

Her ongoing principle in Eleni's upbringing had been to listen to her and go along with what she wanted, whenever this was possible. In reality, it meant that whenever going along with her was too far opposed to rational thinking, she would have to use guile to progress with her. Unfortunately, when guile did not work she had given in to Eleni's demands, despite their remote distance from any logic or reasoning. Clashing openly with her, meanwhile, was not on the agenda. This meant changing quite a few nannies, because Eleni did not like them, and having to forgo some of her vaccinations when she started demonstrating an acute hatred of medical intervention. In fact, she had given her the tetanus vaccine when she was asleep once, but when Eleni woke up and narrated the most horrific nightmare with monsters giving her injections, she had decided that this was a risk not worth taking again.

It had meant various changes to her plans too. She had had to cancel at short notice her attendance of at least two medical conferences that she was presenting papers to, as Eleni's reaction when being told that she would have to be apart from her at night was one of inconsolable hysteria. She had also had to drag her along to another couple of conferences, and she was not sure which had been the worst outcome for her career, cancelling altogether or bringing with her a whiny and bad-tempered child who was constantly stared at as she was the only non-adult member of the audience in the complex lectures about psychiatric disorder.

So, when Eleni had declared in a strong voice at the age of eight that she would no longer tolerate a nanny as none of her friends at school had a nanny at home, Leonora had felt as though a panic button was being pushed inside her head. She tried to explain calmly to her that it was not possible not to have a nanny at all as she was working full-time, and although her father was sometimes at home, he was not to be relied on. She also said that the reason none of her friends had a nanny was that they all came from poor backgrounds, and when both parents were working, as was sometimes the case, they were in fact compromising their children's safety by leaving them alone at home when they were far too young to take care of themselves.

Seeing from Eleni's tight mouth and arms folded across her chest that none of these arguments had worked, she offered to ask the present nanny, Lisa, to allow Eleni to spend more time in her room alone, if she did not want to interact with her. But Eleni would have none of it. She could not impose on her something she did not want, she said, and she proceeded to tell the nanny herself that she was no longer wanted and that if she insisted on coming she would not talk to her or even be in the same room with her. The poor girl had seemed rather ruffled round the edges, and Leonora had to boost her confidence by saying that this was just a developmental phase Eleni was going through, before politely sending her away after tipping her generously. Eleni had not come out of her room to say goodbye, although later on that evening she said that she was feeling sad about it.

From then on, whenever Dinos was not at home, which was at least half the time, Leonora would feel a tightening around her stomach at around 1.30 p.m., as she knew that Eleni would be finishing school and would be heading home alone. Now that she was older, and in Year 6, she was allowed to stay out with her friends for an hour or so after school, but Leonora was not sure if this increased or decreased her anxiety. She was also occasionally invited round by a couple of her friends, but given that these invites could never be reciprocated as she was working full-time and Dinos was unwilling or unable to entertain schoolgirls when he was at home, this had felt uncomfortable too.

Lately, Dinos was more and more absent on business trips to Athens, and although she was glad that his business was doing better again, it meant that the everyday tension she experienced from 1.30 p.m. would have to be placated with daily painkillers for her worsening headaches, and more reliance on her carefully monitored use of tranquillisers to calm her down in the evening. She had to admit to herself though, that up to now Eleni had proved very efficient in taking care of herself, and seemed to follow all her instructions. She had given her what felt like a tutorial about how to use the communal lift. 'Never ever get in the lift with a lone man,' she had told her, 'and you always need to check that the lift is in good order and the floor of the lift is in place. Always look down before you step in.' She had also given her detailed orders about how to unlock and shut the apartment door properly, and how to warm her food on the electric cooker. She had in fact glued a notice just above it reminding her to switch it off. Despite everything, Eleni's latest habit was to call her when she was at home and say that she could not find something she desperately needed – a book or something of the sort. The drama was usually not equivalent to the importance of the missing item.

'I have taken some pills', Eleni said quietly but in a stable voice into the receiver.

Leonora felt spacey, and looked for a chair near her to sit down. 'What kind of pills?' she asked calmly, despite her body's reaction.

'You know those neurological pills you keep in the cupboard, the ones for brain tumours and MS ...'

Leonora no longer felt that she could pull through this. 'Have you taken those pills?' she interrupted, still in a calm voice that did not feel her own. These pills were still at an experimental stage. Even a couple of them could prove lethal for an eleven-year-old. Why had she not thought before to keep her large medicine cabinet locked? It had not occurred to her that it would be of interest to anyone else in the house.

'I looked at these pills and I considered taking them, but they looked too frightening. I just took some aspirin instead.'

'How many?' Leonora asked, feeling the blood pumping in her ears.

'I don't know, as many as there were ... thirteen, I think.'

As the dizziness subdued, another feeling started surfacing in Leonora's body: hot red rage. Her daughter had just crossed the boundary of her admirable ability to be patient and understanding. She did not care in the least why she had taken the pills – it must have been some stupid pre-adolescent whim for sure; all she cared about was that no trouble would come of it. She had caused her enough trouble as it was.

She remembered the only time she had ever smacked Eleni. They were walking along a small-town high street, after a long day in a conference, where it had felt like her daughter had demanded her constant attention. Eleni stopped abruptly in front of a shop window. It was a pet shop. Two creatures in front of her were doing acrobatics in a large cage. She was transfixed. 'What are they?' she asked her mother, standing completely still and staring at them.

'Guinea pigs, I think.'

'I want them, please. I don't want any other present ever, just them.'

She had tried to explain nicely how it was not possible to get a pet just like that.

'I hate you', Eleni had screamed at her. 'You never ever

want me to be happy.' And then, before she knew it, she had done it: slapped her across her face with the back of her hand. She was wearing an emerald ring, the stone sharp at the edges. The next thing she saw was the gush of blood spilling out of Eleni's lip. No degree of apologising had absolved her guilt or the embarrassment of having to take her daughter to the conference the day after with a noticeably fat lip.

'Do not worry', she said into the receiver now, in a cold professional voice. 'Thirteen aspirins are hardly going to kill you. We just need to bring you over here and pump your stomach.'

'What?'

'What did you think, Eleni? You have just taken an overdose. The treatment involves a long tube being pushed down your throat.'

'No way.'

'When exactly did you take the aspirins? I mean, how long ago?'

'Just ten minutes ago', said Eleni, sounding very frightened.

'So if you don't want any pumping, here is the plan', Leonora said, trying to think on her feet. 'You go to the dairy shop round the corner now, no delays, and you buy three litres of milk. You will have to drink it all, glass by glass. I am on my way there, you need to have drunk it all by the time I am home in twenty minutes. Otherwise pumping your stomach is the only option, I am afraid. Is that a deal?'

'Yes', Eleni said, now weeping.

'Oh ... and do not forget your keys', she added in an alarmed voice.

***

The three empty milk bottles and an empty glass with some white residue at the bottom were the first things Leonora saw when she entered the kitchen in a fury. Then it was Eleni, standing by the kitchen table, wide-eyed and still as a statue. Even her daughter's defiance and stubbornness, Leonora thought to herself, could be somewhat tamed by the bubbling anger she was feeling inside her, which she was sure Eleni could hear like the sound of the boiling milk rising above the surface just before spilling over.

16
The encounter

London, March 2010

Eleni was in the middle of cooking an elaborate meal, one of those which she knew in advance Chloe would turn her nose up at. Yet cooking had always been for her a soothing space she could immerse herself in when the going was tough. Just like my father, Eleni thought, and cringed.

Chloe's yell made her turn abruptly and drop the wooden spoon, which landed with a bang on her naked toes. Drops of hot olive oil splashed on her foot and made her jump. 'What's the matter?' she said to Chloe, thinking for a moment that she had fallen off her high chair. Chloe normally loved sitting on her high chair watching her mother cook. Eleni would give her various scraps of food, cuts of vegetables and fruit, pieces of bread and cheese and the occasional fancy crisp or biscuit, and Chloe was usually happy to pick and nibble and watch her mother move about the kitchen. She had been crankier lately though, and Eleni had wondered if she could sense her preoccupation.

'Out', Chloe said. She turned the gas flame down to minimum. Thankfully her North African stew was nearly ready. She had used a whole packet of saffron to flavour the stewing chickpeas and vegetables. Saffron apparently had antidepressant qualities, she had read in passing somewhere. She followed Chloe to the living room. Chloe had been a late walker, but since she had mastered the skill a month ago, she was very stable on her feet. Yet she was still at the stage when Eleni needed to follow her with her eyes everywhere. She put the mat and Chloe's large basket of toys down and sat at the end of it. Chloe ignored it to start with, and went on exploring the room. Maybe she would have to resort to TV for a bit, Eleni thought to herself. Her mind was very busy.

'Do you want to play?' she said to Chloe, winding her favourite red caterpillar up. Chloe turned and grasped it, finally sitting on the mat. Eleni lay down alongside it. She was feeling tired. She had not had a full night's sleep since hearing about her father's critical health deterioration. Soon enough Chloe was near her, and then on top of her, giggling as Eleni tickled her. 'Row the boat', Chloe gestured, and Eleni sat up and placed her on her lap. At moments like this, it still felt like they inhabited the same body.

Pregnancy had been a dreamy experience for Eleni. She had never felt more alive in her body, more whole before. Towards the end of it, when the baby's kicks used to wake her in the middle of the night, she had started getting into a rhythm with her, able to predict when she would move and how she was lying in her stomach.

The moment labour started she had felt that she and baby had established a dialogue to the exclusion of anyone and anything else. She had thought that she would be anxious, but all worry had dissipated, as she was convinced that she would know if something was wrong. Labour was a primitive experience and any interference from the outside, other than Nicolas rubbing her back, had felt to Eleni a huge intrusion. There was a sense of absolute abandonment to the waves of pain, riding the wave, going higher and higher, and then falling graciously along with it, taking a breath in before the next one came.

When she finally entered the pool, she reconnected with a wordless, intense dialogue with the baby. She could hardly hear the voices giving her instructions from the outside. It felt like she and baby were floating in this primordial water, primitive anaerobic creatures, fully immersed. After the top of the baby's head had appeared a few times, Eleni gave an almighty push, despite instructions to take it slow, and the baby shot out at the bottom of the pool like a fish. She had just had about time to catch Chloe and bring her slowly to the surface before her head hit the bottom of the pool. On rising to the surface, Chloe had let out a loud scream, despite all expectations that, like most water-birth babies, she would be calm and quiet. It felt like she was protesting about coming into the world so abruptly and unexpectedly. Her first memories of Chloe were all populated by water. Both of them inhabited a lukewarm, bloody, slimy liquid world straight after the birth, when Chloe had her first feed and helped her mother expel the last remains of pregnancy, the placenta.

Love for a man, an erotic connection – could that

measure up to the love for a baby? Despite the long list of reasons she had given herself not to, she had ended up booking the other workshop with Martin Wheel. 'Our Inner Artist: Dreaming and Creativity' was the title, and it would take place tomorrow. The idea of exploring her dreams through artwork in a group was hardly appealing to her, especially in her current low mood. She had to admit to herself that it was more out of a desire to see him again that she had booked it, rather than putting herself in a group when she was feeling so vulnerable. What was it about this man that had become so compelling to her? He was a total stranger, and yet something about the way he had looked at her, the way he had observed her art in his first workshop, was gripping. A kind of connection had been made.

'I see the two of you are having fun.' Nicolas, standing in the doorway, made her start. She had not heard him come in.

'Well, I was cooking a Moroccan stew for all of us but she would have none of it.'

He leant down and gave her a kiss on the lips. Chloe came between them.

'Dada!' He picked her up and she immediately got herself busy playing with his glasses, trying to lift them off the bridge of his nose.

'Moroccan stew? Isn't it a bit ambitious to expect Chloe to eat?'

How funny, Eleni thought to herself: Nicolas was not even sure he wanted children before having Chloe, and yet now his face would always light up when seeing her little face upon his arrival back from work. It was also the highlight of the day for Chloe. She brushed away a pang of jealousy.

'I know. But I think it's good for her to challenge her tastebuds. If I am honest, it was also for me: therapeutic cooking.'

'How are you feeling?'

'The same: worried, I guess, preoccupied. Nothing seems real.'

They both jumped at the sharp sound of Nicolas's glasses hitting the floor. They leant down together to see if they were broken and their heads banged, which made them giggle.

'This is very real, Eleni', Nicolas said, pointing at Chloe.

This is very real, Eleni. His remark echoed in her mind as she heard them upstairs singing 'Three little ducks went swimming one day' while running Chloe's bath. Was that his way of supporting her or criticising her? Why not accept that she had the right to fall apart when her father was dying? How much could a person take? She had reminded him of the workshop she was attending tomorrow just before he took Chloe upstairs for her bath, and he seemed happy that she was doing something proactive to deal with her feelings. If only he knew.

***

She arrived at the workshop ten minutes late the following morning. She was annoyed with herself for taking so long to decide what to wear and then having a nightmare journey on the Tube, finally reaching the workshop's ground-floor venue in the leafy north-west of London all sweaty and out of breath. Everyone seemed to be calm and composed when she entered the room, and she squeezed past two women sitting near the door in order to occupy the only available seat in the circle. Martin nodded at her while he continued talking. Did he recognise her? she wondered. They would begin by introducing themselves and saying why they were there, and then they would proceed with sharing a dream. In the second part, they would produce some artwork, any kind, through the material shared in the dream session. Finally, they would reconvene as a group.

'I am on an Atlantic beach at low tide', Eleni heard herself *saying. 'I am walking on the bottom of the ocean and the floor is embedded with shells and seaweed. It is slippery. There are quite a few rocks around the beach. I climb on a tall, pointy rock and sit on it talking to a friend on the phone. I look out along the beach and I see people struggling to walk on the muddy ground or occasionally being swept by the waves. I tell my friend that I need to join them. I climb down the rock and I start walking with great difficulty. I reach a bend where the waves are crashing against the rocky cliff. I cannot see behind the cliff and I reach the decision that I need to keep walking. As I turn, I get swept away by huge waves, and I find myself in deep sea. There is no land in sight and I scream in terror.'*

In the morning, she had woken up screaming, 'I am going to die', and she had made Nicolas jump up in bed as well and look at her in alarm. Once she had got past the initial terror of it, she was fascinated that she had had such an intense dream just before the workshop. Bringing it to the group had brought something alive, and everyone was now talking, death clearly being a theme they all shared. A couple of people had focused on her rather intensely and had asked her about her perception of death and previous experiences. It had quickly become established that her father was dying. She noticed Martin in her peripheral vision observing acutely the happenings in the group. 'Death and Eros go together, Freud has said', he remarked, when a man was reluctant to share the details of an erotic dream he had had the night before.

She slipped away during the lunch break in search of some precious solitude, rare and expensive since having a baby. Back in the workshop for the second part, she was engrossed in finishing off her third painting when he approached her. She had already produced an image of a grey, turbulent sea and a grey and purple horizon, and a second image of the seabed, mud and soil embedded with open and smashed shells, slimy seaweed and some dead fish and jellyfish. It was the third image that had absolutely gripped her though, and which she was finishing off when Martin approached. A naked woman was sitting on a pointy rock, her hips and legs merging with the rock, her vagina suggestively sitting on the top of the rock. Her hair was long and wavy like Medusa's, her breasts full and lying heavily on her stomach, one of them leaking milk and blood. When Martin approached, she was in the process of adding a few drops of blood to the rock near the woman's vagina, as well as some green and blue algae. He leaned forward and she could smell his discreet scent. 'Is this you?' he asked.

'I don't know – perhaps.' Eleni replied, looking him in the eye.

'You know,' he said in a quiet voice, 'the thought occurred to me when you were narrating your dream that a woman sitting on a rock is how female masturbation was allegedly invented; but I did not want to suggest such an association to your dream, not before I saw this image.'

'This is not much to do with pleasure though.'

'You are quite right', he said. 'Maybe the story of female masturbation is less to do with pleasure and more to do with independence – independence from men.'

Eleni felt herself cringe as though his gaze had physically touched her. He paused. 'I can see now why you don't want to be a therapist', he continued. 'Producing art like this can be therapeutic enough.'

So he did remember her, Eleni thought with excitement; but she only smiled politely. 'I need to move on now', he said. 'But I would like to talk some more about your work, if possible.' He pulled a business card out of his pocket and gave it to her. 'Call me if you are interested', he said, and walked off.

'Okay, I may well do', Eleni whispered, not knowing if he had actually heard her.

For the rest of the afternoon she maintained a cool exterior while feeling the pounding of her heart and the rush of blood in her belly.

17
Separation

Thessaloniki, March 1978

They were lying in bed after having sex. This was already his second cigarette. Nefeli was curled up facing him, her head cradled on the crease between his chest and his armpit. At this moment she resembled a kitten in need of protection, Dinos thought. Sex had always been earth-shattering with her, the ultimate bond between them. They just fitted with each other. They knew what each other's body wanted.

He had not withdrawn in time, yet again. He really ought to stop doing that. He must get a grip of himself. But the ecstasy of the moment, her response to him, the way she orgasmed, always seeming totally abandoned in whatever was going on in her body, it always made him let go of any self-discipline. Two abortions already in the space of the six years since Eleni's birth should have improved their self-control. On both occasions she had threatened to leave him. She would go back to London and have her baby there and start her life over, she would say. Why was that such a threat, anyway? If only she could leave and start her life all over again. If only she could.

He had been feeling it again, the tightening across his chest. He had used his inhaler soon after sex, but the tightening had not gone away. He had gone to their family doctor at Leonora's insistence a couple of weeks ago. He had known about the bronchial asthma, but this time there was worse news. His heart was enlarged, the doctor said. Not sure why – but he needed to lose weight and stop smoking, as he was at an increased risk of heart attack. It was also bound to make his asthma worse, he said: the heart would adversely affect his lungs and vice versa, a chicken-and-egg situation, or something of the sort.

'Are we going out for a meal?' he said, stabbing his cigarette out on the porcelain ashtray inscribed with the hotel's initials. 'I will take you somewhere special'. A special treat to break especially sad news, he thought to himself. 'I need to talk to you', he added. 'Do you fancy fish by the harbour? I stopped by on my way to meet you and I reserved us an amazing catch.'

She sat up in bed, her breasts gently succumbing to gravity, but still firm and pointed. She always liked to show them off.

'What's up?' Nefeli asked. 'First time I've seen you use this puffing thing. You look preoccupied, worried.'

'I will have to use it often from now on, I am afraid. I went to see the doctor and it is not good news. My heart is enlarged and it will make my asthma worse.'

'Is it about her?' she persisted, the word 'her' coming like spit out of her mouth. 'Is she making your life difficult again? What else does she want from you, huh?'

'Look, I cannot be late today. I may even have to force myself to have a second lunch at home. Let's go to the restaurant and I will talk to you then.'

They walked out of the hotel lobby together, keeping a safe distance from each other. As they made their exit, he left a generous tip for the receptionist, timed to stop him in his tracks before he asked in his well-practised, contemptuous tone if the couple should be expected back to their room later on in the day, and before reminding them that they had still not provided the hotel with an identity card as required.

The sun was shining outside, although white clouds were gathering on the west side of the city. It will probably rain again in an hour or so, he thought to himself. He never got such things wrong. If only he could read women's intentions as easily as he did nature's. He could feel the penetrating March chill under the heat of the intense mid-afternoon sun.

The restaurant was only a five-minute walk from the hotel. He could not walk for long nowadays without getting slightly out of breath. He opened the door for her while the waiter greeted him respectfully.

'You are smoking too much, you know', Nefeli said. 'I think it has started affecting your health.'

He lit a cigarette as soon as they sat down at the table, and for a moment he forgot that she was there. He nodded to catch the waiter's attention. 'We have agreed the order already. The usual stuff, and the catch I have reserved, grilled on charcoal with olive oil and lemon sauce as usual. Oh, and your best bottle of white. What do you recommend?'

'We have a new island white, Santorini Nyhteri. You must try it, sir. It is delightful.'

'Bring it on then.'

'Look', he said turning abruptly to face her. 'We had an argument, worse than the usual ones.'

'Oh'.

'She was so antagonistic. Some of the things she said made me lose it. I will never forgive myself.'

'How bad was it?'

'I hit her, Nefeli', he said, holding his head in his hands. 'Eleni witnessed the end of it. She was upset. I will never forgive myself.'

She kept staring at him blankly. The expression on her face was peculiar, not compassionate, slightly sarcastic perhaps. He was feeling tearful. This would not go well, he could see it already.

'You and your wife and your big dramatic arguments. Why are you together anyway?' she finally said.

He took a deep breath to suppress his rising irritation.

'The reason we argued was you, Nefeli. The fact that you come to the house so often, every day really, to see Eleni. Leonora is not happy about it. She says it was not our agreement. And she is right, it was not our agreement.'

'Eleni is my child.'

The waiter approached the table with a clouded bottle of white and an ice bucket. He poured a little wine into one of the glasses and offered it to Dinos. Dinos took his time moving a gulp of wine around his mouth, and nodded. They drank absentmindedly. He exhaled the smoke from his lit cigarette noisily.

'You have started driving me mad like her', he said after a while. 'Eleni is not your child. You gave her over willingly. She has been raised by Leonora.'

'Well, I don't remember ever signing any adoption documents. I am not as stupid as you think, Dinos. I know that the child is legally mine.'

Dinos nodded to the waiter impatiently. 'Can we have some bread, please, and a couple of dips. This wine is nice, but it is getting to my head.'

'Which dips would you like, sir?'

'Any', he said unwittingly raising his voice. 'The spicy feta one and anything else that is nice and fresh.'

He turned to Nefeli. 'I was just going to get to that, Nefeli, very well timed of you. And good to know that you are so calculating, that you were taking advantage of my kindness and generosity, the fact that I did not want to upset you by making you sign adoption papers, that I trusted you not to do anything stupid.'

'Calculating? Not me, Dinos. You are confusing me with your wife. She calculates her every move like a chess player. I am just a naïve victim. That's all I am. I thought you had not yet made your mind up whether to leave her, whether to start a proper family with me and Eleni and all the other babies that I could give you if only you would let me. I thought that was why you had not gone through with the adoption.'

Dinos sighed in frustration. 'I have been consistently clear with you, Nefeli, that you ... that we cannot bring Eleni up together.'

'Clear? You are clear about nothing, Dinos. You are just confused and confusing.'

The waiter coughed discreetly. 'Here is your spicy feta dip, sir, and some warm bread ... and ... and the chef recommended this little crab mayo salad as your second appetiser. It is made with today's fresh crab', he said.

'Thank you.' Dinos waited for the waiter to be a bit further away from the table before speaking again. He picked one of the warm rolls, its scratchy, fragrant crust breaking gently between his fingers to reveal the warm, sticky, white interior. He dipped it absentmindedly in the crab salad.

'Mmm, it is so good and fresh, try', he prompted Nefeli, but she ignored him. 'Listen: Leonora went to a lawyer. I had no idea until a few days ago.'

'And so?'

'She says she did that on the back of trying to tell Eleni last summer that she is not her biological mother.'

'Did she?'

'I know. I had no idea. She claims that she did not want to tell me because it did not go well.'

'Bullshit! All these evenings I have been spending in your house, Dinos. I have not used them only to be with Eleni, although that has been the only delightful bit – I have also used them to study your wife's character. Nothing she does is left to chance. It's all premeditated.'

'Anyway, the point is that Eleni had a really bad reaction. She told her that she would not accept the idea that Leonora did not give birth to her. She told her that she would kill herself if Leonora dared to tell her that again.'

'Now, honestly, Dinos, do you truly believe that? Eleni, a fiveyear-old, threatening suicide? Besides, Eleni spends most of her waking hours in other women's company. Your wife is a workaholic, did you forget?'

'Nefeli!' Dinos said, trying hard not to lose his cool, 'we are not here to do a character assassination. I am trying to explain to you a very serious situation. The solicitor she went to specialises in adoption and custody of children. He advised her that as my spouse and having raised my child for more than five years she has rights over the child. He advised her to press for the formal adoption or file for divorce. Besides, she says she is really worried about Eleni's well-being, how dependent she is on her and what would happen if she had to lose a mother once again. '

'Bullshit!'

'Cut your western-suburbs language, Nefeli. Leonora's concerns are both sensible and considerate. She is asking that you sign the adoption documents and sever all contact with our family.'

'What?' Nefeli mumbled. Dinos noticed that she had turned white despite the warm mid-afternoon light falling on her face. 'I could not possibly do that, Dinos. Coming to your house every single evening for the last six years, I have got to know Eleni. I have seen her growing up, and I could not possibly stop seeing her now. Anyway, your wife uses me as her slave, you must know that. She gets me to wash the dishes and to do all the household chores. I am there to be humiliated by her. She must be really enjoying it. What is there to complain about?'

'Leonora says that you are intervening more and more in her relationship with Eleni. That you antagonise her and that you are trying to win Eleni over.'

'How exactly do I do that – by washing the dishes and mopping the floor?'

'I don't know. As you must have noticed, I deliberately avoid being there when you visit. My presence would make things very awkward. It would add to an already awkward situation.'

'So why do you choose to believe her? Huh?'

'She says that you try to bond with Eleni and to undermine her bond with her mother. Sorry, but Leonora is Eleni's mother now, Nefeli.'

A large silver plate with a whole chargrilled fish lying on a bed of lettuce arrived, along with a green salad and steamed potatoes. The waiter offered to bone the fish and serve it, a service that Dinos knew was offered only to the restaurant's faithful customers. They ate for a while silently. He could taste the freshness of the sea bass in his mouth, he could smell the sea, and for a while he managed to lose himself in the pleasure of his senses.

'Today's catch, as promised', he murmured.

She remained silent.

He needed to go through with this, he reminded himself silently. 'Leonora says', he eventually went on, 'that you put the living-room cushions down on the floor and teach Eleni gymnastics and yoga. And you give her lengthy baths, and giggle together. She says that she even overheard you singing to her in the bath a certain love song that went something like: 'Your mother the murderer that took you away from me ...' Is it true that you are doing such silly things?' he asked angrily.

He could see the change in her face. She was chewing her food slowly and steadily and she had her blank expression on. A teenage expression, but she was no longer a teenager for God's sake, he thought to himself. He had no patience for teenagers, a recent nonsense term, yet another construct of modern urbanity. When he was her age, the concept was non-existent. He was seventeen years old when his parents finally broke up. But the worst of it was, in a way, before that. His mother, always meticulously dressed throughout his childhood, always the first to be up with the sunrise, her golden hair perfectly groomed in an elaborate updo, always looking pristine and fresh, his mother, the most beautiful woman in the village, had been transformed into a crying wreck who stayed in bed all day long in her nightie, he and his sister having to take turns to take food to her bedroom so that she didn't perish. His father had already started effectively living with the other woman, a *putana*; it was the talk of the whole village. His mother would rarely leave the bedroom, but on the few occasions she did, it was to give him a lecture. 'Remember, Dinos,' she would say to him, 'you are the only man in this household now. You have to take the family affairs on and make sure you don't become a tramp like your father.' That was when he dropped out of school. His mother's pleading eyes had finally done the trick. He needed to be a man.

Nefeli put her fork down and took a good sip of wine. She looked him straight in the eye. 'I am not doing anything wrong', she said. 'All I am doing is playing with Eleni. She needs it, you know. This child is like a canary in a golden cage. Her mother works long hours and when she is at home she is constantly busy with housework to keep you happy. She has had more nannies than I care to remember, and there is no other child her age around to play with.'

'We always looked for the best nannies for Eleni.'

'Yeah, and they come and go. They are good at keeping Eleni clean and fed according to your wife's instructions, but no good at engaging with her, not in any way.'

'You are doing it again. She is actually right, I can see it now. You are trying to undermine her.' He paused and took a deep breath in. 'Look, anyway. All this doesn't matter any more really. Things have got to change. She has threatened to take Eleni away and divorce me if you continue coming into the house. She said the family solicitor helped her realise that she was a victim. It is totally unacceptable, he told her, for the birth mother of the child to keep visiting regularly. The child will grow increasingly confused and fragmented. She will need psychological help. He advised her to file for divorce and to claim the child. She said that if she had effective witnesses that she had taken good care of Eleni, and if the birth mother was incompetent, she would almost certainly win the case. She will find plenty such witnesses, Nefeli.'

'Oh.'

'She has a strong case, he told her. Her husband's repeated adultery with the birth mother. Leonora knows about your abortions, you know. I don't know how, but she does. They would look into your background, the counselling you refused in London, everything. It could become very unpleasant, Nefeli, believe me.'

He paused again, looking blankly at a fixed spot on the floor. 'That was when I ended up hitting her. And then she screamed at me. "Take your incompetent mistress and your bastard child and go and live with them. This child will thrive in between your sex and gourmet-food sessions, I am sure."'

'It sounds bad', she said, looking slightly more concerned now.

He held his head in both his hands as though he could no longer support it. 'I have been thinking about all this over and over. I have hardly slept for two nights.'

'I told you, I knew something was up.'

'Listen. The solution is obvious. There is only one, and it is best for all concerned. You have to go back to London. Phone Mrs Marika, see whether she will have you back. Even if you have to pay rent this time. I will take care of it, even though business is not as stable as it used to be.'

He paused and looked at her again as she sat very still with glassy eyes. 'It is really best for all concerned, Nefeli. Think about Eleni. If you care as much about her as you say, you will realise that this is best for her. She needs to grow up in a stable family with good values. You know how efficient and reliable Leonora is. This is what children need, stability, someone to rely on. But also it will be best for you. You are still young. You can go there, study, find a job, even marry someone. You can start your own family, Nefeli.'

She started to cry silently now. 'And us? What about us?'

'There is no us', he said firmly. 'You knew it all along that I was married. You came to me to get some life experience, and this is what you got. You can move on now. I will support you and you'll be fine. Oh, and I need you to sign the adoption documents first thing on Monday morning. I have already made an appointment for both of us with Mr Antonopoulos, my solicitor. It is long overdue.'

They turned down dessert and walked out of the restaurant looking at the ground. 'I will give you a lift,' he said, 'even though I am late. I am parked nearby.'

'I am fine', she said. 'I need some fresh air. I will walk a bit and then take the bus home.' As they parted without kissing or making eye contact, a fine drizzle started falling on the city's dusty pavements.

18
Dying

London, March 2010

'Your father is dying, Eleni. They discharged us from the hospital and they gave us no hope that things will get any better.'

The phone call had caught Eleni breastfeeding Chloe, and she was trying to juggle both, holding the handset in her left hand and supporting Chloe feeding on her right breast.

'Is this definite? Have they given you a time scale?'

'They say it is definite, Eleni, but I want to believe otherwise. We are expecting a home visit from the doctor tomorrow, who will confirm what's happening.'

Eleni felt the first pang of anger hit her in the chest.

'This is very confusing for me, Mum. You are saying that he is definitely dying but maybe not – and you are a doctor too. What am I supposed to do? I am feeding Chloe right now, if you want to know.'

'Well, all he talks about is how much he wants to see you. He doesn't know that I am calling you; if he did, he would ask you to come as soon as you can.'

Before she knew it, Eleni had started yelling at the top

of her voice.

'You two are really so selfish, especially you. Oh, but I forgot, you never had a baby to know what it's like, did you? All you did was dump me on nannies and piss off to work. You have no idea what it's like to have a baby really relying on you, even for all her feeds.'

Chloe had stopped feeding; she had drawn her head back and she seemed to be observing, trying to listen to what her mother was saying. This baby had been there before, she seemed to understand everything. She was especially astute in sensing Eleni's moods. Now that she was older, she could only feed in a dark, quiet room with no distractions. The feed was doomed now. Eleni knew it all too well.

'Here we go again', Leonora murmured.

'Exactly, here we go again.' Eleni continued, yelling. 'You and Father were so selfish that you dragged us as an emergency to Greece in the middle of winter, a day after Christmas, when Chloe was just recovering from bronchitis. He was dying then as well, you told me.'

'I cannot know for sure when he will die, Eleni. I am not God. All I can do is hope for the best and tell you what the doctors are telling me. Do you not want me to keep you informed?'

'So now you throw the ball back at me. This is your way, isn't it? I am a bad daughter, not caring about her dying father. When have you two ever cared about me since I had Chloe? You haven't even bothered to come and visit me for more than three days. Childcare is not your thing really, is it?'

'Eleni, you know how excited I was when you had Chloe.

How much I would have liked to spend more time with her. I truly love babies, especially your baby. He was in a bad way then, I could not leave him.'

'Sure, you love my baby. Do you even know her? Anyway, I am telling you once and for all. I am not a VIP with a suitcase in my hand who can fly to Greece at your every whim. I am the mother of a young one, with very little childcare available and even less support.'

'I know how difficult it is to have a baby. That is why I am trying to bother you as little as I can.'

'No, you don't', Eleni screamed at the top of her voice, feeling hot, angry tears well in her eyes. Chloe jumped off her lap and looked at her in surprise. 'All you ever knew about was your high-flying career and being jealous of your own daughter for giving birth when you couldn't.' On that note, she slammed the phone down.

'I am wondering if I should go back to therapy', she told Nicolas the following morning, after yet another restless night.

'Why don't you go and see Laura again? She knows you well.'

'The thought has crossed my mind, but I am not sure if she will take me. It was not the best of endings.'

'I am sure she will.'

'I am not sure I want to either. I have a feeling I have to go through this alone', she said, feeling a tear make its quiet way down her cheek.

'You are not alone, Eleni', Nicolas said, leaning forward to wipe her tear and giving her a light peck on the lips.

You are not alone, Eleni. Nicolas's voice echoed in her ears as she went through the longest-seeming morning ever, repeatedly restraining herself from calling her mother. When Eleni had called back the previous day to half-heartedly apologise to Leonora for slamming the phone down on her, her mother had said that she would call her in the afternoon of the next day, straight after the doctor's visit. Eleni had decided to go and visit the café in which her work would next be exhibited, in Hampstead, near the top part of the heath, a visit that could possibly wait for a few days but which would help keep her busy, to master the seconds and the minutes ticking relentlessly slowly on her mobile's screen. Despite waiting for Leonora's phone call all day long, the ringing of her phone at two p.m. exactly, just as she had started strolling downhill from the café, made her heart judder against her chest.

'Hello. Mum?'

Leonora had her white-collar professional voice on. 'Eleni, the doctor just left. He said there is little that can be done for your father now. It is a matter of days, if not hours, before he slips into a coma. He can only breathe through the oxygen mask and his oxygen level is far too low.'

'Oh.'

'However, I have not lost hope. Your father has defied medical science before, as you know. I will see if we can get a private ambulance to transfer him to hospital. Once we are there, we can come up with something. I will be reviewing the situation with the lung specialist ...'

'What is it?' Eleni interrupted hearing a groaning-like

noise in the background.

'It's your father talking to me. I will go and check. Hang on a minute.'

Eleni waited for a minute or so. 'What is it? What does he say?' she asked anxiously.

'He says if I transfer him to hospital, he will die on the way. Listen, can you come over? He really, really wants to see you. That's all he's been talking about. Hang on a minute, he wants to talk to you.'

Dinos's voice on the phone was clear and loud, as though he was just next door. Nobody would guess that he was dying. 'Eleni,' he said, 'please take the next plane and come over. I have less than twenty-four hours to live. I want to see you before I die. I will wait for you.'

Eleni swallowed hard. She tried to speak, but found it hard to keep her voice level.

'It isn't as simple as that, Dad. I need to make arrangements for Chloe. I will try.'

'I am sure you will make it on time. You are a clever girl', he said, and hung up.

Eleni could hear him getting out of breath at the end of his last sentence. He always had a way of saying things that irritated her – as though attending to her dying father had anything to do with cleverness.

'My father says he has less than twenty-four hours to live', she said to Nicolas in a steely voice, increasingly breathless from her swift walking. 'He says I have to be there by tomorrow morning.'

'You don't have to do what he says if you are not ready.'

'I have to, Nicolas', Eleni said sharply. 'People die only once.' She paused. 'The good thing is that I had an intuition at the weekend. Out of the blue I decided to go to Boots, without even knowing what I needed. I didn't tell you, but I bought a portable breast-pump. Thank God for that.'

'I don't follow', Nicolas said quietly.

'Chloe is still breastfeeding twice a day. Did you forget? I will not stop because he is dying. I will not let his dying do that to us.'

'Eleni, that's not that important. I will take care of Chloe. Just sort yourself out.'

'It's terribly important', she yelled at him down the phone, sobbing uncontrollably now. She noticed a couple of pedestrians turning to look at her and then lowering their heads in embarrassment. What was it people found so embarrassing about grief? Was there any feeling that was more universal, more familiar than that?

'You don't understand', she continued, yelling into the receiver. 'He made sure I was not breastfed. I will not let him stop me from breastfeeding Chloe as well.'

'Eleni, please try to calm down. Your father is not doing this on purpose to hurt you.'

'It feels like he is', she murmured.

After being reassured that Nicolas would take care of all the practical details, she continued to walk. She was suddenly thankful to Hampstead for providing her with such a long stretch of straight, downhill walking. She needed to walk, just walk for a bit without talking to anyone. There was a strange stillness in her mind. She needed to be alone with herself. She could hear only the rhythmic sound of her footsteps, the cars' engines roaring nearby, and a soothing buzzing inside her ears, blood pumping through her head.

She shrivelled at the sound of her mobile ringing again. *Nicolas* was written on the screen.

'No direct flight until late tomorrow', he said. 'The only option is to travel to Athens tonight, arrive there after midnight, spend four hours at Athens Airport overnight and catch the first morning plane to Thessaloniki at six a.m. Can you postpone?'

'Just get me the ticket. I can leave home in about an hour. Chloe is with Bella at the moment, but she is due to leave at three. Can you come home?'

'Okay. I will book it and be on my way. Are you sure you want to travel tonight? It sounds onerous.'

'Yes.'

***

The plane was about to land at Athens Airport. She did not like flying in the pitch dark. It reminded her of death in the best of circumstances. Her mind was spinning throughout the flight, and a much-desired nap completely escaped her. She had managed to give Chloe a quick feed just before leaving, but her breasts were bizarrely full again. Was this a bodily expression of already missing her baby? She must now be sound asleep, on her back with her arms stretched open, a position of such innocence and vulnerability. She cannot possibly know that her mother is far away, flying on a plane in the dark and windy Greek sky at nearly two o'clock in the morning, she thought. Could she sense the danger? All it would take was for the pilot to get something wrong, the plane's engine to fail, and Chloe's life would never be the same again. She had been on a plane the last time her real mother had held her in her arms before giving her over. Everything must have gone dark for her after that trip, at least for a while. That first plane had crashed and had taken her down with it.

Layer 3

Before we get forgotten, we get changed into kitsch. Kitsch is the platform of communication between the being and the forgotten.

Milan Kundera, *The Unbearable Lightness of Being*

19
Therapy

London, October 1999

Laura had booked, not without much trepidation, a consultation with one of the top therapists in her field. For years, she had admired his writing, which felt like a breath of fresh air. She knew she was more than lucky to have managed to book an appointment with him. Yet she was feeling frozen at the thought of her prospective exposure. Was talking to a stranger really better than talking to her long-term practice supervisor, who knew her well and had a high regard for her clinical work?

She had in fact created this impasse by consistently avoiding discussing with her supervisor the patient she now urgently needed to talk to somebody about. How could she ever broach the subject with her supervisor without appearing dishonest, given that she had already been seeing the patient for two years, and mostly twice a week? She couldn't talk about it, especially now that she was in such a mess. Strictly speaking, she did not have to talk about her entire caseload with her supervisor, as she was now a senior therapist herself supervising others in the field. However, it would be hard to justify not mentioning the one patient that she was most intimately involved with.

She had valued her long-term supervisor, one of the trainers at her institution, now semi-retired; but she had to admit to herself that her primarily Kleinian approach, even if she called herself middle-school, had lately felt to Laura like intercourse in the missionary position: safe and trusted, but going through the motions to some extent. Despite this, she could not deny that it was her own failure to keep proper boundaries and to resist becoming entangled with a patient that had been the main reason for her silence.

She rang Martin Wheel's bell, her hand shaking slightly. Although in his latest writings he had declared himself an artist and not an analyst, he had a reputation for clinical excellence, unusual kindness, and intensity of presence in the room. As he opened the door of his top-floor studio, his outline almost fading in the luminous background, Laura was stunned by the flood of light in which the room was bathed. Her eyes could not focus on him, but kept wandering around one of the most intriguing and inviting spaces she had ever been in. There was a central skylight from where the sunshine of a breezy October day was filling the room. The space looked much more like an art studio than a consulting room. Canvases with what seemed like unfinished work lay on the floor near his desk, and there was an array of books on the numerous shelves, and some spread on the dark, stripped floorboards. A few tall, wide-leaf plants in dustbin containers decorated the corners of the large, airy room. He led her towards the wide window, where, initially unnoticed by Laura, there was a large leather burnt-orange corner sofa at an uneven angle, its one side significantly longer than the other. She rightly guessed that this was where she was supposed to sit.

She finally focused her eyes on him, noticing his dark-blue eyes, nicely wrinkled at the edges, and the typically male sharpness of his features, and she smiled politely.

'I am a great admirer of your work', she said, realising that she was sitting very tense and rigid, right on the edge of the sofa.

He smiled back. 'Thank you. What brings you here?'

'I will put it as straightforwardly as I can', Laura said, taking a deep breath in and sitting back, finally feeling the sofa supporting her back. 'I am in a bit of a mess with one of my patients and I haven't been able to talk it over with my long-term supervisor for fear of being judged. I have heard a lot of good stuff about your acute clinical judgement, but also your independent spirit, and I was hoping that you could perhaps help me.'

'Okay. Can you tell me a little bit about yourself first – your work, how many years you have been practising, and so on?'

'I trained in the classical psychoanalytic tradition and I have been working as a therapist for nearly twenty years, although it has only been in the last two years that I started developing my own private practice. Actually, thinking about it, my private practice is linked with what I came here to talk about', Laura said. 'She has been a catalyst for my practice in a good and in a bad way.'

'Who has?'

'Sorry, I am so preoccupied by this patient', Laura said, already feeling embarrassed. 'I will say a bit more about myself before I get to her. Basically, I have been working full-time at the University of London's counselling service for nearly twenty years. I was lucky to get the job almost immediately after qualifying. I gained a lot of experience, although as you may know, it is a constant battle against the system, and in the end you have to accept that long-term work, what we have been trained to do, is a luxury.'

'Hmm.' Martin nodded.

'I suppose part of me liked belonging to a team and the sense of security it gave me, and for the first few years after qualifying I didn't want to think outside the box.'

'I see.'

'But I always knew that I was missing out on something in not developing my private practice. I guess I lacked the self-confidence. And then you meet the odd patient whose history or even the way they are in the world blows you away and you think, "Wow! This is a private practice patient. I wish I could see this person in my own consulting room and develop the relationship that needs to be developed without interruptions."'

'Did the patient you came to talk about evoke these thoughts in you?'

'Yes, exactly.'

'What is it that makes her so special?'

'Putting it like that makes it all sound quite suspicious – I mean my attachment to her; but yes, you are right. I suppose she became a bit special to me. Shall I give you a bit of her history?'

'Yes, please. In any way that feels right to you.'

This was a revelation to Laura. She was used to supervisors having their dogmas about how clinical work was to be done and discussed.

'She was twenty-five when she came to see me two years ago. The truth is that I was only seeing her for an assessment, as I had no space available at the time.'

'So how did you come to take her on?'

Laura hesitated. 'Well, by the end of the assessment session I knew that I wanted to work with her; and she also asked if she could see me again.'

'Was it that you felt moved by her?'

'Yes, absolutely. The problem was that I had to keep giving her different slots every week for some time. I had to make a real effort to find a slot for her.'

'So she knew from the beginning that she was special to you.'

'I suppose', said Laura, feeling surprised that the thought had not occurred to her before.

'What brought her to therapy?'

'An affair.'

'Oh. Was she not rather young to be having an affair?'

'Well, she was in a long-term relationship from a young age, and then she met an older man and she had a fling with him.'

'Why did she not split up with her boyfriend?'

'She said she could never be with the other man. It was

just that she was so infatuated, she could not get over him, and she was very confused about it.'

Martin interrupted. 'Can I have a name for her?'

'It is kind of Helen ... let's say Helen', Laura said, feeling that her nervousness had not quite abandoned her. 'Look, I had better tell you more about her history. It is very complicated.'

'Go on', Martin said leaning forward.

'She is adopted on her mother's side, but her father is her biological father. And this is what makes things complicated. He is somebody who had many affairs when Helen was little, and her conception was the outcome of one such affair.'

'Did she get to know her birth mother?'

'She has known her all her life; but it was only at fourteen that she found out the truth about who she was.'

'So it sounds like what brought her to therapy was that she started acting like her father. Monogamy was no longer satisfying to her.'

'I suppose. I hadn't actually thought of it like that before. The problem is our relationship though. That is what brings me here. I have completely messed up in my countertransference to her.'

'How do you feel about her?'

'Well, she is very intense, but also open and honest, and one can feel her suffering, it makes sense. I suppose I really like her. I did from the very beginning.'

'Do you know why you felt compelled to hold on to her in the first session?'

Laura hesitated. 'She was interesting and complex and

I felt that I could help.'

Martin focused his gaze on Laura. 'Do you think that there was maybe something in her history that you related to personally, perhaps something unresolved for you that you wanted to work through by seeing her?'

Laura took a deep breath in. She felt her hands shaking. She should not have come here. Martin lived up to his reputation. He really was a brilliant therapist: he could see right through the mess she had created.

'You don't have to tell me if you don't want to', he added softly.

'No, it's not that, it is that your questions make me realise more and more that I have really messed up with this patient. I should not have taken her on. Doesn't Freud say that we can only analyse others after we have worked through our own stuff? So, if I unwittingly took her on to work through something personal, surely that was a serious clinical mistake.'

'I have to say that I don't agree with that', Martin said. 'It is a myth that we can ever be fully analysed and sorted human beings. Freud liked to be scientific, but claims like that can only be pseudo-science. In reality, we work better with people that we connect with, and these are precisely the people who tap into something personal and often unresolved. I can hear a lot of guilt and self-blame in you.'

Laura could no longer withhold her tears.

'I am so sorry', she said in a shaky voice. 'I came here for a professional consultation. I have not even met you before and now I am getting upset.'

'What are you upset about?'

'I suppose your question hit the nail on the head. There was something personal that prompted me to take her on, although I thought I had better control over it than it proved.'

Martin focused his gaze on her. 'Just to say, you don't have to tell me, if you don't want to.'

'No, in fact, I do. If you don't mind, that is.'

'Go on.'

'Well, when I was about the age of Helen's birth mother, I got pregnant. I was in a relationship at the time and the pregnancy became a love test. He was consistent all along. He didn't want a baby. When the pregnancy progressed and it was getting too late for an abortion, he abandoned me. I was in a mess. I had not really thought what it would be like to have a baby. It was all about the power struggle with him, and suddenly I got really panicked about becoming a mother.'

Laura paused, swallowing down a sob. She wanted to tell him, to get it off her chest. To finally tell somebody who would get it, get her rather than try to analyse her. Sobbing throughout her supposed supervision session was out of the question though.

'My parents didn't know, as I was studying at uni and I had avoided going home at the end of term. In the end, it was clear that I could not have the baby, and I arranged for her to be adopted. She was taken away at birth. My whole life changed after that. I was doing a science degree at the time and I decided to switch to psychology, and then I trained to become a therapist. I waited and waited for the pain to subside. I thought it would get better when I had my own children, but now that I am a mother of two, I know that it actually makes it worse. Not a day goes by when I don't long for that baby and I wish that she would look for me and contact me – but she never has.'

There was a brief silence while Martin seemed to be absorbing the impact of what Laura had just told him. He finally spoke. 'Thanks for sharing this with me. It must have been difficult for you.'

Laura nodded. She felt her cheeks burning and she was sure they had turned a glowing hot pink. She hated it that even her skin made her feelings visible.

'So when Helen came for an assessment,' Martin went on, 'did it feel like you were being reunited with your lost daughter?'

'Obviously, rationally, no; but yes: I wanted to know about the impact, what it feels like to have that happen to you, I mean to be abandoned by your mother soon after birth. Part of me really rejoiced in what a beautiful, rounded person Helen was. I was relieved that she was not entirely damaged – but of course, she was in a lot of suffering and I wanted to help. It felt like I owed that to the universe.'

'And so how did it play out between you?'

'To start with there was a positive rapport. I think that she knew that I liked her, and that helped her open up and bring a lot of material to me. It was all moving at an astronomical pace. For some time she was quite distressed about having been obsessed with this man, but she was no longer infatuated with him. He had caused her some damage. He passed on a serious form of hepatitis to her.'

'Did he do that deliberately?'

'No, it was completely accidental. It is a long story. I think that is why she may have become infatuated with him: she could see his vulnerability. Anyway, my hypothesis was that she needed this affair as a poor substitute for a maternal connection, and I think I was right because, as she got more and more attached to me and the therapy, the obsession with the man seemed to shift, and it eventually disappeared. But, that was when it became more complicated.'

'In what way?'

'Well, there is something really physical about her. It is hard to describe it. She is an artist and she works with the form of the female body. I would say that she is somebody really "embodied". As she was getting deeper into the therapy, she started to physically attach herself to the room. She asked me why I don't have a couch, and she told me how much she wanted to lie down. Of course, we don't have a couch at the university counselling service. It is sad, isn't it? It made me really wish for the first time that I had my own practice, so that I could treat people the way they needed to be helped.'

'So it made you feel more embodied too.'

'Yes, I suppose. I felt whole in her presence. She was increasingly uncomfortable in the chair, and then she spotted the floor cushion, which is more decorative than anything else. Nobody had used it before. But she asked me if she could sit there. So she started sitting on the floor, not far from my feet, curled up. She was like a puppy, impossible not to touch. She evoked these deep maternal feelings in me.'

Laura stopped abruptly. She took a deep breath in and suddenly burst into tears. It felt like she had been preventing this warm, liberating flow from her eyes for more than half her life.

'I am so sorry', Martin said, leaning forward. 'Look, this is more complex than I initially thought. Are you happy to meet for a second session? I think we will need it.'

'Yes, of course', Laura said, taking a tissue from her bag. I would be so grateful.'

'What I hear up to now, though, is that you have managed to establish an amazing connection with this young woman. I am sure that this will have been immensely therapeutic for her.'

'I have touched her', Laura said. 'I have held her hand and I have given her hugs.'

'Okay, I hear that. It is not the way I work, but it is not the end of the world either. Many therapists touch their patients.'

'It was a mistake.'

'Did she say how she found the touch?'

'She didn't for a long time, but now she has, and that is what brings me here.'

'What did she say?'

'She said that she found it intrusive and that it bothered her and that she is considering ending therapy.'

'Do you think that your touch was erotic?'

Laura took some time to think. She was feeling calmer now. The worst had already been said. She could never have imagined that she would say that much to anyone.

'I experienced my touch as coming from a deep maternal place. But of course, who is to say that the maternal is not erotic?'

'You are right. Maternal love is the first real love we know, if we are lucky. But I think you are also confusing two things, which is precisely why I am against touching in therapy. Patients and therapists alike get in touch with early feelings and cravings during the process, but of course we are dealing with adults, and in adults, intense love is invariably erotic in its nature. This is what I think she is pointing out to you. That she is an adult and not a baby. I must admit that I admire her courage. It must have been difficult for her to say that to you.'

'Yes, it was. She was shaking all over.'

'But you also did something very brave today. You came here to talk about something very personal and complicated. I imagine it would have been tempting to bury it and talk to nobody about it.'

'I don't want to lose her', Laura said, and her voice cracked again. 'She is considering terminating the therapy.'

'Being a therapist is a heartbreaking business, Laura. We engage deeply with people and we have no control over when they decide to leave us ... We need to stop here, but I am well aware that there is still a lot of material to consider in relation to this patient.'

'Yes, even I had not realised how incredibly complex it is.'

'Can you come next Tuesday at 3.30?'

Laura thought for a minute. 'I will have to cancel a

session, but it is possible.'

'I am sorry. I have very limited availability at the moment.'

'I will be there, Martin, thank you.'

Laura got up and headed towards the door. Her step felt lighter, as though a huge weight had been taken off her shoulders.

20
Paris breeze

London and Paris, June 1997

Eleni kept peering at her freshly manicured nails. This was only her second manicure ever. The first one had lasted for less than twenty-four hours, and since then she had felt that it was not worth the money. For somebody who used her hands every day to do art, a manicure felt like high heels on an elephant. But today was a different day. Today was the day she had decided that she could allow herself to go wild, just for a weekend. Her nails told the story. Bright red, they were, a colour she had never felt comfortable wearing before.

The wavy, soothing motion of the Eurostar on her hips only confirmed her determination. She was a young woman in charge of herself, who knew what she wanted. She had loved trains since childhood. When she was very little, planes were in fact her favourite. She loved looking out of the window and observing the clouds. She loved being in the sky. But after a few bumpy rides in heavy cloud and rain during their frequent trips to Athens when her father was working there, she had decided that she did not like planes that much after all. In fact, she started refusing to get on one all of a sudden.

The time when she loved planes was the time she thought that she could fly. She still remembered vividly fantasising that she was flying in bed before falling asleep as a little girl. Her mother had done a good job to dissipate these fantasies. She managed to convince her that she could not fly, and once she believed her, she did not want to get on a plane any more. If humans could not fly, planes, also made by humans, could surely fail and crash.

Her flying dreams had continued throughout her life though. In fact, she had had one yesterday.

She was riding something that looked like a rocket over water. She was treading water, flying from London to Paris. The colours in the sky were auburn reds and oranges. She was flying while the sun was setting.

It was a truly beautiful dream, and yet there was a sense of threat coming from the red sky and the approaching outline of the city.

She had never met up with Yves since that fateful night in Paris, exactly five years ago to the day. She had received some postcards from him on his travels, North Africa seeming his favourite destination. All his postcards would arrive at her parents' address in Thessaloniki, so she would collect them months after they had arrived. His cards read something like:

Dear Eleni,

I have just been watching a beautiful sunset in Marrakech and I thought of you and our night together.

Je t'embrace,

Yves

She had never replied to him directly, not only out of the wish to disentangle herself, but also because she did not have a private address for him. Imagine writing to him at Vivienne's address! That would take courage. In fact she had also received a couple of joint postcards from Vivienne and Yves playing the parental couple, asking her how she was and hoping that she could come and see them next time she visited Paris. She had entertained the fantasy of writing back:

Dear Vivienne and Yves,

I am not well, thank you for asking. I have hepatitis C. I will have it for life. I got it from Yves. Are you two using condoms?

Je vous embrace,

Eleni

In reality, she had sent back a couple of postcards of the kind that she imagined Vivienne would expect, telling them that she was studying for her PhD. She was lucky enough to have funding. She still reminisced about the nice time she had in Paris and she hoped that they were both well. The postcards had got progressively rarer. In fact, last Christmas was the first that she had not received a card from them.

And then it happened. It was a bitterly cold and cloudy February afternoon. Nicolas was working in her little ground-floor study room and Eleni was preparing an early dinner when the phone rang.

'Eleni, it is Yves', a strange but familiar voice said from

the other end of the line. She froze.

'How did you find my number?' she mumbled, trying not to resort to suspect whispering.

'It was easy. It is in the list of the College's Art PhD students. Is this not your office? I can hang up, if you want me to.'

'It is my home number', Eleni said, now in a steadier voice. 'I work from home, it is easier. I cannot really talk right now.'

And just at that moment, she came up with a firm plan in her mind, a plan that felt as solid as one of the female figures of her artwork.

'I have been thinking about you a lot', he continued. 'I wanted to talk to you. Can I call you another time?'

'It is better if you don't. Give me your address. I promise that I will write to you.'

'Who was it?' asked Nicolas as soon as she hung up.

'Oh, someone who is interested in my work. He may want me to do some art for his café. I said I was busy with writing up my PhD thesis right now, but I would contact him if I got any space.'

'You shouldn't turn work down like that. You are under-promoting yourself', Nicolas mumbled without raising his head from his desk.

Yves's phone call had confirmed to Eleni that something was mutual, as usually happens in such cases. He too had been unable to let go of her. But the obsessiveness and sentimental reminiscence had to stop. Things linger on like this when they are unfinished, Eleni thought the moment she heard Yves's voice from the receiver. If she could only go and finish off what she had started that night in Paris, she would be set free. They would both be set free.

She wrote Yves a very simple and brief, but clear, letter. She said that she was also thinking of him, and yet she was still in a loving, committed relationship. She would not be able to be in touch with him in the future, but she wanted to see him one last time. She was planning to visit Paris for a weekend in June. Would he be able to see her then? She gave him the date and the hotel she would be staying at, on the Rive Gauche, near the Quartier Latin, her favourite part of Paris. Within a week, she had received a reply. 'Mademoiselle, à votre disposition', he wrote with his familiar humour.

Her excited mood was somewhat spoiled as she remembered setting up the plan and the lying and deceiving it took to organise this weekend away. Nicolas was never possessive or jealous unless provoked directly. It was one of the things that had drawn her to him. She could not stand macho men. Yet, this time round he asked her one too many questions about the trip. She told him that she was going to meet Lea, who was going to Paris for an architecture exhibition. It was a chance to have a girls' weekend away. As it happened, this was half true, as Lea was arriving at Paris on Saturday evening and they were going to cross paths. They had agreed to meet for coffee before Eleni's train left on Sunday afternoon.

As they were lying in bed the night before her departure after having made love, Nicolas turned on his side and asked her:

'Are you going to see him then?'

She had felt her blood freeze, yet she had defended her deception ruthlessly.

'What are you saying?' she replied sternly, 'That I can no longer visit Paris without being accused of being unfaithful, just because of a silly mistake five years ago?'

'I am saying that it is likely.'

'I am not in touch with them any more.'

'But it might be a good chance to get in touch now.'

'I think you are becoming possessive because I am going away for a weekend with a girlfriend and not you – and you know how I feel about possessive men like my father.'

'I was just asking', he said in a resigned tone. 'Just remember that your silly mistake cost you a serious disease for the rest of your life. Do not let it cost you any more than that', he added, and turned his back.

As the train was slowing, having reached the suburbs of Paris, Eleni's thoughts had become more solemn and her determination weaker. One thing her mother had repeatedly told her during her childhood was that she should never do to others what she didn't like done to her. Yet, she had convinced herself that this was the best thing she could do to bring this lingering obsession to a close.

Yves had agreed to pick her up from her hotel at eight. She had two hours to shower and think for the last time about what she was about to do and its possible consequences. Everything was arranged. She was equipped with condoms and a double room at the hotel. A friend might be staying with her for one or both nights, she had explained when booking.

Yves was already sitting on the big leather sofa by the reception when she got out of the lift, deliberately ten minutes late. She was wearing a black fitted dress, a short denim jacket and sandals, as the weather was beautifully warm and balmy, exactly as it had been that June night five years ago. She was hoping to look bohemian chic, but sexy at the same time. Yves got up as soon as he saw her and kissed her lightly on the lips. A noncommittal signal of what the deal was between them. He looked as familiar as if she had seen him yesterday, in his wide beige cotton trousers and his light-blue chequered short-sleeved shirt tucked in.

'Comment ça va?' he said.

'I must tell you,' Eleni said hastily, 'my French has become really rusty. Can we speak in English, or we will struggle to have a conversation? From what I remember, your English is magnifique', she added, trying to lighten up her request.

He took her to a Moroccan restaurant in Bastille, by car, as it was quite a long way from the hotel. The conversation was light and flowing as they ordered wine, couscous and some tagines. He asked her about her PhD, then he talked about his travels, and then it was her turn to ask politely after Vivienne. They had nearly finished the bottle of red, Nuits-Saint-Georges, when the food arrived. She had to be careful, Eleni thought to herself. Since her diagnosis, she had never drunk any more than two small glasses of wine in one go, and drinking on an empty stomach, however slowly, had gone to her head. They continued to talk as though they had last met yesterday, throughout the meal.

They had just ordered some mint tea when he topped up her glass and took her hand in his. This was the first time he had touched her since their greeting kiss. His touch felt like an electric current running through her body.

'So, what are you doing here?' he asked, looking her in the eye.

Eleni quivered, and felt her determination melt away. She took a deep breath in and let it out without speaking. She swallowed hard.

'I came to finish what we started five years ago. I came to sleep with you – that is if you want to sleep with me', she replied eventually, resisting the temptation to move her eyes from his.

'It is not like that', Yves said, seeming slightly taken aback. 'I did not go out with you then to have sex with you.'

'Oh.'

'It was because I had profound feelings for you, and they are still there.'

Eleni pulled her hand away. 'So you are saying that you don't want to sleep with me?' she asked.

'No, of course I do. Why would I not? You are very attractive. But you know, it was all very complicated: you and Vivienne having all these conversations, and then me asking you out on your last night. I felt guilty. It felt like you were almost like my daughter, me being Vivienne's partner and her feeling so maternal towards you. She was so sad when you left, you know.'

'But I'm not your daughter', Eleni said trying to lighten the atmosphere. Only seventeen-and-a-bit years between us? You would have been a teenage father.'

They both laughed.

'Listen', Eleni said after a while. 'You are right. It is quite complicated. I have felt very guilty too. You have a partner, I have a partner. But what else could there have been between us?'

He didn't answer, but he leaned over and gave her a deep, lingering kiss on the mouth. Eleni felt her breath being cut away. This is it, she thought to herself. He has made his decision.

'So do you want to come to my flat?' he said when they were back in his car, putting his hand high up on her thigh.

'No, I have booked my hotel room for two, you can be my guest.'

'You are a naughty girl', he said, moving his hand even higher. His erection was visible under his trousers even in the dim light coming down from the lampposts.

***

It was Sunday morning and Eleni was lying very still in the middle of the hotel's double bed on her back, staring at the ceiling. Admittedly, she had not paid much attention to the hotel's style when she was booking it other than to make sure it was decent enough and in her favourite area. But now, after the nights she had had here, the not-that-freshly painted cream walls with their semi-arty, semi-kitsch pictures of Parisian nightlife made her feel more dislocated than ever. She had just been to the bathroom, which smelt of industrially washed and neatly folded towels, and had realised that her period had come early. She knew that she had to get up and start getting ready, as she was meeting Lea for coffee in an hour. But it was as though her ability to give her body commands to move about was escaping her. Instead she kept staring at the thin sunrays creeping through the heavy wine-red drapes. She now knew that she had made a mistake. Sex did not resolve anything. It only made things worse. She was silly to have thought otherwise.

They tried to have sex on both Friday and Saturday night, but on both occasions Yves lost his erection the moment he tried to penetrate her. The foreplay was exciting though. To be touched by another man in different ways, on different parts of her body, felt to Eleni what it must be like to be high on drugs, an exhilarating act of abandoning parts of her to a stranger; letting them merge with his parts and then disappear for ever. She was no longer an embodied Eleni, but a fragmented, elastic person, happy to be transported to unknown places. This is what people on ecstasy must feel like.

Yet, when the moment of penetration came, it was like she had quickly landed back in her everyday body that needed protection and reassurance and survival; that needed to know that he would wear a condom so that he didn't pass on anything else to her; that he wouldn't get her pregnant; that ultimately, there would be reinstated boundaries between them that meant that they could both continue with their lives.

On the first day, he took the condom from her hand and put it on politely, but by the time he attempted to thrust in, his erection was lost.

'I am sorry, I had too much to drink', he said. 'It never works when I have drunk so much.'

They both tried to be as light-hearted and courteous about it as possible. They chatted for some time in bed and then he made his excuses for having to go back to his flat. Eleni was relieved, as she had started to feel anxious about the unanticipated intimacy of having to sleep with him in the same bed all night long. She had also noticed silently how he made no attempt to give her pleasure after he lost his erection. Nicolas would not have behaved so selfishly. Did he not know, she asked herself, that there are other ways than penetrative sex to satisfy a woman? She sensed a feminist disapproval of him. What was she doing here in an unfamiliar hotel, away from the people she loved and who loved her, trying to have sex with a stranger? she wondered with sadness.

Before leaving, he had asked about her plans for Saturday and she had insisted that she wanted to visit her 'personal Paris' as she put it, all the places she had loved during her six-month stay. She had wanted to relieve him from any sense of duty to entertain her while she was here. Yet he persuaded her to meet at five o'clock in an unusual part of town, near Place Pigalle, where major cultural developments were taking place.

'Isn't that where the brothels are?' Eleni asked, laughing, but he reassured her that that was not a planned part of the tour. She had thought that spending time with him the following evening would be awkward, but Yves seemed to be at his most natural when acting as the host. He took her down to a rather derelict part of town where abandoned industrial-looking buildings had recently been turned into galleries and lofts. One could sense the new and exciting vibe when passing bars and cafés with their improbable and interesting look, many of them combining art spaces and a bar.

'I am in my element here', Eleni said, turning her head towards Yves after they had been walking around for a while. 'You know, this is what I have started doing to make a living: exhibiting my art in cafés. I had one exhibition at a café in Athens and another more recently in London. It was surprising how well it sold.'

'I would love to see your art. You have never shown me', Yves said, holding her hand.

'C'est un secret', Eleni smiled.

They spent most of the evening in and around a vast derelict building turned into a multi-combo cultural space, with live music and gourmet food stalls on the ground floor. They had food out of a plastic box with little plastic forks, standing up: delicious steamed cockles with crunchy French fries and mayonnaise. Then they ended up in a quieter bar further down the road, where they each had two small glasses of wine, Eleni noticing Yves's restraint.

Yet, at the hotel that night the same scenario was repeated, only this time, it felt to Eleni, in an even more sterile and unexciting way. The foreplay was rather rushed, and there was a sense of purpose to it. As he was kissing her neck and bringing his hips into alignment with hers, he asked her if they had to use a condom, as he was not fond of them. Eleni felt a taste of anger in her throat.

'Don't you practise safe sex?' she asked as softly as she could. 'You have been to Africa.'

'I know, you are right', he mumbled. 'In fact I have something to admit. I have herpes – but it is in remission, which is why I suggested not using a condom. It cannot be passed on when it is in remission.'

The conversation stopped them in their tracks and they pulled away from each other. Eleni knew that he had again lost his erection. She was already naked and she rushed to cover herself.

'Don't', Yves said, and he cupped one of her breasts; but she had already turned on her back, pulling away from him.

'You also have hepatitis C, isn't that right?' Eleni said in a quiet voice.

'Yes', he said sounding really surprised. 'How could you possibly know that? I must really reduce my drinking. It is sad.' He stopped in his tracks. 'But how could you possibly know this, Eleni? Not even Vivienne knows.'

'I know, because I got it from you', she said in a steady voice.

'What? This is not possible. I only found out a year ago.'

'Yes, but you probably had it for many years before you found out. Remember that night you were bleeding and I was kissing you? I must have swallowed some of your blood.'

'I am so sorry', he said, holding her hand.

After that the mood was solemn. He caressed her hair and occasionally placed his hand on one of her breasts and they eventually fell into a light sleep, lying side by side. It is interesting that intimacy seems to arise between us when there is no sex involved, Eleni thought before drifting off. She did not know what time it was when she sensed him trying to disentangle himself from her and moving noiselessly around the room. She opened her eyes.

'I am off', he said. 'I will be back early, before eight. Let's have breakfast together.'

She kept waking up and falling back promptly into a restless sleep. The light of dawn had penetrated the room some time ago when she heard the door open, and she jumped out of bed, her heart pounding hard against her chest.

'I am sorry, I did not mean to scare you', Yves said. His intention was obvious from the moment he got into bed. He smelt of aftershave and freshly applied shower gel, and he thrashed his tongue deep into her mouth while removing her knickers. Eleni felt a flutter of panic and excitement at the knowledge that she was about to have what she thought she had wanted for a long time now. She tried to respond to his lovemaking, yet there was a sense that this was now his game. When they were both completely naked, he lay on his back, putting a condom on his erect penis, and asked her to ride him. It all happened very quickly after that. The only thing she remembered vividly was the frustrated realisation that there was little excitement for her in the way he thrashed into her and that she was far from reaching an orgasm. In a desperate attempt to reverse this, she took his hand along with hers and placed it on her clitoris. He moved her hand away and his thrashing became deeper and quicker. It was at that moment that the feeling of stillness and deadness moved inside her and settled around her chest like a plinth.

After he had finished, she knew that she wanted to end this as quickly as possible without being rude. She pretended that her train was leaving at ten o'clock in the morning, and so, after a quick breakfast in bed, they started saying goodbye. She expected him to ask her if he could see her again and she was prepared to say firmly that she had come here to end the affair; but he didn't ask. It seemed that on the non-physical level there was an understanding between them that was both profound and intimate. They kissed goodbye and he looked at her deep in the eyes, before making his way out.

***

'What is the matter? You don't look well', Lea said as soon as they sat down for coffee. 'Too many sleepless nights, huh?' she added, smiling wryly. Eleni, feeling that stillness inside her, could not get herself to respond.

'Are you all right? You are making me worried now. Did you see him or not?'

'It was awful, Lea, truly awful', she said, and her eyes filled with tears. 'I don't know why I am doing this to Nicolas and myself.'

'Was he not nice to you then?'

'Oh, no, he was nice, of course, very courteous. He took me to places, we made polite conversation. He told me he had feelings for me.

'So?'

'The sex was truly terrible. The closer it got to penetration, the less intimate it felt. It was as though he was performing on his own and I was a kind of plastic doll.'

'Oh, dear, so he was crap in bed then. It doesn't matter. It will make it easier for you to get over him, I guess.'

'I don't think so', Eleni said. Tears were now rolling down her cheeks.

'Oh God, you are a mess', Lea mumbled. 'Let's go for a walk by the river. I went past it on my way here, it should be round the corner.'

She took her by the hand like a small child. They walked for a while silently.

'Here is what I think', Eleni said after a while, wiping her tears. 'When a man and a woman meet and there is an attraction, it is as though they look to each other to repair their wounds. Yves was on the lookout for someone to love him. No woman can have loved him properly, which is why he doesn't know how to make love. He needed me to love him, but I can't, because I love someone else. I have failed him.'

'What about him failing you? He gave you hepatitis C and no pleasure in bed. How good can that be?'

They walked and walked along the river. There was a fresh morning breeze, ruffling their hair as they walked, turning their backs to the still-rising sun.

21
Birth

London, February 1972

Marika was pacing up and down holding a piece of folded paper in her hand. She unfolded it and read it again:

Dear Marika,

Please forgive my writing and spelling errors. I am a simple woman and I haven't written to anyone for a long time. I wanted to thank you again for hosting Nefeli and for helping her out. She so wanted to come to London to study, even though I thought that she was still too young to be so far away from her parents. I trust though that she is in really good hands with you.

I am enclosing a pashmina for you, some socks for Mario (I hope I am getting your husband's name right) and a scarf for Nefeli. I knitted them all myself. I hope that you will like them and that they will keep you warm.

Tell Nefeli that I had a dream that she had a big belly, as though she was pregnant. It is not a good omen, it means that she will encounter sorrow. Please ask her to be careful.

With my gratitude to you and your family,

Magda

22
The beginnings

Thessaloniki, April 1972

Leonora folded yet another Babygro, putting it away neatly in the new chest of drawers by her side of the bed, adjacent to which lay the shiny red crib. She had left work early, and even worse, she had not yet officially started her maternity leave. Two weeks for maternity-related duties was what was allowed to a female member of staff. As the leave was so tight, she had been advised by one of her contacts in the administration department to claim sick leave to begin with. This was legitimate for caring for a sick child as well, she was told. The main reason she had not informed anybody in the hospital about her prospective leave, though, was that she did not yet believe that she would need it. Given that she was now the Head of the Psychiatry Clinic, one of the most demanding wards in the hospital, she did not want to alert the staff to her absence, and especially did not want to lose face by telling them that she was about to get a baby, a huge and unforgettable life event, which might turn out to never quite materialise. Of course, she had explained the situation to her personal assistant and to Dimitri, one of the new doctors at the hospital, less dog-minded than the old guard, whom she had developed a blooming friendship with. They were going to adopt, she told them, but the legal process was rather onerous and complicated: she did not quite believe that they would get the baby until she saw it crossing her doorstep.

Besides, the fact that she had been elected as the first ever woman Head of the Psychiatry Clinic had already raised many hackles, let alone, God forbid, daring to combine this with maternity duties. Even she had found herself agreeing with her male colleagues in one of the many multi-disciplinary team meetings that she had to convene as Head, that women nowadays wanted to have it all, a career and a baby, but it was just far too much to ask, and unless they got their priorities right they were in danger of compromising both.

When she had chosen to specialise in neurology and psychiatry during her medical degree at university, she could have never anticipated that it would offer her such a flourishing career. She had never done well at anything that involved blood, having fainted twice in her student years when they had to dissect animals in the lab. Dermatology was what her degree supervisor had suggested to her as the area to specialise in, but she had wanted to do something she found interesting. Besides, her supervisor's thinking was transparent. She was a female student on a hardship scholarship. She would have to marry soon and have children. She needed to practise a branch of medicine that was comfortable and unchallenging, to have her cosy consulting room next to her family home, providing comfort creams on prescription. Yet, this was not what Leonora had chosen medicine for. Neurology was fascinating, as so little was known about the human brain, but research was progressing all the time.

She was not really that much into psychiatry. She had always wanted to be a proper doctor, and some of her psychiatrist colleagues, especially those with a genuine interest in psychiatry, were hardly that. They were interested in fluffy, scientifically dubious practices such as psychoanalysis. It was rather ironic in that sense, then, that she had ended up as Head of the Psychiatry Clinic in the hospital. The hospital hosted the only forensic unit in town, and although this had occasionally accommodated real criminals – including a murderer and a serial rapist – most of the inmates were drug addicts, many of them with severe neurological handicaps after years of drug abuse. They could be charming and apparently compliant, and although some of them would try sincerely to get better, they would invariably end up in the unit again after a short time trying to make it out in the world. In some ways, they were not as complicated as other psychiatric patients, as the focus was specific: their addiction and how to manage it.

She always referred the true sociopaths to her male psychiatrist colleagues, as she felt rather at sea and perhaps even a bit repulsed when it came to that kind of pathology. She had been working at the hospital since she graduated for more than fifteen years now. She had been instrumental in setting up the forensic unit, a safe place for the city's junkies, who had kept wandering in and out of the hospital;

so surely her promotion was more than fair enough. Unlike some of her colleagues, she had not cared to establish a secret private practice, an illegal but widespread choice for National Health Service employees, or to accept the also very common 'tip' envelope passed to the white-coated doctor discreetly in the hospital corridor by a desperate member of a patient's family. She had chosen to work with the junkies, those whose families had stopped caring.

For the first twelve years at the hospital, she had put in very long hours, comparable to, if not longer than, those of her male colleagues. Childlessness had worked to her advantage where her career was concerned. In fact she had invested all her young energy in her work. Despite all this, and all the promotions and recognition of her work she had received down the years, she could often hear the whispers behind her back. A woman Head of the Psychiatry Clinic? It is completely inappropriate, people would say.

The sound of the key turning in the door abruptly landed her back in their dimly lit bedroom, with its heavy walnut wood furniture – Dinos's choice of course, opulent and dark like him. She had been expecting this noise all afternoon: her husband returning from his trip, bringing the new baby home with him. Yet she was still not sure if it was really going to happen. Would Nefeli let him take her baby away? What kind of mother could possibly do that?

It was now over two months since the baby was born, and for most of this time Nefeli had lived with her in London. How could she possibly give her up now? Yet Leonora had seen it happen at work. Although she mainly dealt with adults, she had heard colleagues talk about children they were assessing who were suffering the symptoms of neglect and abuse. And she had met in the corridor repeatedly the little boy who was a regular at the hospital, the middle child in a family of seven children, who swallowed lightbulbs and other glass items in desperation to get his mother's attention. It hadn't happened recently, but when she first started working in the hospital it was not uncommon to find abandoned babies wrapped up in blankets, at the steps of the outpatients' entrance. After all, had she not done this herself – aborted her baby, the only one she had ever fallen pregnant with, without a second thought? At twenty-five she had just assumed that her body was invincible, that it would produce as many babies as she liked in the future. How arrogant, how wrong. She ought to stop thinking like that. She had been punished enough. She ordered herself to get up and walk towards the apartment door.

'Leonora, where are you?' she heard Dinos call out in an irritated voice. She saw him standing by the living-room door, a bit breathless as usual, having placed on the floor in front of him a Moses basket. She leaned over and looked in the basket in awe. There, a well-fed baby with fine blonde hair was sleeping peacefully.

'You said she was dark-haired and premature. She doesn't look either of the two to me', she said in surprise.

'Apparently she has been putting on weight rapidly, and the hair she had after her birth is being replaced with new blonde hair', Dinos said, lifting his shoulders. 'At least she looks like my baby now', he added, and smiled proudly.

Leonora peered in the basket again. She was shell-shocked to see two wide sea-coloured eyes staring at her. Was it her imagination or was this baby exploring her face? It was like it was saying to her, 'We have a long way to go together.'

'Just to warn you, she is quite a big crier', Dinos said.

'Yet she has just woken up in a strange place and she has not cried at all!' Leonora whispered.

She undid the straps and leaned down to lift the baby out of the basket. Her head started flopping backwards, and she quickly remembered to put her hand at the back of the baby's head for support. It was a long time since her paediatrics training, and despite having bought several books on childcare in the last few months, she still felt inept. The problem was that she had not quite believed that this moment would ever come, not even ten minutes ago. It had all felt so unreal; one of Dinos's utopian projects that would never come to fruition. He had always been a dreamer, a visionary. But how often did visions become reality?

The baby was still staring at her silently. Was she weighing her up? Was she wondering if she would be a good mother to her? If only Leonora could know the answer to that. She knew that she had to try. She had to measure up to Dinos's expectations of her. He was trusting her with his precious baby. When it came to their relationship, she never felt good enough. She always felt like she was walking on eggshells, that she would do something and disappoint him despite her best intentions. She knew that objectively she was the most giving party in their relationship, yet somehow he would always manage to take the high ground. Loving him was like a race to prove herself, while at the same time having to accept him as he was, with all his faults and infidelities. Loving him was like loving a baby, unconditionally and despite the terrible trouble he gave her.

And now, here was the baby he wanted her to take care of and provide unconditional love for; the baby he had had with his lover. She had fallen for the baby's looks, the wide bright eyes and the blonde soft curls; but now that she had picked her up, the smell of her was unfamiliar. Did she smell of Nefeli? The thought made something inside her go frozen. This baby smelt like her husband's lover, possibly even like the lovemaking the two of them had last night. She was not a fool. She knew that he had spent the night with her. Farewell sex, she hoped that they had.

She walked about the living room rocking the baby, whose head was now resting on her left shoulder even though she was not crying. She had done this mechanically, without registering what she was doing. Dinos had been following them with his eyes.

'Here,' she said, 'take her for a while. I will go and make some milk. She must be hungry.'

'I am not that comfortable holding her yet when she is awake. She is so little', he said.

She placed her back in her basket, but the moment she was about to leave the room, the baby turned her head in her direction and let out a cry, followed by rhythmic, escalating wails. The message was clear enough. She picked up the basket and carried it to the kitchen, putting it safely in the middle of the kitchen table where they could make eye contact. 'Here, baby', she said. 'You must be hungry. I will make some milk for you.' She was astonished to see a vague smile forming on her round baby face.

23
The scent of things to come

Thessaloniki, June 1983

After she let the daughter go in foreign lands abroad
She would only wear black, black like the gloomy sky
Standing still and stiff like the dead
over her husband's grave
Curse I give you, she cried, for my piercing sorrow
Missing a daughter is no less than missing half my body
A daughter fresh like waterfalls, fragrant like a rose.

They were sitting on the marble steps of the ground-floor entrance of the block of flats where Eleni lived, singing the song together and tears flowing down their cheeks. One of the elderly residents on his way up to his flat had stopped to admire 'two beautiful girls in their tidy navy-blue school uniforms singing nicely together'. But when he came close enough to perceive the tears in their eyes through his spectacles, he seemed puzzled and somewhat embarrassed, and he quickly proceeded up the stairs and into the lift without saying goodbye. They smiled in conspiracy with each other. They looked at each other through their wet eyes, and then agreed to sing it again from the beginning, as they had been interrupted.

It was Friday today, and the fifth day of the week that they had sat on Eleni's steps singing the same song again and again and crying. Mr Manos had recited it as an example of poetry and sorrow in traditional Greek song. For some reason, they had both been hooked. While Mr Manos was praising the depth of the song in their Greek class at the beginning of the week, they could hear some of their classmates trying to suppress giggles. 'Like a rose, my ass', Eleni had heard Alexisaying to the boy sitting next to him. She would not have wanted to risk Mr Manos's scolding herself, as he could be the kindest of teachers, but very strict when it came to behaviour like that.

Anyway, this week the last thing she wanted was to get Mr Manos's attention again. She had had enough intensity with all the crying they got into with her friend Electra, feeling compelled to sing the song again and again without even fully grasping its meaning. It was all poetic and metaphorical. And then, in the midst of all this, Mr Manos called her into his office during the long break and kept her there for the whole forty-five minutes. She was so scared when he asked her to go in and see him. She was sure he was going to tell her off about the other day, when she and Electra had sat on the school's fountain taps during the break and they were so dripping wet on their return to class that he had had to interrupt the lesson and go and look for some absorbent paper, which he asked them to put under their uniforms. He had scolded them enough at the time; why did he need to tell her off once more? Overall, she was really fond of him and wanted to please him, despite her occasional misdemeanour, usually prompted by a kind of folie à deux.

'You seem really worried Eleni', Mr Manos remarked. 'I haven't called you in to tell you off', he added humorously.

'Have you not?' Eleni sighed in relief.

'No, of course not. I just wanted to have a chat with you before the big day when you finish primary school. Moving on to secondary is a big moment in a child's life.'

She had always felt in awe of Mr Manos. He had the most intense, magnetic dark eyes, which looked at her as though he could see right through her. Yet she would never feel intruded upon in his presence, just deeply cared for and acknowledged. In fact he cared deeply about all his pupils, but she secretly felt that he had a soft spot for her. Yet this time, while sitting at his office across from each other, him leaning forward, elbows on his knees, looking at her very seriously, she felt somewhat uneasy. She was still not sure what this was about.

'You must know, Eleni, that I think very highly of you. I expect you to excel academically in your new school.'

'Thank you.'

'Even the – let's face it – sometimes crazy behaviour that you and Electra can get into together is a sign of premature intelligence and the first hint of entering puberty rather early.'

'I am sorry, Mr Manos, I don't know what gets into us at times', she mumbled, wondering what on earth puberty was.

'In fact this is why I called you in, this is my only worry: that you are entering puberty early and that bright girls like you can have quite a hard time during adolescence. This is why I wanted to talk to you now, before you leave the school. Your mother has talked to me about your family situation and I believe that I can be of help.'

'My family situation?'

'Yes, Eleni. You shouldn't have to feel that you are carrying a secret alone, that it is not safe to share it with anyone. It is quite safe to share it with me. I already know it and I could help you feel better about it.'

'A secret?' she replied. 'What kind of a secret?'

'A family secret, Eleni. You do not have to carry it all by yourself. You are not protecting anyone by not talking about it. You are the one who needs protecting.'

'But I don't have any family secret', she said, puzzled; but then she stopped in her tracks. His words had just sunk in. She should not try to protect others by not talking. He was right, she had been doing this all her life. She burst into tears.

'You are right,' she said, 'I have been protecting my parents all my life. Their relationship makes me unhappy. They keep arguing all the time. I don't think that they should be together.'

'I am sorry to hear that.' Mr Manos said, lowering his gaze.

'Also, my father is not nice to my mother. He has many girlfriends. Everyone knows about it. I don't understand why my mother puts up with it.'

'You know what I think? I think that you should care

less about their relationship', Mr Manos said in a kind voice. 'They are adults, and I am sure that they can sort it out by themselves. But what about you?'

'What about me?'

'What about your relationship with your mother? Do you feel loved by her?'

'Of course!'

'I noticed the other day how upset you got when I recited the song about the abandoning mother.'

'Oh, was it an abandoning mother? I had no idea', Eleni said, feeling embarrassed.

'Why do you think you get so upset, Eleni, when hearing a song like that?' Mr Manos asked, looking at her intensely.

'I have no idea', Eleni said, perplexed. 'I love my mother. She is my rock. She would never abandon me, although I think she should have abandoned my father.'

'But do you think you may feel a bit insecure in relation to her? Like she might abandon you if they divorced, so that you need to please her and protect her so that she stands by you?'

Eleni thought for a while. 'My mother would never leave me', she said emphatically. 'Yet I always get upset when she is not there, not sure why.'

She walked out with the vague feeling that she had not given Mr Manos what he wanted to hear. Maybe she had somehow let him down. Electra was waiting for her anxiously in the playground by the school building entrance.

'Has he told you off?' she asked. 'Is he going to call me in next?'

'He hasn't told me that he will', Eleni replied.

'So, what did he want to tell you?'

'Oh, just to talk to me about leaving the school and entering puberty and how bright girls like us sometimes find puberty hard.'

'Puberty? What is that?'

'I don't know, I guess growing up, becoming more like a woman.'

'Oh!' They both giggled. 'And so?'

'He just wanted to wrap things up. Apparently he was worried that we both got so emotional about the mother song.'

Eleni noticed how selective she was being about the information she was giving out. It was funny how often she thought of herself as too open, and yet when it came to certain moments like Mr Manos or Electra asking her all these questions, she felt like a snail residing in its shell.

She had been thoroughly enjoying her last year in primary school. It was the first time in her school years that she was a member of the popular group in her class and had made some genuinely good friends. Towards the end of the year, Electra had rapidly become her best friend, and although she found their friendship exciting, she was sometimes scared of the intensity of it all. It was as though when they were together the floodgates were let open and eventually there would be an overflow, sweeping them both away. Often the two of them would skate around the neighbourhood after school daring each other to do something crazy. Electra would invariably win the game, as she was not shy like Eleni and would think nothing of stopping a handsome man in the street and asking, 'Excuse me, sir, would you mind telling me your zodiac sign?'

It was not always fun either. Sometimes when they got back from skating and playing with the others in the park, they would get into a serious conversation about the family problems some of their classmates had, or who loved whom in the class and would they ever be fortunate enough to be loved in the way they craved. Eleni sensed that her mother did not approve of her friend Electra, despite her being the only other middle-class child in her entire class. Electra's father was a university professor and her mother a librarian, and it was clear that Electra had a huge preference for her father, who came across as warm and affectionate.

'I think I know what puberty is', Electra had told her after some thought. 'The other day I came on – you know, I had a period.'

'Wow! And you didn't say a thing!'

'My father went down to the pharmacist's to buy me some pads and then had a serious chat with me about it. My mother had not told me a thing.'

'Oh, that's not nice.'

'Yeah, we never really do talk, Mum and I', she mumbled.

'My mother has been trying to prepare me a little bit; she told me what a period is.'

Their friendship had been rather late-blooming, as for years they had avoided each other in class, despite the chemistry between them. When Eleni had joined the school, her classmates had quickly worked out that she was from a wealthier background than the rest of them, and had soon started calling her 'the rich Eleni', a moniker that only Electra had received previously. It became a frequent joke and they both intensely hated being called 'the rich Es'. Avoiding each other seemed like the only safe way to blend in. Having reached their final year, though, it was certainly a sign of their hard-won popularity to be finally called rather affectionately just 'the Es'.

That June Friday afternoon that found them sitting on Eleni's steps singing once again the song that made them cry, they had already spent some time in the park with their mates after school. Quite a few of the popular boys had joined the group that day, along with their favourite boy in the class, Leo, who was a rare joiner in their outings. Leo had angelic, handsome looks combined with an aloof personality, and both of them had agreed that they loved him, but that they would not mind if he chose either of them over the other. What had become crystal clear to both of them during that park outing on a sunny Friday afternoon was that he didn't have his eyes on either of them. His intimate chat with Melina, another popular girl in their group, had established quickly that she was probably his heart's desire.

They talked all the way home, having put their skateboards under their arms, too gloomy to feel like skating. Electra in particular was really gutted.

'I don't believe it that he didn't even give us a second look', she mumbled. 'All this daydreaming about him and his heart was set so easily.'

Eleni had tried to cheer her up. 'Come on, let's have a

race. Forget about him, he doesn't deserve us. Let's have some fun. It is Friday afternoon!' But her friend would have none of it.

When they finally collapsed on Eleni's steps, the mood was still solemn.

'I have an idea', her friend said. 'Let's commit suicide.'

'What?' Eleni said, not quite believing what she was hearing.

'I mean not truly die, but let's take some pills to show how bad we are feeling. Shall we?'

'Take pills?'

'Yes, painkillers – you know, to numb our pain. Come on', she prompted her. 'I will call you when I am home and tell you what I am taking. Come on, Eleni, let's do this together.'

Eleni could not believe it when she found herself agreeing to it. As usual, the two of them had got into an exhilarated mood that needed some big drama to be fed like a starving lion. The truth was that she was really not that bothered about Leo. She was not even sure if she truly fancied him or if she was just going through the motions. Popular, classically handsome boys like him were not exactly her type. Yet the gloomy mood had slowly crept under her skin and she was desperate to find a way to express it.

'I swallowed 1, 2, 3, 4, 5, 6. Six! It is already an overdose!' She felt good that she was able to do this. '7, 8, 9, 10! – shall I take them all? There are only three left. I may as well. 11, 12, 13! Wow! This feels so strange! I must hang up now. I want to concentrate on how my body feels. I will call you later, bye.'

24
Sweet adolescence

Thessaloniki, January 1986

Dinos took a sip from the little cup filled to just below the rim with foamy and slightly muddy coffee, while sitting at his usual place at the top end of the oval formica table by the kitchen door. He lit up a cigarette and inhaled with delight. It was savouring moments like this, being in his body and feeling the smell and the texture of the coffee passing his lips, temporarily filling his mouth with aromatic bitterness and eventually warming his throat, and sensing the scent of his favourite Assos cigarette filling his lungs, these were the moments that made life worth living. It was as though nicotine fuelled his blood with the right substance for contemplation.

In his last check-up, after Leonora's insistence, the doctor had bullied him again to quit smoking with all the usual scaremongering tactics. He had never trusted doctors. They didn't really get it. They saw people like some kind of machine that they could fix or at least put in good order. If only he would follow their advice, eat the diet of an anorexic and stop anything that gave him pleasure, he would be all right. But what about having a life?

Today, he was having a particularly good day. His mind was full of exciting new ideas. The beef stew and spaghetti he had cooked for lunch was truly delicious, despite Eleni turning her nose up at it as usual. After lunch, he had fallen into a contented and unusually deep sleep. He even had a dream, quite a weird one. Eleni was in his bed, she must have been around five, her blonde wavy hair falling around her face. She had been at her best at that age, beautiful, like an angel. She kept saying, 'Daddy, Daddy, do the aeroplane, Daddy', and he lifted her up with his legs, and then it was no longer her, her face had turned into Nefeli's face.

When he woke up, he realised that Leonora had not joined him in bed for her usual midday siesta. He was expecting to find her in the kitchen, still fiddling about with things, but to his surprise she was not there either. In fact, although she had tidied up some of the leftovers, she had left quite a mess of unwashed dishes in the kitchen sink. He did not want to let this deter him from his good mood though. Leonora had never been house-proud. On the occasions that he had pointed out to her that he was the one who cooked most of the family meals and often tidied up after, and that she should try at least to keep the house in order as she should have known by now that he really disliked mess, she would invariably reply that he should in that case try to be the main breadwinner of the family, as Eleni's school fees did not rely on his business's ups and downs but on her considerable, and steady, salary. She would often add that at least he had found a woman who was nothing like his mother, active and capable and engaged in the world, not a neurotically house-proud and needy ice queen. He knew how easily such remarks could escalate into a major argument, so his strategy lately was to try and let go of anything that he did not find too offensive.

While he was making his coffee earlier on, he had overheard Leonora's and Eleni's voices in what seemed like an intense conversation in Eleni's room. He had found himself smiling in surprise. Almost two hours after they had finished their lunch, those two were still locked in Eleni's room talking. Part of him was really enjoying the closeness that Leonora and Eleni had established from the beginning of Eleni's adolescence. Their decision to move Eleni to an exclusive all-girls private had definitely been the right one. After two years of defiance and conflict with both of them at the end of primary, Eleni had now finally mellowed out, at least in her relationship with her mother. He could not exactly say the same for him. The last few years had been very testing for their relationship, and he had often wished that he could have held on to his sweet little girl for ever. Eleni always responded badly to him establishing ground rules such as needing to dress modestly and checking with them about her outings (especially the evening ones). Every time he told her that she could not be home after ten p.m. while she was still at school, he would get a flood of complaints and resistance from her. All her friends were allowed to go to the disco at least once in a while; she was losing face with them; he had no right to tell her how to dress, and so on.

His fears about Eleni's imminent discovery of sexuality,

with all its dark and destructive aspects, had not been dissipated by the fact that reading books and playing sports were still her favourite pastime. Lately she had become much more sedentary, and several times when he walked into her bedroom he had found her absorbed in writing. Keeping a diary was surely the first sign for girls of getting into the lures of attraction to the opposite sex, he had thought.

His little girl would eventually turn into a woman, and there were very few women around who stood in his mind as a good model for her to aspire to. There had only been a couple of women he had had an affair with who he had looked up to. There was the architect he had worked closely with when building a posh block of flats in Athens's north suburbs. Yet she was weak enough to sleep with him and get entangled, and then, in the end, as usual, they were both hurt and let down. Sexuality made women weak, this was his view. Perhaps it made him weak as well, but it was different for men. How could one be a man and abolish the love for a woman in some form? In fact Leonora was the best model for Eleni. Strong, independent and in control. This was how he wanted his daughter to be.

He was really dismayed when Eleni started breaking the ground rules. She had come back from the hairdresser's a couple of months ago with all her lovely rained-on-hay locks gone and her army-style short hair coloured a bright yellow.

'You look ridiculous', he had found himself shouting at her. 'Do you love making yourself look ugly?'

'Yeah, I love it!' she had shouted back.

'You know that you are breaking the ground rules, Eleni.'

'I couldn't care less.'

He hated it when she was defiant like this.

'Don't push it with me, Eleni. What about school? Have you thought that they may expel you when they see your new hairstyle?'

'That would give me a lot of pleasure,'

'Eleni!'

'It is my hair, Dad, my body. Neither you nor the school have the right to dictate what my hair looks like.'

'You are really letting me down, Eleni. It is a pity, because I had thought that you were an intelligent girl who knew better than that. For your information, there are rules in families and in schools and if you don't learn to respect them you will be in a lot of trouble, young lady', he had warned her, waving his finger at her.

He hated how old and conservative she made him feel. In fact he turned out to be right about the school, as they had called Leonora in to discuss Eleni's appearance. He had to admit, though, that he was partly relieved that she had gone down the route of teenage-clown looks. She looked as androgynous and scruffy as it was possible to be, not heavily made-up and in high heels and mini-skirts, like some of her mates.

By the time Leonora walked into the kitchen, his good mood had evaporated. How could it be that his mind always took him down the darker alleys after only five minutes of pleasure? She sat down without seeming to notice him. Was he invisible, he wondered, or was she sleepwalking?

'You have left the sink full of unwashed dishes', he said

solemnly after a while.

'I told her.'

'You told whom what?'

'I told her everything, Dinos. I told her that I am not her real mother.' Tears rolled down her cheeks.

'Oh. Do you want a coffee?'

Leonora did not reply. She stared out blankly and tears continued to flow one after another from her eye sockets.

'Did you tell her about Nefeli?'

'No, that was the only thing I did not say. God knows why. Maybe for fear that she would run straight into her arms and never want to see me again.'

'Don't be silly, Leonora. You know Eleni loves you.'

'Do I? Anyway, don't expect her to be all loving to you after this. I told her that you had had her with one of the women you had an affair with.'

Dinos got up and poured water, coffee and a tiny bit of sugar in a little silver pot, which he started brewing on a small portable gas ring by the sink, his back to Leonora.

'And how is she?' he asked.

'Upset, tearful. It is going to be as difficult as expected.'

'If I am honest, I don't see the need for all this', he said, while pouring the coffee carefully into a small cup with saucer.

'What do you mean?'

'She knows anyway. She has always known the truth. She is a highly intelligent girl. Is it possible that she doesn't know that Nefeli is her biological mother? Every time they go out together, everyone remarks on how similar they look.

Every time she goes to Nefeli's house to visit, her whole family gather around her. It is a special event for them all. It only takes putting two and two together.'

'That's all well and good, but I can tell you that she had no idea.'

'She was pretending not to know, that's all. And you decided to get in there and stir things up for her.'

'Oh, so now you are chastising me for doing the difficult work. That's handy! She has been pestering me for a couple of weeks with questions, how exactly she was born and all that.'

'You could have come up with something.'

'So you wanted me to lie blatantly. Sure, she would have appreciated me for that, when she eventually discovered the truth.'

'No, no lying was necessary, she already knew the truth. All we needed to do was protect her from the details of it all for a few more years.'

'Oh, I see. You know what I think? That it suits you to say that she knew already, so that you would not have to do any of the hard work.'

Dinos held his head in his hands, feeling as though it was too heavy for him to lift.

'I can see that you are building this to an argument', he grunted. 'All I am saying is that on some level Eleni knew that Nefeli is her mother. She was just not ready to acknowledge it, and you are intruding into her mind with things she has not asked for.'

'This knowing and not knowing at the same time has

been very dangerous for her. It made her volatile and irrational. I would rather she heard the truth and could begin to process it.'

'There is the psychiatrist talking.'

Leonora took a sip from her coffee. 'When Eleni was five I told her that sometimes, when a woman cannot have a baby in her tummy, another woman has it in her tummy for her, and when the baby is born she gives her to her mother. "This is what happened to us", I told her. "I couldn't have you in my tummy, but I love you nevertheless and I am still your mummy." She looked at me for a moment wide-eyed and still, and then she said: "If you ever say that to me again, I am going to fly out of the window." I am not sure if she meant fly like the Bionic Woman she was into at the time, or die.'

'You see, I told you she didn't want to know.'

Dinos lit up another cigarette.

'Give me one as well', Leonora said. 'I need it today.'

He passed her the white packet embroidered with a silver line. Dinos had always liked its simple elegance. She pulled one out and he leaned forward to light it for her.

'Look', he said exhaling the smoke. 'I will talk to her about Nefeli. Give it a few days for things to calm down and I will.'

They both smoked for a while in silence, inhaling deeply every single puff.

25
The encounter

London, February 2009

Nefeli managed to squeeze onto the Heathrow Express just a second before the doors shut. The valerian capsule she had popped under her tongue during take-off had quietened her nerves down. Homeopathy and all sorts of herbal pills had become her best friends during the last few years of going through a late menopause. She knew, though, that her anxiety throughout the trip and the night before had less to do with hormones (although her hormones did not help) and more to do with her recent decisions and the fact that Eleni had, for the first time ever, invited her to stay over with them in her house in London.

It felt like she had been waiting for the invitation for a lifetime. Every time she travelled to London, and it would be at least once a year, she would spend the week before her trip daydreaming about how Eleni and she would go shopping together in the West End, or how they would go for a walk side by side on the South Bank. She still had vivid memories of her pleasant walks in yellow- and orange-leaved autumnal London when she was pregnant with Eleni.

Her fantasies had never materialised though. The most she would see of Eleni when she visited London would be over a rushed coffee at Eleni's local café, where the conversation would be strained and stuck. Eleni would always look at her watch or out of the window, and before Nefeli knew it she would be off to an appointment.

She thought that she actually preferred the adolescent Eleni, full of anger and accusations, to her adult version, polite, restrained and hardly there at all. Any time that she had found an excuse to visit Eleni's house, she was made to feel that she was imposing herself. Dinos would invariably dump various food items on her to deliver to Eleni upon her arrival to London; Eleni would greet her with coldness, and soon enough she would get exasperated at the sight of the considerable volume of olive oil and feta cheese that her father was sending her from Greece. Nefeli often had to rescue stuff from being thrown in the bin.

'Eleni, if you do not want some of this food,' she would say as softly as she could, trying not to exasperate her any further, 'I am sure Mrs Marika and her family would greatly appreciate it.'

This time, something had changed though. Since Chloe's birth, they had talked on the phone several times.

'You can stay with us when you visit London in February', Eleni had interrupted her mid-sentence, as she was hesitantly telling her that she was thinking of organising her yearly trip to London.

The silence was palpable.

'I would love to', Nefeli had rushed to reply, trying to

steady her voice when she eventually woke up from her muteness, before her silence could be interpreted as hesitation or lack of interest.

'Since having a baby daughter, I have wondered more about the beginning of my life', Eleni had added hesitantly. 'It could be an opportunity for us to talk.'

Nefeli had now reached Victoria Station, and she started dragging her heavy, thankfully wheeled, suitcase through the considerable crowd on her way to the taxi rank. She was carrying as usual quite a few things for Eleni, but unlike the previous times, when most of the stuff had been given to her by Dinos in his customary imposing manner, this time it was gifts that she had chosen herself for the baby and for Eleni. Her mother had knitted several baby outfits for Chloe. It felt like telling her mother that Eleni was pregnant had given her permission to get her hands busy, despite Nefeli's insistence that it would be better to find out if it was a boy or a girl first, and to ask Eleni what she wanted. At least her mother was doing everything she could this time round, but it was far too late for Nefeli to recover her lost baby.

On the other hand, Dinos had only given her a couple of things for Eleni that she had specifically asked for: her favourite milk pie, and some almond and orangeflower water triangular pastries, a childhood favourite. Breastfeeding had given her a sweet tooth, she had said. It felt like pregnancy and breastfeeding had somewhat mellowed Eleni. Perhaps she was also responding well to the fact that her father had become somewhat less intrusive, not filling her space with tons of feta cheese and floods of olive oil.

Though Nefeli knew only too well that this was not a change in his character, but only a sign of the recent sharp deterioration of his health.

Things had been rocky between Dinos and her lately. The café that they had had together for the last few years was not doing well. Yet Dinos was unable to admit either that he was no longer fit to work or that it was not fair or realistic to expect Nefeli to be on her feet all day long, running the place for a bag of peanuts. She was no longer a young woman. She had tried to broach the subject with him several times, but every time she was met with a 'do whatever you like' shrug of his shoulders, effectively refusing to discuss rationally with her the process of closing the business down.

And yet Nefeli was feeling grown up for the first time in her life. She could see that she needed to start taking steps to take care of herself now, as, if she didn't, nobody else would. She had done some research into selling the business and the kind of money she might expect if she managed to do so. Dinos had promised her security, but as the prospect of her retirement approached she could now see that this was yet another thing he had failed her in. Their relationship had been platonic for a while now. Nefeli wondered if abstaining from sex with him, sex that had always felt like an addiction, was what had given her, for the first time ever, the determination to take her life into her own hands.

So many things had changed in the last few months. How much of that, she wondered, could she share with Eleni? She had decided to be as honest and open as she could with her about her decision to sell the business and move on. But could she really tell her that, at the age of nearly sixty, she still craved to be swept away by a man, to accept a proposal of marriage and to start her life at last? Somebody who would be available for her and only for her, who would want to spend the rest of his life with her. Could she ever dare to disclose to her that such a man had appeared in her life in the last few months out of the blue? As though, disentangling herself from Dinos, even if only in her mind, could open up the possibility of finally meeting her prince.

She still remembered vividly the first afternoon Andreas had come to the shop, luckily on a day that Dinos was not there. Conversation had flowed between them.

'Things are difficult out there, people losing their jobs, businesses closing down. And I hear it will only get worse. How is this shop doing?' he asked her.

'As you may have guessed, things are difficult here as well', Nefeli volunteered. 'We hardly make any profit any more. Working for nothing is no fun.'

'That's a pity. It is a beautiful café. And I love your pastries. My friend told me about this place. He said go and see, all the pastries are like real homemade stuff, with excellent ingredients. Your business?'

'Mine and somebody else's. I do most of the work, but he is the boss really. And the pastries are homemade. He makes sure only the best goes in them.'

'Your husband?'

'Oh, God, no. He is already married, to somebody else I mean ...' Nefeli felt herself blushing, and she blushed even more.

'Not fair then, if you do all the work. You need to make a living when you work hard.'

'I have been talking to him about closing it down, I have had enough really, but let's say things are a little complicated between us ...'

'Sounds like you could do with getting some of it off your chest. Would you sit down for a coffee? My treat.'

Nefeli still felt astonished every time she remembered that first meeting. Despite her usual suspicion of strangers, she found herself sharing all her worries of the last year. She had sat down and had a coffee with him, something she very rarely allowed herself to do with customers. Her relationship with Dinos had always been the ultimate secret in her life, the reason she could not get really close to any of her friends. It was not allowed, to share the intricacies of her life with anyone. And now, in the space of an hour, she was sharing the most private information with a virtual stranger.

After that, he visited every other day, which made Nefeli feel nervous and excited at the same time. A few times he bumped into Dinos, and Nefeli was impressed by how cleverly he handled it. He hardly talked to her when they both knew that Dinos was observing their every move. Instead, with his naturally charming manners, he struck up a conversation with Dinos and managed to get himself an invitation to Dinos's table right at the back of the café, where Dinos would sit for hours, supervising things while wearing the plastic tube into his nostrils that provided him with the necessary extra oxygen.

She didn't know if Dinos had intuited something, or if he

had developed a natural dislike of him, but even though he normally loved chatting to customers he became politely hostile to him after his first few visits. After that, Andreas had avoided crossing his path, and visited the shop only in the late afternoon after Dinos had left for his midday siesta.

'I hope you don't mind me coming here so often', he said to her after about two weeks of stopping by the café most days.

'Mind? I am delighted to see customers like you.'

'But you must know that I come here so often because I am delighted to see you.'

'Are you?' Nefeli said, feeling herself blushing. She did not remember blushing so often ever before.

'Of course! You are more delightful than the pastries and the sweets!'

This was too much. Surely he was making fun of her.

'I am an older woman, Andreas. And I have not had an easy life. You are welcome at this shop, but please cut the jokes.'

'Nefeli, why would I joke about something like this? I have feelings for you, don't you see? I am a streetwise man, Nefeli, and I like to name things rather than tiptoe around them.'

'I like that in you, Andreas', she said, daring to look him in the eye.

He took hold of her hand over the counter. 'I hope you don't mind. I can see the pain in your eyes, my dear, and I just know that you and I can make each other's pain feel better.'

No man had ever treated her like that before. Her looks

had always attracted attention, even until recently, but it had always been sexual attention. During her second stay in London, she had tried her luck with breaking away from Dinos, but in reality she was too entangled with him at the time to contemplate the complexities of dating. And now, the moment she felt the chains of her entanglement loosen up, here was her prince appearing out of nowhere, making himself available to her. He was such a good listener, it seemed like he had just emerged from the foggy horizon that had been her life up to now, to help her turn things around for ever.

The taxi was slowed down now by heavy traffic. 'Kilburn, 1 mile', Nefeli read on the road sign next to the red traffic lights. She was there. She would be at Eleni's house in less than ten minutes, despite the traffic. She was not sure what was stressing her out the most: that she was going to stay at Eleni's house for the first time ever and it was her one chance to make amends with her; or the decision she had made to talk to Eleni about closing down the business with her father; or the fact that she had to be extra careful not to let it slip that she was now a different woman, a woman in love. Sometimes she thought that Eleni's gaze could see right through her, into the most intimate parts of her soul.

But part of her wanted Eleni to know, to open up to her. She had done this as role-play in her mind, telling her daughter that at last, at the age of nearly sixty, she was becoming the woman she should have been all along, assertive, knowing what she wanted, trusting of herself; the woman that could have been Eleni's mother; the woman that a man could fall in love with.

But how could Eleni ever understand her? She grew up safe and protected, her father's little princess. The only true love in his life, as he so often said. Eleni was the exact opposite of her, her photographic negative: a woman who always knew what she wanted, because she always knew that she could have it. Right from the beginning of her life, she had her father's adoration and her adoptive mother's devotion, and she too, Nefeli, fitting in around her needs and demands like a faithful servant. The girl had grown up being told by everyone how special she was. It was no wonder she had become rather spoiled.

Her thoughts were interrupted by the noise of the taxi braking abruptly in front of Eleni's house. 'I think it is here, madam', the driver said. Nefeli jumped at his words. She only had a little flavour left of the resentment and envy she had felt a minute ago at the thought of Eleni's comfortable life, like a bitter taste at the back of her throat. She quickly swallowed, as though to push such uncomfortable feelings down. And here he was, Nicolas, stepping out onto the front patio in socks only and his shirtsleeves rolled up, despite the bitter cold and the damp of the February dusk, a handsome, professional young man. Eleni's faithful, lifelong partner, another man who was prepared to stand by her no matter what. If Eleni could only see that clearly, she would have been a much happier and less spiky young woman, Nefeli thought to herself.

'Hello, Nefeli', Nicolas said with his usual restrained politeness. 'Come on in. Don't worry about your luggage,

I will take it.' Nefeli went up on her toes and gave Nicolas a peck on the cheek. He towered over her, giving her a rather distant hug.

'I can take it', she said.

'No, no, go straight in. Eleni is breastfeeding, but she should be finishing soon.'

Nefeli stepped into the dark corridor, hesitating for a minute before walking towards the kitchen at the back of the house, where she guessed that Eleni had, once again, decided to hide from her.

26
Separation

Thessaloniki, July 1978

The chips are sizzling in the deep fryer. All lights are off. She can hear the dangerous sizzling, but she cannot locate the pan in the dark. Where is Eleni? There is also a buzzing noise and it is getting louder and louder coming deep from the earth five floors below. Everything is shaking. 'Eleni, get away from the kitchen, you will get burned!' she shouts breathlessly. Dinos is yelling, 'Everyone under the bedroom's door-frame now!' They gather, they hug, holding on tight, the buzz is overwhelming. 'We are all going to die!' Dinos screams. The sizzling gets louder and louder.

Leonora sat up and switched on the table lamp although the morning light had started creeping through the shutters, and a yellow sunray had formed a straight laser line on the wooden boards next to her bed. She was completely drenched. Her wet hair dripping on her forehead, her nightie glued between her breasts, the familiar pink rush of upset spreading on her chest. Thank God Eleni was fast asleep next to her. She tried to discern Dinos's silhouette under the light linen blanket, but he was not there.

'I had it again', she mumbled when she saw him sipping his coffee sat in his usual spot by the kitchen table. 'How many times can I have the same dream in the space of one month?' He offered her coffee, but she declined choosing a glass of ice-cold water instead. Her body was drained of fluid.

Leonora was more than relieved when Dinos offered to take Eleni downtown to buy her summer reads, and they were out in good time for her to pack. She started preparing the luggage frantically. The last week at work was so manic that she had no time to breathe. As much as she felt that she had put all the hard work necessary to leave her house in order, she could not shake off a dark feeling that she was like a captain abandoning his ship while sinking with all vulnerable parties on board. How else was she supposed to feel about all the crippled families camping in the gardens of the hospital, having been left homeless after the most violent earthquake that had struck the city since the beginning of the century? The images of the bruised little torsos of children that had been brought in that night from the site of the block of flats that had collapsed over Nikos's infamously delectable patisserie would stay with Leonora for life. 'We do not have a paediatric unit here', she would tell the accompanying adults trying to make eye contact, to get through to them and, yet, on they would march regardless, like zombies in search of the next feed. Leonora had not seen a dead body since the early days of her medical training, having managed to escape to the realm of what many in her profession saw as pseudo-medicine, that of treating the mentally ill.

Once they had managed their descent to the ground floor, she had persuaded Dinos that the safest place to spend the night after a major earthquake was the hospital grounds. She then gently broke it to him that at times of emergency like this, the Xenofon plan was activated which meant that all doctors were automatically assumed to be on duty. Thank God, Dinos had never been obstructive to her work, being secretly proud of his wife's status and how it rubbed off on him.

She had just finished packing when Dinos and Eleni arrived, Dinos huffing and puffing, a cigarette as always lit and hanging between his lips, holding Eleni's hand and carrying three heavy-looking plastic bags from Barbounakis bookshop. He dropped them by the door to the living room with a bang.

'What have you bought?' Leonora asked. 'The whole bookshop?'

'Well, Eleni wanted *The Secret Seven* and then she discovered *The Famous Five* by the same author, an English one. I bet this child could be reading these books in English if she put her mind to it. She is such a genius at reading. I couldn't deny her.'

Leonora picked up the bags and looked inside them in disbelief. 'How many books in total have you bought?' she asked.

'The whole series, fifteen and five of them. I bet she will have finished them all by the end of the holidays. And I got her some fairy tales too.'

She felt exasperated. Her voice was controlled and

contrived when it came out. 'I think these books are too advanced for a six-and-a-half-year-old, even if you do think she is a genius. Besides, it must have cost you a lot of money. You never know when to stop, do you?'

He was now sitting in the grey velvet armchair across from the TV, his legs up on the colour-matched footstool. He exhaled some smoke from the new cigarette he had lit up. 'Give me a break, Leonora. This is my only child. I want to treat her to the best. I don't come from a stingy peasant family like yours. Anyway, what's for lunch? We must head to the airport in less than an hour and then make sure that we drive to the resort before it gets dark. My headlights are playing up.'

Eleni had peered in the bag and taken a few of the books out. She was now on the large sofa, legs up on the wall, head hanging towards the floor, holding a book open in front of her face.

'Are you doing gymnastics or reading, Eleni?' Dinos scolded her, but he got no reply.

'Mummy, Mummy!' Eleni exclaimed. 'We are going to the airport to see Nefeli fly in an aeroplane. I have never seen an aeroplane before. Isn't that exciting!'

'Yes, darling, I know', Leonora said absentmindedly. Then she turned to Dinos. 'There is some leftover rice and salad, if we have to have lunch', she said dryly. 'But we need to hurry up and I can't leave dirty dishes for a month. Also, not sure Eleni will eat it.'

'No, no,' Eleni interrupted, 'Daddy got me a kasseri toastie and coffee ice cream.'

'In fact I don't need lunch either', Leonora added. 'I had a quick something while you were out. Do you want to finish off the rice then?'

'No, I would rather fix some fried eggs for me. Do you want some, Eleni? They are delicious!'

'Yuck!'

'She really does not like eggs, Dinos.'

'Only because she has not tried my fried eggs yet', he said, walking towards the kitchen.

'Make sure you don't leave too much mess behind, Dinos, we need to get going soon', she said, letting her exasperation seep through her voice.

***

They were at the airport just before five. The late-afternoon heat had triggered a column of steam to rise up and blend with the haziness on the horizon.

'We are heading for a thunderstorm', Dinos had commented on the way there, his weather predictions being uncannily accurate most of the time. Nefeli was nowhere to be seen.

'Has she gone already?' Eleni asked with palpable disappointment in her voice.

'Are you sure she has definitely decided to take this flight?' Leonora asked Dinos without trying to disguise the irony in her voice. 'Perhaps she only wanted tickets for the two of you and now she has changed her mind and sold her boring single ticket back', she added.

'Will you stop it now?' Dinos mumbled, anxiously

inspecting the departure lounge.

'She is here', Eleni shouted, pointing at Nefeli walking slowly towards them, not seeming to be in a rush, a frozen smile on her face.

'Do you realise that you are going to miss your plane?' Dinos scolded her. 'God, you haven't even checked your luggage in yet', he added, looking at the big suitcase she was dragging along.

Nefeli dropped the suitcase and her hand luggage in front of them, and held out a red paper bag containing a shiny, rectangular, silver package crossed by a red satin ribbon ending in an impeccable bow.

'This is for you, Eleni', she said, going down on her knees and passing the parcel to Eleni.

'Really?'

'Yes. You are allowed to open it while I go to check my luggage in. Then I will come back and I will explain to you what it is for.'

'Perhaps you could explain that to us first', Dinos said, but Nefeli turned her back and walked towards the check-in point, dragging her heavy suitcase along. There was no queue any more, as the last passengers checking in for the flight to London were just leaving the counter.

Eleni was trying to open the parcel with immense excitement, ripping pieces of the wrapping paper off and throwing it on the floor. Leonora turned a blind eye, and she was sure Dinos was too absorbed to notice. Eleni got stuck trying to open the cardboard box, as it was well sealed with tape.

'Mummy, help!' she exclaimed. Leonora took the box

from her, removed the tape and lifted its lid.

'I didn't ask you to open the box!' Eleni cried, now only a breath away from a major tantrum. Leonora, sensing the storm coming, quickly closed the lid.

'I didn't see what is inside', she said smiling. 'Here you are. You can open it yourself', and she handed the box back to Eleni. Eleni, somewhat pacified, opened the box and for a while observed quietly the dark-blonde doll with its wide-open blue eyes and hand-knitted clothes.

'It is a beautiful doll', she said quietly.

Leonora could not help it. 'How thoughtless of her', she said. 'We already have so many dolls that we do not know where to put them all. In a while we will have to start stepping on them to move around the flat.'

'It is a beautiful doll, Leonora', Dinos said quietly. 'Let's leave it at that.'

'It may look like an ordinary doll', Nefeli interrupted, having just come back to join them unnoticed, 'But you see, Eleni, this doll is very special. I will show you why.'

'You really want to miss this plane, don't you?' Dinos said, his voice having become irritated again.

'No, I do not. They cannot leave without me now that I have put my luggage in.'

'So ...' she took the doll out of the box. 'You see this cord, Eleni?'

'Yes ...'

'You can try to pull it.'

Eleni pulled the cord.

'Gently, you don't need to pull too hard. Let it go now.'

Eleni let out an 'oooh!' as, in releasing the cord, the doll said something in a clear, loud voice in a foreign language.

'Wow! A talking doll', said Eleni. 'She said something strange, what was it?'

'She said "I love you" in English; and she can say other things too. Every time you pull the cord she says something different, and that way you can learn English really well. So when you grow up you can come and visit me in London. Will you?'

'For sure I will', Eleni said, and they hugged.

***

Leonora, Dinos and Eleni were now standing close to each other by the airport's large floor-to-ceiling window. The haziness on the horizon had got even thicker.

'I will really struggle to drive to the seaside without headlights', he said.

'We can always go back home and drive there tomorrow', Leonora offered. She was feeling as though all the energy had been drained out of her body. It must be the effect of a sudden drop in adrenaline, she observed silently. No adrenaline was needed any more, not now that it was all at last finished.

'No, better to get on with it. I will drive slowly.'

'Look, look!' Eleni's voice broke the numb dialogue between them. A plane sped up on the runway and soon enough the wheels were leaving the ground, its nose pointing upwards. They all watched silently as the plane flew higher and higher, eventually disappearing into the foggy horizon.

'That is Nefeli. She is flying up there, all the way to London', Eleni sang in her child's voice.

27
Dying

Thessaloniki, March 2010

Eleni rang the buzzer on the fifth row, labelled 'Hatzis', outside the apartment block where she had spent her entire childhood. For the last few years she had referred to it as 'my parents' flat'. It had been too many years since she had lived in it to be able to call it 'home'. No reply. She must try to calm down, she thought to herself, but she could feel the veins under her skin contracting.

The night she just spent in Athens Airport was certainly one of the worst of her life. Her flight from London landed in Athens at two o'clock in the morning. The first flight to Thessaloniki was at six a.m., so she had to spend three and a half sleepless hours surrounded by the homeless who had come to the airport lounge in search of some shelter from the unusually bitter March cold. Some of them had approached her for money, and when she tried to lie down on the cold and steely lounge seats, unable to bear for much longer the burning sensation of exhaustion in her body, she had quickly realised that it was simply not safe to even attempt to sleep in what had become a reception hall for the city's damaged and lost.

She was the only traveller around. No one else seemed to have an emergency like hers. No one else's father was dying so that they had to leave their family and their home and spend the darkest hours of the night in an airport lounge. She had become homeless among the homeless. What would happen when the one person who had chosen to give her life was no longer there? Would it mean that part of her would die too? She had tried to push these thoughts away, but they had haunted her throughout the night. She hated being sentimental, especially when away from Nicolas and Chloe in the middle of the night. They were her life now. She would have to stay alive for them.

She had called her mother as soon as she arrived at Thessaloniki airport at 6.45 a.m. She was expecting her: why was she not answering now? She rang the buzzer again her finger lingering on it for a few seconds. This time she was let in immediately. Her breasts were feeling swollen and hard. She would have to set up the breast pump as soon as she walked in. In the past she had cringed at the idea of extracting her milk, and the few times she had tried it, it had made her feel like a cow. What was the point of breast-feeding if she had to rely on such machines? But now, under the circumstances, she was almost looking forward to the hard, sucking motion of the pump. It would make her feel close to Chloe, allow her to almost smell her baby's scent, and feel far, far away from death.

By the time the lift arrived at the fifth floor, Leonora was standing by the door, holding it open. They hugged and kissed, going through the motions.

'What's the matter? Why are you not opening the door?' Eleni asked, trying to control the irritation in her voice. 'I was out there buzzing for five minutes.'

'I was in the room with him. The ventilator is very noisy, I didn't hear. How are you?'

'How is he?'

'He has just fallen asleep. You can come and see him, but brace yourself', Leonora said, looking her in the eye.

Eleni found her way to the bedroom guided by the noise of the ventilator. Her father was lying on his side wearing loose white boxers and a white sleeveless vest. He did not seem to feel the chill of the early morning, as his covers had been kicked to the side. Both his arms were covered from wrist to shoulder in bruises at different stages of healing, a collection from his recent visits to hospital, Eleni guessed. His legs, so familiar to her from childhood, normally chunky and robust, were stick-thin, looking as immobile as the legs of a paraplegic. His stomach was protruding abnormally, as though his emaciated hips and legs could no longer support it. Eleni was staring at his sight standing frozen by the bedroom door. She felt something bitter rising from her stomach to her throat. Was she going to be sick?

Before she knew it she had stormed out of the room, her heart pumping fast, in search of her mother. She had just started wondering where she was, when she spotted her through the kitchen door, out on the balcony smoking a cigarette. She pushed the balcony door open and stood in front of her.

'What are you doing?' Leonora protested. 'It's really cold out here. You are not wearing a coat.'

'What have you done to him, huh?' Eleni cried, keeping her arms tightly folded across her chest. 'The creature lying in there is no longer my father. The creature lying in there's been beyond a living state for a long time now.'

Leonora burst into tears.

'Why – just tell me why –' Eleni continued unperturbed, 'are you not letting him go? Do you think it's fair to keep him in this state, just to satisfy you?'

Leonora went on crying, and Eleni felt a pang of guilt in her stomach.

'I know, he looks bad,' Leonora said, wiping her nose with the back of her hand, 'but we need to exhaust every hope, Eleni. He wants to live.'

'You are not listening! There is no hope! I could see that the second I walked into the bedroom. My father has already died. Just let him go, all right', Eleni said, now in a softer tone. 'Anyway, what happened to his legs? They were still normal when I visited three months ago.'

'It's the steroids', Leonora said, eyes fixed on the floor. 'He had a very large dose of steroids to keep him alive. They have this effect, emaciating the legs and distending the stomach. For the last month he could hardly walk at all.'

'You didn't say', Eleni whispered, almost to herself.

A head popped through the balcony door. 'Leonora, he is calling you.' Xena, her mother's youngest sister. She hadn't even noticed that she was here, and now she was talking to Leonora as though Eleni standing right in front of her was invisible, yet another ghost wandering in the flat. They both went back in, Eleni walking past her aunt, no greeting from either side exchanged. Death takes everyone's mask away, Eleni thought to herself. She had not seen her mother's youngest sister for years, but she still remembered vividly the unpleasant vibe she used to get from her when she was a child. Whenever she addressed Eleni, on the few occasions she remembered her around in her childhood, it was either to reprimand her or to scrutinise her. Even when she was little, she knew all too well that she was seen as a difficult child by her mother's family – and perhaps as a nuisance that her mother could have done without, by this particular aunt. She was a childless woman, bitter about life for as long as Eleni could remember, perhaps consoling herself with the thought that childlessness and a divorce were better options than the adulterer husband and the mistress's child that Leonora had chosen to put up with.

Leonora entered the bedroom walking swiftly, and Eleni was standing right behind her.

'Leonora, Leonora, help me, I can't breathe', Dinos shouted in a choked voice full of panic.

'Of course you can breathe', Leonora replied, wearing her professional tone and trying to appear cheerful. 'Look, you are wearing the mask, it's giving you oxygen. Shall I help you to sit up?'

Xena joined them in the room, and the two of them with obviously well-trained coordination, but still not without considerable effort, managed to sit Dinos up without pulling any of the machine's wires out. Eleni watched, standing by the door, supporting herself against the wall. As soon as he was sitting up, Dinos opened his mouth wide, trying to take in as much air as possible. He looked like a fish taking its last suffocating breaths out of the water.

'Eleni is here', Leonora whispered to him, as though Eleni, standing only two metres away from her, would not hear her.

'Where? I can't see her.'

'She's just there, Dinos, standing by the wall.'

Eleni approached the bed hesitantly. 'Leave me alone with Eleni now', Dinos said breathlessly, gesturing more towards Xena than Leonora.

'Shall I close the door?' Leonora asked.

'Yes, we'll call you if we need you. Sit down, Eleni', he said, turning to her and pointing to a chair by his bedside that Eleni had not noticed earlier. Still hesitant, she sat down. Her throat felt so constricted that she didn't think she could swallow even her own saliva. She sat very still, frozen. Dinos took her hand in his. His hand felt much smaller than Eleni had remembered, but it was still her dad's hand.

'So, you made it.'

'So, I made it', she replied, her voice coming out stiff.

'How is Nicolas, and the baby?'

'They are fine.'

'Are they here yet?'

'No, they may come, but it couldn't be arranged at such short notice.' *They are only coming for your funeral, Dad,* she thought silently.

He seemed agitated. 'Yes, but there is no time. I want to

talk to Nicolas, to tell him a few things about you before I go.'

'Dad,' she said quietly, but firmly, 'it's Wednesday today. Nicolas cannot be here before Friday.'

He took a while to process the new information. 'He's a nice bloke. He will take good care of you, I'm sure', he mumbled, talking mostly to himself. 'Listen, Eleni, I've got something to tell you. In order to make a good cake, you need at least three layers – more is better, but three will do, it will make it moist and rich enough. Your story is like a cake. You need to see at least three layers when you look at it. Any less than that and you are not seeing it clearly. Any less than that, and you are not getting the full taste.' His sentence was interrupted by running out of breath. 'Okay, Eleni? Do you understand?' he said, still breathless. 'You need to taste all the layers, okay?'

'Yes, Dad', she just about managed to say, before starting to sob.

'I want you to remember that when I go. And one more thing: be nice to Leonora.'

The word hit Eleni like a punch. Her father had always referred to Leonora in her presence as 'your mother'.

'Get me Leonora now', he said, using her name again.

Eleni left the room rather quickly. 'He wants you', she said to her mother, who was busying herself in the kitchen. 'I'm going to use the other room to pump some milk out. Nobody is allowed to come in while I am doing so.'

'Okay. I have made a bed for you in there. You must need sleep. Make sure you shut your door. There will be visitors any time soon.'

Soon after pumping her milk out and talking to Nicolas briefly on the phone, Eleni fell into a numb, iron-like sleep with no dreams. It was more than twenty-four hours since she had last slept.

***

She woke up at the sound of whispering voices and creaking doors. It took her a while to realise where she was, and it was mostly the familiar smell of freshly washed sheets in her bed that orientated her. Her mother had left a robe on the side of her bed, which she put on over her nightie before stepping out barefooted on the cold marble floor of the corridor. Various people seemed to be gathered in different rooms of the apartment. On the side of her father's bed, a blonde woman was sitting, her back turned to her and holding his hand. It took her a while to recognise her as one of their closest family friends, whom she had not seen for years. She walked on, not wanting to interrupt. In the kitchen, her mother, Xena and her father's sister, Jenny, were gathered around the table. Her aunt Jenny had tears in her eyes. It felt like Eleni was still in a dream, walking into a parade of people she had long left behind in childhood. Aunt Jenny got up as soon as she saw her and gave Eleni a warm hug.

'Hello, Fidgety', she said.

Hearing the special nickname her aunt had for her was enough to reduce Eleni to floods of tears. She had not felt this vulnerable since she was fourteen. The presence of her aunt gave her a feeling of warmth in her heart. In childhood, she had spent long summers at her aunt's house near the beach, playing pirate games with her two cousins. These were some of the fondest memories she had. Yet she wondered if it was this, or the fact that her aunt was the only other person in the house who was a blood relative of her dying father. Was it, she thought, that when it came to death one's biological origins really mattered?

After some time wandering around the apartment, stopping by her father's bed quite a few times and finally getting dressed, Eleni had started feeling stifled. She needed some fresh air and to get away from the crowded flat. Yet it was hard to get away without knowing roughly what the situation was with her father beyond the prevailing feeling that he was close to dying.

He kept going in and out of sleep, calling out names of friends and family every time he woke up. Some of the names were of people who had already died, making Eleni feel even more haunted. He repeatedly called out for his mother, who had died not that long ago. Every hour or so, he would cry that he was suffocating and that the air was simply not enough, and Leonora and Xena would quickly come in and help him to sit up. He refused all food and drink other than the few drops of water that Leonora would pass between his lips with a sponge at regular intervals. He had called her name as well quite a few times, but Eleni had not sat next to him for any length of time since the early morning. She would pop in, say hello, and then walk out again. While in the room with him, it had felt like the air was not enough for her either.

She had picked up a few messages on her mobile from friends she had texted about her arrival. Her friend Athena, her closest friend from high school, had offered to meet her in the neighbourhood for a drink around six o'clock, if she felt like going out. 'I'm not scared of death. It's come my way far too often', her friend had texted back after Eleni had tried to make excuses, saying that she was in a state and not good company at all. Death revealed people's true colours, Eleni had begun to realise.

The doctor had finally arrived at three o'clock. This was a young locum doctor, in place of his regular physician, who was off sick. Dinos picked up while the doctor was visiting, appearing chatty and asking lucid questions. The doctor was friendly, but not reassuring. As he rose to leave the room, Dinos asked, 'Is there any hope, Doctor? Can I make it this time?' He hesitated. 'I'm sorry, Dinos. Your oxygen levels are far too low. It's just a matter of time', he said in a low but steady voice. Dinos leaned back in bed and closed his eyes. He fell almost immediately into a deep, exhausted sleep.

As soon as the doctor walked out of the room, he asked to talk to Dinos's immediate relatives. Leonora and Eleni, already standing next to him, led him to the living room and closed the door behind them. 'Doctor,' Leonora said, 'can't we try to transfer him to hospital? Put him on an artificial breathing machine? He really wants to live.' Eleni bit her lip in an attempt to silence herself as she felt her anger rising like foam again. 'I am sorry, but there is nothing more we can do for him', the doctor repeated. 'His lung function is at a level that he could never again breathe independently. Even if we were to prolong his life for a little bit, he would fall into a coma and he would never wake up from it. It's a miracle really that he's still alive. His lung function is only three per cent.'

Leonora lowered her head, seeming disappointed. 'But miracles sometimes happen, Doctor', she murmured.

'Mum, you are being irrational', Eleni hissed between her teeth.

'However, what I wanted to discuss with you two,' said the doctor, speaking up now, 'is sedation. To die of lung disease is one of the most agonising deaths. The patient feels suffocated and he gets very distressed.'

'What would be the sedative's effect, Doctor?' Eleni asked.

'Well, it would calm him down and induce sleep very quickly. As you can see, he's clearly distressed. We need to assist him to die peacefully and with dignity.'

Leonora and Eleni looked at each other, trying to suss out what each thought.

'No', said Eleni. 'My father has been a fighter for all his life. He wants to fight until the end, not to be put to sleep like a dog.' She felt the vein in her neck pulsating hard, and was surprised at the violence of her feeling.

'I agree', said Leonora in a milder tone. 'Why put him to sleep before he's ready for it? He is incredibly lucid for his state of health. Don't you see, Doctor, he's trying to communicate.'

'Yes, it is true that he is incredibly lucid for someone with so little oxygen circulating in his blood, but I think this is yet another symptom of how distressed he is. Remember, you need to do the best for him. It is our standard practice to help people die peacefully.'

Eleni was sensing the rage building up to toxic levels in her blood, yet at the same time feeling incredibly relieved that she and her mother were in total agreement for the first time that day.

'Are you asking for our permission to sedate him, Doctor?'

'Yes.'

'Well, you don't have our consent. We both think that not sedating him is the best we can do for him', she said in a clear voice, at the same time rising to mark the end of the conversation.

'Thank you for your concern, Doctor, but we are doing the best we can for him', Leonora repeated. They looked at each other and smiled in conspiracy as soon as he was out of the door.

'He's so stupid', Eleni could not help but comment.

'Standard practice', Leonora mumbled matter-of-factly.

In the hour following the doctor's visit, her father was dipping in and out of a restless sleep. He seemed to have regained his movement, tossing and turning. From time to time, he woke up abruptly and shouted, 'No, go away', gesturing as though trying to push someone away. Xena approached him, perplexed. 'Who are you talking to, Dinos?'

'Death. He's coming to take me. He's standing right next to my mother and father. No, go now', he shouted again. The only person who managed to stay in the room with him for any length of time was his sister, Jenny, who was sitting by his bed quietly, her eyes resting on his face. She's saying goodbye to him, Eleni thought to herself.

At around five o'clock, Dinos opened his eyes again and seemed to manage to stay awake for a while. He asked for Leonora, who was wandering manically round the house, keeping herself busy. She came into the room ready to help with one of her nursing tasks. Eleni, who also happened to be by the room when he called for her mother, was observing, standing by the door.

'I just wanted to say goodbye', Dinos said.

'What?'

'I'm sorry for everything I did that hurt you.'

'Oh, Dinos, don't say that. You're not going anywhere yet', she said, patting him on the shoulder, and she walked swiftly out of the room, disappearing into the kitchen.

Eleni gathered all the courage she had and went to sit by his bedside. Jenny moved discreetly out of the room. She took his hand in hers. This time round, his hand was no longer warm. He was already drifting to sleep.

'Daddy', she said.

'Who is there?' said Dinos, not sounding lucid anymore.

'It's me, Eleni.'

'Eleni. You are not Eleni', he said emphatically. 'My little Eleni is dying with me.'

Eleni felt as though she had been hit by an electric current. She quickly stood up and walked out of the room. She needed some fresh air and a drink for sure. She texted Athena, *On my way to Totty's.* As she was shutting the apartment door behind her ten minutes later, her father had already fallen into a deep sleep, somehow different from his sleep before, quiet and peaceful.

Athena was waiting for her inside the café, at a small round table by the window, as the wind and whipping rain would make standing outside very inhospitable.

'God, it feels like January!' Eleni said as soon as she approached the table, still holding her raincoat tight around her and shivering.

'In fact it's the first day of spring, the equinox today. Isn't it ironic?' Athena commented. She always seemed to know things like that. She rose and they kissed.

'The first day of spring!' Eleni said, looking outside the window. 'Yes, I guess ironic in more than one way.'

She unbuttoned her coat and sat down looking around her. She had never been inside this café before. It was one of those places which had started with grand intentions, maybe architect-designed: expensive marble counters and stripped wood floors, Moroccan-style tables and of course, as always in Greece, lots of fancy ashtrays and smoke rising up to the ceiling. She felt her eyes swim. She was yet to get used to the level of smoke in any Greek café. The waiter approached the table.

'I will have some tea', Athena said.

'And a double gin and tonic.'

'Oh. Add a shot of brandy in my tea then. The weather calls for it', Athena said.

'I need it', Eleni smiled. 'And I could do with one of those', she said, looking at the couple chain-smoking at the next table.

'A cigarette? Is it that bad?'

'I have to say it's really nice, but also strange sitting here with you. It feels like I have been transported to another life; a life where I don't have a baby and I can have a gin and tonic at six o'clock in the evening with my mates.'

'A life where your father is dying.'

'Yes, that too. He has come close to death so many times before that I need to pinch myself to remember that this time it is for real.'

'How is he doing?'

'He was lucid in the morning, but now he has started to lose it. He just told me that I am not Eleni. His Eleni, he said, is dying with him.'

'Oh, no! How horrible! He always saw you as part of him, didn't he?'

'I suppose.' Eleni had knocked back her gin and tonic in five minutes and it had gone straight to her head. She now realised, too late, that she had hardly eaten anything all day. Aunt Jenny had brought some sweet and savoury biscuits and a couple of those were the only things that had passed her lips the entire day. Not that anyone else in the house, and her mother especially, seemed to remember such routines that kept body and soul together. She suddenly felt tearful.

'Listen,' she said to Athena, 'it's so kind of you to come all the way here, but I think I need to head back. I asked them to call me if they think he's about to die, as I want to be there, but it could happen unexpectedly. The doctor said it was a matter of hours now.'

'Sure', said Athena. 'I hope you won't mind me asking,

would it be okay if I came up with you? Say hello to your mother?'

'Oh, no! You couldn't possibly. It's so disturbing to hear him yell and gasp for air. I wouldn't want to inflict it on anyone.'

Athena looked teary. 'I was only six when my father died, as you know. I was only told well after it had happened. I was not even allowed at the funeral. I always wished I could have been there and said goodbye. I am not afraid of death, I told you already.'

Eleni looked at her friend in wonder. She had not heard her talk so movingly before.

'By all means, come upstairs then. It would be a great help and support to me', she said.

Eleni let them in, still feeling strange using the apartment key after so many years. It was unusually quiet. All the visitors had left. Jenny was still sitting by her brother's side. She found her mother and Xena sitting in the living room. Athena and her mother hugged and kissed warmly. It only now felt like she was back home, Eleni thought. She suddenly felt a surge of anxiety and she rushed to her father's side. She knew something was different.

'What happened?' she asked her aunt. 'Is he still alive?' she added, looking at her father's still body.

'Yes,' Jenny said calmly, 'but he's no longer waking up. Leonora tried to wake him up several times, but she couldn't. I think he's fallen into a coma. It won't be long.'

Athena came into the bedroom carrying a chair from the kitchen, and joined Eleni's aunt at Dinos's bedside.

Eleni walked out of the bedroom, feeling like keeping herself busy. She had to express milk again if she wanted to keep her supply up. The thought made her realise that Chloe and Nicolas were not there, and their absence felt like a stab.

The buzzer rang.

'Are we expecting anyone?' she asked her mother.

'It must be the night nurse. She comes at eight p.m. and leaves at six a.m.'

A chubby, middle-aged woman with a strong accent walked in and went straight into the bathroom to get ready for her shift.

'Where is she from?' Eleni asked her mother.

'Armenia.'

'Oh!'

'She is very good at her job', Xena chipped in.

The nurse went in the bedroom, and for a while she stood by Dinos, looking at him. Everyone gathered in the bedroom around her.

'He's very close', she said loudly, not addressing anyone in particular. 'Any time now.'

Jenny looked at her. 'Is there anything we should do?'

She hesitated. 'In my country, we give the dying person some red wine. It helps them pass away. If you have some and you allow me, I could try.'

'But he hasn't drunk anything for hours.' Leonora protested.

'He loved red wine. I would go for that', said Eleni.

She suddenly had a strange sense of exhilaration. Someone was here who was willing to help her father die.

Leonora brought two bottles of red wine to the bedroom.

'It's usually Mavrodaphne, the black grape variety', Athena commented, seeming to have heard of the ritual too.

Leonora went back for a corkscrew and they picked one bottle, looking very dark red and aged. The nurse poured some of the wine into a clean bowl and dipped the sponge Leonora had used to give Dinos water throughout the day. Everyone gathered around the bed to see what she was doing.

'Dinos,' she said, 'I am going to give you some wine. It will help you go peacefully, if you are ready to go.'

She rubbed a little of the wine on his lips with the sponge. There was no response. A dark red trickle, like blood, rolled down his chin. She wiped it clean. She waited for a bit and then tried again.

'Dinos, I am going to give you a little bit more wine now.'

She held the sponge above his face and tried to place a few drops between his half-opened lips. This time, Dinos moved his lips ever so slightly and took the wine in. There was no spillage. Everyone looked on in awe. The nurse walked out to dispose of the sponge. Leonora, Xena and Eleni followed her out of the bedroom. Before Eleni had even reached her bedroom in search of some private space, she heard her aunt Jenny saying in a clear and steady voice, 'He has just passed away. It's over.'

Athena seconded this. 'Yes, he's no longer breathing.'

The two of them were the only two people sitting by Dinos's bedside when he finally decided to take his last step into the unknown, dark space.

Layer 4

Childhood when we grow up is 'heaven' that we cannot stand, it hurts us in a unique way rather than pleases us. The forever gone stabs us quietly.

Zyrana Zateli, *interview*

28
Dying

Thessaloniki, March 2010

It was one of those mornings on which Thessaloniki and London appeared like sister cities, weather-wise at least. Low grey cloud hung over the city. The sun was nowhere to be seen. The wind was bitterly cold and the high humidity evaporating from the grey sight of Thermaikos Gulf made the sharp wind especially sinister in its ability to penetrate right through to one's bones. It was not unusual, in fact it was quite customary, to see women dressed in all black around the city's modern-built cemetery, which occupied a large field overlooking the sea on the outskirts of town. It was rather unexpected, though, to see them walking one behind another, as though in some kind of funeral procession.

Leonora was walking in front, eyes fixed in space, the handle of her black bag clutched in her fist, a bunch of white and red gladioli under her arm. She seemed completely oblivious to the fact that there was no longer any pavement. She was now walking on the edge of a muddy field unfolding next to the slip road. Some ten metres behind her was Xena, breathless and exasperated, trying to catch up with Leonora's swift steps and trying to talk some sense into her. Even further behind, walking slowly, feeling indifferent and by now resigned to her fate, was Eleni. After having yelled at her mother to stop walking in that direction, as it was obvious that there was no pedestrian passage and it was bound to be the wrong way, she had stopped trying to catch up with her. Aware that she would probably get out of sight in a while, she kept turning to look behind her, hoping that a taxi would stop by, but there were hardly any cars at all on this muddy, out-of-town slip road.

After a while, she came to a halt abruptly, and after making a full turn she walked all the way back to the main road and stood just before the bend leading to the slip road. She buttoned her black coat up. The coat, borrowed hastily from her mother's wardrobe, old and smelling of mothballs, was loose on her upper body. She had forgotten to wear a scarf and the wind hit her directly on her bare neck and upper chest. A taxi at last! She hailed it standing at the very end of the pavement. The taxi stopped abruptly in front of her and she got in, sighing with relief.

'It is so good to find you', she said. 'Can you please turn at this slip road. We need to collect two women walking by the muddy field, and then can you please take us all to the pre-funeral reception centre, wherever that is?'

'One can drive down the slip road to find it,' the taxi driver said, 'but it is miles away and that road is not for pedestrians.'

'I told them so!'

'Whoever dropped you at the cemetery should have

taken you there, love. It is too far to walk.'

'Well, my mother wanted to buy flowers by the main entrance, so our first taxi left', Eleni said shrugging her shoulders.

The taxi driver turned round and took his time in giving her an examining look. Eleni felt exposed, but the human contact seemed to do her good. Normally she was not one for talking to strangers.

'Did you just lose your father?' he asked.

'Yes. How do you know?'

'You are wearing all black and you seem to be in your thirties, the age that one tends to lose one's father', he said mildly. She smiled in agreement.

'How old are you, if you don't mind me asking?' he said.

'Thirty-eight.'

'Well, I am thirty-nine and my father is in hospital. We are expecting him to go any time soon.' He let out a sigh.

'I am sorry to hear that', she said. 'It is tough when it happens.'

He finally started the car and sighed again.

'It's also hard how mad they get when they reach this final stage, the end of the road.'

'I know!' Eleni said.

'Mine is refusing treatment. He woke up in hospital and he was acting like a madman, pulling all his tubes out and demanding to be taken home. He's also refusing to eat.'

'Oh, that must be hard. Mine was completely the opposite. He wanted to live no matter what. He died trying to live. That was hard too, very painful to watch. Stop! They are here.'

Xena was now walking just behind Leonora who had slowed down somewhat. Eleni opened the taxi's door. 'Get in', she said. 'He will take us there.' As an afterthought, she got out of the taxi first and sat in the front seat next to him, leaving the back seat for the two women. She was acutely aware of the tension between her mother and her. Since her father had died two nights ago, her mother had gone a bit mad as well. The best thing Eleni could do to manage the situation was to stay out of her sight for as long as she possibly could. There were many decisions to be made though, and every time they needed to talk, Eleni could not help but explode at Leonora's blatant irrationality. It was hard to watch her mother disintegrate like this, and even harder to feel that she could not have her support at one of the most difficult moments of her life.

When her father passed away, and after her aunt announced the fact, Eleni had walked into the room. Even though she had not had a close-up experience with a dead body before, she could immediately confirm her aunt's announcement. The difference from his comatose state before was subtle, as the ventilator was still on, sending out a rhythmic, reassuring sound. Yet Eleni knew just by looking at him that her father was now dead. Leonora had walked in just after her, and sat by the bed, putting her ear to his chest.

'He is not dead, he is breathing', she said hysterically.

'It is only the ventilator. He has passed away', the nurse said softly.

'How do you know?' Leonora said, raising her voice. 'We

need to call a doctor straight away. He may still be breathing.'

'Mum, stop it at once', Eleni said in a firm tone. 'You are a doctor for God's sake. Use your common sense. Dad has just died.'

The calm atmosphere was now spoiled and panic prevailed. There was some debate about whether to switch off the ventilator or not, and it was finally agreed that they needed to call his regular doctor to confirm his death.

Eleni remembered the rest in a haze: the doctor coming after a while to confirm the death, barely able to walk as he was off sick, bedridden with severe backache; switching off the ventilator, saying goodbye – he was fond of her father, she thought. Heated discussions about when to have the funeral – as early as possible, so they could keep to the traditional custom of exposing the body to be greeted by friends and family. Phone calls to England, crying down the phone to Nicolas – the earliest he could come was Friday, in two days, so the funeral was agreed for Friday afternoon. Her friend Athena hand-washing the only black dress Eleni had brought, having now discovered that it was covered in stains, in the grim family bathroom full of her father's urine containers. People arriving near midnight upon hearing the news. Drinking brandy in the living room with relatives that she had not seen for years.

And then, suddenly, the undertakers arriving, many of them, on their doorstep, ready to take the body, ready to take her father away. What a job, she remembered thinking, waiting by the phone at all hours of the day and night, trying to smell out the next dead, the next source of income coming their way. They were keen to get a move on, and as they were taking him, Eleni could hear her mother wailing in the kitchen. On a sudden, unexpected impulse, her own turn at irrationality, she ordered them to stop, to put him down at once. They were already out of the door, near the communal staircase, ready to carry him down five flights of stairs. Surprised, they stopped, putting the covered body down on the cold, pigmented cement. She knelt down on the floor, uncovered his face and, in an unprecedented gesture, she gave him a kiss on the cheek. His face felt cold and hard, already inanimate, like marble. She remembered pumping milk late at night, thinking guiltily of the brandy and gin her daughter would get if she ended up drinking it, thinking of Chloe, her little round face with the big dark eyes, trying to smell her baby smell.

The taxi turned abruptly on a dirt road in front of a large imposing building.

'The pre-funeral reception', the taxi driver announced. 'Good luck', he said to Eleni as she opened the taxi door, and patted her lightly on the shoulder. On the way in, they stopped to read the names on the long row of flower arrangements that friends and family had sent for the funeral. It felt like a long list of people Eleni had encountered throughout her childhood. Suddenly she felt exhausted, as though she could not go on for much longer, and she wished she could turn back, stop the taxi and ask him to drive her all the way back home.

There was not much of a prelude before what they were here to do. As soon as they went past the entrance hall, they walked into a room where the body of her father was lying flat inside the coffin surrounded by white lilies. How handy, Eleni thought, that his favourite flower also happened to be the most customary for funerals.

The only time Eleni had been to a funeral before was at her maternal grandfather's funeral when she was sixteen in the little town where her mother grew up. The reception was held at her mother's childhood house, as the custom was. She remembered that even then, although she was so young, she had found the ritual to be right emotionally. A chance to say a last goodbye in person, to remember the face that once was. The ritual was now disappearing rapidly, especially from Athens. People were put off from looking at the dead. They wanted to be done with it as quickly as possible. Eleni sat still for some time on a chair by her father's coffin, staring at his face: a face so familiar to her and yet so strange and alien. She didn't know if she was imagining it, but he seemed to her to have an angry expression – furious for having had to die in the end.

Yesterday had been the first day of living life after her father had died. Trying to stay out of her mother's way, Eleni had strolled downtown early, where she would later meet Lea. She wanted to spend some time alone in the city first. On her way downtown from her parents' flat, she had experienced an unprecedented, hard-to-name feeling. It was a mixture of liberation and nostalgia. She had childhood memories from every single corner of her parents' flat. She walked past the place where she used to do ballet, the little park where she used to skate with her classmates, Electra's parents' flat, her old friend's traces long lost. As she walked some more, she came to the outskirts of the university town where she used to go skating and wandering around with her friends at the end of Year 6, and a bit further down, her favourite school, the state primary. She had walked past all these places before, when visiting her parents as an adult, yet she had never really felt them as important to her. It felt like the first time she had revisited her childhood as an adult. Her father's death had finally turned her into an adult. It had finally set her free from being his daughter, being his little girl. Or had it?

Eleni stirred as she felt two hands on her shoulders, rubbing the tight knots of her muscles away. Who could be massaging her at her father's death reception? She turned her head.

'Nicolas, you are here at last!' she said, and threw herself into his arms. His eyes were not looking at her though; they were fixed somewhere else in space and they were full of tears. Eleni followed his gaze. It didn't take long for her to realise that he was staring at the open coffin.

'Oh, last time you saw him, he was alive', she said, and gave him a tighter hug. 'Where is Chloe?' she asked in an alarmed voice.

'I didn't think it appropriate to bring her here. She is outside with my mother.'

'I need to see her.'

They walked out of the main reception and into the hall's entrance, where she could see Chloe standing somewhat stiffly on Nicolas mother's lap. Grabbing her baby up in her arms was the first act since she had received her mother's phone call in England that made her feel like her life had some rhythm and normality again. Questions like had she eaten? had her nappy been changed? when was the last time she napped? soon crept back into her mind and transformed her once again into what she had been for the last year and a bit: Chloe's mother. Now, she had a life again, a partner and a baby and things to attend to in her everyday life. Yet another part of her was still in touch with her solitary self of yesterday, wandering around the city centre on her own, then eating a slice of pizza standing up with her friend Lea, like they used to when they were teenagers; strolling along with her on the seaside promenade, looking at the boats and the horizon, not talking much; and finally sitting down at the top of the steps leading down into the sea, full of dirt and humidity, where occasionally old men would stand still under the sun holding a fishing rod.

Her life had been interrupted. There was the life she had as Chloe's mother and Nicolas's partner, a mother and an artist living in London, and there were the smells and sounds of a city she had long abandoned coming back loudly, the crumbs of her childhood memories, once, not that long ago, nicely ordered and put in a drawer, now demanding her urgent attention again.

By the time the funeral began, it had started drizzling down and the wind had got even stronger. Nicolas, driving a rented car, lost his way in the vast grounds of the cemetery, not having anticipated that it would be so hard to find. As he drove down lane after lane, looking for Dinos's burial site, Eleni realised that all funeral crowds looked the same, a little black cluster of people, their open umbrellas held tight against the wind.

'Do you realise that I can't possibly miss my own father's burial?' she yelled at him, panic suddenly overwhelming her, as it dawned on her that they might not find the site in time. He touched the brakes firmly and took a sharp right, having finally spotted the funeral site. The ceremony was well under way as Eleni managed to squeeze past the crowd holding Chloe in her arms. She placed herself next to her mother just a minute before they started to lower the coffin into the hole in the ground. Nobody seemed to have noticed her absence, yet everyone turned to stare at her now. 'A baby at a burial! It is not right', she overheard an old lady whispering.

As the coffin went down on its long journey, she saw her mother's two sisters holding Leonora by her elbows, as though she would collapse otherwise. 'Help me bury him and say goodbye', the priest encouraged the crowd. Following another tradition, the crowd started throwing fistfuls of wet soil onto the coffin.

'Here, Chloe. You can help me. Here', Eleni said, steadying her daughter on her feet. She had recently learned to walk. A couple of months before Eleni had left England, she had taken her first, hesitant footsteps. Life ending and life beginning always seemed to come together, Eleni thought to herself.

'This was your granddad. Do you remember him? He is going down to the earth for a long sleep. Can you help

Mummy throw some soil to make his bed softer?'

Chloe took up the task with enthusiasm. Supported by her mother, she picked up soil and threw as much as she could onto the descending coffin. Eleni did the same. The two of them were amongst the last few people around the hole, throwing soil onto the coffin, unperturbed by the drizzle and the wind while the funeral crowd dispersed.

29
Sweet adolescence

Thessaloniki, March 1986

Eleni got back to her room after they had shared a wacky omelette, as Leonora had come to call them, not without a pang of considerable satisfaction for having at last found a trick to get Eleni to join them. Eleni was increasingly reluctant to join family meals. Every other day, Leonora would find the wrapping paper of a packet of crisps or chocolate under Eleni's duvet when tidying up her room after she had refused to eat lunch with them saying that she was not hungry.

Leonora had been discreetly following Eleni for the last month, and the upshot of her observations was not pleasing. One thing she had learnt from medical school, and she had devotedly integrated that knowledge during the years of her psychiatry training, was that observation was the quintessence of sound medical practice. Action was rarely required, but when observation was accurate, subsequent intervention could be timely and successful. And now the signs she was observing in her daughter's behaviour were not promising, and the problem she was facing was that, unlike in her medical practice, where she always seemed to know what to do next, in Eleni's case it still escaped her what intervention would indeed be timely and successful.

Eleni had become even more solitary and reclusive than she already was before she found out the facts about her origins. She had stopped her weekly meetings with Lea, although to Leonora's relief their friendship seemed to continue through regular long chats on the phone behind firmly closed doors. Family meals had become a battlefield, as Eleni would refuse to eat anything other than the most basic of meals with them. She would spend hours in her room reading and keeping a diary. Leonora had occasionally got a brief glimpse, when Eleni had the diary open on her desk, only to get a sense of the most gloomy of drawings next to words that she imagined to be at least as dark. Once, upon entering her room after Eleni had left for school, she found the purple padded floral journal named Jardin seemingly forgotten on Eleni's desk and her hands took action on their own, picking it up and trying to open it, until she realised to her actual relief that it was locked. Clearly her presence in Eleni's room was no longer as welcome as it used to be not that long ago. It felt like she constantly had to tread on eggshells, even in her most ordinary approaches to her, as the last thing she wanted was to end up like Dinos, an outlet and unfortunate target for Eleni's irritation and adolescent contempt. Then, any chance for a successful and timely intervention would be ruined.

For the time being the omelettes seemed to work well, as a small but not insignificant step in restoring their family life. Cooking had never been Leonora's thing. Besides, Dinos would have been disappointed if she were to take over his favourite creative outlet. However, Eleni was refusing blatantly to eat any of Dinos's food, and Leonora could see that behind the brave face he always put up against any of Eleni's rejections of him, her behaviour at mealtimes had started getting to him. So one day, when Eleni said again that she wanted nothing for dinner, Leonora asked: 'What about a wacky omelette?' Omelette had been one of Eleni's own first culinary attempts. Experimenting with food and going in for unusual tastes had been a like of hers since she was little. Was this yet another reaction against Dinos's love of traditional, good-quality food? Leonora wondered. As she had hoped, she had managed to extract a smile from Eleni's face, and for a few evenings she had agreed to have dinner with them. Her first attempt was a concoction of beaten eggs with a mixture of pan-fried vegetables and cheese, shared over the dinner table along with freshly toasted bread. It worked, despite Dinos's deprecating comments about the combination of ingredients she used.

Her husband was now in his fifties and he was yet to learn the value of diplomacy. It was no wonder that any success he had had in his life had come through working alone, and also no wonder that any success had always been flimsy. Now that Leonora could rest on her laurels at the thought that some family peace had been restored, she needed to tackle the next problem, which was, as usual, Dinos. Talking to him was never easy, as it felt like any diplomacy he lacked had to be employed doubly by her.

'I am rather worried about Eleni, Dinos', she said, clearing her throat.

'Worried about what?' he said absentmindedly.

She tried hard to suppress her irritation. Was he being serious? 'Well, I am worried about the effect my revelation had on her. The tension between you and her does not help things at all.'

'Well, I told you it was not the best time to talk to her.'

'You could have done your bit, Dinos', she said, finding it impossible not to raise her voice. 'You promised to talk to her and you haven't. All you can do is pick arguments with her all the time.'

Dinos let a belch out, and undid the top button of his pyjamas.

'Have you finished?' he said sourly. 'If you don't mind I am going to watch some TV. Your omelette has given me terrible indigestion. I have promised to talk to her, and I will when the time is right', he added, getting up.

Leonora rarely found washing dishes gratifying. As the warm soapy water fell on her hands, warm tears ran down her cheeks and the flow felt like a relief. Keeping on top of her life was the one thing she had always wanted, yet the one thing that always seemed to escape her. When Dinos had told her that he had a baby in line for her, there hadn't been much hesitation on her part in accepting his proposal, despite what everyone else thought. The situation was complicated, she knew that, but her decision was easy. How could she not have chosen a life with a baby of her own and a husband and a place in the world over bringing down in ruins everything she had known since her early twenties? A childless middle-aged woman, a divorced woman. What could a career do to compensate for such failure? All she had ever wanted was a solid corner in the world, and yet being married to Dinos was like walking on a stretched rope over the abyss. She had worked so hard to be Eleni's main, if not only, point of reference, and here she was, her daughter barely fourteen and her wounded mind already closed off to her.

As she was putting away the dishes, she was struck by what seemed like an unusual silence coming from the living room, despite the reassuring background noise of the TV. She instinctively stopped what she was doing and walked to the living room. As soon as she reached the doorway, her mind started working on medical overdrive. Dinos was sitting on his usual armchair in front of the TV, his feet up on the footstool, apparently asleep with the TV control sitting on his lap. His paleness was almost shiny against the dim living room light.

'Dinos!' she shouted, and she shook him by the shoulders. He half woke up, but he appeared disorientated. Rushing back to the kitchen, she opened the medicine cabinet and quickly unwrapped a pill. She ran back to the living room and slipped it under his tongue.

'I am calling an ambulance', she told him. 'I think you are having a heart attack.' The nitroglycerine seemed to have done the trick and he was now fully awake.

'I am fine', he protested. 'I had terrible indigestion and some chest pain and then I got dizzy. I am fine now.' His speech was still a bit slurred.

She picked up the phone to call an ambulance and he became agitated.

'Call a doctor, okay? I don't like hospitals.'

'I will take your blood pressure and decide.'

His blood pressure was eighty over fifty, abnormally low.

'This could be an infarction', Leonora murmured. 'You could die if we don't go to hospital.' She hesitated. 'I am calling an ambulance and I am going to talk to Eleni', she said decidedly.

The ambulance had just arrived, its chilly blue light reflecting on the building's glass front door as Leonora and Dinos, somewhat wobbly on his feet and with a thick cardigan over his shoulders, walked slowly out into the night mist and into the waiting car.

30
The scent of things to come

Thessaloniki, June 1983

The moment Eleni hung up the phone, it was like reality hit her in the face. She had indeed taken the aspirins, thirteen little white pills swimming slowly down her oesophagus and into the lining of her stomach. Suddenly, she was struck by how alone she was in the house. She spotted her lunch sitting on the kitchen table untouched; a covered plate with a piece of crusty bread wrapped in a napkin next to it. Her stomach gurgled. Was it her imagination or had this gurgle come along with some soreness, a warning of worse pain to come?

The silence hit her like a deafening noise inside her head. She was utterly alone, she and her body completely vulnerable to the little pills. She lifted the handset in an almost robotic motion and dialled her mother's work number. One more second of this loneliness and she would go mad. The phone was engaged. She had not expected that. She hung up and realised that her hands were shaking as she dialled the hospital's switchboard number.

'Can I please talk to the Head of the Psychiatry Clinic?'

she said in a shaky voice.

'Who is this?'

'This is her daughter and it is urgent.'

She was finally put through to her mother's secretary.

'Eleni, is that you?' Maria's familiar voice said. 'She is in the middle of an important interview, sweetie. Can I get her to call you back?'

'No, I need to talk to her now. It is urgent', she said feeling very close to tears now.

Her mother's voice came through almost immediately with its familiar mixture of helpfulness and exasperation. The phone call did not last for more than two minutes: her stomach would be pumped if she did not act immediately, she needed to go and buy some milk and drink it, she needed to act. Was it her imagination or was her mother's voice on the phone cold like the sharp edge of a broken glass?

Eleni acted like an automaton, following the instructions, her mother's professional voice replaying in her mind. She took her keys from her school bag – 'don't lock yourself out', Mother had said – took the lift down the five floors and ran to the cornershop, barely a minute's walk from their flat. Was it triumph she had heard in her mother's voice when she instructed her to drink three litres of milk at one go? She had refused to drink milk at all in the last year of primary school, much to her mother's disappointment. So now Mother could have it her way, all the milk Eleni had missed out on in the last year swallowed down at once.

'Are you going to manage to carry all these cartons, little girl?' the milkman asked her suspiciously in his raspy old man's voice.

She was upstairs in no time, the three cartons sitting on the table next to her lunch. She fiddled with the top of one of the cartons, a little pool of milk spilled on the kitchen table. Her stomach gurgled again. 'You should never have an aspirin on an empty stomach', her mother's professional voice said in her ears. She finally started drinking. One, two, three glasses. There were at least four glasses in each carton. Was she going to manage this? The idea of getting sick while alone in the house panicked her beyond belief. She could not afford to be sick now. The phone kept ringing while she was swallowing down the milk, her task becoming increasingly difficult. When she was finally down to the last glass, she sensed the panic that had taken over her body starting to lessen. She was going to be all right, perhaps, she thought.

She shivered all over as a huge wave of nausea overtook her. Was she going to be sick after all? 'When you are feeling sick, take some deep slow breaths in and out', she heard in her ears again. She closed her eyes and inhaled deeply, letting out a long slow exhalation. She now remembered why she hated milk. It always gave her this sense of nauseous queasiness in her stomach. She was standing by the kitchen table, still too anxious to sit down, staring at the three empty red cartons of milk, acutely aware of the dead silence in the flat, when she finally heard the key turning in the door.

31
Birth

London, February 1972

Marika was pacing up and down, having forgotten she was still holding the folded piece of paper in her one hand, when Mario came into the kitchen.

'What's the matter? Basta! Calmati!' Mario said in exasperation. His affectionate use of Italian words to soothe her every time she worked herself up into such agitated state usually had an instant effect, but it didn't do the trick this time.

'From Magda', she said pausing to look him in the eye and waving the piece of white paper. 'I have made a mistake, Mario. I have made a mistake', she repeated, and exhaled.

'What does she say?' Mario asked her in a touchy tone. 'Does she accuse you of anything? You have to remember, you only did the best for her daughter. She came here in such a vulnerable state. If you had talked to her mother, she would have flown off for sure. You gave her shelter and lots of care. What more could you have done?'

Marika sat by the kitchen table across him letting out a sigh.

'Her daughter has just had a baby that she is going to give away. This is worse than an abortion, worse than keeping the baby as a single mother. How much more could I have failed her?'

'Marika', he said in a decisive tone. 'I won't have any more of this. I have had enough of you taking on the sorrows of the world. How did you fail this girl? She came here already pregnant. You didn't even know her before. She doesn't want to keep it. What can you do about it? You can't force her to bring up this baby. It won't be any good.'

Marika shook her head silently, looking at a fixed space on the floor, feeling no less exapserated.

'What? What is it now?'

'Nothing. It's just that I don't understand it. How can she give her baby away like this?'

'Maybe it's better to give it away, if she can't bring it up by herself', Mario said.

'Or maybe it is all to do with this man she's having an affair with, you know, the rich man, the one who's going to take her baby to give it to his wife. She is signing all the documents for him now. She is doing exactly as she is told.'

'Well, isn't that what he gave her all the money for?'

'And so? It is not a legally binding agreement. I told her that she did not have to listen to him. She could stay here. I could put her up. She doesn't have to ever see him again. She doesn't owe him anything.' She sighed again. 'She's doing all this because she is in love with him. It's such a shame.'

'How is her relationship with this man any of our business, Marika? I told you already, you let the problems of other people affect you too much. Don't you have a family of your own to care about?'

'But don't you see? He is exploiting her.'

'They exploit each other. She takes his money, remember?'

'Don't say that, Mario. She is a young, vulnerable girl; she is lost. Anyway, it is past teatime and we are sitting here talking without even a cup of tea.' She got up and put the kettle on, looking forward to the soothing gurgling of the boiling water. She brushed away a hint of guilt. She had burdened Mario enough with her agonising thoughts, especially as she knew deep down that he never really agreed with her choice to put Nefeli up, let alone with all the hospitality she was offering her. Yet, she could just not switch off. She opened a large patterned red tin and took some scones out. 'Homemade', she said proudly, trying to lighten up. She took the butter dish and a jar of strawberry jam to the table, and after a while she expertly poured some tea in Mario's cup.

'No cream for the scones?' he asked.

'We ought to cut down. Your cholesterol is high.' After some hesitation she took a pot of cream out of the fridge, not quite sure which one out of the two of them needed the extra treat.

'What shall I do, Mario?' she said after pouring some tea for herself as well. 'Shall I call her mother and tell her the truth? She will find out sooner or later.'

'Why don't you just forget about her? She will leave very soon. Make yourself unavailable after that. You need to learn to protect yourself and your family, Marika. This girl has only brought us trouble.'

'You know I can't cut Magda out like that. She is my only good friend from Thessaloniki. The only link I have with where I come from, with my roots, Mario.'

All at once she was teary. They both sipped their tea slowly, the scent of Earl Grey and watered-down milk filling the room.

'You have been a bit sad lately, Marika, haven't you', he said after a while. 'I'm sorry I didn't notice earlier; I expected you to be happy. I thought that we had a good life together. Working hard, having the boys, seeing them grow.'

'They don't even speak Greek, Mario, and they are all leaving me. It's only the little one who is around, and he'll be on his way out soon.' She started sobbing, trying desperately to suppress the shuddering of her shoulders.

'Don't be silly, Marika. It's good they are leaving, it means that they are becoming grown men, independent. All due to your hard work.'

'It's easy for you to say. I still remember them like yesterday toddling around the house. And now our life is over and they are gone.'

'Ah, now I see why you got so attached to this girl. You found in her someone eager to be mothered.'

'You know me, I always wanted a girl, and she's such a beautiful, delicate-looking girl. The baby girl I never had.'

He got up and looked for something in the kitchen drawers.

'What is it you are after?' She felt agitated, guessing the

answer to her question. 'Don't tell me you are looking for a cigarette. You will be looking in vain. I have thrown them all out now.'

'I know. Where can I find one, in Spyros's room?'

'You are acting desperate. What has come over you? You quit a long time ago, remember?'

He sat down in a resigned way, stooping his shoulders. 'It makes me sad, Marika, to see that you are not happy. All these years of hard work and the constant demands of the boys, and now, when we finally get some peace, what do you do? You bring this deranged girl into our house and she becomes your problem.'

'Mario! She's not deranged!'

'Well, she's bad news, I can tell you that. She's used to playing the victim. She takes no responsibility for her actions and then she expects others to sort her out. You have four children, Marika. Could you ever do that? Give your children up for money?'

'No, but I also had you, my rock.' She patted the back of his hand. 'Whereas she is in love with a man who wants to exploit her.'

'She has chosen to have an affair with a married man, Marika, knowingly. I tell you, this girl likes the good life. Have you not noticed? She has not even been making her own bed while she's been staying here.'

'I told her not to!'

'And she took advantage of that. That's what she does with people!'

'You don't like her, do you?'

'I don't like the effect she has on you.'

She got up abruptly, starting to carry the cups to the sink. A familiar tightening was spreading across her chest.

'I have made up my mind', she said as though talking to herself. 'I will call Magda tomorrow morning and tell her the truth. She needs to know what her daughter is up to, what she is about to do with her life. I just need to sleep on it. Tomorrow I will have a clear mind and I will know exactly what to say to her and how to handle it. In the meantime', she continued, trying not to sound out of breath, 'I need to look for my inhaler. We should stop buying cream, Mario. I think it brings my asthma on.'

'It's Nefeli who brings your asthma on, my dear! It's Nefeli', he said, sighing.

32
The beginnings

Thessaloniki, May 1972

Leonora's mother had finally agreed to come and look after the baby, but only for a couple of weeks, she had warned her. This time of year was always busy in the fields.

Leonora was now expected to go back to work. She had, to start with, taken two weeks of sick leave and she knew at the time that she was being optimistic. She hadn't even been pregnant, but even if she had been, it would not have made much difference. She knew from experience how women employees who kept taking time off to look after their children were seen: as a nuisance and as cheats. She had heard it often mumbled at management-team meetings. So-and-so had to decide, did she want to be an emancipated working woman or a stay-at-home mother? She couldn't have both, it was not fair. In fact, she had been part of that same management team among those arguing against double standards for men and women. Yes, we give opportunities to women, but they have to prove themselves, be up to it. She had always objected though, when someone, usually male, from the management team wanted to sack a female employee for taking too much time off for maternity-related duties. Just don't promote her, she would say. Leave her at the bottom of the climbing ladder permanently, she will get the message.

The problem was, she had already been promoted. She had been given a position that no woman before her had ever occupied, Head of the Psychiatry Clinic. When she called to ask for another two weeks' sick leave, she had tried to suss out how things were going. She had spent some time talking to one of her confidantes, Dr Nicolaides, one of the junior doctors in the general pathology clinic who was thought of as one of the most promising.

'How is it going, Dimitri?' she had asked. 'Have you heard any rumours about my absence?'

'Kind of', he had replied.

'Come on, you have to tell me. We are friends, remember?'

'Are you sure you want to hear?'

'Yes, of course. I need to know.'

'Well, I heard through the grapevine that your rich husband has bought you a baby and he wants you to stay at home and bring it up. That you are not going to come back to work. Rumours are that you are about to resign, and that you are just biding your time. Is it true?'

'Of course not! This is not true, Dimitri, although I know how pleased some people there would be if it were the case. They can't wait for me to be replaced.'

'Well, you know, it was always a bit of a scandal. A woman Head and all that ... But you have proven yourself. It is just that now you have to live up to it.'

'And I will, Dimitri! Do me a favour, will you? Can you spread the word that I am coming back very soon and that I am looking forward to kicking some asses more than ever.'

'Okay. But honestly now, how is it going? It can't be easy.'

'Well, it was hard to settle the baby at first. But she is a good one, Dimitri, a real beauty. You must come and see her. She and I have hit it off. It is just childcare that has been my problem. Everyone has let me down, but it's getting sorted now. I will be back in two weeks, I promise.'

She was lying, of course. Nothing had really been sorted out yet. Even worse, practicalities were not the real issue. Yes, it was difficult to find somebody experienced enough to leave such a young baby with. She was barely three months old. The main problem though was all the disagreements and arguments she has had with Dinos since they had received the baby. Regardless of the rumours at the hospital, Dinos had never asked her to quit work. But he was acting very precious about who to leave his baby with, and after the latest developments it had transpired that he had an agenda too. She should have foreseen that, how short-sighted of her not to have seen it coming.

To start with, and while she was still settling Eleni into a routine, her mother-in-law had come to stay with them. Her mother-in-law's visit would have been a nightmare at the best of times, and this was far from that. Her critical gaze would wander round the house, stopping expressively at every little dusty corner or anything that had not been tidied away.

'Our house is our façade onto the world', she would say. 'A dirty or ugly façade, and this is who we show ourselves to be', and she would give Leonora a condescending look with her cold, seawater-coloured eyes.

Their relationship had started off on the wrong foot even before they had properly met, and it developed even more disastrously on her first visit when Leonora and Dinos were newlyweds. Dinos had conveniently arranged to be travelling overnight and so she had to spend the whole evening after work in her mother-in-law's company. It was awkward to say the least, and her comments did nothing to warm the atmosphere.

'Dinos was brought up like a prince', she would tell her. 'We had maids to start with, but soon I did not need them any more. Nobody would keep the house as well as I did. My children always slept on freshly washed best-quality linen. They ate only the freshest seasonal food from our farm, all expertly cooked by me, of course. Now, that you are Dinos's wife, you will have to learn all these things. He is used to having only the best, and I can see that you have a long way to go.' All she could reply was, 'Yes, Mother', having to swallow hard not to spit out that her mother-in-law's perfectionism when it came to housekeeping meant that she was utterly oblivious to her children's real needs.

Despite her striking subservience, her mother-in-law had managed to subsequently accuse her of being the cause of all the bad arguments she was having with Dinos.

'Dinos never used to talk to me like that', she would say. 'He was the most respectful of boys. It has to be your fault.

You are badmouthing me behind my back.'

Admittedly, she was not entirely wrong on this. Leonora was fed up with Dinos's blind devotion to his mother and idealisation of his family, when clearly they had failed him so badly. All she had done was to point out to him the reality of the situation, which was that his mother had always demanded that he fend for her. He still worked hard to provide her and his sister with a considerable monthly wage, and they were yet to thank him.

'When did she ever care about you?' Leonora would demand. 'Did she worry about the effect their separation had on you, or about the fact that you had to sleep on benches like the homeless to keep her and your sister happy? She behaves as though she only has one child, your sister, and you are a kind of servant that has to provide for her.'

'That's not true, Leonora. I was a boy, and the eldest. Somebody had to take care of them', he would say, but his eyes would well with tears.

This time round, though, her mother-in-law's visit was more disastrous than any time before. Dinos had begun with high hopes, believing that she would be keen to stay with them and take care of the baby.

'She will not do it, Dinos', Leonora told him. 'She is already taking care of your nephew, and she is used to living with them. Why did you not ask her on the phone?'

'These things are not discussed on the phone, Leonora. Face to face is the way to do it', he had replied grumpily.

'Yes, but we are wasting precious time. I need to sort

childcare out. I am expected back at work.'

'I have asked her to bring plenty of clothes so that she doesn't need to go back to my sister's. You will see, you will be back at work within a week.'

As much as the practicality of such an arrangement would suit her, Leonora wished that she was right, as the thought of having her mother-in-law staying with them permanently made her stomach churn.

Dinos had started on the right foot, trying to appease his mother.

'Look, Mother,' he would say, 'not only does this baby have your name, but she also looks like you. She is going to be blonde with green eyes. I can only hope that she will also be a beauty like you', he would add half-jokingly.

His mother had smiled one of her smiles that never reached the eyes, and then she had let out one of her usual sighs.

'Ah, luck and a good husband is what a woman needs. Beauty is transient and quite useless, if you ask me.'

On the second evening of her visit, Dinos had decided to broach the subject with her. Leonora had stayed tactfully in the kitchen doing the washing up with Eleni strapped into her baby bouncer on the kitchen table, positioned so that she could see her as usual. This baby could not be in a different room from her without wailing at the top of her lungs from day one. It did not take long for the tension in the voices in the living room to reach her ears, and soon after that, Dinos started shouting. She walked into the living room after a while, holding the baby bouncer in one hand.

'What's going on here? Why are you shouting?' she asked in an alarmed tone, pretending to know nothing about their conversation. Her mother-in-law did not look up, sitting stooped and holding her white silk handkerchief, embroidered with her initials, against her wet eyes.

'Every time I come here Dinos upsets me', she said after a while. 'That's why I don't like to visit you.'

'Why are you shouting at your mother, Dinos?' Leonora asked. She always liked to play mediator between them. 'It is not fair to upset her like that.'

He gave her a look. 'She will not do it', he said angrily. 'She will not stay with us to take care of Eleni.'

'Are you sure you don't want to take some time to think about it, Mother?' Leonora asked her politely. 'You will have the best of times here. We will get a housekeeper to do all the housework. You will not get tired at all. All you will have to do is look after the baby for a few hours, that's all.'

'I can't possibly leave Jenny, Leonora, you know that. She is pregnant again. Who will look after her children? You have money, you can hire childcare.'

'As you wish, Mother', Leonora said, being careful not to let out a sigh of relief.

Dinos wasn't usually forthcoming in sharing with Leonora his conversations with his mother, but this time round he was too upset to keep it a secret. He could only eventually talk to her when they were both lying in bed, with Eleni sleeping soundly in her baby cot next to them.

'The woman is insane', he said, shaking his head. 'I made her an offer to double the monthly amount I give her, and it would all go into her savings too, as she will not need to spend a penny while she is staying with us. I even said I would give some money monthly to Jenny so that she can get childcare. She would not even take a minute to think about it, Leonora. She was so adamant.' It was one of the few times lately that Leonora had felt for him, as he looked truly sad and hurt.

'Still, you shouldn't have shouted at her. Let her be. You know what she is like.'

'I shouted because I told her that I am going to stop her monthly aid, as we will need a lot of money for childcare, and she said that I could not possibly do that to her. Did I want her and my sister to die? she said.'

'Oh!' Leonora said.

'I lost it Leonora. I saw red, I almost thought that I was going to hit her.' I said: 'I now have my own family. Jenny's husband can sort her and you out. I was not born to be your fucking saviour.'

'Good for you!' Leonora said. 'It was high time you told her that.'

'She will be leaving tomorrow, first thing in the morning.' He leant on his side, looking for something.

'What are you doing?'

'I am going to have a cigarette.'

'Did we not say not in the bedroom? It's not good for the baby.'

'Just tonight,' he said. 'I do not want to get up and bump into her or something.'

Leonora's sympathy for Dinos dissipated quickly

though, in less than a few days. It was early afternoon and he had come back home while she was in the middle of walking Eleni round the living room to burp her.

'She is becoming quite unsettled after her feeds, I have noticed', she told him. 'Since I have been walking her around holding her upright like this, she lets out a couple of good burps and she seems to be fine after that.'

He smiled. 'The two of you have hit it off, haven't you', he said.

Leonora smiled back. She could see now that he had been right all along. Getting a baby even in this way, having her own baby in her arms, was certainly worth it. If only she could trust him a little more.

'I have talked to a couple of the girls in the office and they told me not to worry, they will find me a nanny in no time; plenty of women in the hospital who have recommendations to make. I told them I want the best. I said we don't care how much it costs as long as it is somebody experienced and highly recommended.'

'I have been thinking about it, Leonora, and I really don't think that it is right to leave my baby with a stranger. Look at her, she is tiny.'

'And so?' Leonora asked in an alarmed tone. 'My income is the only stable income we have. Your business is always up and down, you know that. Besides, we had agreed, hadn't we, that I would be keeping my job?'

The baby had fallen asleep on her shoulder, lulled by their conversation, so she placed her gently in her cot in their bedroom.

'What are you saying, Dinos?' she asked when she came back to the living room.

'It hasn't been a good week for me, Leonora.'

'I know that.'

'Today Nefeli contacted me. She's very upset. Her parents know all about it.'

'And so?' They would have found out about it sooner or later. 'They must be relieved that their daughter has been taken care of and that she has conveniently found a way to dispose of her mistake.'

'Do you really think it is that simple, Leonora? How many times have you cried and reminisced about when you disposed of your mistake?'

She unexpectedly felt really angry. 'What is this about? I don't want to hear about this woman or her feelings. Besides, I thought that you were not going to be in touch with her.'

'I haven't been. She has been in touch with me. She and her mother. Her mother is threatening that she will take the baby to raise it herself, Leonora. I bluffed it out, and I can only hope that these people are uneducated and ignorant enough not to start investigating about the legality of the adoption.'

'Why? What do you mean?'

'I didn't want to tell you not to worry you, but the baby cannot be adopted before she is four months old.'

Leonora suddenly felt nauseous. She should have trusted her premonitions. She should have known better than to believe in Dinos's utopian plans.

'I should have known better than to ever trust you', she said quietly.

'There is no reason not to trust me, Leonora. It is all arranged. Nefeli will do it, I promise. All the documents are ready and it's just a matter of a month's waiting now. We just have to be careful with these people. They are scum. We don't know what they are capable of.'

Leonora was suddenly feeling very tired and as though all the blood had drained from her body.

'What is it you want from me, Dinos?' she asked, feeling resigned.

'Nefeli just wants to be able to see the baby, that's all. I thought that if we employ her as our nanny, she will earn some money that would keep her parents happy, and at the same time she would obviously be the best person to take care of the baby. She has already done it for two months.'

'You are kidding!' Leonora said in disbelief.

'No, I am not. What I am saying makes sense.'

'I don't believe you said what you just said. I will tell you what, Dinos. You had better not say that to me ever again or I will walk out on you and your baby and I will leave you to sort it all out by yourself. I will be a fly on the wall while you two sweethearts raise her together. You haven't even changed a single nappy yet. Oh, I forgot, what did your mother say? You are a prince.' She had managed not to raise her voice, but while talking she had gone out to the corridor to put on her shoes.

'Where are you going?'

'Out. I need some fresh air. There are leftovers in the

fridge and her next feed is due at five o'clock. You can read the instructions on the packet of the formula.'

'Where are you going, Leonora? Where will you be until five?'

'Oh, and I might not be back this evening. Don't worry, I am sure you will work out how to take care of a baby.'

She was feeling really dizzy now, and she thought that she might faint if she lingered there much longer. It had happened to her before at moments of distress, usually at the sight of blood. Her life was feeling like that now, like a medical procedure that was getting out of control and was likely to end up in a haemorrhage.

'Leaving and not talking to me is not going to sort anything out, Leonora. It will only make things worse', he said before she slammed the door behind her and walked out into the lobby, running down the five flights of stairs, not bothering to wait for the elevator. Once the fresh spring air hit her, her queasiness started dissipating, but panic set in. Where was she going to go now?

33
Separation

Athens, October 1978

Dinos had not had one good night's sleep since Nefeli left the country. Dreams, nightmares, had been waking him up night after night, forcing him to spend the rest of the night until early morning smoking and soothing himself with cold leftovers from the fridge. His weight was creeping up.

When he had arranged all the details for Nefeli's departure, he had also planned to move to Athens to take on a major property development that had landed in his lap. This was money that could not be missed. A block of luxurious flats in posh Kolonaki, built according to the American dream model with en-suite bathrooms and walk-in wardrobes, a project unheard of in Greece before. How lucky for him to be in the right place at the right time. He was dining with his friend Kostopoulos, a multimillionaire, who was looking for a property developer to take the project on.

'Dinos,' he had said, 'do you want this project? You are one of the few around who do elegance the right way. There will be lots of money involved, of course.'

Dinos had hesitated for a moment. 'But, I will need to

move to Athens for this, no? It will probably take a couple of years to carry out.'

'Yes, indeed. You will need to move here. Would you mind? I will help you out with the good life in the capital. The two of us will have fun!' Kostopoulos said, laughing a throaty laugh and giving him a wink.

'It's just that Eleni is still very young. I want to be around.'

'Couldn't your wife move over here with you?'

'No, she is working full-time. She is a psychiatrist; she has an important position.'

'I will tell you what, Dinos. With the money you will make, you can fly your wife and daughter to spend every weekend with you. How old is your little one?'

'Six and a half.'

'Good age to start going to the theatre. I will give you my booking agent's number. Lots of good stuff for little ones in Athens: music, theatre, dance. It is a bit dead culture-wise up there in the north, isn't it? It will give your daughter the right start in life. Deal?'

'Deal! It sounds good!' Dinos said, feeling genuinely excited now.

Then he had come up with a plan. If he managed to get Nefeli out of the country in the summer, he could move to Athens soon after that. It would be easier to move in the summer, as Leonora and Eleni could come and spend some time with him and help him settle before Eleni started school in September. It would be easier for him all round if he moved to Athens after Nefeli left. A fresh start, that's what he needed.

For the first month after she left, he had managed to keep his promise to himself. 'Cut it off, don't call her, a clean end, a fresh start', he kept ordering himself; and for a while it worked. But then, just as he thought he was getting over her, the tormenting feelings started kicking in along with the nightmares and the sleepless nights. The dreams were recurring: he was driving fast in Sounio near the sea and he could not stop stepping on the accelerator. When he finally pressed the brake, it didn't work and the car would speed out of control round a sharp bend, eventually crashing into the metal barrier and flying into the sea. He would wake up with his breath cut, not knowing for a while whether he was on land or in water.

In another dream with several recurring versions, Nefeli was dating a man whose face he could not see. The man would offer to walk her back home, and then lead her into a dark corner, where he would strangle her. He would see her face turning blue and lifeless, and he would jump up in bed, cold sweat running down his forehead.

After the second recurrence of the dream with Nefeli and a sleepless night smoking in the kitchen until the early hours, he picked up the receiver and dialled Marika's number. It was not easy to find the time to call, as Leonora and Eleni were staying with him for the last week of Leonora's summer leave, before Eleni started school. The flat he had rented in Athens was tiny, just a small double bedroom, a box kitchen with a small table in the corner, and a living room as tiny as the bedroom. It would be plenty for him when he was eventually alone here in the winter. He had to pretend that he was feeling under the weather, not untrue either given his sleepless night, as he drove them to the bus station where they would catch the bus for the beach. He felt a pang of guilt when he waved them goodbye, realising that it was a Saturday and the bus was packed. And of course it was never easy to fool Leonora.

'Everything all right?' she asked him when they got back, giving him one of her cold looks. 'The sea was very refreshing. It would have done your nerves a lot of good', she added.

Was she being sarcastic? he wondered.

He was so embarrassed to have to call Mrs Marika's number. She had always been restrainedly polite with him on the phone, but of course this was when things were different, when Nefeli was pregnant with his baby and after she gave birth but before he had taken the baby away. He was desperately hoping that Nefeli would pick up the phone, but of course, as he had expected, it was Mrs Marika who answered.

'Can I speak to Nefeli, please?' he said, putting on his most authoritative voice.

'Who is this?' the voice in the receiver replied coldly.

Of course she knew perfectly well who he was. 'Mr Hatzis', he said, remembering the need to sound formal and imposing.

'She is not here, I am afraid.'

'When can I call her back?'

'Never. You can never call her in this house. She is not here.'

'Come on', he said losing his patience. 'I know that she lives with you, she is probably right next to you as we speak. I think you are making a mistake, Mrs Marika. Nefeli may no longer be that young, but she thinks and behaves like a young girl. She needs protecting.'

'Yes, she needs protecting from you', Mrs Marika said; but before finishing her sentence, Nefeli was on the phone.

'Hello. Dinos?' she said.

'Yes, it's me.'

'I thought you would never call again.' There was a pause. 'How are you?'

'I ... I am worried about you. I keep having nightmares. In some of them you get murdered.'

'It's probably because you have murdered me already.'

'I don't like it when you talk to me like that, Nefeli. Are you keeping well, keeping yourself safe?'

'Yes, I am in good hands, as you know.' After that she hesitated. 'I had better go', she said with determination.

'Yes, me too.'

He hung up feeling somewhat lighter, as though he had done something to keep at bay the night terrors and the feeling of abandonment that was pestering him. For the last month, when he was spending time with Eleni and Leonora, he kept having the feeling that something was missing, as though someone who was part of their family was no longer there.

The idea that this phone call had resolved things turned out to be wishful thinking. For a couple of weeks he felt better; but soon after, the urgency to get in touch with Nefeli, to see her, even to touch her and hold her in his arms, like he so often used to, returned. The broken and sleepless nights had started affecting his work and sense of well-being, and finally, before Leonora was due to return from her summer leave, he had to admit that he was not feeling well and asked her for some tablets to help him sleep.

'It sounds to me more like depression than anxiety', she said, thinking aloud. 'It is bound to be because your girlfriend has gone away. How sad!' she added, openly sarcastic this time. Before their exchange had time to escalate into an argument, she wrote a few prescriptions, giving him detailed instructions under what circumstances to take each pill.

'Use those with caution,' she warned him, pointing to some tiny, pretty pink pills, 'only if you are desperate. They are very soothing, but highly addictive and your resources to deal with addiction have always been limited.'

As much as it irritated him hearing Leonora put on her professional persona, it also felt strangely reassuring.

'Don't worry', he replied. 'I am planning on using hardly any of them. It's just comforting to know that I have them and can use them if I need to.'

Things only got worse once Leonora and Eleni went back to Thessaloniki at the beginning of September. Now it was not only the nights that bothered him, but his days were hard going too. Tears would surprise him by rolling down his cheeks with no warning while he was having his morning coffee. He would eventually manage to pull himself together and get dressed, ready to visit the building site, well after midday, when the builders were about to finish their shift and head back home for their lunch and siesta. Every single flaw he noticed in the work would irritate him beyond belief. Yelling at them before leaving the site had become a daily ritual.

A week or so after Leonora and Eleni had left, he called Nefeli again. This time Mrs Marika passed the phone straight to her.

'How are you? I miss you', he said.

'I am okay. Not too bad. How is Eleni?'

'She just started proper school. Leonora says she doesn't like it very much. She keeps hiding behind her back when the school bus comes to collect her.'

'Oh dear! The poor thing! Maybe it is the wrong school for her?'

'No, it is the best private. You know we have always given her the best. Anyway, what are you up to?'

'Trying to start a new life, I suppose.'

'And are you succeeding?'

'It's difficult, but I try.'

'Does this mean that you are dating someone?' he asked, trying not to sound menacing, but feeling a surge of uncontrollable jealousy poison his every cell.

'Kind of.'

'I warn you, Nefeli, be careful. My nightmares haven't stopped since you left. You could easily be a victim of exploitation. Just be careful who you trust.'

'You know from first-hand experience that I can be a victim, huh? Don't worry. I'm being careful this time round.

I had better go.'

After she hung up he was thrown into the worst state of obsession he had ever experienced. All he could think of was Nefeli making love to another man. Scenes of her lovemaking, the sounds and the abandonment in her face when she reached an orgasm, would flood his mind. Work was now the best therapy he had available, as the pills would make his mood worse. He threw himself into supervising the building site, going there at dawn, even before the builders had arrived, until late lunch time. He also phoned his friend Kostopoulos.

'Hey, how are you, mate? You promised to entertain me while I am in Athens. My days and nights are very dry at the moment.'

They met that evening at a cabaret: whisky flowing, beautiful girls dancing for them. They seemed to know Kostopoulos well and they later on took them to a VIP booth where two of them, whom Kostopoulos had chosen, whispering in Dinos's ear 'these two are the best', stripped for them and then, sitting on their knees, started to undo their shirts. He ended up in one of the rooms upstairs, having mindless sex, a professionally executed blow job and then a quick hard climax while she rode him. His head was spinning on the way back home. He usually liked sex with a bit more context: dating someone, taking her to expensive restaurants, then sleeping with her and spending all night with her. Getting close, falling in love, for a while at least, until he moved on to the next one. This was his pattern. Paid sex left him feeling numb and bruised.

After that night, he called Nefeli again and again, almost daily. He wanted to know who she was dating. Sometimes she would talk to him in her sad little voice, enquiring about his life and the weather in Greece and Eleni. When he bombarded her with questions, she hung up on him and then for a few days she would not come to the phone. He panicked. Suddenly the thought occurred to him that she really could cut all her ties with him, disappear into thin air. He could not allow that to happen. It had been silly of him to listen to Leonora and let her go. For one thing his daughter would almost certainly look for her when she grew up. They were a kind of family, the four of them. It had to stay that way.

He called Mrs Marika again.

'I beg you let me speak to her. It is really important.'

'Well, she no longer wants to speak to you, I am afraid.'

'I understand, but there is something she doesn't know that I need to tell her. Please?'

'All right. Just a moment, I will ask her.'

'Nefeli', he said as soon as she was on the phone. 'Please do not do this to me again. Do not hang up on me. I miss you terribly. Nefeli, you need to come back. Eleni will also miss you a lot when she grows up, if you are not around.'

'Eleni does not even know who I am to her.'

'Of course she does – she will. Please come back. It will be like before between us, even better.'

'It was not good before. Are you planning to leave your wife then?'

'I don't know, maybe. I can't promise that right now.'

'And I don't want to be talking to you right now. I told you,

I am trying to start a new life here. You asked me to leave, remember?'

'Please don't hang up. We have to talk again in a few days. There is so much to say. You will come to the phone. Do you promise?'

'Okay.'

'Maybe you and I should not be together', he told Leonora one day on the phone. They had not met at the weekend as was customary. 'I thought having Eleni would sort everything out, but I can see now that I am not suited to the married life.'

'Well, we are hardly together anyway', Leonora said bitterly. 'You only come to me when you need me. We no longer have a sex life. The only thing we have in common nowadays is Eleni. What will happen to her?'

'I don't know', said Dinos, and he started sobbing on the phone. 'I don't want to lose you, Leonora. We have been together all our lives, so many good and bad moments we have had together, but I think I am losing my mind. I don't know what is happening to me.'

The thought occurred to him that maybe the easiest thing to do would be to end his life. A life so tormented was not worth living. He called Nefeli again and again, losing his cool and weeping down the phone, begging her to come back.

'Please have sympathy for me, Nefeli. I can't leave Leonora, I won't lie to you. We haven't even been a couple for many years, but I don't know, it is the sense of security it gives me to be around her.'

'Is it her steady salary then?'

'Nothing to do with that. I can earn more than her just by snapping my fingers. It is just that she is a steady person.'

'Then you have made your choice.'

'My choice is you, Nefeli. I really need you to come back, I can't live without you. I have been thinking of killing myself.'

'Oh, don't be silly.'

The black thoughts continued to haunt him. He had a feeling that Nefeli had been thinking secretly of returning; something in her tone of voice on the phone had conveyed that to him. Yet everything had already changed. Leonora would no longer accept her in the house and he was not sure what her return would do to their precarious marriage. What would happen to Eleni if they split up? His idea of giving her the perfect childhood could easily turn into a reality of chaos. She was a settled little girl now, attached to her mother like an oyster to a rock.

The pressure building up in his head felt like an active volcano. One morning, after taking the sleeping pills Leonora had warned him to use sparingly the night before, he woke up feeling so groggy that he decided to spend all day in bed. He would only get up every couple of hours for a cigarette break and to raid the fridge, and would eventually return to a restless sleep filled with nightmarish scenes. By late afternoon he was dizzy with despair. He picked up the phone, hoping to talk to Leonora. She needed to know something about his mental state. Eleni's nanny picked up instead.

'Leonora is not here yet', she said. 'She must be on her way back though. She had a late work meeting.'

'Tell her to call me back, will you? Can you pass me Eleni? I need to speak to her.'

It was enough to hear her little-girl voice to reduce him to tears. At least he could feel something strong and meaningful though, love for his daughter rather than just anguish and despair.

'Yes, Daddy?'

'Yes, it's me, darling. Have you eaten lunch?'

'Yes.'

'All of it?'

'It was steak. I don't like steak very much, but I ate a bit. That and potatoes.'

'That is a special steak Daddy buys for you. It is the best. You must eat it.'

'Okay, Daddy. What time is Mummy coming home?'

'Any time now, my darling. Listen, I am calling you to tell you one thing. Your daddy is not feeling very well. I may not be around for long, but one thing you must remember if I die is that I love you more than anything else in the world', he said, swallowing down the cracks in his voice.

'Why you may die, Daddy? Are you sick?'

'I am kind of sick, my darling, but do not worry about me. Just remember what I told you, okay?'

It was no more than ten minutes after he hung up that Leonora called him back. Her tone of voice was like a razor cutting through a metal surface.

'I hear you told Eleni that you might die. She is quite upset. What's going on?'

'I am feeling truly awful, Leonora. I cannot bear it any

longer.'

'Well, listen. You are depressed because you are missing your stupid girlfriend so much. You may not believe it, but I care for this child. It takes a lot to raise her and you have no right to upset her like that. You didn't even come to see her last weekend.'

'I needed to talk to her, to tell her I love her. I tried not to upset her.'

'Well, there are many choices available to you. One, go and find your girlfriend, even take Eleni with you and raise her together.'

'I am not planning to –'

'Well then, the other solution is to kill yourself, if that is what you feel like doing. I have left plenty of pills for you in your drawer. Eleni will miss you a bit, but she will get over it quite quickly. She doesn't see you that much, remember?'

'You fucking cruel bitch!' he yelled, and he put the phone down on her.

Leonora's phone call had done him in. He was boiling with rage and despair. He got dressed quickly. Next thing he knew, he was behind the wheel and driving fast on the seaside road towards Piraeus. It was exactly like in his recent nightmares, the car spinning out of control, hitting the barrier and crashing hard into the sea. Only this time he was feeling in control. He did not want to die. He had to see his daughter first, and Nefeli as well. He drove the five hundred kilometres to Thessaloniki almost non-stop. He was there just after midnight.

34
Therapy

London, October 1999

Laura was sitting on Martin's wide-angled leather sofa for her second session with him. She was less nervous this time, although it was a long time since she had finished her analysis and she was feeling somewhat unused to the sense of someone seeing right through her. The nice thing about Martin, she thought, was the deep respect for the person he was talking to that transpired through his every word. It was the combination of respect, kindness and acute perceptiveness that made him one of a kind.

Yet Laura was not sure that she would want to have him as her supervisor, even if a place was offered to her. She had asked herself why on the way there and she thought that the reason was really her lack of self-confidence. She was not sure that she could bear to have a supervisor who could see right through her. She would have to work on this, if she wanted to develop her private practice. Her countryside upper-middle-class upbringing with parents who were mainly interested in the norm and the right order of things had left her struggling to trust her own judgement.

Any divergence from convention – such as getting pregnant at twenty – had to be concealed, as it would be seen by her parents as a violent disturbance of their sanitised world. At least her analysis had brought her in touch with the emotional deprivation of her childhood and, as she grew older, she saw less and less of them. She always kept up her duty as their daughter though: postcards throughout the year, visiting at Christmas and occasionally on their birthdays. What she admired so much in Eleni and Martin was precisely what she lacked: their uninhibited freedom to be themselves. The thought of Eleni sent a pang to her stomach. She should not have tried to hold on to her. She was not a good therapist for her. She should have referred her away from early on.

'Have you had any thoughts since our first session?' Martin asked, interrupting her self-accusatory daydreaming.

'Well, I suppose I still have quite a bit of guilt and remorse about how things have gone, but overall it was a huge relief to talk to you and your observations were really thought-provoking.'

'I am glad to hear that.'

'What I wanted to discuss today was the implications of how things turned out with Helen.'

'Go on.'

'If you remember, she first came because she became infatuated with an older man while she was in a long-term relationship at the same time. Your comment that this was her way of struggling with monogamy like her father was really spot on, but it was not a thought that had occurred to me at the time. The way I saw it was that this was a talented and intense young woman who had become infatuated with somebody who was clearly not good for her, despite being in a relationship. I saw it as a sign that her relationship was not good enough.'

'Did she tell you that she was not happy in her relationship?'

'Not exactly. They always argued quite a bit. Her partner is like an English public school boy, very unemotional. I thought that he couldn't give her the intimacy that she needed from a relationship.'

'I think what comes across to me is how you saw Helen as a little girl and you wanted to take her under your wing and protect her. She provoked these deep, maternal feelings in you, but at the same time it was a re-enactment of your past. I wonder what this maternal preoccupation felt like to Helen. Whether she felt that you were not respecting her boundaries.'

'Yes, that is exactly right. My comments about her relationship, that maybe she was not emotionally fulfilled and that maybe she needed a partner that could respond to her intensity, were interpreted by her as me prompting her to split up with her boyfriend.'

'Did you not want her to split up?'

'Well, I still believe that what I said about her relationship was right.'

'But it doesn't matter as much whether an interpretation is right or wrong; what matters more is what it does to our relationship with a patient. Where was she likely to place you through what you said to her. Were you likely to remind her of a figure from her past who perhaps failed her or abused her?'

'So you think that I repeated in the transference something from Helen's past?'

'I was wondering, for example, what the relationship between Helen and her adoptive mother is like.'

Laura thought for a minute. 'Complicated, I suppose', she answered. 'Helen came with a rather idealised version of her mother. She described her as a kind of Mother Teresa. A mother who would put up with anything that Helen threw at her and who would always be there for her. I felt from the beginning very suspicious of the mother's motives. What kind of a woman would take the baby her husband had with his lover?'

'You are quite right to be suspicious of the mother, but you are diverting again from Helen's experience', Martin remarked.

'I suppose Helen deconstructed her relationship with her mother through the therapy. She came to see her mother as a much more complex person. She was ready for it, I think. She felt that her mother was in an indirect way manipulative and controlling and that she had tried to turn her against her father and her birth mother and to use her as an ally in the complex power dynamics within the family. I agree with all of this.'

'So, if her mother was manipulative and controlling, it must be particularly important for someone like Helen to be able to think for herself and to stand on her own two feet, right?'

'Yes, I think that is correct.'

'I suspect that this is who you came to represent in the therapeutic relationship: the mother who took Helen under her wing and who didn't let her have a relationship with her father; the mother who wanted to keep her a prisoner through her own self-interest.'

Laura looked at him horrified.

'Sorry', Martin said. 'I don't mean to discourage you or put you down. I am just trying to think along with you from the information that you gave me about what might have gone on between you, and you have reached this point of crisis, despite having done such important work together.'

'Oh, I don't feel that you are putting me down', Laura rushed to say. 'It is just that I am horrified about how accurate what you are saying is. It puts everything into context. Many things I have said to her, she must have experienced as a re-enactment of her mother's smothering and control. In fact, one of the mistakes I have made is that I think I let her sense my anger with her father and his behaviour towards women. Sorry, Martin, but I think her father is such a bastard.'

'Like your boyfriend, who abandoned you? Who would not have the baby with you?' Martin said softly.

Laura looked at him. If any other supervisor had said that to her, she would be overwhelmed with dread and shame. Yet she did not feel even a bit criticised by Martin, as all these revelations coming one after another and causing her pain and shock on impact were delivered with unquestionable kindness.

'Yes', she mumbled breathlessly. 'And then I scrutinised her boyfriend. I have acted exactly like her mother, wanting to take her under my wing and to have her for myself.' Laura paused and then added, as though talking to herself, 'The only thing that doesn't fit is the erotic. This is what had confused me.'

'Can you say something more?'

'You know, what I mentioned last time, that there was physical contact between us – I didn't experience it as erotic at the time, but as deeply maternal, nevertheless very intense, and irresistible. There was something I would say almost seductive about her sitting curled up on the floor cushion like a little girl, burying her head between her knees and then looking up at me with wet eyes. I almost resent it.'

'Did it remind you of your lost girl?'

'Possibly', Laura said in a shaky voice.

'Many supervisors would endorse the view that the patient seduced you into something, the patient's sadism and so on. I am afraid I do not agree. Freud moved from his early trauma and seduction theory to an intra-psychic theory to suit his needs and those of the medical establishment, and also, not to turn away the aristocrats who brought their offspring to him. He realised that if he persevered with a theory that suggested that his patients had been abused in their childhood, he would provoke outrage. However, in moving away from the early trauma theory, he inadvertently moved away from the actual experience of his patients. The vulnerable little girl that you saw in Helen is what Winnicott has called her 'real self', the abandoned baby on the lookout for a mother. On that level, you have made a really strong connection to each other and I think this is wonderful and it doesn't happen often. But then, it is what we do with it as therapists, especially when it stirs up painful feelings and longings in us; also, all the doctrines, how we have been taught about what to do with it. This is when it can go wrong.'

'Do you think it has gone terribly wrong?' Laura asked, feeling the dread of her worst fear creeping in.

'Not at all. I think you have done many things right. You have not been defensive or punitive or tried to analyse Helen away. But at the same time, you have re-enacted something from her relationship with her mother. You have wanted to take Helen under your wing, and to her this has felt possessive.'

'So is there a way to reverse this?'

'I think that you can still do one thing that will make a big difference regardless of the outcome. You can be honest and non-defensive with her. I think this will work wonders with someone like Helen.'

'Do you think that the erotic stuff was provoked by me?'

'Oh, I meant to comment on the erotic, but we got somewhat diverted. I think that the erotic is Helen's way of getting close to people and making sure a connection is established. If you think that we develop our sexuality from the first close physical relationship with our mother, then it makes sense that in a context where one feels vulnerable, this erotic stuff may come up.'

'Sorry, Martin, but this sounds to me like classic psychoanalytic theory', Laura said. It was the first time that she had dared to challenge him, and she was used to expecting some form of retaliation. He surprised her by breaking into a wide wry smile.

'You are quite right. I didn't mean to lecture you on psychoanalysis. I am sure that you have had more than enough of that stuff in your training already.'

She really liked this man, she thought to herself.

'I guess what I meant to say,' he continued in a lighter tone, 'was that it doesn't seem strange to me that there was some erotic energy between you, as your connection was based on this early maternal stuff, but maybe the hugs you gave her made her project this onto you and fear that you were sexually attracted to her, and that this could get out of control.'

'So is there something you think that I could do about it now? Is there any chance of reparation?'

'First of all, can I ask you a difficult question? You don't have to answer it, if it feels uncomfortable.'

'Go on', Laura said, already feeling on edge.

'Do you think there has been on your part some sexual attraction other than the maternal feelings?'

Laura thought for a minute. 'I don't know', she said hesitantly. 'I am heterosexual you know, like Helen ... and also, anyway, I would never sleep with a patient.'

Martin waited for more, looking at her patiently.

'Okay, if I am to be completely honest about what I felt, it was like I wanted to have her all to myself, not share her with her boyfriend or with her parents who had failed her. I wanted to become the most important person in her life, and for a while it felt like I was. Very irrational, I know. But isn't it that when therapy works, we become temporarily the most important person in the patient's life?'

Martin was leaning forward, looking at Laura sympathetically but seeming slightly bemused.

'Why did you want that, Laura? Why be the most important person in her life?'

Laura felt distressed. 'I don't know', she said in an unstable voice. 'Fear of losing her, I guess. I think it is to do with that lost baby. Not wanting to lose that connection again.'

'I am aware of not having much time left, but we should try to see this constructively before we finish. My advice is the following: if she wants to end the therapy, you should not try and persuade her to stay. You need to let her go. It will actually be good for you too. Is she chooses to stay, then I believe you can make real progress by acknowledging what I believe she has already sensed, that you have become in the transference a bit like her mother.'

'Yes, I can see that clearly now. I need to acknowledge that some of my interventions might have felt rather controlling or possessive to her. And yes, I can see that I need to let her go.'

'Do you think that you may need supervision for this patient if you continue working with her?'

'That sounds to me like you think I have messed up.'

'No, I was just wondering if some of these issues would

have been better handled if you had sought help early on. She is a complex patient and she has tapped into something deeply personal for you.'

'Could I come and see you?'

'I am afraid I have a full schedule at the moment.'

'I imagined so.'

'I could book you the odd one-off slot. But if you need ongoing supervision, it would be better to find someone else.'

'Not everyone is like you, Martin, that's the problem.'

He smiled and walked her to the door, holding it open for her. It had felt to Laura like a very full session and one that she would not forget.

35
Paris breeze

London, September 1996

'What's the matter with you again?' Nicolas asked.

'Nothing. The usual', Eleni replied without turning her head to face him.

'Have you really spent all day sitting on the bench looking out of the window?'

'Yes', she said. She was feeling lifeless, as she had done every single day over the last three months, but somewhat provocative as well. Nicolas evoked that in her.

'This is ridiculous!' he said, puffing and walking up and down the living room, as though to counteract her stillness. 'I am losing my patience with you, Eleni. I really am!'

'You never had much, did you?'

'But to be patient about what, Eleni? What's the problem? You are not even telling me.'

'You know bloody well what the problem is: I can't write and I don't feel like doing anything much really.'

'But why?'

'Stop asking "why", "why"!' Eleni shrieked, no longer able to resist raising her voice.

'Have you eaten?' he asked in a milder tone while finally placing his raincoat on the hanger by the front door.

'No. I am not hungry. You know that I hardly ever feel like breakfast.'

'You mean you don't feel like breakfast or lunch. It is past five o'clock, Eleni! You can't starve yourself all day! Sometimes I feel like calling your mother and telling her all about the state you're in.'

'Oh! I didn't know it was that late. Of course, it must be: you are back home, your infamous nine-to-five schedule. You love your routine, don't you?'

He paused, as though contemplating how to respond to her irony. Then he said quietly, 'Why are you trying to pick an argument?'

'That's all we have been doing for the last few months, Nicolas, arguing. Sometimes I think that we would be better off calling it a day.'

'Yes, that's all we have been doing since you came back from Paris. What happened there, Eleni? Was he not nice to you? You have been depressed ever since.'

'Stop saying that!' she yelled, and she got up. 'You are making me upset!'

'Did your plans to have sex with him fail then?'

'I don't know what you are talking about.' She kept her back turned to him as tears rolled down her cheeks.

'You keep trying to find an external cause for our problems, Nicolas', she said after a while. She would try not to turn this into an argument, she promised herself. They really needed to talk like they used to, although she was not sure what, if anything, could be said. 'The fact of the matter is that you have a perfectly nice study here with all your books, and since the summer you have decided to go to the department to do your writing up every single day of the week on a nine-to-five schedule, as though you have a full-time job; all so that you can avoid me. This is what the cause of our problems is.'

'Really! Is it?'

'Stop being sarcastic! I am trying to talk to you. Yes, that is what the problem has always been, that you don't want to be intimate with me, or with anyone else for that matter. You don't do intimacy, do you?'

'Bullshit!' he yelled. 'I have been very intimate and loving to you. It is you who keeps spoiling it by being unfaithful! I can't trust you any more!'

They were both yelling now at the top of their voices, but Eleni found it hard to keep track of what, if anything, they were saying.

'Besides,' he said 'I cannot possibly work in this house when all you do is hang about in your pyjamas all day long doing nothing.'

'Well, I am an artist, you know, not a kind of robot that works on a schedule after pressing a button! I work when I have inspiration. What looks like nothing to you might be some very creative thinking, something you don't know much about, do you?'

'Yes, sure, call it that if it suits you. Just like your father, homebound all day, doing nothing other than wallowing over some kind of supposed sadness in your life!'

'How do you know what my father was like? You haven't even met him!'

'I know about him from you, Eleni, and I know that you are depressed and that unless you do something about it, it will only get worse', he said in a milder tone.

She sat on the sofa and her body finally seemed to release, sobs shaking her shoulders and salty warm tears running down her cheeks. He looked at her, standing still near the sofa.

'I'm not feeling well', she said after a while. 'I'm dizzy and my heart is pounding.'

'Of course you are not feeling well. You haven't eaten all day, for God's sake! Pull yourself together, Eleni, won't you?'

'Why do you have to be so nasty?' she mumbled, covering her wet, flushed face.

He walked to the kitchen and opened the fridge, looking carefully inside. 'We said we would cook spaghetti bolognese tonight', he shouted to her from the open door. 'I will start making it now, but it will take time. Do you want some toast for now?'

'Yes, please', she said without moving from the sofa. He sounded calmer now, but still quite irritated with her, she thought to herself.

She was just starting to feel a little bit better, as though some life was slowly returning to her body, when he handed her the toast.

'Thank you', she said with half a smile.

'That's okay. Just remember though, that I'm not your mother and I am not Mother Teresa like your mother was either.'

'I know you are not my mother', she replied with a wry smile, 'My mother would never be half as nasty as you are.' She lifted her arms and hugged him before he had time to walk away. 'You haven't even kissed me since you walked in', she said, planting her lips on his. She always liked to feel his warm skin and breath on her face. It was good to be reminded of this right now.

They spent the next hour cooking side by side in the small kitchen, managing not to bicker. She set the table with care, and then lit two candles and put some Sinatra on.

'Are we celebrating something?' he asked.

She shrugged her shoulders. 'Just that I am feeling a bit better since you came in. Besides, I like to lay the table nicely. Did you forget?'

He shrugged his shoulders too. 'It's just that you haven't done it for a while. You haven't been yourself for a while.'

They sat across from each other, their glasses filled with ruby red wine, their plates full of steaming spaghetti topped with sauce and grated parmesan. Nicolas was telling her about his meeting with his supervisor earlier in the day, mimicking as he spoke his supervisor's authoritative voice. Eleni listened to him for a while, eating slowly; she then put her fork down abruptly.

'What's the matter? I hope not a fly in the food?' Nicolas said, smiling.

'I phoned the University Counselling Service today', she said. 'I made an appointment with somebody called Laura Barker. You are right, I am depressed. It is like something has taken over me, like I am possessed', she said quietly.

'That's good', he said hesitantly. 'It's the right thing to do. Why did you not tell me for all this time though?'

'You are right about the other thing too', she continued, looking down. 'I have slept with him. That's why I am depressed. I am depressed about what I have done to myself, what I have done to us.'

He stopped eating too now, and looked at her.

'Go on', he said calmly.

'Well, you know, you suspected it all along. I went to Paris to have sex with Yves.'

'Why?' he asked quietly, but his eyes were glassy as he stared at her.

'I don't know. It felt like unfinished business. I thought if I had sex with him I could put it behind me, close that chapter for ever.'

There was a long silence that felt to Eleni like the quiet before a storm erupted. 'Can you please say something?' she begged.

'It sounds to me like you decided to go for a weekend of fun, while you could have stupid Nicolas believe that you needed a break with your girlfriends, because, poor thing, you were stuck with your writing up.'

'It wasn't like that, Nicolas. It was not fun. It was truly awful.' Her voice shook.

'Oh, really! Poor you! A weekend of planned sex, how awful!'

'I'm sorry, Nicolas. It was a mistake. I still haven't worked out what to do with my connections to other people, what to do when somebody gets under my skin like that.'

'Well, you seem to have the answer, don't you? You just go and fuck somebody!'

He got up quietly. She felt desperation and panic rising through her throat.

'Where are you going? Please don't go, Nicolas!' she cried. 'I have only ever loved you; that's the problem. Otherwise it would be easy: split up and experiment. I have only ever wanted to be with you.'

He picked his raincoat up from the hallway hanger and walked out quietly into the misty evening breeze.

***

She was not sure for how long she had been sitting still, before eventually gathering the necessary energy to carry the half-full plates of cold, congealing spaghetti to the sink and emptying their contents in the bin. She hated the smell of leftover food hanging about, even under such dire circumstances. The sense of emptiness and loneliness inside her was like a gaping wound. She could not bear the silence. She switched on the TV and sat staring at it mindlessly for what seemed like hours. The images kept changing. All she noticed was the parade of electronic colours hurting her eyes. Every time she heard the rhythmic sound of somebody's steps near the house, her heart raced. She finally switched the TV off, feeling nauseous from staring at it for so long, and looked at Nicolas's old-fashioned analogue clock sitting by the corner bookcase. It was nearly one a.m.

She was now curled up on her side of the bed. She could

not resist running her hand from time to time over Nicolas's empty side of the bed, cold and crisp under her touch. If only she could cry, she thought to herself; but tears would not reach her eyes. All the sorrow seemed to be buried in a deep, shady part of her that she could not reach. She must have fallen into a shallow sleep, as she woke up startled by the sound of the front door closing and locking. She turned to look at the alarm clock on Nicolas's side-table. It was five past four. She listened as his heavy steps stopped by the living-room sofa. She waited, holding her breath, but she could not hear anything else. She waited some more, still holding her breath, hoping to hear the creaking of the staircase under his feet, but no noise was forthcoming. It felt like hours had gone by, but the clock read four fifteen. Unable to bear it any longer, she walked in her bare feet down the stairs and into the living room.

'Is it you, Nicolas?' she whispered. She was standing in front of the sofa, where he was lying on his side, curled up, wearing all his clothes but his shoes, his raincoat buttoned up.

'Please come upstairs to bed, Nicolas.'

'I am all right here, thank you.'

'You seem cold. Please come to bed. I will come down here if you don't want me in bed with you.' Her voice cracked. 'Please, Nicolas', she insisted.

He walked upstairs silently and lay in bed in his boxers and white T-shirt, keeping away from her and facing the ceiling. Eleni lay on her side, her back turned to him. Tears rolled freely down her cheeks, wetting her pillow. After what seemed like hours, he turned on his side and put his arm gently around her waist.

'Stop crying, will you? You have cried enough for tonight', he said tenderly.

'Where have you been for all these hours?' she asked.

'I've been walking.'

'Walking for eight hours? You must be exhausted.'

They could see the pale light of dawn creeping in through the curtains.

'I love you, Nicolas', she whispered. 'I will never do that to you again, I promise. I will go and have therapy and sort myself out.'

'Let's sleep. Shall we?' he mumbled.

He hugged her closer. Just before drifting off a panoramic image of the two of them flashed up in Eleni's mind, as though she was watching them from above the bed, lying on their sides like two teaspoons fitted perfectly into each other. She sensed the early morning sunshine penetrating the bedroom window like a caress on her face, but it did not disturb her heavy, entangled sleep.

36
The encounter

London, February 2009

Nefeli had offered to babysit Chloe, while Eleni was doing work. She did not really understand Eleni's work. It usually involved playing around with pictures on a computer, a far cry from what Nefeli thought of as art. Today, she told her, she needed to do something physical and so she could hear her tapping at some material, while pacing about in the loft which she had converted into her studio. Despite not understanding it, Nefeli was proud of Eleni's work. She sensed that it was what her daughter had retained of her before her umbilical cord was cut so violently.

She had always imagined that to be invited to spend time with Eleni would make her very happy. Yet after a few hours in Eleni's house, stuck watching the baby sleep, ready to intervene if she woke up and before she started crying, at moments like this she felt suffocated. It felt like the walls of the house were closing in on her and unless she managed to work her way out they would start squeezing her to death. It was not the first time Nefeli had experienced claustrophobia. About a year ago, it had become so bad that she would have stopped working at the shop altogether if it had not been for an amazing homeopath who had sorted her out. All the doctors could offer was to say that it was because of the menopause and it would pass, and to offer her more and more tablets that she knew would make her feel worse.

It was just as she had started feeling better that she had encountered Andreas. It was exactly as her self-help books were telling her: the moment you start loving yourself and accepting it for what it is, is the moment your life can change for the better, the moment you might find true love. So here he was with his Vespa parked outside the shop, his wonderfully bohemian grey ponytail; here he was coming back to the shop every day just to see her. The knight she had been waiting for all her life.

Had it been a good idea to leave just at that moment and come to London, a place so saturated with dramatic events from the life she wanted to leave behind? Was it a good idea to be here now, even if she was seeing Eleni's baby, even if she had been invited to Eleni's house for the first time ever? What if he forgot about her and never visited again after her return? Perhaps it had not been the best time to leave Thessaloniki, yet this was the one chance she had to try and make amends with Eleni. She needed to talk to her about the changes that she knew were coming.

She took another deep breath to disperse the heavy feeling in her chest, but the walls around her did not seem to get any lighter. She considered moving the sleeping baby to the kitchen where there was more light and she could look out into the garden, but the last thing she wanted was to wake her up. The other day, Eleni and Nicolas had left her with the baby to go out for a meal, their first in ages, they said. Eleni had left a bottle with her own expressed milk in the fridge and had given detailed instructions about how to warm it up if the baby woke up and started to cry. It was barely an hour after they left before the baby woke up with a start and began wailing even before opening her eyes. No amount of rocking and walking her up and down had made any difference, and when she had finally left her in the cot to go and warm the milk up, the wails had got even more hysterical. Nefeli was not even able to get the bottle into her mouth, as she was turning her head away and straightening her little arm, pushing the bottle away in rage. Nefeli had felt hot flushes and cold sweat all over her body, while her heart pounded in her chest. It was as though she had been transported back to Mrs Marika's house, to her tiny little room with a strange baby she had no idea what to do with, only this time she was no longer young and her menopausal symptoms were driving her mad. In the end, she had resorted to calling Eleni on her mobile and saying that Chloe would not stop crying and that they needed to get back. It was their baby, after all. She could hear the coldness and irritation in Eleni's voice.

'Can't you give her the milk?' she had said. 'Our main course hasn't even arrived yet.' And then, after some hesitation: 'Don't worry, we are on our way.'

On their return, when, very embarrassingly, Chloe was lying peacefully in her Moses basket, having cried herself into a deep and somewhat bruised sleep, Eleni had given her the cold shoulder in her usual icy, polite way.

'At least you could have tried giving her the milk', she had remarked. 'It is so hard and unpleasant to express.'

Of course, I could expect no better from you, Nefeli, the baby deserter. Leonora would have been so much better at it, she had imagined Eleni thinking.

There had been good moments too though. Eleni was a good cook, as Nefeli had heard from Dinos so many times. He was so pleased, he kept saying, that Eleni had turned out to be an amazing cook, as it showed that all his efforts and the gourmet meals that he had cooked for her throughout her childhood had not gone to waste. He only wished, he would always hasten to add, that if she had to choose something artistic and ignore her exceptionally academic mind, she could have chosen something decent like being a chef, which would have brought her more money. Despite hearing all this, Nefeli had never tasted any of Eleni's food until this invitation to spend a week in her house. Every morning she had been woken by the smell of something delicious like home-made pancakes with baked cinnamon apples, a recipe Eleni had been given in Paris, or freshly baked blueberry muffins with a crumble top. Eleni claimed that it calmed her down to cook such elaborate breakfasts, and since she was often woken up by Chloe before dawn it gave her something to do with herself. Yet Nefeli could not help but also secretly think that through cooking her breakfast, her daughter was expressing the love for her which she had had to repress in all her years under Leonora's dictatorship.

One of these mornings, after Nefeli had thanked Eleni

sincerely for the breakfast and while the two of them were lingering at the kitchen table with a pot of coffee after Nicolas had gone to work, Nefeli had tried to talk to her. She had started the conversation by telling her how ill her father was, but she had got back an instant dismissive and impatient response from Eleni.

'I know that. I have been told it all my life', she had replied, shrugging her shoulders and rolling her eyes.

Nefeli had persisted. 'Eleni,' she had said, 'I think it might not be long until, you know, the inevitable.' Sensing that she had managed to engage Eleni more as she looked at her with sad, wide eyes, she had forced herself to continue.

'The shop has not been doing very well. For the last year it has produced nearly no profit.' Eleni was quickly impatient again.

'Are you going to talk to me about my father's health or about your finances?' she had asked in her usual 'don't give me bullshit' tone.

'The two are connected', Nefeli had continued in a steady voice, trying to assert herself. She had always felt so intimidated whenever she was in Eleni's presence, since Eleni had found out that she was her mother, when she was fourteen. 'What I am trying to say,' she had gone on, 'is that your father is not well enough to be at the shop any more, even though he does not want to admit it, and I have been exhausting myself working very long hours for nothing. Besides, it is clear now that he's approaching the end of his life that he needs your mother to take care of him. Leonora and he are the couple and I am the spare third party.'

'Has it not always been so?' Eleni asked. Another cutting remark, yet this time she looked genuinely puzzled. Nefeli felt a pang of anger.

'Believe me, there were times in the past when your father really, really needed me, like when I left for London to start my own life. You were about six at the time. You all came to the airport to say goodbye and I had bought you the doll that spoke English. Do you remember?'

Eleni nodded.

'Well, then I tried hard to forget and to start a new life, but your father would not let me. He kept calling me every day and even threatened that he would kill himself if I didn't go back to him.'

Eleni interrupted, looking quite upset now.

'Nefeli, I really don't want to hear all this now. I don't want to hear about your weird triangle. I have spent enough years in therapy analysing it. The way you and my father and mother have chosen to live your lives in this entanglement is really none of my business. I have a new baby now and I want to concentrate on her and on the future.' She paused. 'Anyway, why are you telling me all this? Is there something I need to know?'

'What I am trying to say is that the situation we have, this triangle as you have just called it, can no longer exist.'

'Why not?'

'Because I no longer want it and it doesn't make any sense.'

'It never did.'

'Well, you said that you don't want to talk about the past,

so don't get me started', Nefeli said, staring at her daughter with teary eyes. All the things she wanted to tell her about having had to stick to it so that she could see her, she had to repress as she knew that she would only get back anger and disbelief in return.

'What I am trying to tell you, Eleni is that I have decided to close the shop down and sell the business if I can, get some money for my retirement and move on. Once I close the shop, I will not be seeing your father any more. Anyway, our relationship has been platonic for some time now.'

'Nefeli, I told you already, I don't want to know', Eleni replied in an exasperated tone. 'Does my father know about this? He hasn't mentioned anything to me.'

'Yes, I have told him, but he doesn't agree with it.'

They were interrupted by Chloe's weak, bubbly cry as she had just woken up in her Moses basket, which sat on the table between them. The pale late-morning February sun creeping into the kitchen through the French windows into the garden had woken her up, but instead of her usual cries, she was smiling and babbling at them as though she was happy to see these two women sitting together around the kitchen table. Eleni got up.

'I must give her a feed', she said. 'Anyway, I have had enough of this talk for today.'

'I will clear the breakfast table.' Nefeli offered, getting up as well.

'Okay, but don't hand-wash the dishes like the other time. We have a dishwasher, you know. Just load it.'

'Okay, okay', Nefeli murmured. She had never seen the

point of dishwashers. By the time the plates were rinsed and placed in it, she could have washed them. Anyway, the warm soapy water, and keeping things clean and tidy, had always helped her relax.

She sighed and looked at the sleeping baby and the fading light outside the window. It would be dark soon and she could count off another day at her daughter's house when her desire to rekindle the connection with her had not quite materialised.

Eleni interrupted her thoughts by walking quietly into the room and peering at the Moses basket.

'Is she still sleeping?' she said in a voice that could not conceal disappointment. 'It's over two hours since I left you with her.'

'Well, she has been stirring from time to time and looking as though she might wake up, but then falling asleep again.'

Eleni sighed. 'This baby sleeps too much during the day and stays awake during the night as a result. I must work harder to change this now that she's not a newborn any more. She's such a night owl.'

Nefeli fought a bout of nausea as the walls again felt like they were about to fall on her. She had been debating silently whether to attempt to continue the interrupted conversation with Eleni or to make her way out of the house for some last-minute shopping.

'I am thinking,' she said hesitantly, 'that I must go and do some shopping as there are only two days left before I head back, and tomorrow I must go and see Mrs Marika. I promised her. She's not feeling too well.'

'What's wrong with her?'

'Oh, just the usual. Her asthma is getting worse, pains and niggles, just old age I guess.'

'Well, then, go, go. It's already four-thirty and the shops close at six.'

'But ...', Nefeli replied, feeling nervous, 'I don't feel that we have finished the conversation we started the other day. So tomorrow, if you have some time before I set off, I have got some more things to tell you.'

'You make it sound so formal, Nefeli. All you want to say really is that you decided to split up with my father. Anyway, I've had some thoughts about this too, so let's talk tomorrow. But now, come on, make a move', she added, shooing her out of the door in a half-humorous gesture.

***

The following morning, Nefeli walked into the kitchen, where Eleni was already sitting by the kitchen table having tea. She looked pale, with large black circles around her eyes. Before Nefeli even had time to say good morning, Eleni started filling her in.

'This baby is going to kill us', she said. 'She was up until three, screaming her head off. Did you not hear her?'

'No', Nefeli said rather surprised. 'I had to take my herbal pills to help me go to sleep last night, and it was a deep sleep after that.'

'And now,' Eleni continued, as though she had not heard her, 'she's sleeping so peacefully in her cot that I felt sorry for her and left her there for a while, despite my determination to establish a routine.' Before she had finished her sentence, a long wail was heard from the room upstairs.

'You see!' Nefeli said, smiling.

'That's strange', Eleni said, seeming even more worried. 'She has cried so much in the last day. How would I know if something was seriously wrong with her?'

'Come on. She's just a baby. Babies cry', Nefeli said, and regretted it instantly, as on her way out to attend to Chloe, Eleni gave her one of her condescending looks before swiftly exiting the kitchen. She did not get to see Eleni after that, as she left swiftly for her promised visit to Mrs Marika's house. When she let herself back into the house around nine o'clock, she found Eleni and Nicolas slumbering on the sofa, mindlessly watching TV, her feet resting casually on Nicolas's lap. If only Eleni knew what she had got, Nefeli could not help but think.

'Have you had dinner?' Eleni asked absently, without moving.

'Oh, yes. I had food for ten as usual at Mrs Marika's house.'

'We are exhausted, but we may have cracked it', Eleni muttered. 'First evening ever that Chloe is up in the room asleep without us.'

No invitation to join them on the sofa was forthcoming, so after a few more minutes of light chat Nefeli excused herself and said that she needed to drop off early as she was travelling tomorrow.

The following morning was the last of Nefeli's stay. She had made sure that she had packed everything ready to go before making her way down to the kitchen. She had woken up with a feeling of disappointment and apathy, a weird sense of deadness below her chest, something that she had not felt for some time now. It felt like something was amiss in her visit, although she had spent more time with Eleni and her baby daughter than ever before, at least since that fateful morning thirty-seven years ago, when she had left her sleeping baby in the back of Dinos's car.

She walked downstairs with heavy steps, noticing on her way down that the smell of freshly brewed coffee and something delicious baking in the oven meant that Eleni at least must have had a better night. She found her doing things around the kitchen while carrying Chloe in a sling, her baby eyes wide open for a change, observing her surroundings.

'Do you want me to take her?' Nefeli offered.

'No, it's all right. We are bonding', Eleni said, seeming in a lighter mood.

They both sat down at the table already set with butter, jams and freshly made toast as well as a cafetière of fragrant coffee. Eleni put Chloe on her breast almost mechanically, while sipping from a cup half filled with what looked like lukewarm black coffee. These modern mothers, Nefeli thought, they seem to think that the primitive ways of raising children in Africa are the way to do motherhood. How weird! She had observed with disbelief during this week staying with Eleni a few other trendy London mums breastfeeding their children in the fancy cafés near Eleni's house while sipping their coffees and chatting. Breastfeeding was thought of as distasteful, if not shameful, in her young days – certainly not the way to show off one's boobs in posh London cafés.

'Will you take the muffins out of the oven?' Eleni asked her. 'She seems to have an appetite today.'

Nefeli got up and lifted the tray out of the oven, looking for a plate, on which she placed them carefully one by one.

'They look truly delicious!' she commented, feeling some genuine admiration for Eleni's baking ability.

'I am aware that you are leaving in a few hours and that you wanted to talk to me', Eleni offered. 'It might be our only chance, while the baby is so hungry', she added in a lighter tone.

She always had a way of making her feel stressed, Nefeli thought to herself. Just like her father.

'I … I just wanted to tell you that the way you have known things for most of your life is coming to an end. I just wanted to prepare you for the changes that are coming.'

'I guess my father's life is coming to an end.'

'Yes, that as well. But also this messy threesome situation – this is also coming to an end. I can no longer tolerate it, Eleni, so this time round I will truly be the deserting party.'

'Good for you, if you can make that choice', Eleni said, although Nefeli thought that she could hear some irony in her voice.

'You don't believe I can do it, do you?'

'I'm trying not to get irritated, Nefeli, but I am really wondering why you are telling me all this. I'm not your confidante and we are not exactly friends, are we?'

Nefeli felt her pulse quicken. She had not expected such

a reply. She had thought that she had finally caught Eleni in a good mood.

'I am telling you because it is going to affect you. The shop will have to close down and your parents will have to withdraw into their flat. They will be an ordinary retired couple, as they should be at their age.'

'Reality is good, I think', Eleni said in a milder tone.

'And I will no longer be around', Nefeli added.

'Oh! So, where will you be?'

'I don't know. Taking care of myself, trying to have a life for once.'

Eleni appeared lost in her thoughts and then spoke hesitantly. 'I don't mean to sound patronising or discouraging in any way, but I have had many years in therapy and I am now able to recognise things in myself and in other people; I am able to see beneath the surface. The thought I had when you talked to me the other day, the thought that is becoming even stronger now, is that you are really scared of my father dying. You cannot bear to be there and see him die because all your life you were his little girl.'

'No, you were his little girl.'

'Quite! I should be his little girl, because I am his daughter and he is my father!' Eleni said with indignation.

'All I am trying to do, Eleni, is to tell you how much you matter to me, and you are being so hostile, as always', Nefeli said, quietly feeling very close to tears.

'You are trying to tell me you care for me? I have failed to hear that. All I have heard you say is that you are planning to turn my life upside down, now that I have had a new baby and am feeling vulnerable.'

'I think it's best for everyone, Eleni, if reality and order prevail. The reason I am telling you all this is not to upset you – and I'm sorry if I did – but to ask you if I can still be in touch with you after I have left your father.' She swallowed hard and tried to hold her tears in as hard as she could. The sensation was physically painful and her eyes hurt.

'I will have to take some time to think about it, Nefeli', Eleni said quietly.

'But you have to be in my life, you are my daughter', Nefeli said, her voice rising involuntarily.

The baby had finished feeding some time ago now, but Eleni was still holding her in her lap, now asleep, in the breastfeeding position.

'I will think about it, okay?' she repeated after a while, getting up decidedly to mark the end of the conversation.

Layer 5

There's just this for consolation: an hour here or there when our lives seem, against all odds and expectations, to burst open and give us everything we've ever imagined, though everyone but children (and perhaps even they) knows these hours will inevitably be followed by others, far darker and more difficult. Still, we cherish the city, the morning; we hope, more than anything, for more.

Michael Cunningham, *The Hours*

37
Dying

Thessaloniki, 23 March 2009

My dear Eleni,

Please forgive my silence. My life has been rather eventful since I left your home in London about a month ago. I am still thinking of you and little Chloe every day though and I wish you well.

I am writing to fill you in about the latest events, as I would not like you to hear a distorted version of what went on from your parents. You will have heard already that your father and I are closing down the café. This is long overdue, as it was not making a profit for some time now. However, it was not easy to get your father to agree, and once we finalise the closing down I will not be keeping in touch with him any more. Your parents are already in the process of moving all their stuff back to your family flat.

I also wanted to let you know that your father and I had a conversation about splitting up, if you can call it that, and I had the chance to tell him freely my opinion of him and his actions. I know you told me when I was over there that you did not want to hear about my relationship with your father, but I just need to tell you one thing, as it concerns you. When I had the conversation with your father, I told him that it was not only me who thought that he behaved like a bastard, but his own daughter, that you feel the same and you despise him for the way he has treated women. Isn't this true, Eleni? Isn't it high time that he knew the truth? I needed to tell you this, because he may mention it to you, and so it is better if you hear it from me first.

I have one more thing to tell you: a few months ago, I met a very nice man who has shown a real interest in me. He has supported me and stood by me during this difficult time of closing the business down with your father. When you come to Thessaloniki next, I would love to introduce you to him. I am sure that you will like him a lot. And I have some big news for you, Eleni. In the last week, he has proposed to me. Can you believe it? A real marriage proposal! I trust and hope that you will be coming to my wedding, Eleni, when we have a date for it. I know that this may be a lot of change for you to take in at once, but you must agree that it is for the best.

The main reason I am writing to you, though, is to make sure that, now that I am parting ways with your father, you and I can still stay in touch. All my life, I have tried to be part of your life, Eleni. There is not one day that goes by that I do not think about you.

I would like to conclude this letter by stressing the following: you are my daughter, my flesh and blood, and I did everything I could to stay by your side and see you grow up. Doing this took over the last thirty-seven years of my life, Eleni. I will be turning sixty soon, so I may not be around for that long. We should make the best of the time we have left together, Eleni.

Please don't let your parents' manipulation and a misplaced sense of loyalty to Leonora deprive you of the most important relationship in your life, the relationship with your own mother. Now that you have become a mother yourself, you know full well what it takes to give birth to a child. You also know how precious it is to see your daughter grow and develop. Looking forward to speaking to you and seeing you soon.

With my love,

Nefeli

38
Therapy

London, October 1999

They were both sitting down, facing each other at an angle. The box of tissues discreetly placed on the side-table between their chairs looked identical to the one Eleni had so hated when she first came to see Laura just over two years ago. Thankfully, Laura had one of her beautiful flower arrangements sitting next to it, and this made the room feel to Eleni more like the personal space that she had inhabited for the last two years. Her eyes kept focusing on the floor cushion and it felt almost painful to drag them away from it. The minutes on the clock kept ticking by. She was aware of Laura's breathing, her attempt at neutrality, her trying not to prompt her or intervene. Eleni was holding her arms tightly crossed against her stomach, and her legs crossed as well. She was wearing all black today. What other colour could she wear? It was gone ten past, her session was wasting away, she must talk ... Twenty past ...

'I am sorry. I am really tongue-tied today. My mind was bursting with issues on the way here and now it's all gone', she finally said.

'Maybe there is so much feeling that it's hard to put it into words.'

Eleni looked around the room. 'In fact, silence allows me to take the room in, to register the atmosphere here … In case I never come back', she added.

'Does it have to be like this?'

'No, but it may be what I want.' She felt a surge of anger, the first feeling she had experienced after the numbness that had overwhelmed her since she entered the room.

'Okay, but I think it's important to explore what makes you want to leave.'

'People start therapy and they leave therapy. I have been coming here for two years already. I am feeling better. Isn't that a good reason to leave?'

'Yes, but we both know that it is not the reason you are leaving.'

'I told you the reason the other day. Do I need to go into it again?'

'You sound angry', Laura said mildly.

Eleni hesitated, uncrossed her arms and covered her face. 'Look, I'm grateful to you for what you have done for me. I came in a state of soul-destroying obsession and depression and I'm feeling like a free person. I'm so over Yves now. I have been for a long time.'

'But?'

'But … but I suppose I feel that some of the entanglement I came with, the intense feelings I had for Yves without knowing why, were replayed in our relationship.'

'Yes, during the process you developed some very strong

feelings for me; but this is normal in therapy, it's even a sign that it's working.'

'Oh, I see! So you are saying that I was responding as expected! I was a good patient then!'

Laura looked at her intensely and then lowered her gaze. Was she feeling put on the spot or was she getting annoyed with her too? Eleni wondered.

'I don't mean to attack you, but your response just now made me furious', Eleni said in a milder tone. 'You are putting everything on me. I developed these strong feelings, it's all normal and so on. What about you and the role you played in all this?' She crossed her arms again, feeling frustrated now with Laura's continued silence. 'You are not going to help me here, are you?' she finally said in a defeated tone.

'I want to help you.'

'Okay, then you must know what I'm talking about. The thing I found maddening was that you did things here, you said things that were not exactly neutral, they were not to do with your therapist's position. They seemed to have to do with your personal feelings, Laura. Do you see what I mean?'

'Hmm.'

'Well, that was not easy for me. It felt like a crossing of boundaries. It messed me up all over again.'

'I'm sorry if it felt like that to you; however, in the process of therapy, when it is successful, there is always an entanglement, and as long as it is part of the process and it can be worked through, it is okay.'

'Laura, I feel that you are sidestepping the issue. You know how difficult it is for me to talk because I still have these feelings of respect and admiration for you, and I think that may suit you. Let's leave it at that then, shall we? Is it time?'

'Time for what?' Laura said, seeming rather confused.

'Time for me to go.'

'We had discussed having a double session today. You said one was not enough for you to say everything you needed to. Remember?'

'One seems more than enough now.'

'Eleni, I want you to talk, but it needs to come from you. I cannot try to guess what you need to say. It would be yet another intrusion into your space. Don't you think?'

'So you are accepting that there has been an intrusion, right?'

Silence followed. During the silence, Eleni and Laura exchanged glances, taking each other in. At least, this is what Eleni thought that Laura was doing, taking her in, in case she never saw her again. She also thought that she looked sad. Her kind, grass-green eyes were somewhat darker today, opaque.

After a while, Laura said, 'We have to decide either to stop now or to start the second session. I would like us to continue.'

'I'm feeling tired', Eleni mumbled, feeling as though the weight of the world was on her shoulders. 'This is hard work. Therapy is meant to help me get on with my life, but it seems that lately I have been needing energy from my life to deal with my relationship with you.'

'I am sorry to hear that. I think that if you are able to talk today, to name things your way, you may feel less tired and stuck afterwards.'

Eleni took a deep breath in and sighed. 'You did a series of things that I found difficult and intrusive. To start with, I always felt that you were against both my parents. You absolutely loathed my mother and you thought my father was a real bastard, a man who ruined women's lives, that's what you called him right from the beginning. I know that you were trying to help me make sense of my history, but it felt like more than that. And then, you had a lot of sympathy for Nefeli. It was quite clear that you thought that she was the only good guy there. Nefeli and you, the only two people in the world that I should rely on. After a while, it just felt wrong.'

She stopped and looked at Laura, wanting to examine the impact she was having, trying to make sure that she was not being too hurtful, too damaging to her.

'Go on.'

'Well, there was so much more than that. The hugs you gave me, the tears in your eyes. It felt like there was something going on for you.'

'What did the hugs feel like to you?'

'There was a maternal quality, I can see that, but – I don't know how to say this ...'

'Go on.'

'I remember once you put your arms on my sides and looked me straight in the eye. I felt trapped, at your mercy.'

'At my mercy?'

'Yes, like you could do anything you wanted with me ...

to me.'

'I would do something to you?'

'You know what I mean, Laura. I am not saying that you would actually do something, but it was electrifying and it felt unsafe.'

'I see.'

'And then, you tried to turn me against Nicolas as well. You suggested that I split up with him.'

'I thought that there were some issues in your relationship.'

'What do you think the issues are?'

'Those you told me about: that he didn't connect with you, that he is emotionally distant, not really a warm person.'

'He may be all these things, but he is also the only person I want to spend all night with ... When I did what you suggested when I left him, even for a few nights, it felt like one of my limbs was missing.'

'That's what separation feels like.'

'You see, you are doing it again! I don't want to separate from him, I love him.'

'The problem here is, I think,' Laura stopped to clear her throat, 'who I have come to represent for you in our relationship.'

'I am not following.'

'Well, through all my actions and interpretations, I have become in your eyes someone who tries to manipulate you and control you and intrude on your space, someone who is very possessive of you. I have become like your mother.'

'My mother? My mother is not these things.'

'Is she not? Did she not try to turn you against your father when you were little, to dampen your love for him, to make you feel guilty for loving him so much? Did she not try to make you depend only on her?'

Eleni paused. She suddenly felt like a bright new window with a different view had opened in her mind. Laura had never suggested anything like this before.

'I will take you away. You and I alone in the world.' Her mother and her dancing alone in a brightly lit living room, the two of them alone in the house, her mother singing the song, tears running down her cheeks. She must have been five or six. 'I love you, Mummy. Can it be just the two of us? Daddy is bad, let's run away, just the two of us.' The music of the song is playing in her ears.

'Eleni?'

She could just about hear Laura's voice. 'I ... I have gone somewhere, trying to think about what you just said.'

'You have gone somewhere?'

'I was just thinking how much I loved my mother when I was little, and how threatening it was. Maybe some of it has been replayed here.'

'Why was it threatening?'

'At the time, it was not, I guess. It felt like the best thing in the world; but it was all a bubble, a lie.'

'This is difficult stuff. Can you say some more?'

'I feel like I don't want to go there, it's too painful. I think you stirred up this pain of childhood ... the longing ... the fact that I can never have what I want.'

'What is it that you want, Eleni?'

'It's not that, Laura. It is not about what we might want, it is that we can never have it. Suppose when I was little I just wanted to be with my mother all the time. Suppose I wanted to be so special to you that ...'

'That what?'

'I don't know. I can't even visualise what it would be. That you were no longer my therapist, that I was your favourite person in your life.'

'Would you want that?'

'I feel this is what went wrong. You almost made me feel as though I was that special to you. I am dying to know why, but I know that you won't tell me.'

'Let's stay with why you might want to be so special to me, to someone.'

'Don't we all want that?'

'Yes and no. In some ways you were very special to your parents; in some other ways you were not at all.'

'You are constantly taking it away from you and me and how much of what went on between us stirred things up for me the wrong way. I have been sitting here for an hour and a half now, and no genuine exchange has taken place between us', Eleni said angrily. She was feeling tense and stiff and about to burst into tears.

'I want to go now. I am very tired', she added after a while.

'We only have ten minutes left anyway', Laura said. 'What I have been trying to show you is that what has been going on between us, as is always the case in all relationships, is a lot to do with the history of each person involved.'

'So you are saying that you have complicated feelings

for me as well?'

Laura looked at her intensely. 'What I am saying is that you have stirred things up for me, but I am trying to work with these things therapeutically. I am trying to use my feelings to help you explore yours, which is what you are here for.'

'I see, but what if I don't trust that you can control your feelings?'

'Then you will leave with many unresolved issues and you will probably have to go somewhere else to explore what happened here.'

'You mean to another therapist?'

'Possibly. But there is also a chance of trying to work this through together. Think about it, Eleni. Will you?'

They both got up, their eyes focused on the floor. Eleni felt dried up, as though there was no more thought or analysis that her body could bear. She just wanted to go home, take her clothes off and slip her naked body under the cold duvet, spend time in bed doing nothing, stay there until it got dark and Nicolas got home.

39
Separation

Thessaloniki, October 1978

After Leonora hung up, or rather he hung up on her, she walked into the living room, where Eleni was still playing with Lisa, seemingly unperturbed. She was feeling shaken, as though something had changed for ever and it could never be put back together, but she was not sure what it was. She had shocked herself, hearing her calm voice on the phone telling Dinos that he could take all the pills she had left for him and kill himself. Did she really mean it? What if he actually did it? Then it would just be Eleni and her. It wouldn't be that bad, after all. It was not how she had wanted her life to be, but it could well work out better.

'You can go now', she said to Lisa.

'Is everything okay, Mrs Leonora?' asked Lisa, who seemed rather shaken herself.

Leonora absolutely hated it when Dinos gave people material for gossip. 'Everything is fine, Lisa. Dinos just had a little panic attack. We are all fine now.'

'Are we going to lie down for a little rest?' she said to her daughter, who moved manically round the room spreading her dolls around after Lisa had left.

'No, Mummy, let's play. You were late today, so no rest.'

She was right, Leonora thought to herself. It was well past five o'clock.

'Okay, then, it is time for your fruit snack. I will go and prepare it.'

'No, fruit snack today either', Eleni giggled.

Leonora thought that just for today she might let her off the hook. She smiled at her cheekily. 'So,' Leonora said, sitting down, 'Lisa says that you talked to Daddy on the phone and that you were upset by what he told you. What did he say?'

'Daddy said that I should remember he loved me when he is no longer here. He always says that', Eleni replied absentmindedly, piling all her dolls now into a corner of the room.

'Oh! Is that all he said?'

'Yes.'

She could not let it go. Something in her life had changed for ever today, and although she could not put her finger on what it was, she knew it was to do with the life she once thought she had, her life with Dinos. Ever since she could remember, she had craved to be a unit with somebody, just her and that special person, no intrusions. The only way to be special in her childhood was to be helpful, and later on to be in charge, as she was the eldest. Her sisters' arrivals had come one after another with few gaps in between, and although she had established from early on that she was not special to her preoccupied mother, she had also realised that the only way to be special to her struggling father was to be obliging to him. Despite the soft spot she always had for him, being the good girl had never made her feel special enough.

She knew now that the same strategy had not quite worked with Dinos. No matter how self-effacing and helpful she had tried to be, she had never been his only love in the way she had craved. The only creature she had ever been so special to was this child. Despite seeing often enough reflected in the rather sensual features of her daughter's face the passionate, as she had always imagined, union between her husband and Nefeli, this child was now hers and only hers. For all she knew, Dinos could be already lying semi-conscious after swallowing the pills she had left for him, and Nefeli could be already dating her next *amore* in London. For all she knew it could finally be the two of them.

'Come here, I want to talk to you', she said smiling. 'Or rather let's sit by the balcony door.'

This was Eleni's favourite spot. When as a toddler Eleni would be fussy about food and refuse to eat almost anything, Leonora would let her have her food on a tray that she would place on her lap while she sat on her little red chair by the balcony door, watching the world go by. She pulled one of the heavy mahogany dining chairs, chosen of course according to Dinos's extravagant taste, away from the dining table and placed it by the balcony door next to Eleni's little red chair. Eleni sat obediently next to her.

'Mummy wants to tell you something important, Eleni. You know Daddy was upset, because Mummy and Daddy do not always agree about things to do with you.'

'Like what things?'

'Like how to bring you up, and even if Mummy and Daddy should be together.'

'Oh! If you split up, I want to be with you.'

'I know that. Would you mind it if it was just the two of us?

'No!' Eleni said emphatically. And then, after some hesitation, 'But where would Daddy be?'

'I don't know, darling. Is it important to see Daddy?'

'No … it's just that he buys me more ice creams and books than you do. Will you buy me more, if he goes?'

'Of course, I will, my darling.' Leonora smiled.

Eleni got up and started looking for something in her large pile of dolls.

'What are you looking for?'

'My talking doll. I want to see what she will tell me today. Mummy?'

'Yes?'

'Does Daddy make you sad?'

'Sometimes …' What an understatement, Leonora observed silently.

'I was thinking, we could go to London and join Nefeli. He will never find us there.' She was now holding her doll in both arms and she pulled the cord firmly. 'See?' she said, after the doll spoke. 'We can learn English together.'

***

Leonora woke up with a start on hearing the front door shut and heavy steps in the corridor. It took a lot to suppress a scream while her rational mind took over and she thought that whoever had violated their apartment in the middle of the night should not know that she had heard him. Looking around the bed in the dark without knowing what she was looking for, she managed to locate an old wooden curtain rail that had been lying there waiting to be fixed for the last year. She took a peer at Eleni, and was reassured that she was sleeping snugly next to her. She took hold of the curtain rail and, tiptoeing as noiselessly as she could and holding her breath, she crept along the corridor. She could hear her heart pounding in her ears. Then she noticed that the light was on in the kitchen. What on earth was a thief looking for in the kitchen? Holding the rail in front of her, ready to attack, she popped her head through the half-open kitchen door. They both started at seeing each other, and then, to her surprise, they started laughing.

'You gave me a real fright, Dinos', Leonora finally said. 'What are you doing here? What time is it?'

'Nearly one a.m.', Dinos replied, supporting his head with one hand, a cigarette in the other, looking exhausted. 'I drove all the way from Athens. Only one stop for a strong coffee.'

'That's crazy. You could have had an accident.'

'Isn't that what you wanted, me to be killed?'

'No, I said that if that's what you want, it is a valid option after all.'

'I will never forgive you for what you said, Leonora. I was feeling so vulnerable, I could have done it.'

'What is it you want from me, Dinos? I am not stupid. I have gathered that you are so depressed because your mistress has left you.'

'She hasn't quite. You made her leave.'

'Okay. Do you want me to put that right then?'

'Things can no longer be put right, Leonora, I am afraid', Dinos said, sighing.

'Well, as far as I am concerned you two are free to enjoy your love. Just don't ever bring her back to my house again or I will divorce you. And now I am tired. I am going to bed', she added, and walked off.

They slept on opposite sides of their large double bed with their backs turned to each other and Eleni right in the middle. Leonora woke up early as usual, and she was in the kitchen preparing Eleni's milk when she heard giggles coming from the bedroom. When she finally walked into the bedroom, she saw Eleni suspended in the air, her tummy being supported by Dinos's feet, his legs stretching up high.

'Vroom, vroom goes the airplane', he cried between her giggles.

'I'll pick you up from school in my Mercedes today. Okay?' he told Eleni after putting her back down. 'You can have a special ride in the front seat. Eleni squealed in delight, ignoring the bottle of milk that Leonora had placed on her bedside table.

40
The scent of things to come

Thessaloniki, June 1983

'Why did you do it, Eleni?'

'Do what?'

'You know what, the overdose?'

Eleni and Electra were sitting facing each other on a red bench in the park, feet up the bench, legs crossed on the ankle, soles touching, munching on a pack of crisps. They had just split from their mates who had gone on to the larger park across the road to skate, as they both had to be back home within an hour from finishing school. Their skateboards were sitting next to each other under the bench.

'My dad was so upset that he called your mother. They spent an hour talking on the phone. Did you know that?'

'Kind of. My mum said she had had phone calls from parents. She was not happy about that.'

'Your mum is fierce. God, I'm scared of her.'

'My mum, fierce?' Eleni burst out laughing. 'She is the mildest, kindest mum one could ever have. She has never smacked me, not even once.'

'Still, she has her way of being scary. Something about

the look she gives people.'

'The thing is she doesn't like you very much.' Eleni bit her lip. She was often shocked by the candour of her utterances, when she least intended it.

'Oh! Why?'

'She thinks it was your fault that I took the overdose.'

'Do you also think that?'

Eleni could see tears filling Electra's eyes.

'Don't be silly. It's just that I thought we were in it together. It was your idea to take the pills, remember?'

'It never crossed my mind that you were serious about it. It is like when we played that game and we called the spirits. Do you remember that day?'

'Of course I do.'

'Remember when we started calling out to the spirit of the dead and our cup started moving without us touching it?'

'I know!'

'Did you really think that there were dead people in the room moving the cup?'

Eleni shrugged her shoulders, munching on. 'I don't know what I thought. It was exciting and scary.'

'I know! Do you remember when the cup started going to letters and forming words?'

'Yeah! That was very scary to start with, but after a while I lost interest, I did not believe it any more. Was it you moving it?'

Electra smiled cheekily.

'It was you, wasn't it? You are quite something!'

'Only towards the end. I thought it might be fun to get a few words from the spirits. The cup was moving before though, and I was not pushing it, at least not on purpose.'

'So, you might have been pushing it a little bit?'

'We were pushing it together Eleni, don't you think? We were in it together and it was dramatic and exciting and fun. I thought we could do something like that with the overdose. Have a bit of drama together.'

'Taking an overdose is not that fun, believe me', Eleni said solemnly. 'You should have been there when I drank the milk. It was disgusting!'

They both giggled.

'I kept calling you and you weren't picking up. I wanted to see if you were all right. I wanted to see if you needed to go to hospital. You were not picking up and I panicked, I thought something happened to you. Then I started calling people from our class. I called my parents too. I thought we should alert someone to save you.'

'Do you want a "Kiss"?' Eleni said, pulling out of her pocket a long thin bar of chocolate in a pink shiny wrapper. 'I finished all my crisps and I'm still hungry. My dad is cooking today so I am avoiding food at home.'

They both giggled again in conspiracy.

'Is your dad a bad cook?'

'No, he is supposed to be the best. It's just that I don't like his food. He never asks me what I want. Anyway, I must head home soon. When he is there waiting for me, he counts the minutes.'

'Did you really want to die?' Electra interrupted.

'What? No! Oh, God no!'

'So why did you take them?'

Eleni shrugged her shoulders. 'I don't know.'

For a while they kept munching on the chocolate, looking around at the younger children playing nearby, yelling at the top of their voices. A delicious smell travelled to them from the taverna across the street. It was full of locals drinking retsina and dipping their bread on little meze plates. Their laughter and banter was like background music to their conversation.

'That smell makes me hungry', Electra said.

Eleni kept looking towards the taverna. 'I was very sad just before taking the pills', she said quietly. 'That song made me so sad that I could not bear it.'

'I was sad too, but I did not want to die.'

'It's funny. I didn't think I did either, but when I got hold of the strange neurological pills, death was listed as a rare side effect and there was a long moment when I thought very seriously about taking them. I could imagine putting them in my mouth and swallowing; but then I got too scared.'

'God, you make me scared, Eleni.'

'My mum said, if I had taken those I would have been dead now. She has put a big lock on the medicine cabinet and I cannot even get hold of my favourite cough syrup.'

'Good! Cough syrup is yucky!'

They laughed and Eleni felt lighter. They got up and started skating slowly side by side.

'Do you still sing that song?' her friend asked.

'No, not since that day.'

'Sometimes I sing it in the bath and it still makes me cry. It's so strange!'

They sped up and skated past a few pedestrians. An old lady with a tiny dog gave them a nasty look.

'Be mindful of the pedestrians, young girls!' she shrieked.

They stopped when they reached Electra's flat. How strange, Eleni thought, Electra has never invited me in. It was either Eleni's place or the park.

'Does your mum know about how sad the song makes you?' she asked her.

'My mum knows nothing about me, we hardly talk. That's why I think the song makes me sad. It's about the mum I always imagined I should have.'

'Oh!' Eleni said. 'I hardly ever see your mum around, only your dad.'

'Yeah, my dad is my favourite. But sometimes, I miss having a mum who is lovely and caring like he is.'

'My dad is not my favourite', Eleni said … 'I must go. He will be there looking at his watch saying, "You are late, Eleni"', she said in a very thick voice. They both laughed and hugged goodbye.

'No more sad thoughts, huh?' Electra winked as she skated away.

41
Sweet adolescence

Thessaloniki, April 1986

He drained all the liquid from his Greek coffee cup with a noisy gulp. He lifted the cup with his right hand and he looked at the thick coffee mud gathering at the bottom, as though it was a specimen. With a decisive gesture, he swirled the mud around and turned the little cup upside down, pouring the thick liquid into the saucer and eventually placing the cup upside down on a square plain napkin to let it dry. He loved to look at the intriguing shapes gathering in the cup, at moments of low mood like today, and to imagine for a moment that he could see his future clearly pictured there. Sometimes, he found himself lost in the shapes appearing in the cup: little clouds, sheep, snakes and snaky roads. Occasionally, even a little heart shape would form, and the search for someone's initial next to the heart would always lift his mood.

Eleni walked in hesitantly and looked at him anxiously, as though preparing for a swift exit.

'Welcome, my little swan with the proud neck'[['Καλώς τήνα την πέρδικα που περπατάει λεβέντικα', είναι το απόφθεγμα που εννοώ εδώ, Χρύσα.]], he said smiling. 'Sit down. Do you want something to eat?'

'Dad, every time you see me, you ask me if I want something to eat. I have put on weight. Haven't you noticed?'

'I'm afraid extra weight runs in our genes, my love.'

'No. it runs in eating too much and, in my particular case, in having stopped exercising. You must be glad about it. That's what you always wanted me to do, isn't it?' she said grumpily.

By the sound of it, Dinos thought, she was not in any better mood than him. She never was lately. She was always irritable and grumpy, ready to pick up an argument, especially with him. Whatever happened to his little girl? He had to make an effort to talk to her. He had promised Leonora to do it, and as much as he didn't feel like it, now seemed like a good moment. *Carpe diem*, as the Romans said.

'Sit down, Eleni, will you? I want to talk to you', he said to his daughter, who was still standing up stubbornly by the kitchen table.

'I just came in to take a glass of water really. I didn't know that you were here.'

'I don't bite, you know.'

'Sometimes you do', she said, giving him a sideways look and pulling up a chair to sit wearily on its edge, almost at the other end of the round Formica kitchen table.

'I am still thinking about your birthday. Maybe we should throw a late party for it. With my illness and everything, it did not turn out to be the most spectacular of birthdays, did it? Just taking Lea out for pizza and cake, not like the parties

I used to throw for you.'

'Dad, that was ages ago, at primary school.'

'Well, you haven't wanted to have a big one since joining secondary.'

'That's because I don't like anyone there other than Lea.'

'It's a lovely school, Eleni. I don't know why you have taken it so much the wrong way.'

'I am not going to answer that: it will lead to an argument. You know it was not exactly my choice to go there. Anyway, it was not just your heart attack around my birthday this year. You and Mummy did your best to spoil my birthday before that.'

'Me? What did I do?'

'You know exactly what I mean, Dad!' she said in an exasperated tone.

'No, I don't. I don't agree with what your mother did, talking to you about your birth, if that is what you are referring to.'

'You don't think that she should have told me? Hasn't the lying gone far enough?'

'I don't think that you are at the right age for her to tell you. Besides, you always knew.'

'What do you mean I always knew?'

'You are a bright girl, Eleni. How could you not have known who your mother was? It was always so obvious.'

'I always knew that Leonora was my mother. That was what I was always told.'

'You know what I mean, Eleni: your birth mother. Don't play games with me', he said, trying hard to control his rising irritation.

'I don't play games with you. You do!' Eleni shouted.

'I am trying not to have a fight with you, Eleni. Really, what is it that makes you want to pick fights with me all the time? You know damn well that I love you more than anything else in the world. Don't you?'

'No, you don't!'

'Yes, I do, and you know it. I have told you so since you were as little as a teddy bear.'

'You don't even know me, Daddy. I am a stranger to you', she said in a shaky voice. Dinos thought that she was about to burst into tears. Oh, dear! Talking to her would not be easy!

'Don't be silly, Eleni. I think you have been reading too many gloomy books lately. You are right, you should go out and exercise more. You used to love that skateboard of yours. Whatever happened to it?'

Eleni managed a half smile, a rare sight these days. 'Anyway, I thought you wanted to talk to me about something. I am in the middle of a very interesting book and I need to get back to it', she said in a softer tone. She now managed a full wry smile.

'What is it about? Don't tell me – something dreadful again!'

'Jean-Paul Sartre. Do you know him?'

'Yes, of course', he replied, feeling anxious in case more questions came his way. His prematurely interrupted education had always been his Achilles heel. The last thing he wanted was to feel embarrassed in front of his daughter, who was fast becoming very bookish and sophisticated.

'What is it about?' he dared to ask, being aware of postponing the conversation he needed to have with her.

'It's called *Nausea*. It's all about the dreadfulness of the human condition.'

He shook his head to show his distaste.

'Now, is this appropriate reading for a fourteen-year-old? Should you not be reading something cheerful to lift your spirits? It's no wonder you are always grumpy!'

Eleni covered her face to conceal what appeared to be a schoolgirl's nervous laughter. After a while, when the hysterics started to die down, she said with eyes that were wet from laughing, 'You are not exactly into philosophy, Dad. Are you?'

He tried to ignore the condescension in her voice.

'No, I am not. Life is for living.'

'But maybe people like to live their lives in different ways. You are not good at seeing how different we are, Dad.'

'We are not as different as you like to think, Eleni. Anyway, if you want to talk philosophy, your granddad would be more than happy to spend hours talking to you. He is a gloomy book-reader like you. You are his favourite, you know. The other day he was telling me how he wants to hand you down your great-grandmother's poetry.'

'Yes, I would love to have it. She is the one person in the family I always wanted to meet and she died before I was born. How unlucky!'

'Even I didn't get to meet her, Eleni. She died young. But I think you are right, you would have liked each other.

Granddad says you are just like her. I just hope not as mad as her. She was known for throwing food out of the window and yelling at the top of her voice. Everyone in the village could hear her.'

Eleni laughed with delight.

'It's good to see you laugh, Eleni. I haven't seen a smile on your face for some time now. Listen, do you want to know who your birth mother is?'

'Of course, I do', she said rather abruptly, all traces of her laughter having quickly deserted her face.

'It's Nefeli.'

'What? Nefeli?' She seemed shocked. 'You don't do long speeches, do you?'

'Not for something that is blatantly obvious.'

'Stop saying that!' she yelled, and got quickly up.

'Please don't leave, Eleni. We haven't finished talking.'

'You and Mum and Nefeli, you are all perverts, I hope you know that!' she yelled again, and she left, slamming the kitchen door behind her.

He lit a cigarette and picked up the cup to examine it. How handy for Leonora to be taking an extra-long siesta, he thought to himself. When she came back from work, she said that she had a headache and needed to lie down in a dark room. Her siestas were getting longer and longer. During the short winter days, it would already be pitch dark when she woke up from one after coming back from work.

He sighed. What a pity! It had almost felt like he was having an enjoyable conversation with his daughter after such a long time, just before she had stomped out, slamming the door behind her. Of all the business plans and creative ideas he had had over the years, having his daughter was the one plan that had gone well. Yet the degree of blame and attack he had received for it was endless. And now Eleni had probably joined the crowd of women attacking him for what he had done.

Obviously, everyone, even he, would have preferred a child in less complicated circumstances. Who knows, if that first child Leonora had conceived had not been aborted, maybe the two of them would have had a completely different life: two children, a family car, a countryside house, the typical life of the Greek middle classes. The reality though was that such a life would never suit him. He could never imagine himself settling for monogamous, suburban smugness, being the routine-loving breadwinner Leonora had always wanted him to be. But who knows, if that first child had been born, maybe he would have turned into a proper family man of the ordinary kind. Or would he?

In his thirties he was at his most popular. He had money, looks and charm. Women were queuing for a date with him, even for a night with him. It would have been so easy to find someone else to have his children with. Would this have made him a better man? Abandoning his infertile wife to have children with a better catch? Yet he knew that it was not exactly out of charity, nor out of love, that he had chosen to stay with Leonora. He had never felt secure without her. Over the years, she had become the one person in his life he could always fall back on. How many people like that does one encounter in one's life? And when you do, is it wise to let go of them? In some of the nasty arguments they had had over the years, Leonora had attacked him for his need of her.

'You only stay with me because you weren't mothered as a child', she had said to him in her usual coldly curt way. 'I am not your mother though. I am your wife and I am sick and tired of being treated like someone to dump all your difficulties on while you are choosing some more exciting company to have fun with.'

He didn't notice at first the kitchen door opening quietly. Eleni poked her head in and then hesitantly came in to stand warily by the door.

'You are back', he said, slightly startled. 'That's good. Have a seat.' Eleni sat grumpily, supporting her chin on her hands, her elbows placed on the table. It was obvious from her red eyes and swollen face that she had been crying.

'Aren't you glad that Nefeli is your birth mother rather than some unknown person you could never have access to?' he dared to ask.

'I don't want anyone other than Leonora to be my mother', she said in a voice hoarse from crying.

'Leonora is your mother, Eleni.'

'You are right though. I have been pretty stupid not to have known. Almost every time I go out with Nefeli, people comment on how similar we look. Usually they think she is my older sister though. Isn't she young to be my mother?'

'She was only twenty when she gave birth to you, and a young twenty as it were.' He paused and then said hesitantly, 'Nefeli is a good person, Eleni, and she's been around you all your life. It's like having two mothers really, even better than having one.'

'Don't give me this bullshit or I'm going to leave again!' Eleni cried.

He felt his blood pumping inside his head. Maybe teenagers should still be disciplined with some good old-fashioned smacking. This girl could certainly do with some.

'Stop swearing at once! There are rules in this house, remember?' he said to her, his voice giving her a firm warning about the limits of his patience.

'Anyway, I'm only back to ask you why you couldn't choose one wife but had to have two. If Nefeli is my birth mother, why did you have to keep her as your girlfriend as well? Don't you have enough of those?'

'I don't like the tone of your question, Eleni', he grunted. Where the hell was Leonora? It was nearly seven o'clock.

'My question is valid though. Isn't it that in adoption cases, the birth mother doesn't usually hang around, and certainly not as the father's girlfriend?'

He suddenly realised how frazzled and close to tears he had been, even before he had got into this gruelling dialogue with Eleni. What a mistake, to have started the conversation in the first place. Leonora should have taken the brunt of it, she was the one who had chosen to disclose.

'You are not adopted, Eleni', he said, trying to be patient. 'You are my daughter. I made sure that Nefeli stayed around for your own good. I wanted her to be available to you when you needed her. It was you that I was thinking about all along, if you want to know.'

'Don't give me that, Dad. Did you even ask me if I even

wanted to be alive, to be born? All you can ever think about is what you want. Did you have any idea when you conceived your brilliant plan how messed up it would make me feel?'

He was past the point of no return now. He had lost his cool.

'What more do you want from me, Eleni?' he shouted. 'I made sure that you always had the best and I brought you up and cared for you. Two mothers are better than none. That is what you would have had if you had stayed with Nefeli: no mother! Stop being ungrateful', he yelled at the top of his voice.

Eleni was staring at him without speaking. Tears started flowing, one by one, and before he knew it he was sobbing like a small child.

'I took everything on my back, everything!' he cried between sobs.

Eleni sat very still and upright, tears rolling quietly down her cheeks, arms crossed tightly against her ribs. Leonora entered the kitchen, seeming freshly woken up and startled.

'What's happening? What are these shouts?' she asked. 'Why are you crying, Eleni? Dinos? God! You two are like little children. One cannot leave you in a room together for more than five minutes or you start going for each other's throat!'

'Why don't you go back to your siesta, Mum?' Eleni said bitterly. 'It's only four hours since you started your afternoon nap. Clearly not enough for you. Go back to it!'

'Stop being rude to your mother, Eleni', Dinos said. 'She has not been feeling well. She had a headache. Stop being rude to everyone in this family!'

Eleni got up and walked out of the kitchen, this time quietly but firmly.

42
The encounter

London, May 2010

Eleni rang the bell of his east London studio. In her brief walk from Old Street Tube, it felt like she was on a roller-coaster, her stomach jumping and her heart skipping. She had spent weeks handling the business card Martin Wheel had given her with his work telephone number inscribed at the bottom right-hand corner, taking it out of her purse to look at it for a few seconds and then quickly putting it back in. She had finally dialled the number. He gave her an appointment in two weeks' time. He did not seem in a hurry to meet her after all.

She was breathless when she reached the top of the two flights of stairs to his studio, her pulse loud in her ears as she was going up. They nodded at each other, exchanging a short glance, and she was led to one end of a burnt-orange leather corner-sofa beside the large loft window overlooking the square. The room was filled with light despite the white cloud that covered the city. He focused his gaze outside the window, as though he had not seen the view before, and Eleni found herself following his example and directing her gaze on the urban landscape in the square. Through her peripheral vision, she could sense an array of books and unfinished works of art scattered around the room. Under normal circumstances, she would have been interested in allowing her eyes to wander around such a beautiful studio, but for now they were fixated on the expanse outside his window.

'Isn't it a cliché to have a loft in Hoxton Square?' she heard herself saying. She bit her lower lip. Why was she being sarcastic?

'Well, when I got my studio here twenty years ago the area was really run down and not trendy at all. It's rather sad that it's become the Mecca for wannabe artists', he replied non-defensively.

'I am probably just jealous. I love the area, and your studio', Eleni said, trying to repair the damage. 'I'm not quite clear why I'm here though', she added. 'Is this a session?'

He leant forward and as he moved a tiny whiff of a discreet male scent travelled her way. 'It can be what you want it to be', he said, focusing his eyes on her this time.

'Still not clear, sorry.'

'I'll try to keep it simple. Last time you came to my workshop, I was struck by your artwork and the dream material you brought.'

'Thank you.'

'I thought that you were a therapist with years of experience, but you told me that you were not.'

'No, I'm not.'

'Have you ever been in therapy?'

'Yes, for quite a few years.'

'I see', he said, and pulled slightly back. He hesitated. 'You're right. We need to clarify what you are here for today. In the second workshop you attended, there was all this creative material pouring out of you, but it was also clear that you were in difficult circumstances. Your father was on the verge of dying, right? Has he passed away now?'

'Yes', she nodded.

'That must be difficult', he said leaning forward. 'Do you think therapy is what you need at the moment?'

'If you thought I needed therapy, surely you would not have invited me here to suggest I have some with you', Eleni said in a low but steady voice.

'Quite', Martin replied.

Eleni felt his gaze burning her. 'So you haven't invited me here for therapy. What am I here for then?'

'Look, it's not customary for me to invite people to my studio', Martin said. It's usually others who seek me out. The reason I invited you here today is that I have felt this intense connection with your artwork and with you. I'm not sure why or what it means, but I am old enough to know that it happens rarely in life to feel so moved by somebody, and that when it happens one needs to cherish it.'

Before she knew it, Eleni was in tears, big sobs shaking her body, floods of warm salty liquid running down her face and onto her clothes. He got up and brought her a box of tissues, discreetly leaving it next to her on the sofa. Eleni blew her nose and cleared her throat.

'I'm sorry', she said quietly. 'I don't know what's got into me'.

'You must have been through a lot. Perhaps my timing was out to suggest that you come here so soon after your father's death.'

'It's not that, it's what you just said. This strong connection, I felt it so clearly the moment we crossed paths. What are we to do with such connections? Do they mean anything, or are they just a fantasy?'

'My philosophy in life is that we need to cherish our connections with other people, whatever these connections are.'

'But what can we do with connections with people we can never be with?' Eleni asked, thinking aloud. Tears started running down her cheeks again and she covered her face. 'Maybe I should go', she said between her fingers. 'I'm over-emotional today.'

'Come here, will you?'

They both shuffled up the sofa towards each other. He put his arms over her shoulders. Their hips touched. A rush of intense heat ran down Eleni's body. Like a déjà vu, she remembered that the only other time she had felt such maddening intensity was when she was first dating Nicolas. *I will not be able to resist him. I will not be able to resist him,* the thought sounded loudly inside her head. She opened her mouth to talk, but he lightly placed his finger on her lips.

'Sshh, don't talk', he murmured.

With one hand he now very gently stroked her hair, picking up small locks and letting them fall again to the sides of her face. Eleni felt her breath had been cut away. Slowly her panic subsided, his stillness next to her reassuring her he was not about to make a sexual move. He smelt like a dampened piece of wood on a clear winter's day in the park. She inhaled deeply. When it came to sexual attraction, smell was all that mattered, she thought to herself. Slowly and gently she moved her body away from his. He let go of her. They now sat a cushion apart from each other on the sofa.

'You have beautiful hair', he murmured.

'You remind me of my ex-therapist', she said in a hoarse voice. 'She also used to touch me as though I was a little girl.'

'I'm not your therapist, Eleni. I thought I made that clear', he said sharply.

Their eyes met. His eyes were moist and shiny. She could see desire in them.

'And I am not a little girl. Being touched like that turns me on.'

'But you are not ready to make love, are you?'

'No', she said, looking down, suddenly feeling as though she would start crying again.

'I thought as much. Sometimes there is this connection between people. I just wanted to show you how I felt. That's all.'

'I need to go now', Eleni said.

'Take care', he said as he accompanied her to the door. As she was going out, he patted her lightly on her lower back and she felt his hand linger.

She turned abruptly, stepping back – two feet of distance, that's what they needed or else they would be kissing in seconds.

'Martin ...'

'Yes, Eleni ...'

'It is not just our connections with people we need to cherish, is it? It's always more complicated than that.'

'Is it?'

'Yes, what about our attachments, or others being attached to us. What are we to do with all of that? What about commitment and responsibility?'

'All I can say is, it is our connection that brought you here today.'

'Yes, I can see that.'

'Let me know when you are ready for us, Eleni.'

'By when?'

'By when?'

'Yes, give me a deadline. Sometimes I need a deadline or else I put things off indefinitely.'

'Well, I am going to do some travelling in the autumn, September time. I need some space, some fresh inspiration for my art. I will not be around for a couple of months. Let's say I may change my mind, if I hear from you before then.'

'Thank you, that's helpful. Goodbye, Martin', she said, turning again. She could feel his gaze burning her back as she started walking down the stairs.

43
Birth

Thessaloniki, April 1972

Dinos left her at the crossroads, just before the square red-soiled alley which her family's second-floor flat overlooked. It was the closest he could get without becoming visible from the balcony, where no doubt her mother would be sitting inspecting the late-morning happenings in the neighbourhood. By this time the lorry drivers had usually left for their next shift and the pre-school children would be out in the alley, their shrieks and giggles rising high in the air.

Nefeli looked at the alley, almost as if wanting to verify the landscape she was expecting; but whatever was there, she did not take it in. All she knew was that everything looked so familiar and so alien at the same time. She was almost dragging her suitcase across the alley. It was so heavy that she had to stop every ten metres, drop it and, after taking a deep breath in, lift it again with her other arm. He had offered of course to drop her by the building's entrance, but she was too scared that she would be seen. It was not as much the danger that she would be seen in the car with an older man, she did not care about that, not any more, but there was a baby in the car. How would she ever explain that? Imagine one of the neighbours peering into the car, saying, 'Hello, Nefeli', and then noticing that she was sitting next to a baby basket with a baby in it. On closer inspection, they would see that she was holding the sleeping baby's hand in her hand and that tears were running down her face. How would she ever explain that?

How weird it was, this morning, when they went to the registry office and she found herself signing to confirm that she was indeed Eleni's mother, who was now a Greek citizen. She wasn't quite expecting that, she had to say. She thought she would put her signature under a paragraph declaring that she was no longer her mother and could never be her mother again. But no, she was now officially the baby's mother in Greece, her own country; and yet, six hours later, she was giving the baby over for ever.

'This is just the first stage of the adoption process, Nefeli', Dinos had grunted between his teeth when she had dared to ask him. 'All the documents are ready. All just stages you need to follow, things you don't understand, legal things. You already declared in England when she was born that you were giving the baby over for adoption, remember?'

Of course she knew this moment would come, but now that she was walking back home, just as though she was coming back from a school trip, she knew something had changed. The smell of powdered formula and green soap-washed nappies was all over her, and the warmth of holding the baby in her lap had not yet deserted her body.

The moment she reached the building's entrance hall,

she disposed of her suitcase, just by the front door. She did not care if it had been stolen by the time somebody came downstairs to fetch it. She could not carry it a moment longer. She let herself in the flat as quietly as she could. She was hoping that nobody was in, which would give her some time to get her bearings. She almost let out a scream on seeing her mother sitting in the armchair across from the TV in the living room. The flat gave off its familiar smell of enclosed space that had not been aired enough, and of chlorine solution, her mother's favourite cleaning product.

'Why did you not call us to get you from the airport, Nefeli?' she asked without getting up to greet her. 'Where is your luggage?'

'I left it downstairs. It was too heavy to carry.' she mumbled. 'I didn't want to bother you. I knew that father would be at work. It was just easier to get a taxi.' She was still standing by the doorway, frozen, far away from her mother. 'Won't you get up to greet me?' she said after a while in a shaky voice. 'It is nearly a year since I was last here.'

'You had better come and sit down here. We have lots to talk about.'

'I am just worried about my suitcase.'

'Your suitcase will be fine. Nobody is in at this time of day. Anything important in there?'

'Well, yes, some presents of course, for you and Dad and my sister, and quite a few new things for me too. London's shopping scene is so exciting.'

'No baby in there, I hope?

'What?' she said, and she felt the tiredness and the sleeplessness of last night hit her like an electric shock.

'Come and sit down, Nefeli. You are standing there as though you are about to be beaten up. You have put on weight though, in your midriff, I can see that.'

'Mrs Marika has spoilt me rotten.' She walked cautiously in and sat on the edge of the fluffy beige sofa as far away from her mother as she possibly could. God, she had almost forgotten how much she loathed her.

'So where did you find the money to buy us all these presents, huh?'

'Mrs Marika was very kind –' she started saying, but her mother interrupted.

'Mrs Marika is a very kind person, but she doesn't have any extra cash to give to you to buy us presents. She has four sons to raise. Putting you up was more than enough, with all the burden you placed on her.'

'Stop interrogating me or I will just go back where I came from!' Nefeli shouted, gradually feeling the numbness subsiding and rage rising rapidly to her head. 'I was working before I left for London, remember? I had a very generous salary. Stop being jealous of me and what I have. That's what you have done all my life.'

'Who, me, jealous of you? I feel sorry for you, and for myself for having you as a daughter. You have disgraced us, Nefeli. Having a baby with an older man and then giving it away as though it is a kind of puppy. Not even bitches do that.'

'What?' she said voicelessly. Her cheeks were burning badly. She had now just received the blow she was expecting since she walked in. 'Mrs Marika told you? I didn't expect her to –'

'Of course she did. The poor woman! You put her in such a difficult position. You stressed her out beyond belief. You got her to believe that, poor you, you were not getting along with me and if she did the honourable thing and told me, you would disappear into thin air. Little did she know that you were taking advantage of her all along.'

'I wasn't lying to her, we never got on.'

'You never got on with me, Nefeli, although I always gave you the best. I worked my backsideoff to raise you.'

'How? By spending all morning in your negligée chatting the lorry drivers up?'

There was a silence for a minute that felt like the silence preceding a murder in a cinematic thriller.

'It's a good thing that since Mrs Marika talked to me two days ago, I have been experiencing the most severe back pain that forces me to stay still for most of the day,' her mother said eventually, 'otherwise I would have got up and given you the slap you deserve. You have always fabricated things about me. You were the one who was jealous. What lorry drivers, huh? I worked for long hours in back-killing jobs until the factory closed down. And then I took up sewing at home to be around you and your sister when you were both little. I worked so much that my eyes and hands started to give up. The chatting-up of the lorry drivers was me walking to the balcony to get some fresh air. It was not my fault that they were hanging out there and I was a beautiful woman.'

Nefeli was sitting silently with her head hanging forward between her shoulders.

'Does Dad know too?' she said after a while.

'Of course he does. I could not keep such a thing from him.'

'Poor Daddy, having you as a wife and me as his daughter.' She covered her face and burst into tears, a welcome release of the tension within.

'That was always your problem, wasn't it? Your daddy deserved better than me. Your father and I loved each other. It's time that you get your head round that.'

'I am tired. I will go to bed', Nefeli said getting up.

'What are we going to do, Nefeli? What are we going to do about the baby?'

'There is nothing to "do". She has been adopted', she said quietly, her eyes like glass staring at the void. She was near the living-room door when her mother said:

'We could have her here. I have been thinking about it. We could keep it quiet for a bit, and then say that I had the baby. That is technically possible still, you know. I will talk to your dad. I am sure I can get his head round it.'

'No', Nefeli said, still as a statue. 'I don't want you to raise my baby. She is better off where she is going. Besides, it is all done and dusted, and legally binding.' She walked off before her mother had the chance to reply.

To her surprise, she found her bed nicely made with the embroidered sheets with her initials on, which her mother had put aside for her 'dowry', and a clean, ironed nightie waiting for her on her pillowcase. She took her clothes off and put her nightie on. The moment she lay in bed, her body felt stiff and heavy as iron, and within minutes she had fallen into a deep and dreamless sleep.

She woke up with a start, searching in the dark. The void next to her bed struck her. It felt like an abyss. Where was she? Where was the baby? Then she heard the knock at the door, and realised that the tapping noise had been there when she woke up. Her mother popped in.

'It is well past lunch time, you need to eat something. I came in earlier and you were asleep. Also, your father is here. He wants to see you.' She paused and looked at her. 'Are you all right?'

Nefeli could not speak. The nausea was overwhelming and the buzzing in her head deafening. She went past her mother, standing by the doorway, and rushed to the toilet, but before she had time to reach it there was a huge release, her stomach's contents spilling out of her mouth.

'I am sorry,' she said, 'I will clear it all up, I am sorry', not knowing who she was talking to. Instead, she sat on the cold, slate corridor floor, holding her knees to her chest and weeping uncontrollably. Her father, a tall and slender figure, emerged from the living room and lifted her back onto her feet, holding her gently by the shoulders.

'Go to bed, Nefeli', he said. 'You are feeling sick.'

Her father's presence felt like the first soothing experience since she had started to have the contractions on a cold February night. He helped her into her bedroom and tucked her in.

The next time she woke up, her mother was sitting by

her bedside and the warm smell of chicken soup was filling the room.

'What time is it?' she asked.

'Nine p.m. Are you a bit hungry now?'

'I suppose.'

Her mother stayed, watching her eat the soup. Nefeli felt grateful for her silence. When she had finished eating, she said, 'Do you know about Anthony, Nefeli?'

'Who is Anthony?'

'Anthony is the baby I lost, just before having you.'

'Mother, don't start again, please!'

'I just want to tell you one thing, just one. I was about six months pregnant when I went into labour, and he was born still as a statue. A beautiful baby boy, I will never forget his face. Nefeli, please don't lose touch with your baby. Losing your baby is like losing yourself.'

Nefeli kept staring at her, her eyes feeling as though they were made out of glass that would break if moved.

44
The beginnings

Thessaloniki, May 1972

Leonora's steps took her to the hospital.

'You are back, Mrs Hatzi, at last', the porter exclaimed. They always had a good rapport, the two of them. He often gave her sneaky lifts home when it was too hot or too cold to walk back pleasantly, leaving temporarily the boy from the canteen to watch over the hospital's entrance. She had also used him occasionally as a handyman, given Dinos's inability to fix anything in the flat. She had always tipped him well, despite his insistence that he did not want any money from her.

'Not quite, Christo. I am not quite back yet', she mumbled, and she proceeded quickly before he had time to ask her any more questions. Her legs were driving and she was merely following. She went past the hospital's lower garden across from the canteen, with the red benches under the shadow of the birch tree, almost always occupied by some of the outpatients or their relatives, munching on something from the canteen and smoking. As she was walking on the main hospital driveway leading up to the old hospital building overlooking the town and the sea, going past the newer outpatients' building, she realised, even in her agitated state, that she would soon be seen by some of the staff, and questions would follow.

It suddenly hit her how much she had missed her job. The real advantage of working in what was called by locals 'the Turkish forest hospital' was how beautiful the surroundings were. The hospital probably had the largest and most luscious gardens in the city, leading up to the pine forest which surrounded its grounds. When sitting on the outdoor benches among birch trees and blossom on a spring day, one could see clearly the city's most well-known landmark, the White Tower, and beside it, the blue and silver dazzle of Thermaikos Gulf.

Leonora could remember falling in love with the place when she had first started there as a junior doctor. She had settled quickly and had soon enough stopped caring that it was not the city's top research hospital. In fact, for the first few years and before she got married to Dinos, she had lived in one of the forest cabins behind the hospital that were provided for free to the hospital's single female staff.

Soon after she had moved out to live with Dinos in their first marital home, there had been some very dark moments at the hospital. A serial killer had struck the city. The crimes had started in the forest just behind the hospital, as it attracted young couples who would find a place to make love down one of the steep dirt roads deep in the forest late in the evening. His first attack was on one such couple, who had been found dead at the side of their car, the woman having been raped. Panic and dread had spread through the hospital. Female employees doing late shifts were advised not to walk home alone.

On top of that, there were rumours flying around that the serial killer was one of the doctors at the hospital, as whoever was committing the murders clearly knew a lot about human anatomy. Fear and suspicion spread around the wards. Then there were sightings of a lone man walking around the forest cabins where young nurses lived. Two of the nurses reported that they had seen the shadow of a man outside their cabin at night, and it was only after switching on all the lights and talking loudly that he had eventually run away.

And then it happened. Leonora was nearing the end of her evening shift one day when she heard that there had been an incident in one of the cabins. She offered to go and help, and she joined the group of male staff who made their way there, to find a couple of nurses outside one of the cabins in a state of extreme hysteria. They had seen a man leaving the cabin, running up the hill. One woman who lived in the cabin had gone and knocked on the door, but there was no reply from her roommate. They had not dared to go in and they had alerted a passer-by for help.

When security finally arrived and they opened the door, the sight they confronted haunted Leonora to this day. She would still from time to time get a flashback of the scene which would make her blood freeze and bathe her body in cold sweat. There were bloody footsteps all over the cabin; the walls were smeared with blood too. As they slowly walked in, they saw the young womam sitting on the floor, her body leaning against the wall, squashed by the side of her bed. Her eyes and mouth were wide open, her eyes frozen in an expression of utter terror, brains and blood leaking out of her head. It was the first time since she had finished her medical degree that Leonora had fainted – to her great embarrassment when she came round, as a couple of staff had had to get busy with her instead and help her recover.

Feeling strongly that she wanted to help, she had offered to interview potential suspects in the psychiatry clinic along with a male colleague. That was when the nightmares started. Men chasing her in the street trying to rape her, her legs turning to jelly and being unable to run away; a man lying on her, heavy on her chest, his foul breathing blowing into her mouth.

She went off Dinos almost completely. Sex was not exactly her priority – but also, if she was honest, they were fundamentally different in this area. She was quite scientific and rational about it. Sex was really a primal instinct, one of those remaining active in humans. When she saw the trouble it created, not just extreme incidents like sex crime, but much more ordinary ones like affairs, broken hearts, unwanted pregnancies, surely any civilised human would have to wonder whether it was all worth it. Dinos of course, would see the whole thing very differently: it was all about savouring, taking one's time, treasuring and indulging in it. Sex and food were his true loves.

There was a time that sex was intense and wild between

them, when they were both like adolescents. And the result, a baby killed through abortion. She would never forgive herself for such stupidity and the infertility it left her with as a life sentence. As for Dinos, his sexual urges became more and more distasteful to her, salivating after increasingly younger women, following faithfully in the footsteps of his father. He had rather surprised her by never fighting his corner about the quick, quiet burial of their sex life. All that sex reminded her of now was serial killers and dead babies and Dinos's infidelities. Surely their relationship was more dignified without it.

She took a sharp left just past the outpatients' building in good time to avoid colliding with a small group of white-collar junior doctors walking towards the hospital exit. She was now on a tarmac road that even in the middle of a bright and sunny spring afternoon seemed insufficiently lit. On both sides there were ugly, badly built storage sheds. This road was hardly ever used by the hospital's medical staff. It was usually the cleaners, builders and other technical staff that came this way to fetch equipment from the storage rooms. She knew exactly where the road led, and despite its sharp steepness she managed to keep her pace. In less than two minutes she was on a tiny footpath in the forest. She remembered how in her junior years at the hospital, staff would use the little forest footpaths for a post-lunch stroll. Of course, that was before all the little cabins in the forest were deserted and taken down on the orders of the council. It was sad, and the new staff didn't even know about the path, or that one could walk into the forest directly from the hospital.

She had now slowed down, walking steadily and inhaling the spring smells of the blooming flowers. Thin-stalked red poppies and tiny daisies and chamomile touched her feet as she walked, trying not to step on them. When she was little, her sisters and she loved to get hold of a daisy each and play the 'he loves me, he loves me not' game. She would always try to cheat when down to the last few petals and end up on 'he loves me'. She was the eldest, and accustomed to be the leader in all their games, so it was hard for any of the other kids to take her up on it.

They were sitting on the grass with her best friend Kate, peeling the daisies slowly. Kate pressed her shoulder gently.

'Really lost in thought today, huh? Are you thinking of him?'

She had just met Dinos the night before, the God-like boy. He was the most handsome man she had ever come across. His hair was the colour of sun-kissed straw, his long, thin face suntanned, his lips full and sensuous. It was last day of high school and they were sneakily watching the show at the 'Little Island', the only proper music cabaret in her sleepy town, which happened to be just across from her house. She had dressed up for the occasion, a Friday evening of a fragrant June day.

She was wearing her only pair of white shiny high heels, pointy toed as was the fashion at the time, and a navy-blue dress with a white embroidered collar, showing off her ample bust and small waist. Her father had paid a lot of money to buy her these clothes for her seventeenth birthday. Her mother had disapproved. 'She is too young for such expensive clothes and we don't have the money', she had overheard her saying. Her father had a soft spot for her though. 'You married me at seventeen', he told her mother. 'Besides, they will be handed down.' Another three girls, her younger sisters, would be wearing these clothes for years to come. She was wearing them for the first time ever today though, and she was dreading that they would get soiled, as she was standing up with a couple of her mates, squeezed beside the cabaret's back window, desperately trying to peep through.

'Would you girls like to come in?' he had said.

He had given them a start, as they thought to begin with that he was one of the porters and that he was about to have a go at them.

'No, we don't have the money to pay the extravagant entrance fee', Kate had said giggling. Kate was so naïve, Leonora had thought, and always ready to utter what did not need saying at all.

'Come on in then', he had said. 'I will pay the fee and you can sit at my table at the front and have a drink as well.'

On their way to his table at the front, squeezing past the standing crowd, Kate kept elbowing her.

'He's gorgeous!' she kept whispering in her ear, giggling at the same time. 'Is he a prince or Jesus Christ? He so looks like Him!'

Leonora had gone into a state of starry-eyed, transcendental existence from the moment she had set eyes on Dinos. That meant that she could never recall afterwards much of what went on that night. All she remembered was that both her friends were besotted with him, openly flirting and trying to get his attention, but that he had made it clear from the first moment that he was only interested in her. When the music finally stopped late at night, far later than she was used to staying out, he offered to walk her home.

'I only live across the road', she had said, but in order to have more time with him she chose a longer way, following one of the back-roads that went up the hill and then descended steeply into the little cobbled street where her house was. They sat by a derelict front yard, on a low stone wall at the top of her road, just out of sight of her parents' bedroom window.

'I love your town', he told her. 'First time I have been here.'

'So you are not local?' she asked him, her imagination running already at high speed.

'Oh, God, no!' he said, almost laughing in shock. 'I come from far, far away, from the Peloponnese.'

'The Peloponnese!' she exclaimed. 'That is really far. What are you doing here?'

'Long story; let's say I accompanied my mother who is visiting some relatives.'

When she got up to go, he leant over to kiss her, but she refused.

'I'm only seventeen, you know', she said, and she gave him a peck on the cheek instead, smiling.

How many times since then had she regretted denying him that kiss? Why could she never let her hair down? She had always been reserved.

She came to a halt. She just knew it was there. She looked

to her right, only to have it confirmed by the old pine tree with the inscription 'T♥R' still clear on its flaky bark. She turned to walk down the path that started on her right, but to her surprise there was no path any more. She walked carefully between the pine trees, inevitably stepping on some of the smallest wild flowers, and in less than a minute she was there. No sign at all to acknowledge the fact that this was once upon a time, not that many years ago, a little cabin in the forest where young nurses used to live to avoid the city's extraordinarily high rents and thus to save some money for their prospective wedding. A cabin where, not that long ago, a young woman had been murdered in the most violent way imaginable by the only true serial killer that Greece had ever known.

'I will marry you', Dinos had said to her that first night. 'You will be the girl that I will marry. I know that.'

Despite her serious and reserved demeanour, she had let out a giggle.

'You will have to wait for that a long time', she had told him. 'I have got one more year of school and after that I am going to medical school.'

'Wow! That's why I like you', he said. 'You are determined. You know what you want. Not many girls do.'

That day of witnessing the crime had changed her life for ever. It was that day that she had finally decided that relationships were not worth it. Love was yet another overused word. 'This is what men do to women in the end', she had thought to herself.

She was now sitting on the brown, dry soil, not caring

about her clothes in the least, and she must have been crying for some time, as the tears had soaked her white cotton blouse. She took her cardigan off. The heat of the afternoon was nearly as intense as in July and her shoulders and head were burning hot. She remembered that she was comfortable wearing her cardigan all day at home. How strange that in the spring, the houses' walls retained the coolness and damp of the winter, even when, outside, summer seemed to be on its way. Houses are like our bodies, she thought: they seem to remember things that happened a long time ago. She could still hear his voice from that balmy June night, still remember her desire to touch his wavy hair, and yet all this between them had been gone for a long time now.

She was holding her cardigan on her lap, examining a large white patch on the crease of the right shoulder and sleeve. What was it? Then it dawned on her: baby sick. She was holding the baby, burping her, and she must have got a bit sick on her shoulder before falling asleep. She looked at her watch. Ten past four. She will be waking up soon, hungry for her next feed. Will he know how to hold her? Will he remember to support her head? The urge was overwhelming. She must go back. There was a tiny little creature that needed her and only her. No one else had, no one else would.

45
Paris breeze

London, May 1999

'Post coitum omne animal triste est.'

They were lying in bed, both naked. Eleni had her back turned to him, his arm round her waist, their hands interlocked. She could feel his warm breath over her left shoulder as he kept shifting locks of her hair away from his face.

'What?' Nicolas asked.

'It is Latin. It means 'All animals are sad after intercourse.'

'Oh, I thought that you were falling asleep, but now you are reciting proverbs in Latin.'

'I am not reciting. I am telling you how I am feeling. You are not good at picking it up.'

'Is this the beginning of an argument?'

'If you want it to be ...'

'No, you want it to be!'

She turned abruptly to face him, moving his arm away. 'Look, I am telling you that I am feeling sad. I always feel sad after sex. Do you ever get that?'

'Don't think so. Why are you feeling sad?'

She shrugged her shoulders in disappointment. 'Don't

know.'

'Is it that you didn't like it?

'Actually, come to think of it, the more intense the connection is, the sadder I feel.'

They were lying in the double bed in their bedroom in the middle of the afternoon of a Wednesday in late May, a rare occurrence. They had put the blinds down to obscure the view from innocent passers-by going about their business on a working weekday. In the last six months, and since his PhD had consisted more of writing up than research, Nicolas had started working some days from home, although Eleni still felt that he secretly preferred to work from the office. When he stayed at home, she would happily make space for him in the little study next to the living room, her permanent work-space, and she would retreat to their bedroom where their second computer was, pretending to be busy writing up.

In fact she had spent almost all of this morning playing Solitaire on the computer. Her last session with Laura was being replayed painfully in her mind. She had been stuck again with her writing up for the last month and she was beginning to give up on the idea of trying to make progress with it. Therapy and Laura were now occupying the intense space in her mind that Yves had once inhabited. If she constantly felt emotional intensity and longing for other people, was that not a sign that her relationship with Nicolas was wrong? She had asked herself this question almost obsessively since her last session on Monday.

'I think I am feeling sad because sex is always so good

between us, it's like our bodies fit ...'

'Isn't that great?' he interrupted her, pinching her playfully on her naked stomach.

'Ouch!' she complained playfully. She took hold of his hand, pondering whether to say any more or to just drop it.

'No, it's not that good, because after sex I feel lonely. It feels like the bit that we do well together has just ended, and then we have a long stretch of all the bits that we don't do that well.' She could not let things drop after all.

'So if I said that I hadn't quite finished what I was doing and that we had promised we would get back to work after that little break, but you seem to want to spend the afternoon in bed talking, you would tell me that this is one of the bad bits, right?'

'Probably!' Eleni said, shrugging her shoulders, feeling her irritation rising.

'It seems to me that effectively I am not allowed to work any more today. You see, this is why I prefer to work from the office.'

Eleni got up and started dressing, having her back turned to him.

'Am I getting the silent treatment now?' Nicolas said, still lying in bed naked.

'Just go back to your work. I don't want an argument', she said quietly.

'In a minute. I am just enjoying the view.'

'I'm not in the mood now, Nicolas. You have spoilt it for me. Let's both go back to work.'

'Come on', she said after a while, seeing his hesitation.

'Off you go, out of my work-space'. She uttered this playfully, trying to lighten things up, but no lightness remained in the atmosphere between them.

She was cooking a vegetable and black bean enchilada with spicy guacamole to cheer herself up, an elaborate Mexican recipe she had found in her newest cookery book, when Nicolas walked into the kitchen and gave her a light kiss on the neck.

'It is only five thirty', Eleni said. 'You can work for one more hour, then rush off to buy some tortilla chips for what I am cooking.'

'I can't. It smells too delicious', he said. 'What time are we eating?'

'Whatever time you bring back the tortilla chips and some wine. I feel like it.'

'Mmm, me too!'

They were sitting down across from each other, savouring the enchiladas and drinking some Chilean red, the latest craze, when he asked her how her writing was going.

'It's not going', she said matter-of-factly, munching on. 'I haven't written a single word today, or for the last month. I am stuck.'

'So what were you doing upstairs?'

She hesitated. 'Playing Solitaire', she murmured.

'I thought that you were getting better with the therapy. You didn't seem as depressed any more. I haven't seen you playing Solitaire since the days after Paris.'

'I know. I started again in the last month.'

'Why did you not tell me?'

'What, so that you could tell me off?'

'Is that what I am doing?'

'Most of the time you do. You told me off earlier on when I said that I was feeling sad.'

'No, I didn't. I just felt a bit criticised I guess, because you were sad after sex with me!'

'Anyway, let's not go into it again', Eleni said, feeling resigned.

'You are kind of sad now, aren't you?' Nicolas said after a while.

'I keep thinking about something Laura has said. You reminded me of it when you pinched my stomach earlier on in bed.'

'What did she say?'

'You know the other day, when we went to the Turkish restaurant, I asked you if my tummy has got any bigger and you said, "Yes, a bit." I was so upset after that, my whole evening was ruined.'

'All I meant was that that there is a bit of flesh on you now, that's all. As you know, I love being able to pinch it.'

She half smiled and he went on, seeming encouraged.

'I hated it when you were eating next to nothing. Remember how I used to count your ribs and your vertebrae in bed?'

She smiled fully now, but quickly got serious again. 'It's your way, Nicolas. You never make me feel appreciated as a woman. It never feels like you are in love with me.'

He looked down, a shadow cast over his eyes.

'But I am', he said quietly.

'You know what Laura said? She said that you are the kind of man who will never give me the warmth and affection that I need in order to feel secure. "There are plenty of men out there who would. Why stick with him?" she told me.'

'Do you want my view, Eleni?' he said, getting up and starting to take the dishes to the sink. She could feel how upset he was, and her heart sank. He always had to do something at moments like that. He could not sit still, like a little boy in distress.

'I think that you allow people like Laura or like Yves to get under your skin and mess with your mind. And while you let that happen, you will never be able to enjoy the good things you have in your life – that's what I think.'

She sat there for a while watching him pick up the plates and carry them to the sink, busying himself in the kitchen, putting things back in the fridge. Her eyes had filled with tears that had started running down her cheeks. He came back to wipe the table and he stopped in his tracks.

'What's the matter?' he asked.

'Yesterday I called the accommodation office to ask if there are any rooms available. I was told that from the first of June there will be a couple of rooms in Doherty Hall. They will be filled quickly again by the summer students. I need to decide if I want one now.'

'What are you talking about?'

'I think that I have just decided that I am going. We are stuck here, Nicolas. I am stuck. I need the space to decide if this relationship is what I really want.'

'I love you, Eleni. That's why I have stayed with you despite everything you did in Paris. Don't go.' He hesitated. 'Go, if you need to', he corrected himself quietly.

She threw herself into his arms. 'I love you too, but I need, too', she mumbled. They stood by the kitchen table hugging each other. The hug felt to Eleni like a century-old cocoon before the inevitable fall into thin air.

***

She packed a small bag with clothes and toiletries. It struck her as rather surprising how little she needed when it came to solitary living. Although she was in turmoil, she was craving her own space with a door she could shut behind her. A room with a view to her mind that would unleash her flow again, channel it into words, into her art. A room where her mind was not painfully filled by the absence of another. She loved having her own room in Paris for the six months that she lived there, the sense of self-sufficiency that having her own space gave her. Come to think of it, Yves and Vivienne had been impinging, dragging her out to engage with mess again rather than the retreat she had been craving.

The room she was allocated was tiny, but it overlooked Butler's Wharf, and although she could not directly see the river from her window she could smell stale water in the air, a smell she loved only second to the smell of the open ocean. She quickly retreated into the very basics of existence, as she had always tended to during the periods of her life that she had previously lived alone. She would start her day with black coffee, sip it slowly, and make some toast when she felt hungry, usually close to midday. A very late lunch of some quickly thrown-together salad of some sort and then a chocolate bar while reading a book was her evening treat. Food tasted good in its simplicity, and if you only had it when absolutely necessary. As she had expected, her writing started flowing, like the flow of the nearby Thames whose sound she felt that she intuitively tuned in with. She was usually up by six – the intense penetration of light into her bedroom at this time of the year had always been an impediment to restful sleep – and with a full cafetière next to her, she would start writing still in her nightie, feeling the chill of the laminate floor against her bare feet.

Part of the stuckness in her writing was to do with a split she felt in her mind between the history of the female form she was examining and her own artwork, which she was using to underline the argument about the difficulty of successfully representing female subjectivity. This time, she worked differently. She took the original forms of the images she was examining from her artwork and spread them on the little patch of floor between the desk and her bed. One was a collage of a pregnant body made out of magazine and newspaper extracts; another, a painting of a mother and a baby just born, lying on a bloody bed, still connected through the umbilical cord with the body of the mother, the baby's face deformed in crying, looking out in space, mother looking with empty eyes her separate way. She had called this *Non-intervention.* Then, the photographic image of a pregnant woman in whose transparent body one could see all her vital organs, her veins as well as her uterus with the developing foetus. She had used advanced computer technology to create this, not a medium she was comfortable with, but at least she was happy with the result. *Objectivity* was the title of this one, and the image spoke for itself. Finally, her favourite, *Alice*, a photograph-like painting of a little blonde immaculately dressed girl walking on the seabed full of mermaids, babies sleeping on seaweed and couples engaged in intercourse, the girl looking around with eyes wide open. She now found that the landscape she had created was nightmarish as much as it was dreamy. Surrounded by her four favourite works of art, those she had chosen to examine in her thesis, Eleni kept writing.

She talked with Nicolas every evening on the phone, but she had cancelled both her weekly sessions with Laura, finding, rather to her surprise, that she did not feel like going to see her. She indulged in the solitude of her existence during the day, but the nights were another matter. As soon as she switched off the light, she would fall into a restless sleep, waking up several times in search of Nicolas's body. While lying in the dark fully awake, she would count the ticks of the clock, waiting for morning to come, and she would eventually fall asleep again just before dawn. She had to admit to herself that despite the self-satisfaction of her day's confinement, in her nightly existence she missed Nicolas terribly.

They had arranged to meet for a stroll by the river on Saturday evening, a week after she had left the house they shared. He looked drawn in the face, and tired.

'Are you not eating?' she asked him. 'You look rather

pale and thin.'

'I am eating all right. I am not sleeping very well', he said.

'Me neither', she admitted.

She remembered that first evening they had got together after their brief separation, with a warmth that comforted her heart. Their stroll by the river, eventually holding hands, the take-away fish and chips, then inviting him over to her room – but 'no sex', she told him. Sleeping in her single bed, their bodies intertwined, waking up with her head on his chest. They eventually settled into a routine of meeting just before sunset every evening after a long day of work, having a walk and dinner together, and then ending up in her room where, as space was scarce, they would squeeze into her single bed. By the time she was due to see Laura again, she had finished a first draft of her thesis, and was feeling closer to Nicolas than ever before.

Layer 6

ARMOURED

1

Keeping a dark or secret profile.

2

Hardened for the elements; soft-centred.

3

Inviting attack by being prepared for it,
provocative.

4

Heavier.

5

Sustaining belief in the inside and
the outside, the invulnerable space and
the essentially unprotected body.

6

Clothes as noise.

7

Undressing revised.

Judith Clark & Adam Phillips,
The Concise Dictionary of Dress

46
Reunion

Thessaloniki, September 1978

Homework

Write ten sentences about you and your favourite hobby

I live on the fifth floor with my mummy and daddy.

I love flying.

The other day, my mummy took me to a film where people flew off tall buildings.

My mummy said that flying off tall buildings is dangerous and I should never do it.

I love the Bionic Woman and she can also fly.

In the summer my nanny, Nefeli, flew off to London in an aeroplane.

One day I will fly off to London in an aeroplane too.

I want to learn how to fly by myself like the Bionic Woman.

When I do, I will fly to London to find Nefeli.

She will be so surprised.

Eleni

47
Dying

Thessaloniki, August 2010

London, 23 April 2009

Dear Nefeli,

I am sorry for taking so long to reply. I needed to think about your letter very carefully before getting back to you. I was surprised to hear that you now have a new partner and that you are about to get married, as you did not mention anything when you were visiting. If this is what you want, I am glad for you. As for your relationship with my father, I told you before that it is not my place to comment. I have to say though that I cannot help but feel taken aback that you are choosing to leave him the moment he has become very frail and is close to dying.

You are asking me to consider my relationship with you and how important it is to be in each other's life. You are suggesting that it would be out of guilt that I might choose not to see you now that you are parting ways with my parents. I thought about what you are saying very carefully as I would not want to act out of guilt or resentment. Now that I have my own daughter, I understand very well what a big thing it is to carry a baby in one's body and to give birth to her. Birth in particular is a heroic act of love.

For all my life, Nefeli, I have been trying to figure out what it was like to be in your body and then to come out of it and lose you so abruptly. I have been doing this with my art, as you so astutely noticed when you were in London, and in the therapy I have had for many years. It was there that I began to understand that I have been on the lookout for you all my life. You have always been there, Nefeli, in your absence, in all the imaginary and real strangers with whom I have felt a unique connection, in all my recurrent nightmares of a plane crashing.

Looking back to my childhood, I only have faint memories of a kind of relationship with you. My memories are from when I was very little. I remember you giving me a bath and singing to me, and also I remember with delight doing gymnastics and yoga with you on the sofa cushions that you used to lay on the living-room floor for me. You may be surprised to know that I also remember with sadness the day we saw you off at the airport and I was told that you were leaving for ever. You gave me my talking doll, which I still have in my childhood room, and we all waved goodbye to you watching your plane take off.

After that day, Nefeli, I never felt like I had much of a relationship with you, although at times I wondered if I should try harder. After that, I always saw you as my father's girlfriend and as someone my father obliged me to keep in touch with. This didn't change much after I found out who you were. Come to think of it, you being my father's girlfriend also alienated me from him. It was all about you two and there was no space for me. Whenever the two of you were together throughout my childhood and adolescence, the only person available to me was Leonora.

I am writing to tell you that with great sadness I have decided not to keep in touch with you. You need to know though that I am not choosing Leonora over you. I am choosing reality, the life that I already have and the imperfect relationships with the people who are available to me. I think that you have also finally made your choice about what it is that you want in your life. I do not think that there is much space within the choice you are making for a relationship with me other than perhaps being in each other's mind. Inhabiting a ghostly corner of my mind is the only place I can give you from now on, Nefeli. The same space I have given you all my life.

Wishing you best of luck with embarking on your new life.

Take care,

Eleni

For a moment Nefeli could close her eyes and imagine that it was raining, despite the oppressive August heat and the sun burning the smooth black surface of the back of her blouse even though it was past six p.m. Nobody else seemed to feel the need to come to the city's cemetery on an August evening. She was the only person around as far as her vision would stretch. If a passenger looked at her from one of the many planes that were making their way down to the city's airport, their engines roaring above her head, she imagined that she would look like a black dot in a vast graveyard.

It was for at least an hour that she sat still by Dinos's grave. The worn-out paper was soaked from her tears, producing a rhythmic tapping noise as they fell on the page, a soothing rain noise. How many times had she read this letter in the last year and a half? Since Dinos's death, she had ceremoniously unfolded it every time she heard Andreas's bike engine turn on, a sure sign he would be out for a couple of hours.

Andreas did not often leave the house and her side. Thankfully, though, he did not yet need to, as the money she had made through selling the business would last them for another year at least, but besides, he was the only man she had ever known who was as happy as she was, and even more so, in their warm, cosy cocoon. They now rented a flat of their own, her own space at last at the age of nearly sixty. All her life she had chased after a shadow, and now she had all she ever wanted right by her side all day long.

It was a rainy Thursday afternoon when the café's accountant had called her.

'Dinos died yesterday evening, Nefeli', she told her. 'An agonising death, as you would expect.'

'Oh', she said, aware of Andreas watching her closely from his comfy living-room armchair.

'The funeral is tomorrow afternoon. Are you coming?'

'I don't think so', she mumbled. 'I am busy tomorrow.'

'Who was that?' Andreas asked as soon as she hung up.

'Oh, just the accountant from the shop. Some business with the shop's last accounts. I must go and sort it out some time soon, but for now I have put it off. Things like that can wait, don't you think?'

'Let them wait for ever, I would say, my darling. Your life now is here with me. Didn't I save you from that shop and the nightmare you were living?'

'Yes, you did', she smiled.

'I have heard that Dinos died, Andreas', she eventually mumbled after a week of locking herself in the toilet to have a silent cry.

This was the one thing she knew not to talk to Andreas about: Dinos and her past life. When she eventually let it out that she had heard of his death, tears fell on her open palms as she was sitting next to him on the living-room sofa staring blankly at the TV. She had then rather unexpectedly seen a glimpse of what he must have been like in his previous life, a life he had for sure solidly left behind for ever.

'And so?' he said abruptly.

She sensed him tensing, his breathing getting quicker and more shallow.

'Don't tell me that you are shedding tears for that fucking shit who messed up your life. Crying for him and his mad wife and his bastard child. How ridiculous!'

'Well, the child is also mine.'

'Enough!' he shouted, and she jumped out of her skin, more scared by the sight of his eyes, which had turned shiny like the blade of a knife, than by his sharp shriek.

He came even closer to her, his torso touching hers, his breath tickling her nostrils. He put his hands round her neck, no pressure applied, and yet cold sweat started dripping down her back.

'Listen to me, Nefeli, you are my wife now. Stop thinking about that shit or I could send you to lick his grave for the rest of your life!'

He apologised to her later on in bed, when he slipped a warm hand under her nightie and she pretended to have a headache. He started massaging her temples.

'I am sorry I shouted before. I did not mean to scare you. Don't you see I was upset because I love you so much?'

And today was the first time she had come to Dinos's grave, nearly five months after his death. It was the first time since then that Andreas was out of town, visiting an old friend of his who had fallen ill. Not that she had planned at all to come here. The day after Andreas's departure, the day she was meant to be catching up with her mother and sister whom she had not seen for weeks, she found herself dressing in all black. I am going to visit Dad's grave, she told herself. I am going to lay some flowers on it, my dear Daddy, buried there all alone. But the moment she arrived at the cemetery, she knew she would enquire about the site of Dinos's grave. When she finally pinned it down, she was struck by the sight of the grave next to his. The grave of a six-year-old child, completely covered with fresh flowers, and the picture of a boy with luscious chestnut locks in a baby-blue frame placed prominently in the glass cabinet at the head of the grave. How often must his mother come here to keep the flowers fresh in such oppressive heat? Nefeli wondered.

Six: the age Eleni was when Nefeli left for London that second time. She could still remember as if in a photograph the sight of Eleni's flowery red dress when she leant down to give her the doll, her wide eyes staring at the shiny packet. She could still sense tickling her nostrils Eleni's baby scent. At six, it had not yet changed much. In a decisive movement, Nefeli crumpled Eleni's letter and placed it neatly in the small hole she had dug at the right corner of Dinos's grave, where the soil, dry and dusty from the intense summer heat, had retained a few tiny molecules of moisture. This was where this letter belonged: in her previous life, which she now needed to bury for ever.

48
Sweet adolescence

Thessaloniki, 12 April 1986

My dearest diary Jardin,

My life for the last three months has been a roller-coaster. Most of the time, I am in a super bad mood and if I happen to get a glimpse of any joy and lightness in my day, it evaporates before it has even touched ground.

A few days after my birthday and as things had become just about bearable at home, which in my book means managing to be in the same room with my parents for about five minutes, everything was quickly spoiled again. My dad had a heart attack! I was lying in my room reading my latest favourite author, Albert Camus, when my mum came in and said that they had to go to hospital because Dad was not feeling well and that she would be back as soon as she could. She came back at 6 o'clock in the morning. I heard her coming in as I had barely slept. She looked so pale! This woman is truly heroic. She should have gone to work as a doctor in a Third World country rather than waste her time in this dysfunctional family. She told me that Dad had a heart attack and that she would have to go back to hospital after she got me ready for school. She said that it was not a serious one and that he would be fine, but he would have to be very careful from now on. I was surprised that I burst into tears as so many times recently I have wished him dead. Maybe I felt a little guilty that my wish is now coming true?

Anyway, as you may imagine, my dearest, since he has come back home, he is even more moody and unpleasant than he was before. He spends all day watching TV, reading the paper or cooking. And now, Mum nags him all the time, 'don't eat this', 'you must stop smoking', and of course what he does is the exact opposite. The more I try to avoid him, the more he wants to chat with me and tell me the same stories again and again about his childhood on the farm near Olympia and how crazy granddad was and all that. You won't believe, my dear Jardin, how utterly depressing and grim everything at home is.

About a month ago, my dad sat me down and told me point blank that Nefeli is my birth mother! Nefeli, the woman I knew all my life as my father's official girlfriend, the woman my mum hates so much, is the woman who gave birth to me! If is she is so loathed and loathsome, is it then any wonder that I have come to truly loathe myself and my body? What else can I possibly be than the loathsome product of her innards? Can you see how dark my thoughts have been, my dear Jardin? It is so good I can say all this to you, as you are the only one I can trust with all my thoughts.

In the last three months though, with the spring coming, I had some excitement, but it did not prove long-lasting. Normally spring is my favourite time of the year, and I always feel elated, as though something extraordinary is about to happen. Guess what! It almost did! I was invited to a party of one of the boys in my old primary school. I hate parties and I hardly ever go to any, but Electra really insisted. She said we don't see each other as much any more and it would be fun. Well, if you ask me, we don't see each other because she is too busy with her new boyfriend (can you believe it, she has a boyfriend already and he is much older than her, seventeen, nearly out of school!!!!). Anyway, I promised her that I would go. We went together and it was all giggles like the old days, and guess who was there, Leo! Thank God Electra no longer fancies him, because I thought that he looked even more gorgeous than he used to. So Electra and I were sitting there chatting, and some of the others had already started dancing blues. Sometimes I think that's the only reason the boys want to have a party at all, so that they get to squeeze a girl to their front and breathe into her ear while pretending they are dancing. Anyway, I was determined that I was not going to move from my seat, and next thing I knew, Leo was standing in front of me saying: 'Do you want to dance with me?' I thought he was addressing Electra, but no, he was standing right in front of me, looking me in the eye. What would you do in my place, Jardin? I felt my legs go to jelly, but I said 'Okay', and then we danced, and oh ... I can't describe it. It was just out of this world.

That night, I had a dream that I and my friends were in a palace and we were all dressed up like princes and princesses. I was wearing this beautiful dark-blue velvet dress and I was dancing with a prince, but I couldn't see his face clearly, because he had shadows over his eyes. Anyway, I woke up and

I was in this nice spring-like mood for the first time ever in the last few months, and guess what, my dad comes into my room first thing in the morning and says: 'You are meeting with Nefeli today. You haven't seen her for a long time and she wants to see you.'

Can you believe it? Without even asking me if I wanted to! He is such a Nazi pig!

'I've got plans for today', I mumbled. 'I am meeting my friends downtown.'

It wasn't true, but I could always call Lea and see whether we could meet up like we used to on a Saturday morning.

'It doesn't matter', he said. 'You can meet her later for lunch. Tell me the time that suits you and I will arrange it.'

I SO hate that he thinks he can order me about like that. And all this behind my mum's back. She had just left to go to a conference for the weekend. And then I quickly made up my mind. He could bully me to see Nefeli when he felt like it, but he couldn't make me be nice to her or even see her ever again. I would make my position clear to her today. Surely the two of them had talked it out and it was going to be, 'Oh, you know, I am your real mother!' and all that. I would put her in her place.

Anyway, we met, and she took me out to a nice place for lunch, where they do Italian food and some really fancy things like homemade pasta stuffed with cheese, which I have to admit I really liked. I waited and waited for her to start talking to me, but nothing. It was all chit-chat: how are you getting on with your school, and how is your friend Lea, blah, blah. And then – I surprised myself for having the nerve – but I said:

'Cut out the fluff, Nefeli. As you must have been informed, I know everything now.'

First time ever I had talked to her like that, so she started shaking, visibly very upset, but still she would not come out with it. As it turns out, she genuinely did not know that I had found out!!! Can you believe it, Jardin, my father had not even bothered to tell her! I am yet to get my head round how insensitive and cruel this man is! Then I said to her:

'Now, that I know the truth, I have decided never to see you again. I only have one mother, the one who brought me up. You are just my father's girlfriend.'

She got really upset and she was crying and she said I couldn't do this to her and that I did not know the whole truth. My mother, she said, had manipulated the situation from day one and blackmailed my father into staying with her. I am not sure exactly what she meant. Anyway, I ended up feeling very upset too. She begged me to spend the afternoon at her house like I used to, and I have to say that I felt for her. When we went there, she showed me all these albums she has with pictures of me. Can you believe it? She has a whole album with pictures of me as a newborn in London, and she has even kept the little hospital card I wore on my leg after I was born, and a little lock from my first baby hair. I wanted her to give it to me, but she said that when I grow up I could have it. Overall, I had a good time and I have to say that by the end I felt a bit sorry for her.

When I came back home, I don't know why, but I was in this black mood again and I even cried myself to sleep. Then my mum came back from the conference on Sunday evening and she wanted to know how my weekend had been so I ended up telling her that I met up with Nefeli. She asked me how it was and what we said, but I didn't want to tell her. I think Nefeli is right. My mum can be very manipulative and nosy too.

Oh, my Jardin, quite honestly my life is a series of miserable days succeeding one another. I cannot wait to grow up and leave this house. To round things off, I am copying here a poem from my favourite poet, Kostas Karyotakis, which sums up exactly how I feel:

Unhappiness
Deep night.
In a spirit of rage, I pushed my bed away
I opened the cobweb-ridden rooms
No hope
From my window, I saw the shadow of the last passer-by
And I let out a shriek in the quietness
Unhappiness

The horrible word was written with fire in the sky
The trees are pointing up to it
The stars are looking at it
Houses have it as a gravestone
Even the dogs heard it and they are howling
Why aren't the people listening?

49
After birth

Thessaloniki, April 1972

It was a beautiful spring morning, and, rather unusually for Dinos, he decided to walk to the office. Leonora had teased him often enough in the last few years about his sedentary lifestyle and his rapidly expanding belly. 'That car has become an extension of your body', she would tell him. 'Ditch it and go for a walk instead. You will see how much better you will feel. Not only you will breathe better, but your mood will improve too.'

He took a sharp right at the crossroads before Agia Sofia church, one of the city's landmarks, a meeting point for young couples and busy businessmen. To his surprise, it didn't take him longer to walk to the office than it would have taken him to drive there with all the traffic one could encounter at this time of day. Still, having his car nearby made him feel in control. He could drive his eye-catching pine-green Mercedes, only a handful of them to be seen in town, and take himself anywhere he liked. It had been a beautiful spring day like today when he had driven to the harbour to meet Nefeli in the seafood restaurant, and then taken her to a little hotel near the flower market to make love to her. He was convinced that it was in that hotel on that late spring afternoon that she had fallen pregnant with Eleni.

While she was away in London, he had slept a couple of times with the new girl in the office, but sex with her could not compare to what if felt like with Nefeli. Every time afterwards, he could feel Katie's gloominess and could almost hear her self-pitying 'He only wants me for sex. Nobody around who wants to make an honourable woman of me' thoughts. Her gloom would depress and irritate him. Nefeli was one of a kind in bed. She would purr like a kitten and her eyes would shine with delight for hours after. He was going to miss her.

He still hadn't worked out what he was going to do about sex. Life would feel like a sterile hospital ward instead of this sweet and fragrant spring morning without the intoxicating intimacy he had felt with Nefeli and with a few other women over the years. In his relationship with Leonora, the chemistry between them had evaporated. In fact, she was probably quite like Katie in her approach to sex: reminding him wordlessly, yet with acute precision, that intercourse would be the prize for being nice to her; and one way or another he had always failed in this respect. It had been a long time since he had stopped craving this conditional and restrained exchange with her, other than for the very occasional reinstatement of their married coupledom. What he would do to give himself pleasure, though, still puzzled him. Now that Eleni was finally at home with them, he wanted to take gardening leave from any illicit affairs; yet, as much as falling in love with his daughter had filled his heart with delight, he could not see how he could forgo for ever any chance of personal satisfaction.

'Good morning, Mr Hatzi.' Katie's voice interrupted him. He had walked into his office without realising it, so engrossed was he in his thoughts.

'Good morning, good morning', he said, rather embarrassed. He was about to walk into his office and close the door behind him when she stopped him.

'Just a minute. There have been several phone calls from a woman. She refused to leave her name, but she sounded rather distressed.'

'Oh.'

'She will call back. I told her that you are usually here around ten thirty, eleven. Also, a Mr Mavridis stopped by and asked what time you were coming.'

'What a pain, he probably can't pay his instalment again.'

'Is he the long-term borrower?'

'Indeed!'

'Oh, dear! Other than that, the civil engineer called and said that he has finished the inspection and all is progressing well with the building work in Katouni Road.'

'Here is some good news at last', he murmured.

'Are you available for phone calls now, Mr Hatzi?'

'Yes, but I have a meeting with an architect at twelve and I am not to be disturbed.'

He finally closed the door behind him. He preferred to work with female architects, although they were considerably rarer. They were usually more flexible and imaginative, and of course the potential chemistry between them was another bonus. Yet this was the kind of liaison he was more reticent about: an affair with an intelligent, sexy woman like Eva, the architect he was meeting later on. It would not take long for such an affair to signal the end of his marriage to Leonora, and letting go of Leonora was not something he was prepared to contemplate. Their lives were too intertwined now to ever let go of one another without considerable damage to both. A knock on the door shook him abruptly out of his thoughts again.

'Mr Mavridis is here to see you', Katie said, popping her head through the door.

'Come on in, Theo', he said, and pointed to a seat. He loved to call him 'Theo' teasingly. One could call this a euphemism, as Theoharis was not in the least God-like, either in his looks or lifestyle.

'I was just about to order a coffee for myself. They do a nice filter one in the posh café across the road. Katie', he called before waiting for Theoharis's answer, 'Get us two coffees please. Lots of milk and sugar for Theo, black and two sugars for me. Oh, and some of their nice almond macaroons.'

'What's up?' he said to him as soon as Katie closed the door. 'Is it about your instalment? Listen, don't worry about it this time, but you have to pay it eventually. Okay?'

'No, it's not that. In fact I brought you the money. Here', Theo said, and he placed on his desk a badly rolled wad of notes that he had clearly kept in his back pocket for a while.

'Dinos, I have made a mistake to trust you with my goddaughter, Nefeli. You messed up with her and now there will be trouble. I am coming here to warn you.'

'Me, messed up with her? Believe me, that girl was desperate to get in my bed. In fact I gave her the cold shoulder for months because I felt, I don't know, I suppose a bit guilty. She was a kid and I thought she might be better off finding another kid from her neighbourhood to get involved with and get what she clearly craved. But no, she was full of contempt for your suburb and her life there. In the end she asked me out. She offered to buy me a drink.' He burst out laughing, as that moment of awkwardness at the beginning of their affair always filled him with tender bewilderment at Nefeli's adolescent enthusiasm.

'Okay, okay. I knew you two would be a good match. I have an eye for these things, you see. I am not saying you raped her or anything, but getting her pregnant and all that is another ball game. She is so upset. Her parents are so upset. There will be repercussions, Dinos.'

'I am sorry to interrupt,' Katie said, having popped her head in unnoticed, 'but the woman has called again, Mr Hatzi, and she wants to speak to you. Shall I put her through?'

'Don't take the phone call', Theo interjected. 'It is Nefeli's mother. She is mad at you.'

'I will take it, Katie', Dinos said firmly.

'Hello, Mr Hatzis speaking', he said into the receiver.

'Mr Hatzi, this is Magda, Nefeli's mother.'

'Hello. How are you?'

'I am not well, Mr Hatzi. I am calling you as a mother at

this stage. My child is not well after what you have done to her. She is not eating, she spends all day in bed. She is not herself. I am told your reputation is that of a gracious man. How could you have done this to my daughter, Mr Hatzi?'

'Could you put her through on the phone please?'

'She doesn't know that I am calling you. In fact, I am calling from outside the house. She would be mad at me if she knew. She says she doesn't want me to intervene, yet an intervention is necessary.'

'What can I do for you then?'

'Give us back the baby. I am happy to raise it.'

'That is not possible', he said coldly. 'The baby has been legally adopted. I would advise you not to go down that road. You will be banging your head against a brick wall.'

Dinos got a glimpse of Theo manically gesticulating, signalling to him to hang up the phone, as he needed to speak to him.

'Mrs – Magda, if it is all right for me to call you by your name, can I call you back in five minutes? I was in the middle of a meeting and I need to conclude it.'

She gave him the number, explaining that she had sneaked into her sister's apartment using her spare keys while she was out at work.

'What is it, Theo?' he said as he hung up.

'I was trying to talk to you before you took the phone call. Her mother has gone mad. She wants the baby, she says. So far, her father has remained calm, he is usually a very restrained man, but men like that, you know, they can be very patient and then, boom, they explode! You would not want that to happen, it could get messy. He has a soft spot for her, you see.'

'Are you threatening me, Theo?'

'No, boss, not me. I am your agent, remember? An expert in matters of the heart.'

'So?'

'So, if you ask me, this business has nothing much to do with the baby. Leave the poor baby where it is, in your wife's expert hands. This is to do with love. Nefeli is love-stricken, and you are love-stricken too. You two are sweethearts.' He cackled.

'Cut the crap, Theo. I am a married man and almost old enough to be Nefeli's father. The girl needs guidance and support, that's all. It's just that I can't provide this for a lifetime.'

'That's it. She needs your guidance and support. You can't leave her like that after what happened.'

'Quite. I told her I will send her a monthly cheque for the next year, and with the money she could take some courses, develop herself ...'

'The girl wants to see you, Mr Hatzi', Theo interrupted. 'She is dying of love. Here is my advice, call her mother and tell her that you will be meeting Nefeli and Theo to discuss things. I will arrange the rest.'

* * *

He did not manage to get much sleep in the two nights before going to meet Nefeli and Theo at his office. Eleni's frequent crying during the night did not make things any better either. Leonora was managing the baby rather well and she had become an expert on the night feeds that would promptly get her back to sleep, yet as much as he loved the sight of his daughter during the day, her night wails, combined with his unsettled and fragmented thoughts, would only awaken the most barbaric feelings in him.

He found Nefeli and Theo already there on his arrival at the office on Thursday morning, sitting rather frostily on the leather sofa in his waiting room, Katie busying herself at her desk and successfully ignoring them. He noticed that she had not offered them so much as a drink of water, and he had to take a deep breath to suppress his irritation at the abuse of the little power she had over Nefeli, a young, beautiful woman that she probably saw as a competitor. He showed them in immediately, hardly turning to greet Katie, and closed the door firmly behind him.

'How are you, Nefeli?' he asked tenderly.

There was no reply.

'Do you want something to drink?' he persisted.

'I will have that coffee and the biscuits I had the other time, if you don't mind, boss', Theo interrupted. 'They were delicious.'

He walked to the door and asked Katie to order three coffees with macaroons, although Nefeli had still not opened her mouth.

'Nefeli, remember, we came here to talk, so you must tell Mr Hatzi what you are feeling', Theo said, tapping her lightly on the shoulder.

Nefeli's face still looked frozen, her arms crossed tightly

against her chest, her gaze fixed on the floor.

'You must tell me what you want from me, Nefeli', Dinos said, starting to lose his patience. 'Is it that the amount that we agreed on is not enough?'

'I don't want your money', she said between her teeth, and her voice sounded to him like she was spitting in his face.

'Oh!' Dinos said. 'But money, you see, can help you go places in life, study something, have a new life.'

'I told you before that I don't want to be at my parents' place. You said that if I gave the baby over, you would help me get a life, the life that I want.'

'So what is it that you want, Nefeli?'

'I want to work here, like I used to. I loved it here, I learnt things.'

'But I now have Katie, I can't ...'

'All right. Then I want to work as your babysitter. I want to see my baby, Dinos. I don't care if I am not her mother. She is probably better off without me in the long term. I just want to be around her, to see her grow.'

At this point, it was almost as though her frozen posture melted, and she abruptly burst into tears, violent sobs shaking her curled shoulders.

One of Dinos's favourite proverbs – and he loved using plenty of these as they reminded him of his father and his rural upbringing – was 'What the moment brings, time does not'. This was an instance proving the proverb's wisdom. There was something in Nefeli's unplanned display of vulnerability, her self-deprecation and the candid exposure of her needs that melted, temporarily at least, any defences that were in him.

'You can see your baby again, Nefeli', he said gently. 'I promise that I will arrange it. And I will make sure you get a good job one way or another.'

She looked at him with genuine surprise and their eyes met like they used to before. He felt a not-that-old pang of desire flooding his system. He had to see her alone again without the unpleasant intrusion of Theo slurping his coffee and munching on his biscuits, watching them both as though he was engrossed in a soapy romance film.

'Give me a week and I will arrange everything. Come here same time next Thursday and we will talk it through. Okay?'

'Boss, you have a big heart', Theo said, patting him on the shoulder as they were leaving; and Dinos wished silently that he could clear his loan so that he would be spared any more visits from him.

50
The scent of things gone

Thessaloniki, June 1983

Eleni and Electra were sitting under the sun trying to dry their summer uniforms, which were dripping wet from another extended session of water play. This time round they were not alone in it at least, as all their friends had joined in the water fight with giggles and screams. The group had quickly dispersed when they saw Mr Manos on the horizon. Their own uniforms, though, were glued to their torsos like a second skin, and water was dripping down their ankles, wetting their socks too.

'Is the winner the one who's the least or the most wet? If it is the first, we have definitely lost', Eleni turned to ask Electra in an amused tone; but to her surprise, tears were running down Electra's cheeks.

'You are crying?'

'It is the last day of school, Eleni, the last day of school. This was the best year of my life.'

'I know, me too.'

'Ha, ha!'

'What's funny?'

'What you just said! The best year of your life was when you took an overdose?'

'I think it was good because I was feeling everything so strongly. I love feeling things strongly and I can only do it when I am with you.' Now, it was Eleni's turn to start crying with uncontrollable sobs that shook her entire body and made her shiver, as she suddenly felt the cold of the wet clothes stuck to her.

'Eleni, what's wrong?' Electra asked, putting one arm round her shoulders.

'I can't believe it ...', she started to say, her voice interrupted by sobs. 'I can't believe we won't be together at secondary.'

'I know!'

'I so hate my father. He deceived me. We went round to visit this new private all-girls school that has just opened with staff from the original school in Athens. Apparently the poshest in town.'

'Is it? How exciting!'

'No, it was not! I hated it the moment I set foot in there. Cold and impersonal, with huge grounds, out in the middle of nowhere. It reminded me of the boarding schools in Enid Blyton's books.'

'I know what you mean.'

'Anyway, after the tour, we went to talk to the headmistress, and my father said, "Your school is wonderful, exactly what I had in mind for my daughter. I think we have made up our mind, we will register. We loved it! Isn't it, Eleni?" without me uttering a single word.'

'Okay, that's cheeky!'

'That was it, I made up my mind about him. I hate him and I will hate him for ever.'

'But what about your mother? Why did she not support you?'

'Oh, she is just pathetic. She always does what he says.'

'I wish I could come to your school, Enid Blyton-type schools are my favourite!'

'You are kidding!'

'No, I like posh, but my parents won't send me, even though they have the money. They are socialists.'

'And mine are fascists.'

They both laughed.

'I will miss you', Eleni said, and they hugged, crying and laughing at the same time.

The sound of somebody clearing his throat very close to them made them jump up.

'Mr Manos!' they both exclaimed in fright.

'I am going to pretend that I am short-sighted and am not wearing my glasses so I cannot see that you are both dripping wet.'

They smiled in complicity.

'I am coming to enquire why my favourite girls are sad and crying yet again?'

'It's the last day of school, Mr Manos', Electra said. 'We had the best year of our lives with you as our teacher. We are going to miss you so much.'

Eleni kept her eyes down. She was not one for paying compliments, even if she meant them, and especially not if she felt them deeply. Mr Manos had been the best teacher she'd ever had. She knew that she would miss him and that she would always remember him. And yet, in the last couple of weeks, she had felt slightly disappointed in him. After their long and rather stressful conversation in his office, she had expected him to call her back to see him again, or at least come and talk to her. All her classmates had been shocked and concerned when she had taken the overdose, and yet he never once asked her how she was. Could it be that he didn't know? Impossible! She had felt his highly observant and intense gaze on her several times in the last two weeks, but she could not be sure if he was thinking about her or if she imagined he was. All she knew was that he didn't care about her as much as he had made her think he did throughout the year, and on that day when he had called her into his office. She was feeling somewhat deceived by him, left high and dry.

Mr Manos was now bending down, his face level with her lowered head.

'Eleni, why are you not talking? Are you still upset?'

'Yes. I mean, no.'

'Are you angry with me for some reason?'

'No, Mr Manos. I agree with what Electra just said, you did a lot for us.'

'And yet you are leaving school a bit hurt and disappointed.'

How did he know? He was one of these people who could read another's soul. She just wished that one day she could be even slightly like him.

'Yes, because my parents are forcing me to go to a school that I know I will hate and I won't be able to be with my friends.'

He took hold of both of her hands in his, looking at her intensely.

'Listen to me, Eleni. Sometimes in life we cannot choose things to be the way we want them to be and we have to accept a compromise. This is okay, as long as we learn from the experience and grow. You understand?'

'Yes, Mr Manos.'

'I really wanted to help you grow as much as I could, but in the last two weeks I had to accept that there are limitations to what I could do for you, and now I am having to let go of you.' His eyes got teary as he added, 'I trust one thing, Eleni, that you are a very strong and intelligent girl and that you will keep growing no matter what you encounter in your new school. Okay?'

'Yes, Mr Manos', Eleni said in a shaky voice.

'Oh, and in time, when you are ready, you will find out all the truths that you need to know about yourself.'

So saying, he squeezed her hands and then let go of them.

'Off we go now, girls!' he said, standing upright and clapping his hands. 'Back in class for your last lesson with me. It is called "How to survive secondary school".'

51
The beginnings

Thessaloniki, May 1972

Leonora had wondered what she would face when she stepped into the apartment. Frenzy and chaos was what she had imagined. Dinos trying to fix the baby's feed and Eleni screaming at the top of her voice. She was therefore alarmed as she stood in the hallway and complete silence prevailed inside. She took her shoes off and walked on tiptoe into the living room, but there was nobody there. She had started to panic when she heard Dinos's voice from the bedroom.

'Leonora, is that you?'

She let out a sigh of relief and went into the bedroom. He was lying on his side, and next to him Eleni was sleeping peacefully in her cot.

'I thought you were gone', she said, and she immediately felt overwhelmed by emotion. She hated to let him see her cry. The last thing she wanted was for him to know that he had an impact on her. She turned her back abruptly before the tears started flowing, and walked towards the kitchen. The smell of the warmed-up rice and pea casserole reminded her that she had had nothing to eat since early in the morning. He walked into the kitchen while she was serving herself a portion, having just managed to wipe her eyes and compose herself.

'Where did you think I was gone?' Dinos asked.

'I would rather not talk about it', Leonora said, looking down.

'At least you are back', he said, sitting down and lighting a cigarette. 'You must be starving. It's nearly five o'clock. Did you have something to eat out?'

'You bet', she mumbled, and gave him a look. 'Anyway, I'm not back for you, but for the baby. I realised while I was away that she has nobody else to take care of her. She's got a mother who gave her away as though she was a teddy bear, a mother who all she cares about is having sex with my husband, and a father who is incapable of taking care of anybody including himself. Now that I have taken her on, I can no longer leave her.'

'We need to talk, Leonora, things are complicated.'

'No, things are simple. You put this baby in my care and I am now her mother.'

'Yes, but …'

'There is no but.'

'She came to see me, Leonora. She is a wreck. She begged me to let her see Eleni from time to time. Surely we cannot deny her that. It would be inhumane.'

'Well, she made her choice.'

'Leonora, these people are from an underworld. You don't know what they are capable of. They could attack us, they could even steal the baby.'

'You should have thought of that before getting involved with her. All you could think with was with what's in your trousers – but don't get me started.'

Leonora could hear her voice, robust and sure of herself, while inside her everything was crumbling. How often in her own home she had to pretend that she was convening a multi-disciplinary team meeting where high-risk political issues were at stake. With Dinos, as at the hospital, she always had to be the strong one. Nobody there to comfort her and cushion her.

'You knew what you were getting yourself into, Leonora. You knew all along that it was going to be messy. This was not a routine adoption, was it?'

'Could I have had a routine adoption with you, or a normal married life for that matter? You always want things exactly your way.'

'Really?'

She could see that he was angry now. This would escalate into a big argument. He was holding his head with both his hands and she could see tears rolling down his cheeks.

'Oh, of course! Tears are always easy for you. What about me? Who has ever cared about me and my feelings?'

Her food was lying completely untouched in front of her, the rice probably cold and congealed by now.

'All I ever did was care about you and your feelings. You had the abortion to prove that you were independent, and then I had to marry you to prove that I loved you.'

'You never had to marry me. That's why I had the abortion: to make that clear.'

She was crying now, and her tears felt like the most welcome release from stress she had had in the last few months. She could feel her neck and shoulder muscles relax for the first time in a long time.

'I married you because I wanted to have you in my life, but you always wanted more, you wanted status, to come first.'

'Oh! Isn't a wife meant to be first and best?'

'Forget it', he said, and Leonora could feel his irritation.

'No, what?'

'You don't fulfil any of my needs, Leonora, we hardly ever have sex.'

'No, because you are too busy having sex with other women.'

'Is that so? Like you ever want to.'

'You are right. Why would I want to?'

Her tears had not stopped running and it had started to annoy her. He didn't deserve to see her vulnerable like this.

'I am going to see to the baby', she said, getting up. 'She has been sleeping for far too long.'

'We haven't finished talking, have we? What are we going to do about childcare? Nefeli would be the obvious choice, reliable, trustworthy, and she knows Eleni well. She won't be a threat to you Leonora, I promise. She told me herself that she wants you to have the baby as she thinks that she will have a better upbringing with you. She will just be her nanny. You will be the mother, only you.'

While he was speaking, she had her back turned to him, but now she turned abruptly to face him.

'Do you remember that first night we met in the "Little Island"?' she asked, looking him in the eye for the first time since he had walked into the kitchen.

'Of course I do.'

'Do you remember what you told me when we were sitting by the stone wall, just out of sight of my parents' bedroom? You said to me: "You are the one, the girl I will marry. I just know it."'

'We were barely seventeen, Leonora. What has that to do with anything?'

'It has a lot to do with everything. You betrayed that girl and you betrayed yourself.'

'Leonora', he murmured, and he got up to hug her.

'No, don't!' she said, and she pushed him away by putting her arms out in front of her. 'Here is the deal. Your mistress can come here in the early evening when I am back from work and before Eleni's bedtime, and she can spend a couple of hours with her under my supervision –'

'That would be awkward ...' Dinos interrupted.

'It will be fine. I am a civil person. She will need to make herself useful around the house as well. As for any other business between you, I don't want to know', she added, and she walked down the hallway feeling an ice block in her stomach and deep into her heart.

52
Therapy

London, October 1999

'So you are back!' Laura said without managing to conceal the delight within the neutrality of her professional tone.

'Were you not expecting me?' Eleni said hesitantly, standing up by the door feeling awkward. 'I told you that I would call to cancel, if I was not coming.'

'Of course.'

Eleni remained standing, and Laura, already sitting comfortably, looked up at her, puzzled.

'It's just that I am not sure where to sit', Eleni mumbled. 'I feel like I have lost my place on the floor cushion, but I hate these chairs.'

'Why do you think you hate these chairs?'

Eleni sat down on one of the chairs, exhaling noisily in resignation.

'I don't know. It's a standard counselling room, I guess. They are kind of institutional. It is like an adopted place, not a real one, I suppose', she added, smiling wryly. 'Anyway, I am back because a lot of what you said last week made sense. Since then it has been so exciting, one revelation after another. I love it when things fall into place through therapy. It's almost as good as art.'

'Almost as good, huh?'

'Sorry, but I think art is the real thing', Eleni said playfully. She was in a good mood, and radiant, a feeling she had not experienced during a session before. For all the dramatic disclosures and intense moments she had shared with Laura during the last two years, she had never before felt as close to her.

'Well, I am glad to announce that although I will not be able to provide you with the real thing as I am only offering you therapy, I have just started working from my own consulting room and if you prefer to start coming for sessions there, I can assure you that it will be less institutional. Oh, and there is a couch too!' Laura said, smiling.

'Seriously? I would like that.'

'So, you decided to continue with the therapy?'

'Yes, kind of.'

'Kind of?'

'I mean that I still feel the same way about the things that you did, but I was able to talk about it and I felt that you took it on board.'

'Good!'

Eleni hesitated. 'Laura, the thing you said about my mother, how you became like her in the transference, trying to control me and own me, was a revelation; and others followed.'

'Go on.'

'Where shall I begin', Eleni said, and she shifted in her chair, trying to make herself comfortable. After hesitating for a moment, she kicked her shoes off and put her feet on the chair, crossing her ankles.

'Is this all right?'

Laura nodded. 'Of course.'

'Do you remember that key dream I had just before my mother told me that she had adopted me? We went through it several times.'

'The dream with the mirror?'

'Yes. Remember we couldn't figure out who the man with the intense dark eyes wearing the religious gown was? The man who said that he wouldn't tell me the truth?'

Laura nodded.

'You suggested that he might stand for my father, who was holding the truth back from me, but it didn't ring a bell.'

'So?'

'So, I know who he was. My primary school teacher!'

'I am not following.'

'I don't think I have told you this, but when I was in primary school, the last year was really intense and it led me to take the aspirin overdose. It was the first time I sensed that there was something wrong with my mother. Anyway, it was all linked with that teacher. He was a charismatic man, very religious, but in the right way, if one can say that. He had given us this poem to read about an abandoning mother, and it had got my friend Electra and me very emotional just before I took the pills.'

Laura nodded as though she was following now.

'Well, this teacher had invited me into his office just a few days before I took the overdose and asked me about my family and if there was a secret that I wanted to share with him.'

'Oh.'

'So, do you see the connection?'

'Do you mean that he was the man who was trying to tell you the truth?'

'Exactly! But it is interesting that in the dream he was refusing to tell me the truth and he was silent. He wanted to help me, but he got silenced.'

'Interesting!'

'And that brings me to the other revelation. I remembered how my mother had handled things then. She never told my father that I had taken an overdose. She wanted things silenced. That is not normal, is it? One would have expected her to want the teacher to discuss things with me to try and help me out.'

'No, she wanted to have things under her control. I told you so before.'

'Yes, but why? It really hurts me to think that she was just manipulating me', Eleni said, feeling her good mood starting to evaporate.

'Well, trying to understand your relationship with your mother is part of our ongoing work, but we have already had a glimpse of what it felt like through what was played out between us.'

'I think that what this is leaving me with is a sense of never fully trusting anyone. No matter how loving and caring someone might appear towards me, part of me will always think that they have a hidden agenda and are trying to use me.'

'So you can never relax in a close relationship, trust the love that you are feeling.'

Eleni covered her face and stayed still for a few minutes. This is what it felt like every time she had a falling out with Nicolas. She felt fooled to have believed he loved her in the first place!

'It sounds quite pathetic the way you put it', she said quietly after a while.

'It must be sad for you.'

'It was … it is sad … That reminds me of the last revelation I had.'

'Go on.'

'I don't know if it is a revelation really, it is more like a new way of looking at things. I was just thinking of the time a few months ago when I left Nicolas.'

'Hmm …'

'I think that fear of loving and trusting someone was being played out in my relationship with him too. It is almost like in committing to being with him or with anyone in a long-term relationship, he was in my mind becoming like my mother, trying to control me and stifle my connections with other people. So I always felt like I had to try it out, exercise my right to get intimate with others.'

'I see.'

'Anyway, When I went to live alone, it felt like I could choose to leave him, but I didn't want to.'

'Yes, but he came after you, a bit like your mother.'

'No, we both craved each other. There was no pressure, no manipulation.'

'Did you feel I manipulated you into staying here?'

Eleni paused to think. At the beginning of the session, things had felt better between them, but there was a certain hue in some of Laura's comments that made her wonder if she should fully trust her.

'No, I chose to come back because I had all these insights in the space of a week through what you said last week about my transference to you, you being like my mother ...' She hesitated.

'But ...'

'But I don't know if therapy is a process that can be trusted fully. It is a relationship after all, with all its complexities. I think I can only trust you to the degree that you can help me trust myself more.'

'That makes sense', Laura said, smiling.

Eleni walked out of the session feeling lighter than usual. As she was walking past Nicolas's university office, she wondered if she could tempt him to share a quick coffee and a warm scone at the café nearby.

53
London breeze

London, July 2000

Dinos could never have imagined that something he had dreaded so much could be as rewarding as this. He was a nervous flyer, to say the least, and other than the half-hour flight from Athens to Thessaloniki and a few business-class flights to Europe in his thirties, he was far from a frequent flyer. His daughter had made it easier for him as well by not putting pressure on him to visit her in London. In fact, if he was honest with himself, he wasn't convinced that she didn't actually prefer it that her father never came to see where she lived. A flight to London was as a matter of fact something that he had repeatedly turned down throughout his life. He didn't know if this was because the actual flight was longer than to other European destinations or, more probably, because London as a destination was less appealing to him. All his associations with the place were doom and gloom.

'I can't believe that you have never been to London, Dad,' Eleni had teased him in the past, 'having a daughter who is a Londoner both by birth and choice.'

'Your choice of residence is not permanent though. You will eventually return to Greece when you have finished your studies', he had protested.

'You bet!' she had replied provocatively. He didn't quite know if her teasing was an indirect invitation or the only available way in her repertoire to be friendly with him.

It was not to please Eleni that he had finally conceded to attend her PhD graduation ceremony. It was Leonora's insistence that this was a big event that he would regret missing that had finally done the trick. Leonora had grown warmer towards him in the last few years. It seemed like the more his health deteriorated, the more comfortable she was taking the place of his carer with the occasional personal touch. In the last year, he had had to rely on extra oxygen from a machine, as his emphysema had got worse and his heart had grown weaker as a result.

'You can still reverse this if you stop smoking and lose some weight, Dinos', his doctor had said.

'Yes, but I would rather live a short life with some pleasure, Doctor, than a long life that bores me to death.'

Their family doctor was used by now to statements like that from Dinos, so he shrugged his shoulders.

'Your life, your call', he said.

The plane journey was as horrible as he had expected, with frequent turbulence despite his having deliberately chosen one of the front seats. A cigarette would definitely help his tension, but when he attempted to light one up, the air stewardess came immediately to tell him off and point out to him that the smokers' seats were at the back of the plane and were all full.

He had to admit though that London was better than he had expected. Leonora had booked them a truly nice hotel near Piccadilly Circus that had reminded him of the European grandeur he had so enjoyed in his young years, when, already trying to avoid planes, he had driven across Europe in his brand new Mercedes bought from the original Mercedes headquarters in Germany. The food was not as dreadful as he had imagined either. English breakfast, although too rich in animal fat for his liking, was a true feast that he was not used to in the morning, but which was a welcome treat. They had also been to a couple of French and Italian restaurants, where if he was careful enough to order classic dishes through Eleni's excellent translation, the food was tasty enough.

He could not really do much sightseeing, as he got breathless very quickly when he walked, but Eleni had shown them the basics during the taxi ride from the airport. He had been impressed by the sight of the Thames, which had turned out to be much more spectacular than the gloomy river he had imagined. Eleni had come up with a good enough excuse for why they could not visit her in her place.

'The Docklands are really far away from the city centre. It will cost you a fortune to get a taxi there and back', she said.

The most rewarding part of the journey though, was what he was doing right now. Sitting in one of the front seats of the large and imposing university auditorium, as Eleni had managed to book special seats for them reserved for people with disabilities, he watched the parade of students wearing the black gowns he had only seen before on TV and bowing in front of the Vice Principal.

He had protested when Eleni had told them that she had booked them seats for the disabled.

'But I am not disabled!' he said, and Leonora gave him one of her looks; but he could see now that the view, and the amount of space compared to the other seats, squeezed and squashed together as they were, was most rewarding. He was just hoping that he would recognise his daughter when it was her turn to receive her degree, as he doubted he would catch her name when it was announced in an English accent. Just as he was thinking that, he gasped to see Eleni walking up the steps to the stage. His daughter was hard to miss with her unruly dark hay-blonde hair falling all over her face and her slightly uncoordinated walk. Leonora elbowed him.

'I am not blind, I see her', he murmured.

His heart startled him by giving three extra beats, but he soon recognised that it must only be because of the intensity of his feelings. All his life, he had resented his parents for giving him no chance of a real education, being far too preoccupied with their separation to care about his development. Throughout his life, his mind had remained restless, not managing to find an avenue suitable to express his potential. Being creative in business was one thing, but the pursuit of money had left the most able part of his brain underused and unsatisfied. His daughter standing in front of him receiving her PhD was confirmation that at least he had succeeded in doing for her what his parents had failed to do for him. He had helped her to develop her potential.

'Are you all right?' Leonora elbowed him again.

He had not realised it, but tears were rolling down his face and had wet the collar of his shirt.

Eleni walked towards them at the end of the ceremony with a young man, also wearing a gown, by her side. Dinos expected the young man to keep going, but he stopped right in front of them. They both kissed her in congratulation, and he found it hard to loosen his grip until she pulled back.

'Mum, Dad,' she said, 'I want to introduce you to Nicolas. Nicolas and I have been seeing each other for some time now. He was also graduating today. He will be joining us for dinner tonight. I have booked Chinese.'

'Chinese?' Dinos exclaimed, after giving Nicolas a handshake. 'You know very well, Eleni, that I don't eat snakes.'

'Dad, there are no snakes in the Chinese restaurants in London. You will like it, I promise.'

He was aware that the little disagreement they were having about Chinese food was a convenient diversion from the strange feeling he could sense bubbling up in him about the sudden appearance of a strange man in his life.

'Did you know anything about this?' he asked Leonora the moment they reached the hotel.

'About what?'

'You know what I am talking about, Leonora.' He lost his patience. 'The young man.'

'Kind of.'

'Which means?'

'Dinos, Eleni is in her late twenties. Did you think she wouldn't have a boyfriend?'

'Would she? Anyway, it doesn't make sense to have him appear in front of us like this with no warning. She should have come and talked to me first.'

'Perfect timing, Dinos. She is a graduate now and she has some work lined up. An independent woman.'

'Still, she could have told me, all these days she has been taking us out for dinner.'

'Well, you know how your daughter is. She likes to be a bit provocative. My advice to you: do not spoil it for her tonight.'

'Do you think they live together?' he asked after a pause.

'Who knows, perhaps.'

'That's not on. They will need to get married.'

'Dinos!'

'No, I mean it!'

'Since when have you had conservative moral values, huh?'

He needed a good siesta and the maximum dose of his inhaler to brave the evening excursion to the Chinese. Eleni was waiting for them alone in the hotel lobby.

'Is the young man not coming?'

'Nicolas is his name, Dad. He will join us there.'

'You should have told us about it earlier, Eleni', he scolded her. 'I hope you don't live together.'

'Why not?'

'Because you are not married. Have you thought about marriage?'

'Dad, if you continue like that, I am going to cancel the evening out.'

Leonora elbowed him for the third time that day. They entered the black cab waiting for them outside. Looking at his daughter's profile in the dark, he could sense that she was tense and angry.

'He seemed nice enough', he said after a long silence.

'He is', Eleni said. 'Promise to be nice to him, Dad.'

'I am a civil person!' he protested.

The evening passed much quicker and more effortlessly than Dinos had expected. Although the food, as he had imagined, did not agree with his palate, other than a couple of dishes like the duck and the egg fried rice that saved the day, he found himself engrossed in an interesting conversation with Nicolas. The bloke was a scientist of high calibre by the sound of it, and he was eager to answer all his questions about how chemical molecules worked, a subject that had always fascinated Dinos. He had often wished that his daughter had chosen to study chemistry or at least architecture rather than art, subjects that were reputable and solid. At times, and particularly around her birth and then again in adolescence, he wished that she had been born a boy. He thought it would have made their relationship less complicated and would have saved him a lot of worry about keeping her safe. The main feeling he had now, though, while talking to Nicolas, was that of huge relief. He seemed like a safe and sound young man. He did not need to worry as much about her any more.

'How long have you been seeing each other for?' he

asked her in a serious tone when they were finally back in the taxi.

She giggled like a little girl. 'Long!' she said cheekily.

'How long? Tell me', he insisted.

'So that you can tell me off again?' she replied grumpily. 'About ten years.'

He tried not to show his shock and surprise that his daughter had been having sexual relations since she was barely out of adolescence.

'And why did you not tell me, you silly girl? You would have saved me a lot of worry about how you were getting on in London. He is everything I have ever wished for.'

She giggled again and leaned over to give him a tight hug, for the first time, it felt like, in many years.

***

He was lying awake staring at the red electronic letters on the alarm clock across the bed, showing 4.10 a.m. They should abolish such machines from luxury hotels. People should be able to come for a holiday and sleep without being reminded of the time.

'Why are you not sleeping?' Leonora turned on her side to ask him. 'I thought that went really well.'

He felt caught out, unaware that she was not sleeping either.

'I don't know. I keep having this image of Eleni spotting my Mercedes outside the school gate and running to me full of excitement. Her blonde hair shining in the sun and her school bag banging about clumsily. I remember how she blushed when I said we could even give her teacher a lift, and how she waved goodbye proudly to her friends who were boarding the school bus. 'I am going with my daddy, not you', she shouted to them. 'He has come all the way to pick me up.' She must have been five. She never grew up much since then in my mind.'

'Oh, of course, your little girl!' Leonora sighed.

He sat up and switched on the bedside lamp. 'I need a cigarette', he exclaimed. 'Can you see if you can switch off this bloody alarm clock. It is driving me mad. After turning sixty, nobody needs much reminding of the time', he added, inhaling the smoke deeply.

54
The final encounter

Folegandros, August 2010

It was late afternoon, and although on the beach the high winds had brought the temperature down, the roof of the cottage seemed to have absorbed all the intense heat from the sun.

Eleni's face had lit up when she discovered this little fisherman's cottage on the island of Folegandros on page three of her Google search after months of looking, just as she was about to give up. She had been to Folegandros before with Nicolas, when they were both in their twenties. She still remembered vividly the view over the deep-blue sea from their double bed in the narrow, cabin-like room. The sea was anything but mellow. They were often woken up in the middle of the night by wild, screaming winds and the splashing of waves. It was the first time that Eleni had thought of death so intensely, the view of the wild sea making her aware of the evanescence of their being, their vanishing insignificance compared to the ocean. At the time, sleeping in Nicolas's arms after a night terror had felt like enough to keep her fear at bay.

She had been in touch with the owner of the cottage to alert him that they were coming with a toddler in tow. 'No air conditioning or mosquito net,' he told her, 'but you won't need them. The cottage is right by a little cove, exposed to the winds, which send mosquitos away and drop the temperature right down. If anything, you may need some blankets at night. I will leave plenty out for you.' He had omitted to tell her that although the cottage was traditionally built in stone, it had been badly restored with the addition of an ugly metal roof that attracted the heat of the sun. It meant that it became blazingly hot from the afternoon until late into the evening.

It was now their third week on the island and they had just about started to get used to what they endearingly called 'their hothouse'. The intense summer heat had also started to bring some of the warmth back into their relationship, and Eleni could see that despite his lingering doubts about her choice of destination, Nicolas had started relaxing into it.

Following her father's death, it had felt like all her previously close relationships had gone into a state of deep freeze. She could feel this acutely in her relationship with her mother. In the mutually avoided instances that she had spent some time with Leonora, they struggled to talk to each other.

'It feels like you are almost estranged from your mother now', Nicolas had remarked. 'You used to be so close.'

Eleni was feeling the same distance creeping into her relationship with him, despite their frequent arguments and make-up sex sessions persuading her to think otherwise at times. Secretly, she had carried Martin Wheel's card everywhere she went, and the thought of their encounter had played on her mind daily. She had hoped that he would be in touch, ask to meet her again, as though, if he took the initiative, it would absolve her from all conflict and guilt. She knew full well, though, that the responsibility of following up on their encounter fell to her, as he had made his intentions clear. She had set herself this holiday as the last deadline for responding to Martin, and the thought that she might be too late to reach him before he went travelling in September felt like a ring of pressure around her head.

Her friends Lea and Athena had just arrived at Folegandros to stay with them for a long weekend and they both approved of her choice. It was telling, how they had all comfortably fitted in what was just a small two-bedroom cottage. She had left Chloe with Nicolas, Athena and Lea on the beach, saying that she needed an hour to catch up on her much interrupted sleep; but as she had planned all along, she had in fact retreated to the stiflingly hot cottage to write her long-delayed reply to Martin Wheel.

Eleni wiped the dripping sweat from her forehead and, with unyielding determination, carried pen and paper to the kitchen table, the only sturdy surface in the cottage. She poised her hand on the paper and started writing:

Dear Martin,

Since our meeting in May, you have been very much on my mind and it was hard for me to decide how to follow up on our encounter. The atmosphere between us has touched me deeply, and I have been thinking a lot about some of the things you said to me. In particular, I was struck by what you told me; that our connections with people need to be cherished. The connection there has been between us, though, is an erotic one, and what I experienced when I was with you was a sense of falling in love.

You were also right to remark that such a strong connection with another is rather rare in life. For me, it is only the second time in my life that I have fallen in love with someone. The first time was with my current partner whom I still love and with whom I have a baby daughter. For those of us predisposed to a double life through our beginnings, loving two people may be the only possible outcome. Yet, I know someone rather well – my father – who tried to be with two women at the same time, and he died an agonising death as a result.

Of course, we all have the most intense connections with more than one person in our hearts and in our dreams and in whatever we engage with. Yet a romantic relationship is to my mind an exclusive one-to-one situation. I am not sure if you would agree with me about the desire for exclusivity in our most intimate relationships, but for those of us, like me, who have endured an early loss, the desire for such exclusive love can be all absorbing. I find that I am fortunate enough to have this already in my life. Thank you for opening yourself up to the encounter we had. I will always remember it.

With love,

Eleni

She folded the piece of paper quietly and sealed it in an envelope without reading it again. She always preferred first drafts. Stepping outside into the fresher air, she realised that her pareo was completely drenched with sweat and her hands were shaking. She hesitated at the top of the few steps leading down to the small cove at the side of the cottage, absorbing the view. In the predominantly blue and white of the landscape, the bright red strawberries on Chloe's swimsuit and wide-brimmed hat stood out. Chloe had her back turned to her, sitting nicely in the circle with Nicolas, Athena and Lea, busy decorating a freshly built sandcastle.

'Are you okay?' Athena, who had spotted her coming down the steps, asked. 'You look flustered.'

'It is a hothouse up there, but I love it all the same', Eleni murmured.

'That's my girl. Stick to your guns', Nicolas joked, giving her a light kiss on the lips.

They were now, all of them, sitting in a circle, Chloe passing pebbles to Eleni, who used them to draw a round, protective bailey around the sandcastle.

Epilogue

London, September 2015

It was always at around 4 a.m. that Eleni would wake up unexpectedly with Martin's voice echoing in her ears like a bell ringing rhythmically at a funeral to signify somebody's passing away. She could never quite catch what he was telling her, but she knew it made sense to her. Yet, by the time she was fully awake, he was gone again.

Being woken in the middle of the night did not stress her out as much any more. Chloe was a settled little girl now, ready to go in the morning and always happy to greet her friends at the school gate. As for Nostos, the baby boy she had thought she would never have, he had liked his sleep from early on, so she was not worried that he would disturb her for the rest of the night, on the rare occasion she had visits like that. Martin, almost a total stranger. Why would he haunt her mind still? It seemed people who no longer populated her life would visit from time to time at night. And others did not.

She drifted listening to the soft, calm breathing of Nicolas on her left and Nostos, sleeping soundly in his cot next to her. She was not sure at what point she joined them falling slowly back into a restful sleep.

Acknowledgments

Writing this novel has proven to be a long-term project, and so I would like to begin by apologising for not being able to list all those I encountered along the way and whose engagement and support sustained my faith. I would like to thank the first readers of the entire novel in English, Chrysa Tsoukis, Sarah King, Vasilis Sakkos and Jill Ploumistos whose positive feedback and encouragement helped me persevere. Conversations with Sofia Makri, whose comments and observations are always incisive, have had a big impact on my work. Madeleine Dimitroff, Victoria Stainsby and Sally Curtis listened patiently to several drafts of the chapters, and their excitement about and interest in the story made all the difference. Madeleine has always been a warm and welcome host of our writers' group. I would also like to thank Maggie Hamand and the Complete Creative Writing courses for providing feedback and a creative space, where I formulated the final draft. Barbara Latham listened carefully and thoughtfully to some of the narratives that later on took shape in the written word. Adam Phillips's writing and supervision provided an inspiring environment, where I began to find faith in my ability to write. I am very grateful to Stefanos Elmazis and the whole team in Archetypo

Publishers in Greece for offering generously to publish my novel in Greek and doing a fantastic job in bringing it into fruition. I would also like to thank Stefanos Elmazis for very kindly allowing me to use the painting he chose for the front cover of the Greek publication of the book in the English version too. The success of the novel in Greece, whose first edition sold out in less than six months since its publication, has given me the courage to persevere with publishing it in English. Chrysa Tsalikidou, who translated the novel from English into Greek, has been incredibly generous, encouraging and supportive throughout. Graham Frankland, who I was very lucky to have as the copy-editor of my collection of short stories recently published by Routledge, has read and copy-edited the novel, and he has been touchingly positive about it. I would like to thank George Kapetanios for being a stoic reader of several drafts of the chapters, even though reading a partner's work is not always easy or pleasant. Finally, I would like to thank Maria Katsapi and Thanasis Chavales of Akakia Publications for helping me bring this project into fruition in the language it has been written.